Hands of Fate
Daybridge Chronicles: Tales from the Nexus
By: Rae Stonehouse

I0639208

AUTHOR'S NOTE

The Hands of Fate is a special entry in the Daybridge Chronicles that explores a unique supernatural case featuring temporal anomalies. While this novel takes place within the same universe as the Ethan Reeves Werewolf Detective Series and features familiar characters, it diverges from the main storyline to focus on Detective Alice Chen's developing temporal sensitivity. This book can be read as a standalone adventure or as a complement to the primary series.

Readers new to Daybridge can start here without prior knowledge, while longtime fans will discover deeper layers to characters they've come to know. The events in this novel occur between Shadows Between Thoughts and Quantum Detective but follow a separate supernatural mystery.

CHAPTER ONE: TIMEKEEPER'S TROUBLES

The first discrepancy appeared on a Tuesday.

Tobias Merrick's fingers, calloused from thirty years of manipulating tiny gears and springs, paused over the half-disassembled pocket watch. Something had drawn his attention away—a whisper of wrongness that prickled the back of his neck. He glanced up at the wall of timepieces that dominated his workshop.

"That's not right," he murmured.

Three clocks—a Victorian carriage clock, an art deco mantelpiece, and a German cuckoo from the Black Forest—all displayed the exact same time: 11:47. This wouldn't be remarkable except that he'd calibrated each to different standards just yesterday. The carriage clock ran two minutes fast (as its owner preferred), the art deco piece kept perfect time, and the cuckoo traditionally ran three minutes slow.

Tobias set down his tools and approached the wall, the ancient floorboards creaking beneath his weight. The shop smelled of clock oil, brass polish, and the faint vanilla scent of aging wood—smells that normally comforted him. Now they seemed to intensify as his unease grew.

"Coincidence," he told himself, adjusting each timepiece back to its proper setting.

By Thursday, all seventeen antique clocks in the front display had synchronized themselves. Not to the correct time—but to 11:43.

Tobias stood in the center of Merrick's Chronometry, surrounded by the gentle cacophony of ticking. The shop occupied the same narrow storefront on Pendulum Lane where his grandfather had established the business in 1914. Warm morning light filtered through the leaded glass windows, casting honeycomb patterns across the polished oak counters and glass display cases.

He ran a hand through his salt-and-pepper hair. "What are you trying to tell me?" he asked the empty shop.

The bell above the door jingled as Eliza Park, his assistant, arrived for her shift.

"Morning, Mr. Merrick! Brought you coffee." She stopped, noticing his expression. "What's wrong?"

"Look at the clocks," he said.

Eliza, twenty-six and studying horological conservation at Daybridge University, set down the coffee cups and scanned the shop. Her dark eyes widened.

"They're all the same. How is that possible?"

"It's not. I reset them yesterday."

She approached a tall case clock from 1780, opening its face to examine the mechanism. "No signs of tampering. The gearing looks normal."

"I checked them all. Mechanically, they're perfect."

Eliza took a sip of her coffee, her brow furrowed. "You don't think it's... you know... the other side of Daybridge?"

Tobias tensed. Living in Daybridge meant accepting certain realities—vampires on the city council, werewolves running the best butcher shops, witches operating herbal pharmacies. Most residents maintained a careful balance between acknowledgment and avoidance. Tobias fell firmly in the avoidance camp.

"It's a mechanical issue," he insisted. "We're just missing something."

"If you say so." Eliza didn't sound convinced. "But this is the third weird thing this week. Mrs. Winters brought in that Danish table clock, saying it chimes at 3 AM even though it's not programmed to. And Mr. Chen complained about whispers coming from his grandfather clock."

"Mr. Chen is ninety-four. He probably heard the house settling."

Eliza raised an eyebrow. "And Mrs. Winters? She's the dean of paranormal studies at the university."

Tobias rubbed his temples. "Let's stick to what we know. Clocks are mathematical. They operate on principles of physics, not magic."

"In most places, sure." Eliza gestured toward the window and the quaint street beyond. "But Daybridge isn't most places."

She was right, of course. Daybridge had always been different—a nexus point for the supernatural, though Tobias had spent his life navigating around that reality. His father had taught him: fix the clocks, mind your business, don't ask questions about customers with fangs or those who only visit after sundown.

He checked his wristwatch—a practical, modern Seiko with none of the personality of his antiques. "We open in ten minutes. Let's reset everything and see what happens."

They worked methodically, adjusting each timepiece to its correct time. As Tobias wound the final clock, a 1920s schoolhouse model, a cold draft swept through the shop. The lights flickered briefly.

"Did you feel that?" Eliza asked.

Before he could answer, the shop door opened. A tall woman in an impeccable charcoal suit entered, carrying an ornate silver pocket watch on a chain. Her pale skin and the deliberate grace of her movements immediately identified her as one of Daybridge's vampiric residents.

"Mr. Merrick." Her voice carried a faint trace of an accent Tobias couldn't place. "I require your expertise."

"Ms. Blackwood." He nodded politely. "What seems to be the trouble?"

Claudia Blackwood had been a customer for decades, bringing in rare timepieces from her extensive collection. She placed the silver watch on the counter with unusual care, as though it might bite.

"This piece has become... problematic."

Tobias picked up his loupe and examined the watch. The craftsmanship was extraordinary—Breguet, circa 1795, with a perpetual calendar and moon phase. Worth a small fortune.

"What's the issue?"

"It whispers," she said flatly.

Tobias looked up, searching her face for signs of humor. There were none.

"I'm sorry?"

"It whispers, Mr. Merrick. At first, I thought it merely needed servicing—perhaps the mechanism was loose. But the sounds are forming words." She leaned forward slightly. "It speaks of a fracture. Of time unraveling."

Eliza shot Tobias an I-told-you-so look.

"Ms. Blackwood, with all due respect—"

"I am three hundred and forty-seven years old, Mr. Merrick. I do not imagine things." Her dark eyes fixed on his. "And I suspect I'm not your only customer experiencing this phenomenon."

The temperature in the shop seemed to drop several degrees.

"There have been... similar reports," he admitted reluctantly.

Ms. Blackwood nodded. "I thought as much. The Council is concerned. When multiple timepieces begin behaving identically, it often precedes a temporal disturbance."

"The Vampire Council is monitoring my clocks?" Tobias felt a headache forming behind his eyes.

"Not specifically. But we monitor patterns." She gestured to the wall of synchronized clocks. "And this, Mr. Merrick, is most definitely a pattern."

As if on cue, a soft chime rang out from the back room. Then another. And another. Soon, every clock in the shop was chiming, despite it being only 9:50 AM.

When they fell silent, Tobias noticed something that turned his blood cold. Every single clock now displayed the same time: 11:42.

"They're counting down," Eliza whispered.

"To what?" Tobias asked, though he wasn't sure he wanted the answer.

Ms. Blackwood gathered her pocket watch and moved toward the door. "I suggest you find out, Mr. Merrick. Time is clearly not on our side." She paused at the threshold. "I'll inform the Council of what I've seen. Expect a visit from the authorities soon."

After she left, Tobias slumped against the counter. "This can't be happening."

Eliza placed a hand on his shoulder. "Maybe it's time to stop avoiding the supernatural side of Daybridge."

"I'm a clockmaker, not a paranormal investigator."

"And these are clocks doing paranormal things." She pointed to the wall of timepieces. "They're trying to tell us something."

Tobias straightened his waistcoat—a nervous habit inherited from his father. "Fine. If the clocks want to talk, I'll listen. Tonight, after closing. We'll see if there's anything to these whispers."

Throughout the day, customers trickled in. An elderly man brought in a clock that reportedly ran backward every midnight. A young witch claimed that her enchanted alarm clock now spoke in a language she didn't recognize. A werewolf complained that his moon-phase clock was showing a full moon regardless of the actual lunar cycle.

With each story, the knot in Tobias's stomach tightened. The boundaries he'd carefully maintained between his orderly world of gears and springs and Daybridge's supernatural undercurrents were dissolving.

By closing time, every timepiece in the shop displayed 11:40.

"Two minutes lost today," Eliza noted as she prepared to leave. "Are you sure you don't want me to stay?"

Tobias shook his head. "I've been working with these clocks for decades. If they're going to speak to anyone, it should be me."

After Eliza left, Tobias locked the front door and dimmed the lights. He brought a comfortable chair into the center of the workshop, surrounded by his lifelong companions—grandfather clocks that had witnessed centuries, delicate pocket watches that had measured out the minutes of long-dead lives, ornate carriage clocks that had accompanied Victorian travelers.

"Alright," he said to the room. "I'm listening."

For an hour, nothing happened beyond the familiar chorus of ticking. Tobias began to doze, lulled by the rhythmic sounds.

Then, at precisely 11:39, every tick and tock synchronized into a perfect, unified rhythm. The temperature plummeted. Tobias's breath clouded in front of him.

And the whispers began.

At first, they were indistinct—like the sound of distant conversation. Then, words emerged from the mechanical symphony:

"The fracture widens."

"The boundary thins."

"Time bleeds through."

Tobias gripped the arms of his chair, his knuckles white. "What fracture? What do you mean?"

The whispers continued, overlapping:

"The stars align as before."

"The cycle returns."

"Prepare for the unraveling."

A sharp crack rang out as the glass face of the oldest grandfather clock split from edge to edge. Inside, the hands spun wildly before stopping at 11:38.

Every clock in the shop adjusted to match.

"How do I stop it?" Tobias called out, his voice shaking.

The whispers grew fainter, but one phrase repeated clearly before silence fell:

"Find the pendulum that bridges worlds."

The lights flickered back to full brightness. The temperature returned to normal. The clocks resumed their usual ticking, though they remained synchronized at 11:38.

Tobias sat frozen, his world fundamentally altered. After decades of skirting the supernatural aspects of Daybridge, he couldn't deny them any longer. His clocks—his rational, mathematical companions—had dragged him across that boundary.

He reached for his phone with trembling fingers and dialed the Daybridge Police Department's non-emergency line.

"This is Tobias Merrick at Merrick's Chronometry on Pendulum Lane," he said when the operator answered. "I need to report... a temporal disturbance."

The operator didn't miss a beat. "I'll connect you to Paranormal Investigations, sir."

As he waited on hold, Tobias stared at the wall of synchronized clocks. Whatever countdown they were marking, whatever "fracture" approached, he was now entangled in it. The safe, orderly world he'd constructed had its own expiration date.

And according to his clocks, time was running out.

CHAPTER TWO: WHISPERS IN THE WORKSHOP

Morning arrived with unwelcome clarity. Tobias sat hunched at his workbench, bleary-eyed from a night without sleep, turning a small brass gear between his fingers. The telephone call to Paranormal Investigations had resulted in a promise that someone would visit "when resources allowed." Apparently, temporal anomalies ranked low on Daybridge's crisis scale.

The shop remained closed, with a hastily scribbled "Emergency Repairs" sign taped to the door. Eliza arrived at nine, took one look at Tobias, and marched directly to the coffeemaker.

"You heard them," she said, not a question but a statement as she handed him a steaming mug.

Tobias nodded, his usual denial reflex finally exhausted. "Every clock. Speaking in unison."

"What did they say?"

"Nonsense about fractures and boundaries." He sipped the coffee, grimacing at its bitterness. "Something about a pendulum that bridges worlds."

The bell above the door jingled despite the locked entrance. They both turned to see a tall figure glide into the shop—Lord Edmund Ravencroft, one of Daybridge's oldest vampires and Tobias's most prestigious client.

"Your sign says closed, but your lights suggest otherwise." His voice carried the crisp consonants of Edwardian English. "I've brought you a problem, Merrick."

Two vampiric visitors in as many days. Tobias suppressed a groan.

Lord Ravencroft gestured, and his driver struggled through the door carrying an enormous grandfather clock. The piece was magnificent—burled walnut with gold inlay, brass fittings polished to a mirror shine. Tobias recognized it immediately: a Thomas Tompion from 1695, worth more than his entire shop.

"Set it there carefully," Ravencroft directed. After the driver placed it against the wall and departed, the vampire turned to Tobias. "It's misbehaving."

Eliza spoke before Tobias could. "Let me guess—it's whispering?"

Ravencroft's eyebrows rose slightly. "Indeed. Started three nights ago. Most unsettling during my evening reading."

Tobias approached the clock with newfound caution. "What does it say?"

"Mostly unintelligible murmurs, but occasionally clear phrases. 'The hands align.' 'The barrier weakens.' Poetic but irritating." Ravencroft straightened his already impeccable cuffs. "I assumed it needed servicing."

"It's not mechanical," Tobias admitted, running his hand along the clock's carved surface. "Look at this."

He opened the clock's face. The hour hand pointed firmly to 11, the minute hand to 37.

"11:37," Eliza whispered. "They've lost another minute."

Ravencroft's expression shifted from mild annoyance to concern. "Explain."

Tobias quickly outlined the events of the past few days—the synchronization, the countdown, last night's whispering chorus. As he spoke, the shop door opened again, admitting an elderly woman in a floral dress who clutched a porcelain mantel clock to her chest.

"Mr. Merrick," she called, her voice quavering. "My clock is talking! About terrible things!"

Before he could respond, the phone rang. Eliza answered, her face growing increasingly troubled as she listened. "Yes... Yes... We're experiencing the same... Bring it in this afternoon."

By noon, seven more customers had arrived with "talking" timepieces. By two o'clock, the workshop overflowed with clocks of every description—from pocket watches to a grandfather clock so large it barely fit through the door. All displayed the same time: 11:37.

Tobias stood amid the collection, overwhelmed. Lord Ravencroft had remained, his interest apparently piqued by the unfolding mystery.

"A convergence," the vampire mused. "I've seen something similar only once before, in Vienna, 1756. Preceded a temporal slippage that affected half the city."

"What happened?" Eliza asked.

"Time folded in on itself. Some experienced the same day repeatedly. Others aged decades overnight." He examined a French carriage clock with clinical detachment. "Several simply vanished."

Tobias's stomach clenched. "And how was it stopped?"

"It wasn't precisely. It resolved itself after considerable chaos." Ravencroft's pale fingers traced the carved wooden case of his clock. "But there were fewer timepieces involved, and they weren't counting down."

The shop door opened again, revealing a woman in her sixties wearing layers of knitted shawls despite the warm day. Her silver-streaked hair was bound in a loose braid, and numerous crystal pendants hung around her neck.

"Madame Winters," Eliza said with obvious relief. "Thank you for coming."

Madame Esther Winters—professor emeritus of Temporal Anomalies at Daybridge University and the neighborhood's most respected diviner—surveyed the room with sharp green eyes.

"Quite the collection you've assembled, Mr. Merrick." She moved between the clocks, pausing to touch each one briefly. "Yes, they're all connected to the disturbance."

"What disturbance?" Tobias asked.

She gave him a look of mild exasperation. "The temporal fracture forming beneath Daybridge, of course." She gestured as though pointing through the floor. "Surely you've felt it? The thinning between now and then?"

"I fix clocks, Madame Winters. I don't dabble in the paranormal."

"And yet the paranormal has quite decidedly dabbled in you." She chuckled, the sound unexpectedly warm. "Your timepieces are sensitive to fluctuations in the temporal field. They're resonating with the fracture."

Lord Ravencroft nodded. "Like tuning forks of the same pitch."

"Precisely." Madame Winters beamed at him. "Edmund, lovely to see you. Still have that remarkable astrolabe from Constantinople?"

"Naturally. It's currently predicting fourteen full moons next month, which seems excessive even for Daybridge."

Their casual conversation about temporal anomalies and malfunctioning magical artifacts made Tobias's head spin. This was the Daybridge he'd spent his life avoiding—where vampire lords and elderly witches discussed the fabric of reality as casually as the weather.

"Excuse me," he interrupted. "Can we focus on the immediate problem? The clocks are counting down. To what?"

Madame Winters sobered. "That's the concerning part. They're counting down to the moment when the fracture widens enough for significant bleed-through."

"Bleed-through of what?" Eliza asked.

"Time itself. Past into present, possibly future into present." She moved to the window, gazing out at Pendulum Lane with a distant expression. "Daybridge has always had thin spots in its temporal fabric. That's partly why the supernatural community settled here. But something's putting pressure on those thin spots."

Tobias felt a chill despite the warm afternoon. "And when the countdown reaches zero?"

"The pressure becomes too much. The boundary ruptures." She turned back to face them, her expression grave. "Time spills through. People might experience events that haven't happened yet, or relive moments from decades past. Objects from different eras could materialize. In severe cases, entire buildings shift between time periods."

The shop fell silent except for the synchronized ticking of dozens of clocks.

"How long do we have?" Eliza finally asked.

Madame Winters gestured to the timepieces. "If they're accurate, less than twelve days. The countdown appears to be losing one minute per day."

Tobias's mind raced. "There must be a way to stop it."

"Perhaps." Madame Winters extracted a worn leather journal from her bag. "I've been researching similar incidents. Daybridge experienced a temporal disturbance in 1927. The accounts are fragmented, but there was definitely a disruption centered around the Oldewick district."

"That's here," Tobias said. "This shop was here then. My grandfather would have—" He stopped abruptly, an old memory surfacing. "Wait."

He hurried to the back of the shop, to an ancient filing cabinet that contained the business records his father had insisted on preserving. After several minutes of searching, he returned with a dust-covered ledger.

"My grandfather's repair log from 1927." He opened it carefully, the pages brittle with age. "I remember my father mentioning something about a week when all the clocks went haywire."

He flipped through the yellowed pages until he found an entry from October 1927. His grandfather's cramped handwriting filled the margins with notes beyond the usual repair details:

Oct 14 - Unprecedented synchronization of timepieces throughout Oldewick. All display same incorrect time regardless of adjustment. Have consulted with M. Ravencroft and the Winters woman. Suspect involvement of the Pendulum. Must secure the workshop tonight.

Oct 15 - Voices from the mechanisms growing louder. They speak of the fracture, of time folding upon itself. The protective sigils hold, but barely.

Oct 16 - The Coven performed their ritual at midnight. Synchronization has ceased. Timepieces returned to normal function. The boundary is secured, though M. Winters believes this is temporary—"until the stars align once more."

The final entry was written in a shaky hand:

The Pendulum must remain hidden. They must not find it when the cycle returns.

Tobias looked up. "The Pendulum. The clocks mentioned 'the pendulum that bridges worlds.' This has happened before."

Lord Ravencroft leaned forward. "May I?" He took the ledger, examining it closely. "M. Ravencroft would be my father. He never mentioned this incident."

"The Winters woman would be my grandmother," Madame Winters added. "This explains much. The disturbance was contained, not resolved. A temporary fix with an expiration date."

"And that date is approaching," Eliza concluded.

Madame Winters nodded. "The stars align once more. There's an unusual celestial configuration occurring next week—a conjunction of planets that happens every ninety-eight years."

"What's this Pendulum they mention?" Tobias asked.

"I don't know," Madame Winters admitted. "But your grandfather clearly thought it was important—and dangerous."

The shop door opened again, admitting a striking Asian woman in a tailored pantsuit and a tall man whose eyes constantly scanned the room with predatory alertness.

"Tobias Merrick?" the woman asked, flashing a badge. "Detective Alice Chen, Daybridge PD Paranormal Investigations. This is my partner, Detective Ethan Reeves. We're responding to your report of a temporal disturbance."

Tobias gestured helplessly at the room full of synchronized clocks. "It's gotten more complicated since I called."

Detective Reeves sniffed the air subtly, his nostrils flaring. Werewolf, Tobias realized with a start. The detective's slightly too-sharp canines confirmed it.

"Quite the gathering," Detective Chen observed, nodding respectfully to Lord Ravencroft and Madame Winters. "I see Daybridge's supernatural community is already involved."

"The situation affects us all," Ravencroft replied smoothly. "Time disturbances don't discriminate between the supernatural and the mundane."

Detective Chen approached the nearest clock—a delicate silver carriage clock—and placed her hand on its surface. She jerked back immediately.

"You feel it too," Madame Winters said, watching her closely.

The detective nodded. "Like an electric current. But cold." She turned to her partner. "Ethan?"

Detective Reeves shook his head. "Nothing specific. But something smells... off. Like ozone before a storm."

As they spoke, a soft chime rang out from one of the pocket watches. Then another clock chimed, and another, until every timepiece in the shop rang out in perfect unison. When the chiming stopped, every clock face showed 11:36.

"Another minute lost," Eliza whispered.

"It's accelerating," Madame Winters said, concern evident in her voice. "The countdown is speeding up."

Detective Chen pulled out a notebook. "Mr. Merrick, we need to know everything that happened, from the beginning. When did you first notice the synchronization?"

As Tobias recounted the events of the past few days, the shop grew darker, though it was only mid-afternoon. Outside, clouds had gathered, unnaturally thick and swirling with internal light.

"That's not normal weather," Detective Reeves muttered, moving to the window.

"It's not weather at all," Madame Winters replied. "It's a temporal distortion becoming visible. The fracture is affecting our reality already."

Suddenly, every clock in the shop began ticking louder, the sound building to a deafening crescendo. The temperature plummeted. Frost formed on the windows in intricate, fern-like patterns.

And the whispers returned—no longer just audible to Tobias, but filling the room so everyone could hear:

"The fracture widens."

"The past bleeds through."

"Find the Pendulum before the final toll."

"Eleven days remain until the unraveling."

The cloud outside pulsed with eerie blue light. Through the frosted window, they watched as a horse-drawn carriage materialized on Pendulum Lane, ghostly and translucent. The driver tipped his hat to a pedestrian who wasn't there, then the entire apparition faded like smoke.

"1890s," Lord Ravencroft commented. "Based on the carriage style."

Detective Chen's pen moved rapidly across her notebook. "The bleed-through has started. Small manifestations now, but they'll intensify as we approach zero hour."

The whispering clocks fell silent. The frost on the windows began to melt. Outside, the strange cloud dissipated, leaving normal afternoon sunlight.

"Eleven days," Detective Reeves said. "That's how long we have to find this pendulum and stop whatever's happening."

Tobias stared at his grandfather's ledger, the cryptic final entry swimming before his eyes: *The Pendulum must remain hidden. They must not find it when the cycle returns.*

"My grandfather knew something about this Pendulum," he said slowly. "He may have hidden it somewhere."

"Or destroyed it," Lord Ravencroft suggested.

Madame Winters shook her head. "You can't destroy artifacts of that magnitude. They can only be contained or redirected."

Detective Chen closed her notebook with a decisive snap. "Mr. Merrick, your shop is now central to an active paranormal investigation. We need to establish a base of operations here, with your cooperation."

Tobias looked around at his workshop—his orderly, predictable world now crowded with supernatural beings, talking timepieces, and the looming threat of temporal catastrophe.

"Do I have a choice?" he asked.

"The universe has already made that choice for you," Madame Winters said gently. "Your grandfather was involved in stopping this once before. Now the responsibility has passed to you."

Outside, a streetlamp flickered on despite the daylight, its glass casing briefly showing the ornate design of a gas lamp from a century earlier before returning to normal.

The boundary between the past and the present was already thinning. Soon, it would tear completely.

"Fine," Tobias said, straightening his shoulders. "Where do we start?"

"With your grandfather's records," Detective Chen replied. "Everything he wrote, everything he left behind. The answer is somewhere in this shop." She gestured to the synchronized clocks. "These timepieces are trying to warn us. We need to listen more carefully."

As if in response, the whispers rose again, fainter but unmistakable:

"The Pendulum waits where time stands still."

"Seek the place untouched by years."

"The keeper holds the key."

The voices faded, leaving Tobias with a chilling certainty. He wasn't just a clockmaker caught in supernatural events beyond his understanding.

He was the keeper. And somewhere in his past, in his family's legacy, lay the key to stopping time itself from unraveling.

CHAPTER THREE: DETECTIVE CHEN'S ASSIGNMENT

Detective Alice Chen had grown accustomed to the particular flavor of chaos that characterized the Paranormal Investigations Unit of the Daybridge Police Department. Three years into her transfer from Homicide, she'd investigated everything from poltergeist infestations to selkie custody disputes. Yet when Captain Vaughn dropped a thin file onto her desk that morning, his expression suggested something unusual even by their standards.

"Got a noise complaint for you, Chen," he said, already turning to leave.

Alice raised an eyebrow. "Noise complaints go to Uniform, not PI."

"Not when the noise is coming from inanimate objects." He paused at the door. "Clock shop in Oldewick. Guy claims his merchandise is whispering."

"Whispering clocks?" She flipped open the file. Just a single page with basic contact information for a Tobias Merrick of Merrick's Chronometry. "This feels like a prank call."

"Probably is. But we've had three similar reports this week—objects speaking, timepieces behaving oddly. Could be nothing, could be something. Check it out when you get a chance."

Alice nodded, tucking the file into her bag. Low priority, then. She had more pressing cases—a territorial dispute between rival werewolf packs in Riversend and a suspected vampire feeding outside sanctioned zones.

The clock shop would have to wait.

Her desk phone rang. The caller ID showed "St. Brigid's Hospital–Emergent Care."

"Detective Chen," she answered, tension immediately tightening her shoulders.

"Detective, this is Dr. Abernathy. Your partner was brought in this morning."

Alice was already grabbing her keys. "What happened? Is he stable?"

"He's fine—physically. Had an episode at the coffee shop on Fifth. Started shifting in public."

She exhaled slowly. Not an injury, at least. "I'll be there in fifteen."

St. Brigid's Hospital maintained a specialized wing for supernatural patients, discreetly accessible through a side entrance. Alice found Ethan in a private room designed for werewolves experiencing control issues—reinforced walls, minimal furniture, and a subtle silver infusion in the paint that helped prevent full transformation.

Ethan sat on the edge of the bed, hunched forward with his head in his hands. He looked up when she entered, his amber eyes brighter than usual—a warning sign this close to the full moon.

"Before you start," he said wearily, "I know. It was careless."

Alice closed the door behind her. "What triggered it?"

"Nothing specific. One minute I'm ordering coffee, the next my claws are out and I'm growling at the barista." He rubbed his face. "Moon's not for three days. This shouldn't be happening."

She studied her partner carefully. Ethan Reeves had been with Paranormal Investigations for eight years, longer than anyone else in the unit. A third-generation werewolf, he typically maintained impeccable control over his transformations—one reason they worked so well together. Alice provided the analytical thinking and attention to detail; Ethan contributed enhanced senses and physical capabilities that had saved her life more than once.

"Have you been taking your stabilizers?" she asked.

He nodded. "Double dose this week. Something's off, Alice. It feels like the moon is pulling harder than usual."

Dr. Abernathy entered, clipboard in hand. "Detective Reeves, your blood work shows elevated adrenal markers, but nothing that would explain a spontaneous partial shift."

"See? Not just me." Ethan stood, steadier now. "Something weird is happening."

Alice remembered Captain Vaughn's comment about multiple reports of strange occurrences. "Is this happening to other werewolves?"

"Three cases since yesterday," Dr. Abernathy confirmed. "All reporting unusual moon sensitivity despite being mid-cycle."

Alice pulled out her phone, checking the lunar calendar. "Full moon's on the 15th. We're only at first quarter."

"Exactly my concern." The doctor handed Ethan a prescription. "I've adjusted your stabilizer formula. Should help, but I'd recommend staying away from stressful situations until we understand what's happening."

Ethan scoffed. "Doc, I'm a PI detective. Stress is the job description."

"Then perhaps desk duty—"

"Not happening." Ethan pocketed the prescription. "I'm fine now. Just caught me off guard."

After signing the discharge papers, they walked to Alice's unmarked sedan in the hospital parking lot. The October air carried the scent of fallen leaves and wood smoke, with the faintest metallic undertone that Alice had come to associate with Daybridge's ambient magical energy.

"I should drive," she said, noting how Ethan's hands still trembled slightly.

He surrendered the keys without argument—unusual for him. "Where are we headed? Back to the station?"

Alice considered the stack of cases waiting at her desk, then made a decision. "Actually, let's check out this clock shop. Might be a simple matter we can clear quickly."

"Clock shop?"

She filled him in as they drove through downtown Daybridge toward the Oldewick district—the city's oldest neighborhood, where cobblestone streets wound between buildings dating back to the 1700s. Oldewick had the highest concentration of supernatural residents and businesses in the city, its ancient architecture seemingly attractive to those with extended lifespans.

"Talking clocks," Ethan mused, staring out the window. "Sounds like a haunting."

"Or a hoax. Or faulty wiring creating audio pareidolia." Alice navigated the narrow streets with practiced ease. "Either way, should be straightforward."

Ethan suddenly sat up straighter, nostrils flaring. "Stop the car."

"What? Why?"

"Just—pull over. Now."

Alice complied, guiding the sedan to the curb. "What is it?"

Ethan rolled down his window, breathing deeply. "You smell that?"

She inhaled but detected nothing unusual. "Ethan, I don't have werewolf senses."

"It's like... ozone. And something older." His eyes had taken on that amber glow again. "Like when you open a sealed room that hasn't been aired out in decades."

"Coming from where?"

He pointed down the street toward a storefront with a hanging wooden sign depicting a pocket watch. "There. Merrick's Chronometry."

Alice checked the address against her notes. "That's our destination, anyway."

As they approached the shop, Alice noticed the "Emergency Repairs" sign on the door, but light shone from within. Through the window, she could see several people gathered among displays of antique clocks.

"Looks busy for a closed shop," Ethan remarked, his enhanced vision picking up details she couldn't see. "Old woman with crystals, fancy guy in an expensive suit, young woman, and a middle-aged man who looks stressed out of his mind."

"Our clock owner, presumably." Alice knocked firmly on the door.

The shop fell silent. After a moment, the middle-aged man approached, unlocking the door with visible reluctance.

"Tobias Merrick?" Alice asked, showing her badge. "Detective Alice Chen, Daybridge PD Paranormal Investigations. This is my partner, Detective Ethan Reeves. We're responding to your report of a temporal disturbance."

The man—Merrick—gestured helplessly at a room filled with clocks. "It's gotten more complicated since I called."

As they entered, Alice immediately sensed the difference between this space and the street outside. The air felt charged, compressed, as though the shop existed slightly out of sync with the world around it. She recognized Lord Ravencroft, one of Daybridge's oldest vampire residents and a member of the city council, and Madame Winters, whose reputation as a temporal specialist preceded her.

"Quite the gathering," she observed, nodding respectfully to both supernatural dignitaries. "I see Daybridge's supernatural community is already involved."

"The situation affects us all," Ravencroft replied smoothly. "Time disturbances don't discriminate between supernatural and mundane."

Alice approached the nearest clock—a delicate silver carriage clock—and placed her hand on its surface. A jolt ran up her arm, cold yet electric, carrying impressions of somewhere else, somewhen else. She jerked back instinctively.

"You feel it too," Madame Winters said, watching her closely.

Alice nodded, flexing her tingling fingers. "Like an electric current. But cold." She turned to Ethan. "Ethan?"

He shook his head, still scanning the room with heightened alertness. "Nothing specific. But something smells... off. Like ozone before a storm."

As they spoke, the clocks began chiming in perfect unison. When they stopped, every timepiece displayed 11:36.

"Another minute lost," the young woman whispered.

"It's accelerating," Madame Winters said, concern evident in her voice. "The countdown is speeding up."

Alice pulled out her notebook, suddenly aware that what had seemed a minor noise complaint was evolving into something far more significant. "Mr. Merrick, we need to know everything that happened, from the beginning. When did you first notice the synchronization?"

As Merrick recounted the events, Alice's training kicked in. She documented everything methodically while evaluating the situation through the lens of her PI experience. This wasn't a standard haunting or magical mishap. The involvement of Lord Ravencroft and Madame Winters confirmed the severity.

Outside, unnatural clouds gathered with swirling internal light.

"That's not normal weather," Ethan muttered, moving to the window.

"It's not weather at all," Madame Winters replied. "It's temporal distortion becoming visible. The fracture is affecting our reality already."

The clocks grew louder, frost formed on the windows, and then the whispers filled the room—voices speaking of fractures and countdowns and something called the Pendulum.

Through the frosted window, Alice watched as a ghostly horse-drawn carriage appeared on the street outside, then vanished like smoke.

"1890s," Lord Ravencroft commented. "Based on the carriage style."

Alice's pen moved rapidly across her notebook. "The bleed-through has started. Small manifestations now, but they'll intensify as we approach zero hour."

As the supernatural display subsided, Alice closed her notebook with a decisive snap. This case had just become top priority. "Mr. Merrick, your shop is now central to an active paranormal investigation. We need to establish a base of operations here, with your cooperation."

Merrick looked around his workshop, clearly overwhelmed. "Do I have a choice?"

"The universe has already made that choice for you," Madame Winters said gently. "Your grandfather was involved in stopping this once before. Now the responsibility has passed to you."

Outside, a modern streetlamp briefly transformed into a gas lamp from another era.

"Fine," Merrick finally agreed. "Where do we start?"

"With your grandfather's records," Alice replied, slipping into her role as lead investigator. "Everything he wrote, everything he left behind. The answer is somewhere in this shop." She gestured to the synchronized clocks. "These timepieces are trying to warn us. We need to listen more carefully."

The whispers rose again, speaking of pendulums and keepers and keys, then faded into silence.

Alice turned to Ethan, who stood rigidly by the window, his jaw clenched tight. "You okay?"

He nodded stiffly. "The moon. It feels stronger in here. Like it's pulling from multiple directions."

"Temporal distortion affects lunar connections," Madame Winters explained. "For werewolves, it can be particularly disorienting."

"I can handle it," Ethan insisted, though Alice noted how his hands curled into fists at his sides.

She made a quick decision. "Ethan, head back to the station. Fill in Captain Vaughn, request resources."

He started to protest, but she cut him off with a look they'd perfected over years of partnership. "We need backup, and you need distance from whatever's happening here. Tactical decision, not a suggestion."

After a tense moment, he nodded. "Fine. But I'm coming back with the team."

Once Ethan departed, Alice addressed the remaining group. "Let's get organized. Mr. Merrick, I need all your grandfather's journals, ledgers, anything that might mention this Pendulum or the events of 1927."

"Most of his papers are in storage at my home," Merrick said. "But I have the business records here."

"Eliza Park," the young woman introduced herself. "I'm Mr. Merrick's assistant. I can help sort through the shop records."

"Lord Ravencroft," Alice continued, "your connection to the previous incident could be valuable. Any chance your family archives contain information about the 1927 disturbance?"

The vampire nodded. "I'll have my archivist search immediately. Though if my father kept this from family records, there may have been good reason."

"Madame Winters, we need everything you can tell us about temporal fractures—causes, effects, containment methods."

The elderly woman nodded, already extracting more journals from her seemingly bottomless bag. "I've been researching similar incidents for decades. The pattern matches several historical events, including one in Vienna that Edmund would remember."

As they began establishing a makeshift investigation center among the antique clocks, Alice felt a familiar sensation—the focused clarity that came with complex cases. This was why she'd transferred to PI from Homicide. The supernatural elements added layers of complexity that challenged her analytical mind.

She moved to the window, watching as Ethan's figure disappeared around a corner. His reaction worried her. If temporal distortion affected werewolves this strongly, the approaching full moon could complicate matters further.

The shop's many clocks ticked in perfect synchronization, the sound almost hypnotic. Alice found herself staring at the nearest timepiece—an ornate mantel clock with brass cherubs flanking its face. For just a moment, she thought she saw the cherubs move, turning their tiny heads to watch her.

She blinked, and they were inanimate once more.

Eleven days until the temporal fracture reached critical mass. Eleven days to find a mysterious Pendulum and prevent time itself from unraveling. All while managing a werewolf partner increasingly affected by lunar distortion, coordinating with Daybridge's supernatural elites, and helping a reluctant clockmaker accept his apparent destiny.

Just another day in Paranormal Investigations.

"Detective?" Merrick appeared beside her, holding a dusty ledger. "I found something else. A blueprint of the shop from 1912, when my grandfather renovated. There's a space marked here—" he pointed to a section of the rear wall—"that doesn't exist anymore. At least, not that I can access."

Alice studied the yellowed paper. "A hidden room?"

"Possibly. The dimensions don't match the current layout."

"Then that's where we start," she decided. "Get me a hammer."

Across town, Ethan Reeves gripped the steering wheel of his Jeep so tightly his knuckles whitened. The strange pulling sensation had followed him from the clock shop, an insistent tugging behind his sternum that made his wolf strain against its human containment.

Something about those synchronized clocks and their whispered warnings resonated with his lupine nature in ways he couldn't articulate. Werewolves existed partially outside normal time—their monthly transformations governed by cosmic forces rather than human calendars. Perhaps that made him more sensitive to temporal disturbances.

His phone rang—the station calling. He ignored it, instead pulling into the parking lot of Howl, a werewolf-friendly bar on the edge of the Riversend district. He needed information from sources that wouldn't appear in official reports.

The bar's interior was dimly lit even in daytime, the air thick with the scent of wolf and whiskey. Several patrons looked up as he entered, nostrils flaring to identify him. A few nodded in recognition.

Behind the bar, Lowell Grey—pack elder and unofficial keeper of werewolf history in Daybridge—watched him approach.

"Detective," the older werewolf greeted him. "You're looking moon-touched. Still three days out, isn't it?"

Ethan leaned against the bar. "That's why I'm here. Something's affecting the lunar cycle. Or our perception of it."

Lowell's eyes narrowed. "You're not the first to mention it. Three of my regulars called in sick today—partial shifts they couldn't control."

"It's happening across the city. Concentrated in Oldewick."

"Oldewick," Lowell repeated, his expression darkening. "Always comes back to Oldewick."

Ethan's instincts sharpened. "What do you mean?"

The elder werewolf glanced around, then motioned Ethan to follow him to a back office. Once inside, Lowell unlocked an ancient cabinet and extracted a leather-bound book.

"Pack histories," he explained. "Records kept by each alpha going back generations." He opened the book to a marked page. "October 1927. Three nights of what our ancestors called 'the fractured moon.' Every werewolf in Daybridge transformed regardless of the lunar phase."

Ethan studied the faded handwriting. "What caused it?"

"They didn't know. Only that it centered around Oldewick." Lowell tapped a particular passage. "The alpha at the time, Margaret Blackwood, wrote that 'time itself seemed to fold and stretch, with moments repeating and others skipped entirely.' Sound familiar?"

Ethan thought of the ghostly carriage materializing outside Merrick's shop. "Temporal distortion. It's happening again."

Lowell nodded grimly. "The pack histories mention a ritual performed by the Winters Coven that temporarily sealed the disturbance. But Margaret noted it wasn't a permanent solution—just a postponement."

"Until the stars align once more," Ethan murmured, remembering the phrase from Merrick's grandfather's journal.

"You know something about this?" Lowell asked sharply.

"A case. Centered around a clock shop in Oldewick. Timepieces counting down to something, temporal bleeding already starting." He ran a hand through his hair. "There's mention of something called the Pendulum. Does that mean anything to you?"

Lowell's expression changed subtly—a flicker of recognition quickly suppressed. "Why would it?"

Ethan's enhanced senses detected the slight acceleration in the elder's heartbeat. "You're lying."

"Careful, Detective." Lowell's eyes flashed golden. "Pack matters and police matters don't always align."

"This isn't about jurisdiction. If time itself is fracturing, it affects everyone—human, werewolf, vampire, all of us."

The older werewolf seemed to weigh his options before sighing heavily. "The Pendulum isn't just an object. It's a name—one rarely spoken among our kind."

"Why?"

"Because the last werewolf who sought it never returned—at least, not as himself." Lowell closed the pack history. "Margaret Blackwood's mate, John Reeves. Your great-grandfather."

Ethan froze. "What?"

"The histories say he volunteered to help hide the artifact after the ritual. When he returned three days later, he'd aged decades overnight. Died within a week, his mind lost in time." Lowell's expression softened slightly. "Your family changed their territory after that, moved to Riversend. Most younger wolves don't know the connection."

The pulling sensation in Ethan's chest intensified, as though his very blood recognized a long-forgotten call. "I need to see the full account."

"It won't help you find the Pendulum. John never revealed its location, even to his mate."

"It's not about finding it. It's about understanding what we're dealing with." Ethan leaned forward. "This isn't just a PI case anymore. It's personal."

Lowell hesitated, then nodded. "I'll make copies of the relevant pages. But Ethan—be careful. Whatever this Pendulum is, it broke something in John Reeves that even his wolf couldn't heal."

As Ethan waited for the copies, his phone buzzed with a text from Alice:

Found hidden room behind shop wall. Get back here. Bringing in full PI team.

He texted back:

On my way. Have new information. Personal connection.

The moon wasn't full yet, but Ethan could feel its influence growing stronger by the hour—pulled forward by whatever temporal distortion affected Daybridge. His wolf stirred beneath his skin, restless and alert.

For the first time in years, he wasn't sure he could control it when the transformation came.

CHAPTER FOUR: THE HISTORIAN'S THEORY

The hidden room behind the shop wall proved disappointingly empty—just a small storage space with water-damaged walls and a collection of rusted tools. By the time Ethan returned to Merrick's Chronometry, Alice had already called in the department's Temporal Specialist, Dr. Joan Mackie from Daybridge University.

Tobias watched the PI team transform his workshop into an investigation center with a mixture of resignation and disbelief. Three technicians set up equipment around the perimeter—devices that looked more like modern art than scientific instruments, with spinning components and pulsing lights. Another officer methodically photographed each clock, documenting their synchronized time: 11:35.

The minute hand had moved again while they'd searched the hidden room.

"Progress report," Alice said when Ethan entered, noticing his troubled expression.

"Later," he replied, nodding toward a corner where they could speak privately. Once there, he kept his voice low. "The Pendulum has a connection to my family. My great-grandfather was involved in hiding it after the 1927 incident."

Alice's eyes widened. "That can't be a coincidence."

"No coincidences in Daybridge," Ethan agreed, a department axiom. "There's more. The pack histories describe exactly what we're seeing—temporal bleeding, lunar disruption. They called it 'the fractured moon.'"

"Did they mention how to fix it?"

"Only that a coven performed a ritual as a temporary solution." He glanced toward Madame Winters, who was deep in conversation with Lord Ravencroft. "The Winters Coven, specifically."

Alice absorbed this. "So we have two family connections to the previous incident—yours and Madame Winters."

"Three," Ethan corrected, gesturing toward Tobias. "His grandfather was the clockmaker then."

"The universe isn't subtle with its patterns." Alice frowned. "Any mention of what the Pendulum actually is?"

"Nothing specific. But whatever it is, it affected my great-grandfather badly. Aged him decades in days."

Before Alice could respond, the shop door opened to admit a tall Black woman with close-cropped silver hair and the purposeful stride of someone perpetually late for important appointments. She carried a leather messenger bag overflowing with papers and wore a tweed jacket despite the October warmth.

"Dr. Mackie," Alice greeted her. "Thank you for coming so quickly."

"When the PIU calls about temporal anomalies, one doesn't dawdle," Dr. Mackie replied, her British accent crisp. She surveyed the shop with practiced efficiency. "Synchronized timepieces, whispered warnings, and visible bleeding between time periods. Classic signs of boundary degradation."

Tobias approached, extending his hand. "Tobias Merrick. This is my shop."

"Dr. Joan Mackie, Professor of Paranormal History and Temporal Mechanics." She shook his hand firmly. "I've actually cited your grandfather's work in my research on chronometric artifacts."

"My grandfather?"

"Harold Merrick was one of the few horologists who documented supernatural influences on timekeeping mechanisms." She set her bag on the counter. "His papers on sympathetic resonance in pendulum systems were groundbreaking, if largely ignored by mainstream academia."

Tobias blinked. "I didn't know he published academic work."

"Not formally. His notes were collected after his death by the Department of Paranormal Studies." Dr. Mackie extracted a tablet from her bag. "Which is why I found this particularly interesting."

She pulled up an image of a journal page covered in the same cramped handwriting Tobias had seen in his grandfather's ledger.

"October 17, 1927," she read. "'The temporal breach has been sealed, but at significant cost. The Pendulum must be hidden where neither the Coven nor the Pack can access it again. Its power is too great, its influence too seductive. Time was not meant to be manipulated so directly.'"

Alice and Ethan exchanged glances.

"Where did you find this?" Tobias asked.

"University archives. Your grandfather donated his professional papers before his death, but certain documents were sealed until 2025." Dr. Mackie smiled slightly. "Which happens to be this year."

"Convenient timing," Lord Ravencroft remarked, joining their circle.

"Or deliberate," Madame Winters added. "Harold Merrick was a skilled horologist with an intuitive understanding of temporal patterns. He may have calculated when the next fracture would occur."

Dr. Mackie nodded. "My working theory is that we're experiencing a cyclic temporal disturbance—one that occurs at specific astronomical intervals. The previous manifestation in 1927 was temporarily contained rather than resolved."

"Like putting a patch on a dam instead of rebuilding it," Alice suggested.

"Precisely. And now the patch is failing." Dr. Mackie approached one of the synchronized clocks—a delicate astronomical timepiece with celestial complications. She placed her hand on its surface, closing her eyes briefly. "Yes, definite temporal resonance. These timepieces are acting as sympathetic conduits."

"Speaking English for those of us without paranormal degrees?" Ethan requested.

Dr. Mackie smiled. "Time isn't as linear as humans perceive it. It's more like a fabric—flexible, woven from countless threads of potential. Normally, the fabric maintains its integrity, but certain conditions can cause weak spots or tears."

"The fracture," Tobias said.

"Exactly. What you're experiencing is a thinning of the temporal fabric beneath Daybridge. These clocks, being instruments designed to measure time, are naturally sensitive to such disturbances. They're resonating with the fracture—essentially communicating across time periods."

Alice took notes. "And the whispers?"

"Echoes from other temporal locations." Dr. Mackie gestured expansively. "Imagine time as an infinite series of parallel roads. Normally, you can only see your own road. But at points where the barriers between roads thin, you might hear traffic from adjacent paths—voices, events, fragments of other realities."

One of the PI technicians approached, tablet in hand. "Detective Chen, we've completed the initial scans. Temporal distortion is concentrated in a roughly three-block radius around this location, with the epicenter directly beneath the shop."

Dr. Mackie leaned over to view the data. "As I suspected. This site likely sits on a temporal convergence point—where multiple threads of time naturally run closer together."

"Is that why my family has operated here for three generations?" Tobias asked.

"Possibly. People with temporal sensitivity are often unconsciously drawn to such locations." Dr. Mackie studied him thoughtfully. "Your family may have served as unwitting guardians of this convergence point."

The notion that his orderly, predictable clockmaking lineage might have a cosmic purpose made Tobias's head spin. He'd spent his life avoiding Daybridge's supernatural side, only to discover he might be intrinsically connected to it.

"The countdown," Alice redirected the conversation. "The clocks show 11:35 now. What happens at zero?"

Dr. Mackie's expression sobered. "Total boundary collapse. Past, present, and potential futures bleeding together without separation. Imagine experiencing multiple time periods simultaneously—buildings from different centuries occupying the same space, people encountering earlier or later versions of themselves."

"That sounds catastrophic," Ethan said.

"It is. The psychological impact alone would be devastating—human minds aren't equipped to process overlapping temporalities. Physical laws would become unpredictable. Causality itself could break down."

Madame Winters nodded gravely. "The 1927 incident was minor by comparison—just flickering between two adjacent time periods. From the instruments' readings, this fracture connects to multiple temporal points."

"Which means we're not just talking about seeing ghost carriages from the 1890s," Alice concluded. "We could experience bleed-through from any point in Daybridge's history."

"Or its future," Dr. Mackie added quietly.

A heavy silence fell over the group, broken only by the synchronized ticking of dozens of clocks.

Tobias cleared his throat. "You mentioned my grandfather's notes were sealed until 2025. What else did they contain?"

Dr. Mackie extracted a folder from her seemingly bottomless bag. "Mostly technical observations about clock mechanisms responding to supernatural phenomena. But there was one section that caught my attention."

She handed Tobias several photocopied pages. The top sheet contained a detailed technical drawing of a pendulum unlike any he'd seen before. Its bob wasn't the typical lenticular shape but rather a complex crystalline structure with multiple facets. Surrounding it were equations and diagrams that made little sense to him.

"What am I looking at?" he asked.

"Your grandfather's design for what he called a 'temporal anchor'—a device capable of stabilizing weakened points in the time-space continuum." Dr. Mackie tapped the drawing. "He theorized that a precisely calibrated pendulum, constructed of specific materials and oscillating at exactly the right frequency, could reinforce the boundary between time periods."

Alice leaned closer. "Is this the Pendulum everyone keeps mentioning?"

"I believe so." Dr. Mackie turned the page to reveal more detailed notes. "According to these calculations, Harold Merrick actually built this device in 1927. He used it as part of the ritual that sealed the previous fracture."

"And then hid it," Ethan added, "where neither the Coven nor the Pack could find it."

Tobias studied the diagrams with growing amazement. The pendulum's design incorporated principles of harmonics and resonance that he recognized from his own work, but pushed to theoretical extremes. This wasn't just clever clockmaking—it was temporal engineering.

"If my grandfather built this, and it worked once before, we need to find it," he said.

"That's assuming it still exists," Lord Ravencroft cautioned. "Ninety-eight years is a long time, even for powerful artifacts."

"It exists," Madame Winters said with quiet certainty. "Objects of that magnitude don't simply disappear. They persist, sometimes changing form, but always maintaining their essential nature."

Dr. Mackie nodded. "The temporal energy contained in such an artifact would make it virtually indestructible. It might be hidden, disguised, or dormant, but it's still somewhere in Daybridge."

"Then finding it is our priority," Alice decided. She turned to Tobias. "Any ideas where your grandfather might have hidden something of this importance?"

Before he could answer, the air in the center of the shop seemed to ripple like heat waves rising from asphalt. The temperature plummeted suddenly, frost forming on the nearest glass surfaces. The clocks' ticking grew louder, more insistent.

"Another manifestation," Dr. Mackie said, her voice tight. "Everyone, maintain your positions. Temporal bleeding can be disorienting, but it's temporary."

The rippling air coalesced into a translucent figure—an elderly man in outdated clothing, his hands stained with clock oil. He moved about the shop as though unaware of their presence, adjusting tools on a workbench that no longer existed in their reality.

"Grandfather?" Tobias whispered, recognizing him from old photographs.

The apparition didn't respond, continuing his silent work. Then, abruptly, he looked up—not at Tobias, but at empty space near the shop's rear wall. His expression changed to one of alarm. He moved quickly to a cabinet, extracted something wrapped in cloth, and hurried to the wall. As they watched, he pressed a hidden panel, revealing a small compartment into which he placed the wrapped object.

"He's hiding something," Ethan said unnecessarily.

The ghostly figure turned suddenly, as though hearing them for the first time. His gaze swept the room, lingering momentarily where Tobias stood. His lips moved, forming words they couldn't hear.

"What's he saying?" Alice asked.

"I can't—" Tobias began, but Dr. Mackie interrupted.

"He's saying, 'The key is in the chronometer. Beware the wolves.'" Ethan stiffened.

The apparition faded, the temperature returned to normal, and the frost melted from the glass.

"That was remarkably clear for a temporal echo," Dr. Mackie observed, already making notes on her tablet. "Almost as though it was directed specifically at us."

"It was," Madame Winters said. "Harold Merrick had strong temporal sensitivity. He may have sensed this moment from his point in time—known that we would be watching."

Alice was already moving toward the wall where the ghostly figure had hidden his package. "There was a compartment here. Did we miss it during our search?"

Tobias joined her, running his hands along the wooden paneling. "This wall has been replaced since my grandfather's time. Termite damage in the 1950s." He knocked on the surface, hearing only solid wood. "If there was a hidden compartment, it's gone now."

"What about 'the key is in the chronometer'?" Ethan asked. "What chronometer?"

Tobias frowned. "That could refer to any precision timepiece. We have dozens of chronometers here."

"Or," Dr. Mackie suggested, "he could have meant a specific one—perhaps a family heirloom or personal timepiece?"

"The pocket watch," Tobias said suddenly. "My grandfather's marine chronometer. My father inherited it, and then I did." He patted his pockets. "I don't have it with me. It's at home, in my safe."

"Then that's our next stop," Alice decided. "Dr. Mackie, can you stay here with the PI team and continue analyzing the temporal readings?"

"Of course. I'll also work with Madame Winters to reconstruct what we know about the 1927 ritual." She glanced at the synchronized clocks. "We have ten days remaining before critical failure, but the bleeding events will increase in frequency and duration as we approach zero hour."

"Lord Ravencroft," Alice continued, "your resources could be valuable in researching historical accounts from that period."

The vampire nodded. "I'll have my archivists search for any mention of temporal disturbances or the Pendulum. My family's records go back centuries."

"Ethan and I will accompany Mr. Merrick to retrieve the chronometer," Alice concluded. "Eliza, would you—"

A loud crash interrupted her as one of the antique clocks suddenly fell from its shelf, shattering on the floor. Before anyone could react, every clock in the shop began chiming in chaotic discord. Wind whipped through the room despite closed windows, and the lights flickered wildly.

"Massive temporal surge!" one of the technicians shouted over the noise, staring at his instruments. "Multiple convergence points activating simultaneously!"

The air split open in a dozen places throughout the shop, each rift revealing glimpses of Daybridge from different eras—colonial buildings, horse-drawn carriages, early automobiles, and in one disturbing tear, sleek structures of glass and metal that hadn't yet been built.

Through one of the largest rifts, they could see figures moving—people in the 1920s clothing hurrying through what appeared to be this very shop, though arranged differently. Among them, Tobias recognized his grandfather again, now accompanied by a younger woman wearing ceremonial robes covered in arcane symbols.

"That's my grandmother," Madame Winters gasped. "The head of the Winters Coven in 1927."

The figures were clearly in the midst of some urgent ritual. They arranged candles in a precise pattern around a central object that glowed with unnatural blue light.

"The Pendulum," Ethan breathed, his eyes fixed on the crystalline device at the center of their circle.

The scene shifted suddenly, showing the same group but clearly later—exhausted, some bleeding from their noses and ears. Tobias's grandfather cradled the now-dormant Pendulum, wrapping it carefully while speaking intensely to a tall, muscular man whose eyes reflected golden in the candlelight.

"John Reeves," Ethan said softly. "My great-grandfather."

The temporal windows began closing one by one, the discordant chiming subsiding. As the largest rift sealed, they caught a final glimpse of Harold Merrick handing the wrapped Pendulum to John Reeves, who nodded grimly before departing.

When the last rift closed, the shop fell eerily silent. Even the clocks' ticking seemed muted.

"What just happened?" Tobias asked, his voice unsteady.

"The barrier is weakening faster than anticipated," Dr. Mackie said, checking her instruments. "These aren't just echoes anymore—they're full temporal windows. The fracture is expanding exponentially."

Alice turned to Ethan, noting his pallor. "You okay?"

He nodded stiffly. "Just... wasn't expecting to see my great-grandfather."

"This confirms our family connections to the previous incident," Alice said. "Winters, Merrick, and Reeves—all involved in containing the 1927 fracture."

"And now our descendants face the same threat," Madame Winters observed. "The universe has a peculiar sense of symmetry."

"Or the Pendulum itself is drawing us together," Dr. Mackie suggested. "Powerful temporal artifacts often create causality loops, ensuring their own protection or activation."

Ethan's phone buzzed. He checked it, his expression darkening. "Captain Vaughn. Three more reports of temporal bleeding across Daybridge. Public manifestations this time—a Revolutionary War militia appeared in the middle of Riverside Park, then vanished. Nineteenth-century factory sounds emanating from empty buildings. A trolley car from the 1920s materialized on Main Street for thirty seconds, causing a traffic accident."

"It's spreading beyond this location," Alice said.

"And accelerating," Dr. Mackie confirmed, showing them her tablet. "At this rate, we'll reach critical mass before the countdown completes."

One of the technicians approached with another update. "All clocks now show 11:34. They just changed simultaneously."

"Another minute lost," Tobias said. "But it's only been a few hours since the last change."

"Time is becoming unstable," Dr. Mackie explained. "The countdown itself is affected by the fracture—it may accelerate as the boundary weakens."

Alice took charge. "We need that chronometer. Now. Ethan, with me and Mr. Merrick. The rest of you, continue research and monitoring. We'll reconvene in two hours."

As they prepared to leave, Tobias noticed something odd about the broken clock on the floor. Among the shattered glass and gears lay a small key—antique brass, intricately designed, and definitely not part of the clock's mechanism.

He picked it up carefully. "This wasn't here before."

Dr. Mackie examined it without touching. "Temporal displacement. Objects sometimes shift between periods during these events."

"Could this be what my grandfather meant?" Tobias asked. "The key in the chronometer?"

"Possibly, though it seems too convenient," she replied. "Bring it with you but be careful. Objects that travel through temporal rifts can carry residual energy."

As they left the shop, Ethan paused on the threshold, his enhanced senses detecting something the others couldn't.

"What is it?" Alice asked.

"We're being watched," he said quietly. "Northwest corner. Behind the bookshop."

Alice casually scanned the street, noting a figure ducking into an alley. "Think they're connected to this?"

"Everyone in Daybridge is connected to this now." Ethan's eyes briefly flashed amber. "But some connections run deeper than others."

Tobias clutched the mysterious key in his palm, feeling its weight—physical and metaphorical. His grandfather had created a device that saved Daybridge once before. Now that responsibility had fallen to him, a man who'd spent his life avoiding the very forces he now needed to understand.

As they walked to Alice's car, he glanced back at his shop. For a moment—just a flicker—he thought he saw it as it had been in his grandfather's time, with gas lamps and a hand-painted sign. Then it returned to normal, the brief overlay fading like mist in sunshine.

The boundary between then and now was dissolving. Soon, there might be no difference at all.

CHAPTER FIVE: FULL MOON REVELATIONS

Tobias's home stood on Pendulum Heights, a quiet neighborhood of Victorian houses overlooking downtown Daybridge. The three-story Queen Anne had belonged to his family for generations, its gabled roof and wraparound porch unchanged since the 1890s. As Alice parked at the curb, Ethan scanned the street with heightened senses.

"Still feeling watched?" she asked quietly.

He nodded. "Different presence than before. More... primal."

"Another werewolf?"

"Maybe." He rolled his shoulders, trying to release the tension building there. "Hard to tell with everything so distorted."

The October afternoon had taken on an unnatural quality—shadows stretching at incorrect angles, birdsong occasionally playing in reverse. Twice during their drive, they'd passed through patches where the temperature suddenly dropped twenty degrees, then returned to normal a block later.

Tobias led them up the walkway, unlocking an ornate front door with stained glass panels. Inside, the house reflected the same meticulous order as his shop—antique furniture arranged with mathematical precision, surfaces dust-free, every item in its designated place.

"My study is this way," he said, guiding them through a hallway lined with photographs—three generations of Merricks standing before the same storefront, their faces showing the same serious expression despite the changing fashions around them.

Ethan paused at one photo. "This your grandfather?"

Tobias glanced back. "Yes, with my father. Taken around 1945."

"He looks... older than he should." Ethan studied the image closely. Harold Merrick appeared almost ancient in the photograph, though based on the date, he should have been in his fifties.

"He aged rapidly in his final years," Tobias explained. "My father said it was a genetic condition, but..."

"But now you're wondering if it was connected to the Pendulum," Alice finished for him.

Tobias nodded, continuing to his study—a room dominated by a massive oak desk and walls of bookshelves filled with horological texts. A glass-fronted cabinet displayed pocket watches and small clocks too valuable or fragile for the shop.

He crossed to a painting of the Daybridge harbor circa 1900, swinging it aside to reveal a wall safe. "My grandfather's chronometer has been passed down as a family heirloom. I rarely use it—it's too valuable for everyday carry."

As Tobias worked the combination, Ethan moved restlessly around the study. The approaching full moon pulled at him, making his skin feel too tight, his senses almost painfully sharp. Through the window, he watched clouds scudding unnaturally fast across the sky—another temporal anomaly.

"Here it is," Tobias said, opening the safe and extracting a wooden box inlaid with mother-of-pearl.

Inside, nestled on velvet, lay a silver pocket watch approximately three inches in diameter. Its case featured intricate engravings of celestial bodies—sun, moon, stars, and planets arranged in specific constellations. Tobias carefully lifted it by its chain.

"Marine chronometer, 1889. Made by Thomas Merrick, my great-grandfather." He opened the case, revealing a face of remarkable complexity—multiple dials tracking not just hours and minutes, but lunar phases, tides, and celestial positions. "It's accurate to within two seconds per year, if properly maintained."

"It's beautiful," Alice said. "But how is it a key?"

Tobias extracted the mysterious brass key from his pocket, comparing it to the chronometer. "They don't seem related. The key is much older, possibly 18th century based on the design."

Ethan approached, then suddenly recoiled, a low growl escaping his throat.

"What's wrong?" Alice asked sharply.

"That watch." He gestured toward the chronometer, maintaining his distance. "It smells like... time."

"Time has a smell?" Tobias asked skeptically.

"Not normally. But that thing—" Ethan's eyes flashed amber momentarily. "It's like ozone and old books and something metallic. The same scent I detected at temporal bleeding sites."

Alice looked thoughtful. "Is it possible the chronometer itself is temporally active?"

Tobias examined the watch more carefully. "It's keeping perfect time, unlike the clocks in the shop." He hesitated, then added, "But there's something I haven't mentioned. This chronometer never needs winding."

"That's not possible for a mechanical timepiece," Alice said.

"I know. My father told me it was a family secret—some special mechanism my great-grandfather invented. I assumed it was just efficient, but..." He trailed off, turning the watch over to examine its back. "Wait. There's an irregularity in the engraving pattern."

Using his watchmaker's precision, Tobias pressed a nearly invisible seam in the silver casing. With a soft click, a hidden compartment opened in the back of the chronometer, revealing a small, crystalline fragment that emitted a faint blue glow.

"What is that?" Alice asked, leaning closer.

"I don't know. I never knew this compartment existed." Tobias carefully extracted the fragment with tweezers from his pocket. "It looks like a piece of the Pendulum from the visions we saw—same crystalline structure, same blue luminescence."

Ethan backed further away, his body language increasingly tense. "Whatever it is, it's affecting me. Like the moon is pulling harder when it's near."

"A fragment of the original Pendulum," Alice theorized. "Your grandfather must have kept a piece when they hid the main artifact."

Tobias nodded slowly. "'The key is in the chronometer.' He meant this fragment, not an actual key."

"But we still have this," Alice said, indicating the brass key. "It appeared during the temporal surge for a reason."

Tobias studied both objects. "Maybe they work together somehow? The fragment could be attuned to the Pendulum's location, and the key actually opens whatever is containing it."

Before they could explore this theory further, Ethan gasped, doubling over. "Something's wrong," he managed through clenched teeth. "The moon—it's too strong."

Alice moved to the window. The afternoon sun still shone, but now a ghostly full moon had also appeared in the sky—translucent but clearly visible.

"Temporal bleeding," she said urgently. "The full moon from another night is manifesting now."

Ethan's breathing grew ragged, his fingernails lengthening into claws. "Can't—control it—" His voice deepened to a growl as his features began shifting.

"He's transforming," Alice warned Tobias. "Get back!"

"Here? Now?" Panic edged Tobias's voice. "It's broad daylight!"

"The temporal fracture is disrupting the lunar cycle." Alice positioned herself between Tobias and her partner. "Ethan, focus. Remember your training."

Ethan stumbled toward the door, fighting the transformation. "Need—containment—"

"There's a cellar," Tobias said quickly. "Stone walls, solid door. This way."

They barely managed to get Ethan down the narrow stairs before the transformation accelerated. His skin rippled as muscles and bones reconfigured beneath it, his face elongating into a lupine muzzle. With a final, pained growl, he shoved them back and pulled the cellar door closed between them.

"Lock it," came his distorted voice from within.

Tobias engaged the heavy iron bolt. Almost immediately, something large slammed against the door from the other side.

"Will that hold him?" he asked Alice.

"It should. Ethan maintains more control than most werewolves, even during full transformation." She pulled out her phone. "I need to notify Captain Vaughn. If one werewolf is transforming out of cycle, others will be too."

As she made the call, Tobias carefully wrapped the crystal fragment and placed it back in the chronometer's hidden compartment. The brass key he slipped into his pocket.

Alice ended her call with a grim expression. "Reports coming in citywide. Every werewolf in Daybridge is either transforming or fighting it off. The temporal bleeding is getting worse."

From behind the cellar door came sounds of movement—heavy paws on stone, occasional growls, but no further attempts to break out.

"What do we do now?" Tobias asked.

"Wait. A forced transformation like this typically lasts a few hours." Alice checked her watch. "We should—"

The house suddenly shook, as though struck by an earthquake. Pictures fell from walls; books tumbled from shelves. Through the windows, they saw the sky cycling rapidly between day and night, the sun and moon trading places in accelerated sequence.

"Major temporal fluctuation," Alice said, bracing herself against the wall. "The fracture is widening."

After several chaotic seconds, the phenomenon subsided. The sky outside returned to normal afternoon, though distant thunder rumbled ominously.

Behind the cellar door, Ethan had gone silent.

"Detective Reeves?" Alice called. "Ethan, can you hear me?"

No response.

"We need to check on him," she decided, reaching for the bolt.

"Is that safe?" Tobias asked.

"Probably not, but we don't have much choice." She drew her service weapon—loaded, Tobias noted with alarm, with what appeared to be silver-tipped bullets. "Stay behind me."

She slid the bolt back and carefully pushed the door open. The cellar beyond was dark, illuminated only by thin shafts of light from small ground-level windows. The air carried the musky scent of wolf.

"Ethan?" Alice called, sweeping her flashlight across the space.

A low whine came from behind a stack of old furniture. The beam of light revealed Ethan in werewolf form—larger than a natural wolf, with reddish-brown fur and intelligent amber eyes. He made no aggressive moves, instead watching them with an almost human awareness.

"He's in control," Alice said, holstering her weapon. "Ethan, can you understand me?"

The werewolf nodded once, deliberately.

"The temporal surge must have completed the transformation," she explained to Tobias. "But his consciousness remains intact."

The werewolf rose to his feet—nearly seven feet tall standing upright—and approached cautiously. He gestured toward the stairs with a clawed hand.

"You want to come up?" Alice asked.

Another deliberate nod.

"I'll trust your judgment," she said. "But if you feel yourself slipping, you go right back down here. Understood?"

The werewolf made a sound that might have been an attempted "yes."

They returned to the study, where Ethan moved directly to the window, staring out at the cityscape below with intense focus. He tilted his head, as though listening to something beyond human perception.

"What do you hear?" Alice asked.

Ethan made a frustrated sound, clearly struggling with the limitations of his transformed state. He turned to Tobias's desk, gesturing at paper and pen.

"You want to write?" Tobias asked, surprised.

Ethan nodded, taking the pen awkwardly in his massive paw. His writing was barely legible, claws tearing the paper in places:

CAN SEE LEY LINES

"Ley lines?" Alice read. "The energy pathways beneath the city?"

Ethan nodded vigorously, writing again:

PULSING WITH CLOCK TICKS

Tobias frowned. "You can see the connection between the clocks and the ley lines?"

Another nod. Ethan wrote:

MAP. NEED MAP.

Alice found a street map of Daybridge in Tobias's desk drawer and spread it across the surface. Ethan hunched over it, his claws carefully marking specific locations throughout the city—about a dozen points, with heavier markings at five specific intersections.

STRONGEST HERE, he wrote beside one of the heavily marked spots. *PENDULUM ENERGY.*

"You can sense the Pendulum?" Alice asked.

Ethan shook his head, writing:

SIMILAR. ECHOES. FRAGMENTS?

Tobias studied the map. "These five major points form a pentagram across the city." He traced the pattern with his finger. "And at the center—"

CLOCKTOWER, Ethan had already written.

"The Central Clocktower?" Alice clarified. "On Municipal Plaza?"

Ethan nodded emphatically, then wrote:

HEART OF FRACTURE

Tobias felt a chill of recognition. "My grandfather helped design the clocktower mechanism in the 1870s. It's been maintained by Merrick's Chronometry ever since."

Alice's phone rang—Dr. Mackie calling from the shop. She put it on speaker.

"Detective, we've identified the epicenter of the temporal disturbance," Dr. Mackie said without preamble. "It's the Central Clocktower. All readings point to it as the origin point of the fracture."

Alice looked at Ethan, who made a gesture that clearly said, "told you so."

"We're reaching the same conclusion here," Alice replied. "Detective Reeves has... unique perceptions at the moment. He's mapped energy patterns across the city that converge at the tower."

"Fascinating," Dr. Mackie said. "Is he experiencing enhanced temporal sensitivity due to his lycanthropic state?"

"Something like that. What else have you found?"

"Lord Ravencroft's archivists discovered references to a ritual performed in the clocktower in 1927. And Madame Winters has been translating her grandmother's encoded grimoire, which mentions using the tower as a focal point for temporal stabilization."

"The clocktower is the key," Tobias murmured. "It always has been."

Ethan wrote quickly:

NEED TO GO THERE. NOW.

"Dr. Mackie, we're heading to the clocktower," Alice said. "Meet us there with whatever equipment you need."

"I should warn you," Dr. Mackie replied, "the temporal bleeding is intensifying. Downtown is experiencing significant manifestations—buildings shifting between time periods, people reporting encounters with historical figures. The PIU has cordoned off a six-block radius around the tower."

"Understood. We'll approach from the east side." Alice ended the call and turned to Ethan. "Can you maintain control in this form?"

He nodded, though his amber eyes reflected uncertainty.

"The full werewolf transformation might actually be advantageous," she said. "Your enhanced senses could help us navigate the temporal disruptions."

Tobias gathered the chronometer and key. "I should bring tools from my workshop as well. If the clocktower mechanism is involved, we may need to modify it."

As they prepared to leave, Ethan suddenly froze, his ears pricking forward. He dropped to all fours, a low growl building in his chest as he faced the study door.

"What is it?" Alice asked, hand moving to her weapon.

Before Ethan could respond, the door burst open. Three figures entered—werewolves in mid-transformation, caught between human and wolf forms. Unlike Ethan's controlled presence, these creatures radiated feral aggression, their partially transformed faces twisted in snarls.

The lead werewolf spoke, his words distorted but intelligible: "The Pendulum fragment. Give it to us."

Alice drew her weapon. "Daybridge Police. Stand down."

The intruders ignored her, their focus on Tobias and the chronometer in his hand. "The Alpha sent us. The fragment belongs with the Pack."

Ethan moved between Tobias and the intruders, his larger, fully transformed state imposing. He snarled a warning, clearly communicating that they would have to go through him first.

"Your loyalty is misplaced, Reeves," the lead werewolf growled. "The humans will destroy us all. Only the Pack can control the Pendulum."

"Nobody's controlling anything," Alice said firmly. "We're trying to repair the temporal fracture before it destroys Daybridge."

"Lies!" The intruder's patience snapped. "Take it!"

The three werewolves lunged forward simultaneously. Ethan met them head-on, his fully transformed strength giving him an advantage despite being outnumbered. The study erupted into chaos—furniture splintering, books flying, growls and snarls filling the air as four massive creatures fought in the confined space.

"Run!" Alice shouted to Tobias, firing a warning shot that embedded in the ceiling. "Get to the car!"

Tobias hesitated only briefly before bolting for the door, the chronometer clutched tightly in his hand. Alice backed out after him, keeping her weapon trained on the whirlwind of fur and claws that her partner had disappeared into.

They ran down the stairs and out the front door, hearing destruction continue inside. Just as they reached the car, a window on the second floor shattered outward. Ethan leaped through it, landing heavily on the lawn before bounding toward them.

"Is he injured?" Tobias asked as they scrambled into the vehicle.

Alice assessed her partner quickly. "Cuts and gashes, but nothing critical. Werewolves heal rapidly."

Ethan dove into the back seat, barely fitting his transformed bulk into the space. Alice gunned the engine just as the three pursuers burst through the front door.

As they sped away, Tobias looked back at his family home, now bearing shattered windows and a splintered door. "They knew about the fragment. How?"

"Good question," Alice said grimly. "The Pack shouldn't have that information unless—"

"Unless someone told them," Tobias finished. "We have a leak."

In the back seat, Ethan made a sound of frustrated agreement. His claws scribbled on a notepad:

ROGUE FACTION. NOT OFFICIAL PACK.

"How do you know?" Alice asked.

SCENT WRONG. NO PACK MARKERS.

Alice processed this as she navigated toward downtown, where the skyline already showed signs of temporal distortion—buildings flickering between modern structures and their historical predecessors.

"So someone's manipulating splinter werewolf groups, feeding them information about the Pendulum." She glanced at Tobias. "The question is, why?"

Tobias stared at the chronometer in his hands, its silver case now bearing scratches from their hasty escape. "My grandfather wrote that the Pendulum's power was 'too seductive.' Maybe someone wants to use it rather than just contain the fracture."

"Control time itself," Alice murmured. "That kind of power would be tempting to many."

Ethan wrote again:

GRANDFATHER WARNED. PENDULUM CHANGES YOU.

As they approached downtown, the temporal bleeding became impossible to ignore. Entire blocks flickered between centuries—modern storefronts becoming colonial taverns, then sleek futuristic structures, then back again. Pedestrians walked alongside ghostly figures in historical dress, some seemingly unaware of the anachronisms surrounding them.

Alice slowed the car as they entered the cordoned area, showing her badge to officers maintaining the perimeter. Beyond the barricades, chaos reigned. Temporal rifts opened and closed randomly throughout the streets. Through one, they glimpsed Daybridge during the Revolutionary War, British soldiers marching in formation. Another showed the same street during what appeared to be the 1970s, complete with vintage cars and dated fashions.

"The fracture's accelerating," Tobias said, watching a modern coffee shop transform momentarily into a blacksmith's forge before returning to normal.

They parked three blocks from Municipal Plaza, unable to drive closer due to the increasing instability. As they exited the vehicle, Ethan dropped to all fours, his nose to the ground.

"What is it?" Alice asked.

He gestured for them to follow, leading them not toward the main plaza but through a narrow alley between buildings. His transformed state drew startled looks from the few people still in the area, but Alice's badge and authoritative presence kept panic at bay.

The alley opened onto a small courtyard behind the Municipal Building. Here, the temporal bleeding seemed less severe—a pocket of relative stability amid the chaos.

Ethan pointed upward. From this vantage point, they could see the clocktower rising above the Municipal Building's ornate facade. Unlike the surrounding architecture, which flickered between time periods, the tower remained constant—unchanging regardless of the temporal shifts affecting everything around it.

Alice's phone rang—Dr. Mackie again.

"We're approaching from the west side," the professor said, her voice breaking up with static. "Temporal interference is severe. Where are you?"

"Courtyard behind the Municipal Building. Detective Reeves found a stable approach."

"Brilliant! The werewolf perception of ley lines must be guiding him along temporal stability points. Stay there—we'll navigate to your position."

While they waited, Ethan paced the courtyard perimeter, occasionally stopping to scratch marks into the ground with his claws. Tobias realized he was recreating the pattern from the map—a pentagram with the clocktower at its center.

"He's mapping the ley lines," Tobias said to Alice. "Showing how they converge here."

Alice nodded. "Werewolves have always had a connection to earth energies. It's part of why they're so affected by the moon."

Ethan finished his diagram and stood upright, staring at the tower with focused intensity. He wrote on his increasingly tattered notepad:

PENDULUM IS THERE. INSIDE TOWER.

"Inside the clocktower?" Tobias frowned. "That's impossible. I've maintained the mechanism for years. I would have seen it."

Ethan shook his head, writing:

HIDDEN. DISGUISED. PART OF MECHANISM.

Before they could discuss this further, Dr. Mackie arrived with Madame Winters and two PI technicians carrying equipment. The scientists paused momentarily at the sight of Ethan in full werewolf form, but recovered quickly.

"Fascinating," Dr. Mackie said, studying him. "Full transformation during daylight, maintaining human consciousness. The temporal disruption must be affecting the lunar connection at a fundamental level."

Ethan made an impatient gesture toward the tower.

"Yes, quite right." Dr. Mackie turned to her equipment. "Our readings confirm what Detective Reeves has apparently sensed. The clocktower exists in a state of temporal constancy—it's anchored somehow, resistant to the fluctuations affecting everything around it."

"Because the Pendulum is inside," Alice suggested.

"Precisely. It's acting as a fixed point in time, but the effect is degrading." Dr. Mackie pointed to readings on her tablet. "The original containment is failing, allowing temporal energy to leak out and create the fracture."

Madame Winters approached Tobias. "Your chronometer, please."

He handed it to her carefully. The elderly witch held it in both hands, closing her eyes as though listening to something only she could hear.

"Yes," she murmured. "It resonates with the tower. The fragment inside is attuned to the larger artifact." She opened her eyes. "This is how we find the Pendulum—the fragment will lead us to its source."

Tobias extracted the brass key from his pocket. "And this opens whatever's containing it?"

"Likely. Objects that travel through temporal rifts are usually connected to their destination."

Ethan suddenly growled, his attention fixed on the Municipal Building's rear entrance. The door opened, revealing Captain Vaughn of the PIU, accompanied by a tall, elegant woman in her fifties whom Tobias didn't recognize.

"Chen," Captain Vaughn called. "Situation report?"

"Sir," Alice straightened. "We've identified the clocktower as the epicenter. Detective Reeves has mapped the energy convergence, and we believe the Pendulum artifact is hidden within the tower mechanism."

Vaughn nodded. "This is Council Representative Diana Blackwood. The Vampire Council has taken an interest in the situation."

The woman stepped forward, her movements carrying the preternatural grace characteristic of elder vampires. "Time is a particular concern for those of us who expect to live through much of it," she said with a thin smile. "The Council offers its full resources to resolve this matter."

Ethan growled softly, eyeing the newcomers with suspicion.

"Is there a problem, Detective Reeves?" Vaughn asked, raising an eyebrow at his transformed state.

Alice intervened smoothly. "The temporal disruption triggered an unscheduled transformation. He's maintaining control and providing valuable insights due to his enhanced perceptions."

Diana Blackwood studied Ethan with cool assessment. "Indeed. Werewolves have always been sensitive to temporal fluctuations. Your pack connection to the earth makes you excellent chronometric instruments, if somewhat... unpredictable."

Ethan wrote on his pad, showing it to Alice:

DON'T TRUST. SMELLS WRONG.

Alice gave him a subtle nod before addressing the group. "We need access to the clocktower mechanism. Mr. Merrick has the expertise to identify any modifications or hidden components."

"Already arranged," Vaughn said. "The mayor has granted the PIU full authority over the Municipal Building during this emergency."

As they prepared to enter, Ethan suddenly froze, his ears swiveling toward the sky. A deep, resonant tolling began—the clocktower striking an hour, though it was only 4:17 PM according to Alice's watch.

The sound carried unnatural weight, each toll sending visible ripples through the air like stones dropped in a pond. With each resonant bell, the temporal rifts throughout the area pulsed and widened.

Dr. Mackie checked her instruments with growing alarm. "The tower's chronometric field is collapsing. The bells shouldn't be ringing at all—they're responding to the fracture."

Twelve massive tolls rang out, each one seeming to bend reality further. When the final bell faded, every clock in view—wristwatches, the clock on the Municipal Building facade, even the digital display on Dr. Mackie's equipment—showed the same time: 11:33.

"The countdown continues," Tobias said quietly. "We're running out of time."

In the distance, thunder rumbled beneath a sky that couldn't decide whether it was day or night. A storm was brewing—not just of rain and lightning, but of time itself, swirling around the tower that stood as both the cause and potential cure for Daybridge's temporal fracture.

Ethan, his werewolf senses attuned to energies humans could barely comprehend, led the way toward the building's entrance. Whatever awaited them within the clocktower, they would face it together—the descendants of those who had confronted this same threat nearly a century before, drawn together again by forces beyond their control.

The hands of fate, like those of a clock, had completed another cycle.

CHAPTER SIX: THE CLOCKTOWER CONNECTION

The interior of Daybridge's Municipal Building echoed with emptiness; its marble corridors evacuated due to the temporal emergency. Their footsteps resonated against the vaulted ceilings as Captain Vaughn led them toward the clocktower access.

"The mayor's declared a state of emergency," Vaughn explained. "Half the city's experiencing temporal anomalies. We've got Revolutionary soldiers appearing in supermarkets, Victorian ladies wandering through traffic, and reports of dinosaurs in Riverside Park."

"Dinosaurs?" Tobias raised an eyebrow.

"Probably hyperbole," Dr. Mackie said, checking readings on her equipment. "The fracture primarily affects periods with human habitation in this location. But as it widens, more distant time periods become accessible."

They reached an ornate wooden door marked "Clocktower Maintenance–Authorized Personnel Only." Vaughn produced a key ring and unlocked it, revealing a narrow spiral staircase winding upward.

"Two hundred and seventy-three steps," Tobias said automatically. "My family's maintained this clock for generations. I usually come monthly for routine service."

Ethan went first, his transformed bulk navigating the tight spiral with surprising grace. The others followed, carrying equipment and supplies. The stairwell grew darker as they ascended beyond the reach of the building's emergency lighting, forcing them to use flashlights.

"The mechanism chamber is just below the bell level," Tobias explained as they climbed. "It's essentially a giant version of a grandfather clock's works, scaled up to move the four clock faces and coordinate with the bells above."

The air grew noticeably colder as they ascended. Halfway up, they encountered their first temporal anomaly within the tower—a section of stairs that flickered between wooden steps and the original wrought iron spiral from 1876. Alice nearly stumbled when solid wood suddenly became metal grating beneath her feet.

"The boundaries are especially thin here," Madame Winters observed, her breath fogging in the increasingly frigid air. "We're moving through multiple time periods simultaneously."

After several more minutes of climbing, they reached a heavy door marked "Mechanism Chamber." Tobias stepped forward with the key, but found the door already ajar.

"That's not right," he frowned. "This should always be locked."

Ethan growled softly, signaling caution. Alice drew her weapon, nodding for the civilians to stay back while she and Vaughn approached the door.

"DBPD," Vaughn called out. "Anyone inside, identify yourself."

Silence answered.

Alice pushed the door open fully, revealing the clocktower's mechanical heart—a massive iron and brass mechanism filling a chamber thirty feet in diameter. Four enormous gear trains extended outward to the clock faces on each side of the tower. Above, a complex system of cables and counterweights connected to the bells on the level above. The entire apparatus ticked with sonorous precision, each movement amplified by the chamber's acoustics.

"Clear," Alice announced after checking the space. "But someone's definitely been here."

Tobias entered, immediately noticing the signs of disturbance. Tool marks on brass fittings that shouldn't have been touched. Gears slightly misaligned from their optimal positions. A maintenance panel left open.

"Someone's been tampering with the mechanism," he said, running his hand along a brass regulator arm. "Recently, within the last day or two."

Dr. Mackie set up her equipment while the others explored the chamber. Ethan moved around the perimeter, his amber eyes glowing in the dim light as he examined the space with werewolf senses.

"Temporal energy is concentrated here," Dr. Mackie announced, studying her instruments. "This entire chamber exists in multiple time states simultaneously."

"What does that mean exactly?" Vaughn asked.

"It means we're not just in 2025," she explained. "We're also partially in 1927, 1876, and possibly other time periods. The boundaries between them have worn so thin that they're overlapping."

Tobias approached the central drive mechanism—a massive pendulum and escapement system that regulated the entire clock. His watchmaker's eye immediately caught subtle anomalies in the design.

"These components," he said, pointing to specific gears and regulators, "they're not standard clockmaking parts, even for a mechanism this size." He traced the unusual tooth pattern on a large brass gear. "This matches exactly with the pattern in several of my shop's most affected antiques, including Lord Ravencroft's Tompion."

"As if they were designed to resonate together," Dr. Mackie suggested.

"Precisely." Tobias moved around the mechanism, his initial confusion giving way to understanding. "My grandfather didn't just maintain this clock—he modified it. These custom components form a pattern throughout the mechanism."

Diana Blackwood, who had been silently observing until now, stepped forward. "The vampire who commissioned your grandfather's services was Lord Edmund Ravencroft's father, Matthias. Council records indicate he took a particular interest in the clocktower's construction."

"Vampires, werewolves, and witches," Vaughn muttered. "All involved in a clocktower nearly 150 years ago. Why?"

"Because it stands at a power nexus," Madame Winters said, her eyes closed as though sensing invisible currents. "Five major ley lines converge directly beneath this tower. Feel them, Detective Reeves?"

Ethan nodded, scratching into his notepad:

STRONGEST POINT IN CITY. ANCIENT POWER.

Tobias climbed onto a maintenance platform to examine the mechanism's upper section. He whistled softly. "Everyone needs to see this."

One by one, they joined him on the platform. From this vantage point, they could see what had been invisible from below—intricate symbols engraved into the brass surfaces of key gears and regulators. The markings were subtle, incorporated into the decorative elements of the mechanism in a way that would appear merely ornamental to casual observation.

"Protection sigils," Madame Winters identified them immediately. "My grandmother's work, if I'm not mistaken. See how they form a containment pattern across the mechanism?"

Dr. Mackie photographed the symbols with her tablet. "Fascinating. They're arranged to create a temporal barrier—essentially a magical Faraday cage for time distortion."

"But they're degrading," Tobias pointed out, indicating where several engravings had become worn or damaged. "The metal's thinning here, and here. These markings should have been re-engraved during maintenance, but I never knew they existed."

"Your father may not have known either," Madame Winters suggested. "Your grandfather might have maintained them himself, then taken the secret to his grave."

Ethan suddenly stiffened, his attention fixed on the central shaft of the mechanism. He made an urgent gesture, pointing and growling.

"What is it?" Alice asked.

He scribbled hastily:

PENDULUM ENERGY. INSIDE SHAFT.

Tobias examined the central shaft—a six-foot iron column that supported the main drive wheel. "There's no access point. It's solid."

"Are you certain?" Dr. Mackie asked, bringing her instruments closer. "My readings indicate an energy source within the column."

Tobias ran his hands along the shaft, his watchmaker's fingers detecting subtle irregularities in the metal. "Wait. There's a seam here. Almost invisible, but—" He pressed a section of the decorative banding, and a small panel slid open, revealing a keyhole.

"The brass key," Alice said.

Tobias removed it from his pocket, studying its ornate design. "It matches the style exactly."

Before he could insert it, Ethan growled a warning. He wrote quickly:

OTHERS COMING. WEREWOLVES.

Captain Vaughn moved to the door. "How many?"

SEVERAL. MOVING FAST.

"The rogues from your house," Alice said to Tobias. "They must have tracked us."

"We need to secure this location," Vaughn decided, drawing his weapon. "Ms. Blackwood, can you assist?"

The vampire nodded, her eyes darkening slightly. "Gladly."

"Wait," Tobias interrupted. "Before anyone arrives, we should see what's inside the shaft. If the Pendulum is there, we need to know what we're dealing with."

Alice nodded. "Do it."

Tobias inserted the brass key into the hidden lock. It fit perfectly, turning with a series of clicks that suggested multiple tumblers engaging. The front section of the shaft—previously appearing solid—swung outward like a door.

Inside was a cylindrical chamber lined with what appeared to be dark mirrors. Suspended in the center, held by a complex arrangement of brass armatures, was a crystalline object approximately the size of a softball. Its faceted surface pulsed with subtle blue luminescence, matching exactly the fragment in Tobias's chronometer.

"The Pendulum," Dr. Mackie breathed. "It's beautiful."

The crystal seemed to capture and refract light in impossible ways, creating the illusion of depth far beyond its physical size. Looking into it was like peering into a universe contained within glass.

"It's not just suspended there," Tobias observed, examining the armatures. "It's integrated into the clocktower mechanism. See how these connectors link to the main drive train? The Pendulum is literally powering the clock."

"And has been since 1927," Madame Winters added. "When my grandmother's coven performed the containment ritual, they didn't just hide the Pendulum—they repurposed it, using its temporal energy to stabilize the fracture it had caused."

Ethan's growl grew more urgent. He scribbled:

THEY'RE HERE. COMING UP STAIRS.

Vaughn and Alice moved to defensive positions near the door, while Diana Blackwood simply smiled, revealing fangs that extended slightly in anticipation.

"Mr. Merrick," Dr. Mackie said quickly, "take readings of the configuration before we're interrupted. We'll need to understand exactly how the Pendulum is integrated if we're going to repair the containment."

Tobias nodded, pulling tools and measuring devices from his bag. He worked quickly, documenting the precise arrangement of armatures and connection points while Dr. Mackie recorded energy readings from the crystal itself.

"The sigils form a containment circuit," Madame Winters observed, tracing the pattern of engravings across the mechanism. "When properly maintained, they would channel the Pendulum's energy into stabilizing the local temporal field rather than disrupting it."

"But as they degraded," Tobias continued her thought, "the energy began leaking into the surrounding area, creating the fracture."

"Exactly. And now—"

She was interrupted by a commotion at the door. Three partially transformed werewolves burst into the chamber, followed by a fourth figure—human, wearing the robes of an academic.

"Professor Harlow?" Dr. Mackie said with surprise. "What are you doing here?"

The newcomer—a thin man in his sixties with piercing gray eyes—smiled without warmth. "Ah, Joan. I might ask you the same, but the answer is obvious. You've found our prize."

"Department of Temporal Physics," Alice identified him for the others. "Daybridge University."

"Indeed," Harlow confirmed. "Though my interest in the Pendulum extends far beyond academic curiosity." He gestured to the werewolves. "As does theirs."

Ethan moved forward, placing himself between the intruders and the exposed Pendulum. He growled a challenge to the other werewolves, who snarled in response.

"Your pack politics are irrelevant, Detective Reeves," Harlow said dismissively. "This transcends your primitive territorial disputes."

"What do you want, Harlow?" Vaughn demanded, his weapon trained on the professor.

"What everyone wants—control." Harlow's gaze fixed on the glowing crystal. "The Pendulum isn't just a temporal stabilizer. It's the most powerful chronometric artifact ever discovered. With it properly harnessed, one could manipulate time itself—slow it, accelerate it, even reverse it in controlled circumstances."

"That's impossible," Dr. Mackie protested. "The energy requirements alone—"

"Are provided by the ley line convergence beneath this tower," Harlow finished for her. "The original builders knew what they were doing, placing it precisely at this nexus point. Your ancestors," he nodded to Madame Winters, "merely scratched the surface of its potential with their containment ritual."

"The containment was necessary," Madame Winters said sharply. "The Pendulum was tearing apart the fabric of time. It still is."

"A lack of vision," Harlow sighed. "You see a crisis; I see opportunity."

Diana Blackwood had been watching the exchange with calculating eyes. Now she spoke, her voice carrying centuries of authority: "The Vampire Council has monitored the Pendulum since its discovery. We allowed the containment because uncontrolled temporal fractures serve no one's interests. But Professor Harlow raises valid points about its potential."

Tobias looked between them with growing alarm. "You're talking about weaponizing an artifact that's already destroying our city."

"Not destroying," Harlow corrected. "Transforming. The temporal bleeding isn't a bug—it's a feature. Imagine Daybridge where all time periods exist simultaneously. Where history isn't past but present. Where death itself becomes merely a transition to another temporal state."

"You're insane," Alice said flatly. "The human mind can't process multiple time states. We've already got people hospitalized with temporal psychosis from brief exposures."

"Adaptation takes time," Harlow acknowledged. "But evolution always does."

The standoff was interrupted by the clocktower bells suddenly tolling above them, though it wasn't the hour. The massive sound reverberated through the chamber, causing the exposed Pendulum to pulse brighter with each toll. The light from the crystal intensified, casting prismatic patterns across the walls.

"What's happening?" Vaughn shouted over the bells.

Dr. Mackie checked her instruments, her expression grave. "Temporal cascade. The Pendulum is responding to the degraded containment. Each toll accelerates the fracture!"

As if to confirm her assessment, temporal rifts began opening within the chamber itself—windows into other versions of the same space. Through one, they glimpsed the mechanism being constructed, workers in 1876 clothing installing the massive gears. Through another, they saw Tobias's grandfather working alongside robed figures—the Winters Coven performing their ritual in 1927.

The bells continued their unscheduled toll, each resonant peal widening the rifts further.

"We need to stabilize it!" Tobias shouted, moving toward the exposed Pendulum.

"No!" Harlow commanded. "Let it continue. We're witnessing the birth of a new temporal paradigm!"

The three werewolves lunged forward on Harlow's signal, directly toward Tobias. Ethan intercepted them, his fully transformed state giving him an advantage in the chaotic space. Alice and Vaughn moved to assist, while Diana Blackwood watched with the patient calculation characteristic of elder vampires.

Amid the chaos, Tobias reached the Pendulum chamber. The crystal's pulsing had synchronized with the bells, each toll causing it to flare bright enough to cast shadows. He could see now that several of the armatures holding it had come loose—the recent tampering had compromised the containment mechanism.

"Dr. Mackie!" he called. "The integration points are failing!"

She fought her way to his side, ducking as a werewolf was thrown over her head by Ethan's powerful arms. "The original configuration must have balanced the energy flow," she shouted over the bells. "These connection points correspond to the five ley lines beneath the tower!"

Tobias examined the armatures with a watchmaker's precision despite the battle raging around him. "They're adjustable. See these calibration points? They've been deliberately misaligned."

"Harlow," Dr. Mackie realized. "He's been planning this."

A temporal rift opened directly beside them, revealing Tobias's grandfather working on the same mechanism. For a moment, past and present overlapped so completely that Harold Merrick seemed to be standing beside his grandson, making the same adjustments to the same device.

Tobias felt a strange doubling sensation, as though his hands were both his own and his grandfather's simultaneously. Knowledge flowed between them—not as words but as direct understanding. He suddenly knew exactly how the calibration should be set.

"The chronometer fragment," he said to Dr. Mackie. "I need it."

She helped him extract the crystal fragment from his pocket watch. It pulsed in sympathy with the larger Pendulum, its blue glow intensifying as it came closer to its source.

"It's a calibration key," Tobias realized. "My grandfather separated this piece specifically to maintain the proper frequency."

The surrounding battle had reached a stalemate. Ethan held two werewolves at bay while Alice and Vaughn kept the third pinned down. Harlow stood back, observing with clinical interest, while Diana Blackwood had positioned herself near the door—either to prevent escape or to ensure her own.

Madame Winters worked her way to Tobias and Dr. Mackie, her hands weaving complex patterns in the air around the Pendulum chamber. "The sigils need reinforcement," she said. "I can temporarily boost their effect, but someone needs to recalibrate the physical mechanism."

"I can do it," Tobias said. "I understand the system now."

He began adjusting the armatures that held the Pendulum, realigning them to the correct positions while Madame Winters maintained a magical buffer around their work area. Dr. Mackie monitored energy readings, calling out corrections as needed.

"The fragment," Tobias said, holding up the small crystal from his chronometer. "It needs to be reintegrated."

He identified a small receptacle within the armature design—a space precisely shaped to hold the fragment. As he prepared to place it, Harlow's voice cut through the chaos.

"Stop! You don't understand what you're doing!"

"I understand perfectly," Tobias replied without looking up. "You sabotaged the containment to force a full temporal fracture. You wanted to use the Pendulum to control time itself."

"Not control—free it!" Harlow's academic reserve had cracked, revealing zealous intensity beneath. "Time is a prison, Mr. Merrick. A linear progression forcing us along a single path when infinite possibilities exist simultaneously!"

"Time is a framework that allows reality to function," Tobias countered, continuing his adjustments. "Without it, causality breaks down. Nothing can exist in a state of temporal chaos."

The bells tolled a final, massive peal—the twelfth strike. As the sound faded, every clock in view shifted to 11:32.

"We're losing minutes faster now," Dr. Mackie warned. "The countdown is accelerating."

Tobias positioned the fragment in its receptacle. The moment it connected, both crystals pulsed with intensified light. The armatures began to realign themselves, drawing power from the fragment to correct their positions.

"It's working!" Madame Winters exclaimed. "The containment field is stabilizing!"

Harlow's face contorted with rage. "No!" He turned to the werewolves. "Stop them at any cost!"

The creatures renewed their attack with desperate ferocity, breaking past Ethan's defense. One lunged directly at Tobias, claws extended toward the Pendulum chamber.

Diana Blackwood moved with vampiric speed, intercepting the werewolf mid-leap. "The Council has reconsidered Professor Harlow's proposal," she said coldly, throwing the creature across the room with supernatural strength. "Temporal stability serves our interests better than chaos."

With the vampire now actively defending them, Tobias completed the final adjustments. The Pendulum's pulsing stabilized into a steady, gentle glow. The temporal rifts throughout the chamber began to shrink, the visions of other time periods fading like morning mist.

"The sigils," Tobias said, noticing how the engraved symbols remained faded and worn. "They need to be reinforced permanently, not just with magic."

"I can re-engrave them," he continued, reaching for his watchmaker's tools. "But it will take time."

"Which we now have, thanks to your adjustments," Dr. Mackie said, checking her readings. "The acute fracture is healing. We've bought ourselves days instead of hours."

The fighting had subsided. Harlow stood against the far wall, his academic demeanor returning as his plan unraveled. The werewolves, sensing defeat, had backed toward the door under Ethan's watchful eye.

"This isn't over," Harlow said quietly. "The Pendulum will continue to degrade unless properly maintained. The original ritual was incomplete—a temporary solution at best."

"He's right about that," Madame Winters admitted. "My grandmother's journals indicate the 1927 ritual was performed under duress, without all the necessary components."

"What was missing?" Alice asked, keeping her weapon trained on Harlow.

"A proper anchor," the elderly witch replied. "Something to ground the Pendulum's energy permanently, not just redirect it."

Dr. Mackie nodded in understanding. "That's why it's failing now. The containment was designed to last only until the next astronomical alignment—when the stars 'align once more,' as Harold Merrick wrote."

Tobias looked at the Pendulum, now glowing steadily within its chamber. "So we've stopped the immediate crisis but not solved the underlying problem."

"Precisely," Harlow said, a hint of satisfaction returning to his voice. "You'll need me, Mr. Merrick. I've spent decades studying the Pendulum. I understand its potential better than anyone."

"You understand how to exploit it," Tobias corrected. "Not how to contain it."

"They're two sides of the same equation." Harlow straightened his rumpled academic robes. "Captain Vaughn, I assume I'm under arrest?"

Vaughn nodded. "Tampering with a temporal nexus point, endangering public safety, conspiracy with non-registered werewolves... That's just for starters."

As Vaughn secured Harlow, Alice approached Tobias at the Pendulum chamber. "How long will your adjustments hold?"

"Hard to say. The fragment has stabilized the energy flow, but the physical containment—the sigils and integration points—needs complete restoration." He closed the chamber door, locking it with the brass key. "I need to study my grandfather's notes more thoroughly, understand exactly what he did in 1927."

"And what he didn't do," Dr. Mackie added. "If the original ritual was incomplete, we need to identify what was missing."

Ethan, still in werewolf form but calmer now that the immediate threat had passed, wrote on his tattered notepad:

GRANDFATHER KNEW. PAID WITH HIS LIFE.

The implication hung heavily in the air. Whatever secrets the Pendulum held, they had exacted a terrible price from those who last confronted it.

Diana Blackwood approached the group, brushing dust from her immaculate suit. "The Council will provide resources for your research, Mr. Merrick. We have extensive archives on temporal phenomena that may prove useful."

"Why the sudden cooperation?" Alice asked suspiciously.

The vampire smiled thinly. "Let's call it enlightened self-interest. Contrary to Professor Harlow's belief, immortals generally prefer temporal stability. Eternity becomes rather complicated when yesterday, today, and tomorrow occur simultaneously."

Outside, the sky had returned to normal—the ghostly moon no longer visible alongside the setting sun. The temporal bleeding had subsided, at least temporarily.

"We should return to the shop," Tobias suggested. "I have my grandfather's journals there, and the affected timepieces might provide additional insights."

As they prepared to leave, Madame Winters placed a weathered hand on his arm. "You've done well today, Tobias. Your grandfather would be proud."

"I'm not sure what I've done, besides temporarily patch a problem I barely understand."

"Sometimes that's enough," she said gently. "The universe doesn't require us to comprehend its mysteries, merely to face them with courage and wisdom."

They descended the spiral staircase in relative silence, each processing the revelations of the past hours. Ethan led the way, his werewolf form a stark reminder of how the temporal disturbance had affected Daybridge's supernatural community.

Tobias fingered the brass key in his pocket—the key to the Pendulum's chamber, yes, but perhaps also the key to understanding his family's true legacy. For generations, the Merricks had maintained Daybridge's timepieces with quiet dedication, never drawing attention to their deeper role as guardians of time itself.

Now that role had fallen to him, whether he wanted it or not.

As they exited the Municipal Building, the clocktower bells rang out once more—this time marking the correct hour with their familiar, comforting toll. For now, at least, time in Daybridge flowed as it should.

But the synchronized clocks throughout the city continued their ominous countdown, now showing 11:32.

Whatever temporary stability they had achieved, the greater challenge still lay ahead.

CHAPTER SEVEN: TEMPORAL ECHOES

The evening sky over Daybridge rippled with auroral light—blues and greens undulating where no aurora should be visible. Citizens stood in streets and yards, necks craned upward, phones recording the impossible phenomenon. Some called it beautiful; others recognized it as a warning.

Temporal instability made visible.

Alice drove through neighborhoods where reality remained mostly stable, though occasional flickers of other eras manifested on street corners—gas lamps briefly replacing LED streetlights, horse-drawn carriages momentarily superimposed over parked cars. The disruptions were less severe than before their intervention at the clocktower, but still present.

"The stabilization is holding," Dr. Mackie observed from the back seat, monitoring readings on her tablet. "But it's incomplete. We've essentially applied a stronger patch to the temporal dam."

Tobias nodded grimly. "And the pressure behind that dam is still building."

Ethan, now returned to human form as the temporal distortion affecting the moon had temporarily subsided, stared out the window with exhausted eyes. The forced transformation had drained him, leaving dark circles beneath his eyes and a slight tremor in his hands.

"You should get some rest," Alice told her partner.

He shook his head. "Later. We need to understand what we're facing first."

They returned to Merrick's Chronometry to find the shop transformed into a fully operational command center. The PIU had established monitoring equipment throughout the space, with technicians tracking temporal fluctuations across the city. Lord

Ravencroft had delivered several ancient volumes from his private library, which Madame Winters was carefully examining at a cleared workbench.

Captain Vaughn had remained at the Municipal Building with Diana Blackwood to secure the clocktower and process Professor Harlow, who now occupied a containment cell specifically designed for supernaturally enhanced humans.

"The affected timepieces are still synchronized at 11:32," Eliza reported as they entered. "But the whispering has stopped."

"The Pendulum's partial stabilization must have interrupted the resonance connection," Dr. Mackie theorized. "The clocks are still counting down, but they're no longer active conduits."

Tobias moved to his workbench, spreading out his grandfather's journals alongside the technical drawings Dr. Mackie had brought from the university archives. "We need to understand exactly what happened in 1927—what they did and what they failed to do."

"And why the solution was designed to be temporary," Alice added, reviewing her notes. "Harold Merrick wrote that it would last 'until the stars align once more.' That's oddly specific for a clockmaker."

"Not for one with temporal sensitivity," Madame Winters said, looking up from her research. "The alignment refers to a specific astronomical configuration that occurs every ninety-eight years. My grandmother's grimoire describes it as a 'thinning of the cosmic veil'—when boundaries between time streams naturally weaken."

"Creating ideal conditions for either catastrophic collapse or intentional crossing," Dr. Mackie continued. "Many cultures have mythologies about periodic opportunities to commune with ancestors or glimpse the future, often tied to specific celestial events."

Ethan joined them, his voice still rough from the transformation. "The Pack histories mentioned this too—something about 'the night when moon shadows fall backward.'"

"Poetic descriptions of a quantifiable astronomical event," Dr. Mackie said. "The precise alignment happens tomorrow night—Jupiter, Saturn, and Venus forming a perfect isosceles triangle with Earth while the moon reaches perigee."

"So the 1927 team knew the containment would fail during this alignment," Tobias summarized. "But instead of creating a permanent solution, they essentially set a time bomb for future generations to handle."

"They may not have had a choice," Madame Winters suggested. "Temporal manipulation requires specific conditions. Perhaps a permanent solution was impossible without the alignment itself."

Alice's head suddenly throbbed with sharp, stabbing pain. The surrounding room seemed to waver, colors bleeding into one another like watercolors in rain. She gripped the edge of the workbench, trying to steady herself.

"Detective?" Dr. Mackie noticed her distress. "Are you alright?"

"Just dizzy—" Alice began, but her words cut off as the room... shifted.

The modern shop interior dissolved around her, replaced by the same space but decades earlier—oil lamps instead of electric lights, different tools on the workbenches, a coal stove in the corner where now stood a refrigerator. The air carried the scent of pipe tobacco and clock oil.

And people—the shop was filled with people in the 1920s clothing, their voices urgent though slightly muffled, as if reaching her through water.

"—must secure the Pendulum tonight, Harold," a woman was saying, her severe bob haircut and ceremonial robes marking her as a witch of significant standing. "The fracture widens with each hour."

A middle-aged man with wire-rimmed glasses—Harold Merrick, Tobias's grandfather—bent over a workbench, making adjustments to a complex device that pulsed with blue light. The

Pendulum, though smaller and differently configured than the version Alice had seen in the clocktower.

"The containment field is imperfect," Harold replied, his hands steady despite the concern in his voice. "Without the Anchor Star, we're merely redirecting the energy, not truly containing it."

"The Star was lost decades ago," a tall, aristocratic man said—unmistakably a vampire, with the same pale elegance as Lord Ravencroft. "We work with what we have, not what we wish for."

"The Pack has secured the tower," announced a powerfully built man entering the shop, rainwater dripping from his coat. His eyes flashed golden momentarily—a werewolf maintaining human form with visible effort. "But strange things are happening throughout the city. People reporting ghosts, buildings that weren't there yesterday, sounds from another time."

"John," Harold acknowledged him with a nod. "Any sign of Harlow?"

Alice's breath caught. Harlow—the same name as the professor they'd just arrested. Could it be a relative? An ancestor?

"None," the werewolf—John Reeves, Ethan's great-grandfather—replied grimly. "He's gone to ground since the ritual failed."

"Failed is perhaps too strong," the witch—obviously a Winters—corrected. "It was incomplete. Without the Anchor Star, we couldn't establish permanent containment."

"So we're merely postponing the problem," Harold said, still working on the Pendulum. "Kicking it to our descendants."

"Better than allowing the complete collapse of temporal boundaries now," the vampire countered. "Future generations may discover solutions we cannot."

"Or inherit our failure," Harold muttered.

The witch approached the workbench, examining the Pendulum with critical eyes. "The fragment separation is clever, Harold. Using it as both key and calibration tool will ensure the containment remains balanced until the next alignment."

"Ninety-eight years," Harold calculated. "My grandson might live to see it. I should leave instructions—"

"No," the vampire interrupted sharply. "The fewer who know about the Pendulum, the safer it remains. Harlow may have failed today, but others will seek it. Knowledge of its existence must fade into rumor and myth."

"We can't just leave future generations blind to the danger," Harold protested.

"We won't," the witch assured him. "The timepieces will warn them. As the containment weakens, they'll begin to synchronize again. The countdown will resume."

"And if no one recognizes the warning?" Harold pressed.

The witch smiled thinly. "Then they are not the right people to address the problem. The universe has its own methods of selection, Harold. Trust that those who need to know will discover what they must, when they must."

John Reeves approached the Pendulum, his expression troubled. "What about the temporal echoes? People are experiencing memories that aren't their own, seeing events from other times."

"A side effect of the fracture," the witch explained. "Memories are especially vulnerable to temporal bleeding. Some may experience echoes from the past, others from futures that may or may not come to pass."

"And when we complete this temporary containment?" John asked.

"Most will forget, their minds unable to reconcile temporal contradictions," she replied. "But those with sensitivity—like all of us in this room—may retain fragments. Dreams, intuitions, déjà vu."

Harold closed a panel on the modified Pendulum, his work apparently complete. "It's ready. But someone must take it to the tower and integrate it with the mechanism."

"I will," John volunteered immediately.

"It's dangerous," Harold warned. "The temporal exposure at the integration point could be severe. There's no telling how it might affect you."

The werewolf smiled grimly. "Better me than a human. Our kind heals from most injuries."

"Physical ones, perhaps," the witch cautioned. "But temporal wounds are different. They affect the soul itself."

"Nevertheless," John insisted. "My pack is already securing the tower. I'll see this through."

The vampire nodded approval. "Once installed, the modified Pendulum should stabilize the fracture for decades. By the time it fails, perhaps the Anchor Star will have resurfaced."

"And if it hasn't?" Harold asked.

The vampire's expression grew somber. "Then our descendants face a choice we avoided today—whether to attempt permanent containment without it, with all the risks that entails."

The scene began to blur around Alice, voices becoming distant, figures transparent. She reached toward Harold, trying to ask what the Anchor Star was, but her words made no sound in this echo of the past.

Just before the vision faded completely, she saw Harold Merrick turn directly toward her—as though he could actually perceive her presence across time. His lips moved, forming words she strained to hear:

"The star falls where no light reaches. Find it before the final toll."

The shop snapped back to its present-day configuration so abruptly that Alice staggered, nearly falling. Ethan caught her arm, steadying her.

"Alice? What happened?"

She blinked, reorienting herself. Everyone was staring at her with concern. "I saw them," she said hoarsely. "1927. Harold Merrick, a Winters witch, a Ravencroft vampire, and John Reeves. Planning the containment ritual."

Dr. Mackie was immediately at her side, scanning her with handheld equipment. "A temporal echo. You experienced a direct bleedthrough from 1927."

"Not just random bleeding," Alice clarified, accepting a glass of water from Eliza. "It was specific—like the exact conversation we needed to hear."

"As if someone wanted you to witness it," Madame Winters suggested. "Temporal echoes can sometimes be... directed, by those with sufficient sensitivity."

"Harold Merrick saw me," Alice confirmed. "At the end, he looked directly at me and said something about a star falling 'where no light reaches.'"

Tobias looked up sharply from his grandfather's journals. "The Anchor Star. They mentioned it in 1927 as being crucial for permanent containment."

"Yes," Alice nodded. "They said without it, they could only create a temporary solution—redirecting the Pendulum's energy rather than truly containing it."

Dr. Mackie made rapid notes on her tablet. "This confirms my theory. The current configuration is essentially a temporal pressure valve, not a permanent seal. It redirects the Pendulum's energy into maintaining the clocktower's chronometric field but doesn't actually neutralize the temporal disruption."

"What exactly is this Anchor Star?" Ethan asked.

"According to my grandmother's grimoire," Madame Winters said, turning pages in an ancient leather-bound book, "it's a crystalline artifact of extraterrestrial origin—a meteorite with unique temporal properties. When properly aligned with the Pendulum, it creates a stable temporal field that exists partially outside normal timeflow."

"A meteorite?" Tobias frowned. "How would that interact with a mechanical device like the Pendulum?"

"The Pendulum isn't just mechanical," Dr. Mackie explained. "It's a hybrid of science and magic—physical engineering and temporal manipulation combined. Your grandfather was bridging disciplines most consider separate."

"So we need to find this Anchor Star," Alice summarized. "Which has apparently been lost for over a century."

"'The star falls where no light reaches,'" Tobias repeated Harold's cryptic message. "That could mean anywhere."

Ethan had been unusually quiet, his expression distant. Now he spoke hesitantly. "During my transformation, when my perception was enhanced, I sensed something beneath the city. Not just the ley lines, but... gaps in them. Places where the energy flows around empty spaces, like water around rocks."

"Caverns?" Dr. Mackie suggested.

"Possibly. Daybridge is built on limestone. There could be natural cave systems beneath us."

Alice considered this. "A cave would fit 'where no light reaches.'"

"There's more," Ethan continued. "One of these gaps was directly beneath Pendulum Lane. I could feel it most strongly right outside this shop."

Tobias moved to the shop's rear wall, studying it with newfound interest. "This building dates to the 1840s. Many properties from that era had access to the underground—storage cellars, smuggling tunnels during Prohibition, even older pathways that predated the city itself."

"Does this building have a basement?" Alice asked.

"A small storage cellar. I rarely use it—it tends to flood during heavy rains." Tobias moved toward a door near the back of the shop that Alice had assumed was a closet. "This way."

The narrow wooden stairs descended into darkness. Tobias switched on a single bare bulb, revealing a cramped cellar with stone walls and a packed earth floor. Cardboard boxes of shop supplies lined the walls, many showing water damage along their bottoms.

"Not much to see," Tobias admitted. "I've never found anything interesting down here."

Dr. Mackie consulted her instruments as they descended. "Significant temporal distortion in this space. More than the shop above."

Ethan paused halfway down the stairs, his nostrils flaring. "That scent again. Ozone and old books."

"Temporal energy," Dr. Mackie confirmed. "But where's it coming from?"

Madame Winters closed her eyes; hands extended before her like divining rods. "There," she said after a moment, pointing to the rear wall behind a stack of water-damaged boxes. "The energy flows through that section."

They cleared away the boxes, revealing an unremarkable stone wall. Tobias examined it carefully, running his fingers along the mortar lines.

"The stonework is different here," he observed. "These blocks don't match the rest of the cellar. They're newer—perhaps added later to seal something off."

Alice ran her flashlight along the edges of the anomalous section. "Could be a filled-in doorway or passage."

Tobias located a prybar among the cellar tools and carefully worked at the mortar between stones. After several minutes of effort, one of the blocks shifted slightly.

"There's definitely open space behind this," he confirmed, working the prybar deeper. "Help me remove these stones."

Together, they dismantled the section of wall, revealing a narrow tunnel extending into darkness beyond. The opening was roughly rectangular, large enough for a person to pass through by ducking slightly.

"A hidden passage," Eliza whispered, having joined them in the cellar. "Under your shop all this time."

Tobias shone his flashlight into the tunnel. The beam revealed rough-hewn walls extending about twenty feet before the passage turned sharply left.

"This doesn't look like a storage cellar or utility tunnel," Alice observed. "It's too carefully constructed."

"And too well hidden," Ethan added. "Someone didn't want this found by accident."

Dr. Mackie's instruments beeped insistently as she held them toward the opening. "Strong temporal signature. Something down there is generating significant chronometric energy."

"The Anchor Star?" Tobias suggested.

"Possibly. Or another temporal artifact."

Alice drew her weapon. "I'll go first. Dr. Mackie, your equipment might help guide us. Ethan, watch our backs."

"I'm coming too," Tobias insisted. "If this connects to my family's history, I need to see it."

"As must I," Madame Winters added. "The magical protections we may encounter would require my expertise."

Alice nodded. "Eliza, please stay here and monitor communications. If we're not back in thirty minutes, call Captain Vaughn."

With flashlights illuminating the way, they entered the tunnel in single file. The passage was surprisingly dry despite the cellar's moisture problems, suggesting some form of waterproofing or magical protection.

After the initial straight section, the tunnel bent left, then descended via rough-cut stairs. The temperature dropped noticeably as they went deeper.

"We must be below the water table," Dr. Mackie observed. "Yet it's perfectly dry."

"Magical containment," Madame Winters confirmed, touching the wall. "These stones are inscribed with water-repelling sigils. Subtle, but effective."

They continued downward for what felt like several stories, though it was difficult to judge distance in the claustrophobic passage. Finally, the stairs ended at a small landing before a stone archway. Carved into the keystone was a symbol Tobias recognized immediately.

"That's my family's maker's mark," he said, pointing to the stylized 'M' surrounded by a circle. "The same stamp we've put on our clocks for generations."

"Your family built this passage," Alice concluded. "Or at least knew about it."

Beyond the archway lay a circular chamber approximately thirty feet in diameter. As their flashlight beams swept the space, they revealed an unexpected sight—the walls were covered in astronomical charts, constellations and planetary orbits mapped with scientific precision but artistic beauty. The floor featured an inlaid mosaic of the solar system, with the sun at the center and planets arranged in their orbits.

"It's a celestial observatory," Dr. Mackie breathed. "Underground, where no actual stars could be seen."

In the center of the chamber stood a stone pedestal about waist-high. Atop it rested a glass case, cloudy with age but clearly designed to display something significant.

The case was empty.

"The Anchor Star was here," Madame Winters said with certainty. "This entire chamber was built to house it."

Tobias approached the pedestal, examining the case carefully. "There's an inscription around the base."

He brushed away decades of dust to reveal Latin words carved into the stone:

Stella Temporis Custos Aeternitatis

"The Star of Time, Guardian of Eternity," Dr. Mackie translated.

Below this formal inscription was a more recent addition, carved with less precision but greater urgency:

Removed for safety. Return before the third cycle. — H.M., 1927

"H.M.—Harold Merrick," Tobias said. "My grandfather removed the Star in 1927."

"And apparently intended it to be returned before 'the third cycle,'" Alice noted. "What does that mean?"

Dr. Mackie consulted her tablet. "If the cycle refers to the 98-year alignment period, then three cycles would be 294 years from 1927."

"That can't be right," Ethan objected. "Why remove it only to specify it should stay hidden for nearly three centuries?"

"Unless 'cycle' means something else," Tobias suggested. "In clockmaking, a cycle can refer to a single oscillation of a pendulum."

As they debated, Alice noticed something unusual about the glass case. "There's something inside the base," she said, pointing to a small drawer built into the pedestal beneath the display area.

Tobias examined it, finding a nearly invisible catch mechanism. "It's locked, but—" He pulled out the brass key that had opened the Pendulum chamber. "Maybe?"

The key fit perfectly. The drawer slid open smoothly despite decades without use, revealing a small leather-bound journal and a folded paper sealed with wax bearing the Merrick maker's mark.

"My grandfather's handwriting," Tobias confirmed, carefully opening the journal. "Dated October 18, 1927—the day after the containment ritual."

He read aloud:

The Pendulum is secured within the clocktower, its energy redirected rather than truly contained. Without the Anchor Star, this solution will hold only until the next alignment—98 years hence. I have removed the Star from its chamber to prevent Harlow or his associates from finding it. They continue to seek temporal control rather than stability.

The Star cannot be destroyed, nor can it be moved far from Daybridge without destabilizing the local temporal field. I have therefore concealed it where none would think to look, yet where it remains connected to the ley line network.

Should future generations face the fracture's return, this map will guide them. The Star must be restored to the Pendulum before the third toll of midnight during the alignment, or the temporary containment will fail completely.

"'The third toll of midnight,'" Alice repeated. "That's what he meant by 'the third cycle'—not years, but the actual tolling of the clock."

"Which gives us a very specific deadline," Dr. Mackie said grimly. "Tomorrow night at midnight, we have until the third stroke to reunite the Anchor Star with the Pendulum."

Tobias unfolded the sealed paper, revealing a hand-drawn map of Daybridge circa 1927. Several locations were marked with cryptic symbols, with lines connecting them in a pattern that resembled a constellation.

"It's Orion," Madame Winters identified immediately. "The Hunter. He's mapped the Star's location using Orion's configuration, overlaid on Daybridge's geography."

"But which point represents the Star?" Ethan asked, studying the map. "There are seven marked locations."

Dr. Mackie pointed to handwritten notes along the map's edge. "These appear to be astronomical coordinates for each point, correlating to specific stars in the Orion constellation."

"So we need to determine which star in Orion corresponds to the Anchor Star," Alice summarized.

Tobias turned the map over, finding additional notes on the reverse:

The Hunter guards what fell from heaven. Seek the blue giant where water meets stone beneath the hunter's shadow. Three keys open the way—time, blood, and light.

"Cryptic," Ethan muttered.

"But decipherable," Dr. Mackie countered. "The 'blue giant' in Orion is Rigel—the star that forms the hunter's left foot in the constellation."

She traced the corresponding point on the map. "Which correlates to... this location in Daybridge."

Tobias leaned closer. "That's the old harbor district—specifically Fellwater Dock, where the river meets the stone embankment."

"'Where water meets stone,'" Alice quoted. "Fits the clue."

"'Beneath the hunter's shadow,'" Ethan continued. "Could mean underground again, or perhaps in the shadow cast by something else."

"There's a statue in that area," Eliza's voice came unexpectedly through Alice's radio. "Sorry for eavesdropping, but I grew up near there. Harbormaster Plaza has a bronze statue of the city's founder, depicted as a hunter with rifle and game."

"The literal hunter's shadow," Tobias nodded. "And 'three keys'—time, blood, and light. Time likely refers to my chronometer with the Pendulum fragment."

"Blood could indicate a blood offering," Madame Winters suggested. "Many magical protections require it as authentication."

"And light?" Alice asked.

"Perhaps literal illumination," Dr. Mackie theorized. "Or metaphorical enlightenment. We may need to discover that when we locate the site."

As they discussed the clues, a low rumbling vibrated through the chamber. Dust fell from the ceiling as the entire structure shook.

"Temporal quake," Dr. Mackie announced, checking her instruments. "The stabilization is weakening faster than anticipated."

"We need to return to the surface," Alice decided. "If the passage collapses, we'd be trapped."

They hastily gathered the journal and map, securing them in Tobias's bag before heading back through the tunnel. The vibrations continued intermittently, intensifying as they climbed the stairs.

When they emerged into the cellar, they found Eliza looking pale. "It's happening all over the city," she reported. "Temporal quakes causing physical disruptions. The news is calling it an 'unprecedented seismic event,' but it's actually time streams colliding."

They hurried upstairs to find the shop in disarray—clocks fallen from shelves; tools scattered across workbenches. Outside, the auroral lights had intensified, now visible even in daylight as shimmering curtains across the sky.

Alice's phone rang—Captain Vaughn reporting from the Municipal Building.

"The clocktower's going haywire," he said without preamble. "The mechanism is running at variable speeds—sometimes too fast, sometimes backward. Harlow's laughing his ass off in his cell, saying it's 'the beginning of temporal liberation.'"

"The partial stabilization is failing," Alice informed him. "But we've found information about what's needed for permanent containment—an artifact called the Anchor Star. We have a map to its location."

"Then find it," Vaughn ordered. "We've got temporal bleeding events citywide. The mayor's declaring a state of emergency, but what do you evacuate from when the problem is time itself?"

As if to underscore his point, the shop briefly overlapped with its 1927 version—ghostly figures moving through the same space, unaware of their future counterparts. The vision lasted only seconds before fading.

"We're heading to Fellwater Dock," Alice told him. "That's where the Anchor Star is hidden."

"Take whatever resources you need," Vaughn authorized. "I'll send additional PIU agents to secure the area."

After ending the call, Alice turned to the others. "We should move quickly. Dr. Mackie, can you and Madame Winters prepare whatever might be needed for the retrieval ritual?"

"Yes, though without knowing exactly what protections Harold Merrick put in place, we'll need to bring a range of tools and materials."

"Ethan and I will secure transportation and alert the harbor patrol to clear the area."

Tobias studied his grandfather's map, tracing the path from Pendulum Lane to Fellwater Dock. "The map shows a specific approach route along the old canal towpath. It might be significant."

"Then that's how we'll go," Alice decided. "If Harold Merrick went to such lengths to hide the Anchor Star, the path to it may be as important as the destination."

As they prepared to depart, Tobias paused at his workbench, looking at the synchronized clocks still displaying 11:32.

"The countdown's frozen," he noted. "That can't be good."

Dr. Mackie examined the nearest timepiece. "It's not frozen—it's building potential energy. Like a spring being wound too tight."

"What happens when it releases?" Eliza asked.

"The countdown will likely accelerate dramatically," the professor replied. "When that happens, we'll know the temporary containment has failed completely."

Outside, another temporal quake shook the street. Through the shop windows, they watched as a section of Pendulum Lane briefly transformed into a muddy colonial-era track, then a futuristic pedestrian concourse, before returning to its present-day configuration.

The boundary between time periods was becoming increasingly permeable. Soon, it might dissolve entirely.

"Let's go," Alice said, checking her weapon and radio. "We have until the third toll of midnight to find the Anchor Star and reunite it with the Pendulum."

As they exited the shop, Tobias glanced back at his carefully ordered world of gears and springs, now in disarray. Time itself—the very thing he had dedicated his life to measuring and maintaining—had become unstable, flowing not in one direction but in all directions simultaneously.

The irony wasn't lost on him. He had spent years avoiding Daybridge's supernatural side, only to discover he was inextricably linked to its greatest temporal mystery.

Now he needed to embrace that connection—not just to save his shop or even the city, but to complete the work his grandfather had begun nearly a century before.

The universe had indeed selected its players carefully, drawing together the descendants of those who had faced this crisis once before. Whether that was cosmic design or temporal resonance hardly mattered now.

The clock was ticking, even when time itself could no longer be trusted.

CHAPTER EIGHT: RACE AGAINST TIME

The Daybridge University Astronomical Observatory perched atop Crescent Hill, its domed roof gleaming in the late afternoon sunlight. The facility stood apart from the main campus—physically and philosophically—occupying a unique position in academia where scientific rigor met mystical tradition.

Alice's sedan wound up the narrow access road, passing through patches of temporal distortion where the asphalt briefly transformed to gravel or dirt before returning to modern pavement. In the passenger seat, Tobias clutched his grandfather's journal and map, still processing the revelations from the underground chamber.

"The observatory should be stable," Dr. Mackie assured them from the back seat. "It was built on a natural energy convergence point—one of the reasons Daybridge University has always been at the forefront of both astronomical and paranormal research."

"Professor Santos is expecting us?" Alice confirmed, navigating around a section of road that had temporarily become a horse path.

"Yes. He's been monitoring the celestial anomalies since they began." Dr. Mackie checked her watch. "He's one of the few academics who bridges conventional astronomy and astrological interpretation."

"Meaning he believes in magic?" Ethan asked skeptically.

"Meaning he understands that cosmic forces affect earthly events through mechanisms science has yet to fully quantify," she corrected. "In Daybridge, that's less mysticism and more practical reality."

The observatory compound came into view—a main dome flanked by two smaller structures, with a modern research building connecting them. Unlike much of Daybridge, the facility appeared completely stable, untouched by the temporal fluctuations affecting the surrounding areas.

"Why isn't this place experiencing bleeding?" Tobias asked as they parked.

"Astronomical observatories often incorporate celestial alignments into their construction," Madame Winters explained. "Whether intentionally or intuitively, builders place them at points of cosmic stability."

"Plus, this facility has modern temporal shielding," Dr. Mackie added more pragmatically. "The university installed it after the Incident of '98."

"Do I want to know what that was?" Alice asked.

"Probably not. Let's just say it involved accidentally observing the same star at two different points in its lifecycle simultaneously."

A figure emerged from the main building—a tall man in his sixties with silver-streaked black hair and a neatly trimmed beard. He wore a tweed jacket with leather elbow patches over a sweater decorated with celestial patterns.

"Joan!" he called, greeting Dr. Mackie with a warm hug. "Your message sounded urgent."

"It is, Javier. We're dealing with a Level One temporal crisis."

His expression sobered immediately. "Come inside. I've been tracking unusual stellar phenomena that may be related."

Professor Javier Santos led them through the research building into a circular room dominated by a holographic projection of the solar system. The three-dimensional display showed planets in their current positions, with various orbital paths illuminated in different colors.

"Welcome to the Celestial Mapping Chamber," Santos said, gesturing to the impressive display. "The most accurate real-time model of our solar system on the East Coast."

"It's beautiful," Tobias commented, watching Venus track its path around the holographic sun.

"And concerning," Santos added, pressing controls on a nearby console. "Observe what happens when I accelerate the projection forward."

The planets began moving faster along their orbits, days and weeks passing in seconds. As they watched, three planets—Jupiter, Saturn, and Venus—gradually aligned into a perfect isosceles triangle with Earth at one vertex.

"This configuration occurs tomorrow night," Santos explained. "A rare celestial alignment that happens approximately every ninety-eight years."

"The exact timeframe mentioned in my grandfather's notes," Tobias said.

Santos nodded. "Not coincidental, I assure you. This particular alignment creates what we call a 'cosmic lens'—a focusing of gravitational and quantum effects that can amplify certain energies." He glanced at Dr. Mackie. "Including temporal energies."

"We've discovered that a similar alignment in 1927 coincided with a temporal disturbance in Daybridge," Alice explained. "One that was temporarily contained but designed to last only until this alignment recurred."

"That explains much," Santos said thoughtfully. "I've been observing chronometric anomalies in stellar spectrography for weeks—essentially, temporal echoes from celestial bodies. As if we're receiving light from multiple points in their timelines simultaneously."

He adjusted the display again, zooming out to show a wider view of the solar system. "But there's another factor you may not be aware of."

With another command, a comet appeared in the projection, its elongated orbit bringing it near Earth precisely during the planetary alignment.

"Comet Bennett-Zhao," Santos identified it. "Discovered in 2023, with an orbital period of approximately 6,000 years. Its previous passage would have been during the early Bronze Age."

"I don't recall any news about a comet approaching," Ethan said.

"Because it's not particularly spectacular to the naked eye," Santos explained. "But its composition is unique—unusually high in exotic minerals and elements rarely found in solar system objects."

Dr. Mackie moved closer to the projection, studying the comet's trajectory. "You think it's influencing the temporal disturbance?"

"I think it may be catalyzing it," Santos corrected. "Historical records from ancient Mesopotamia describe a 'star that broke time' appearing in the sky, after which people experienced visions of past and future events. The dating corresponds with Bennett-Zhao's previous passage."

"The ancients would have interpreted temporal bleeding as divine visions or omens," Madame Winters noted.

"Precisely." Santos pointed to specific data scrolling alongside the projection. "What makes this passage particularly significant is that the comet crosses directly through the triangular configuration formed by Jupiter, Saturn, and Venus—creating a perfect four-point resonance pattern."

"Meaning what, exactly?" Alice asked, focusing on practical implications.

Santos's expression grew grave. "Meaning the temporal amplification will be significantly stronger than during the 1927 alignment. Perhaps an order of magnitude greater."

Tobias felt a chill despite the room's comfortable temperature. "So the containment wasn't just designed to last until the next regular alignment—it was specifically calibrated for this enhanced alignment with the comet."

"That would be my assessment," Santos agreed. "Your grandfather must have calculated this astronomical convergence, even without modern computational tools. Remarkable foresight."

"Or he experienced a temporal echo himself," Dr. Mackie suggested. "Glimpsed this future moment and prepared accordingly."

Alice brought the conversation back to immediate concerns. "When exactly does this alignment peak?"

Santos manipulated the projection, accelerating it further. "The perfect configuration occurs at 11:58 PM tomorrow night, with maximum resonance at precisely midnight."

"Midnight," Tobias repeated. "The third toll of midnight—that's our deadline for reuniting the Anchor Star with the Pendulum."

"Anchor Star?" Santos's interest visibly heightened. "You've found a reference to the Stella Temporis?"

The group exchanged surprised glances.

"You know about it?" Madame Winters asked.

"It's something of a legend in astronomical circles," Santos explained, moving to a bookshelf and extracting an ancient leather-bound volume. "Referenced in texts dating back to medieval times as a 'star that fell to earth and bent the flow of moments.'"

He opened the book to a hand-illustrated page showing a crystalline object radiating blue light, with figures in period clothing genuflecting before it.

"Most modern astronomers dismiss it as allegorical—a mythologized description of a meteorite impact. But those of us who study both the scientific and mystical aspects of celestial phenomena have long suspected it was something more significant."

"It's real," Tobias confirmed. "My grandfather helped hide it in 1927 after using it in a ritual to contain a temporal fracture similar to what's happening now. We've found a map to its location."

Santos's eyes widened. "That's... extraordinary. The Anchor Star is described as having unique chronometric properties—essentially existing partially outside normal timeflow, allowing it to 'anchor' temporal energy without being affected by it."

"Which would make it the perfect counterbalance to the Pendulum," Dr. Mackie concluded. "One manipulates time, the other stabilizes it."

"Together, they could create a permanent containment field," Santos agreed. "But the timing is critical. The alignment creates both the problem and the opportunity—it weakens temporal boundaries, but also provides the energy necessary for permanent sealing."

Alice studied the holographic display showing the approaching alignment. "So we have until the third stroke of midnight tomorrow to find the Anchor Star, bring it to the clocktower, and complete the ritual."

"Yes, and you must be precise," Santos warned. "After the third toll, the alignment begins to degrade. The window for permanent containment closes rapidly."

"What happens if we miss that window?" Ethan asked.

Santos's expression grew somber. "Based on what we're already seeing, a complete temporal collapse in the Daybridge region. Past, present, and potential futures would bleed together permanently."

"Could people survive that?" Alice asked bluntly.

"Physically, perhaps. Mentally..." Santos shook his head. "Imagine experiencing your birth, life, and death simultaneously. The human mind isn't equipped for non-linear temporal perception on that scale."

The professor moved to another console, bringing up data charts on a wall-mounted screen. "I've been tracking the temporal disruption through its effects on astronomical observations. The pattern is clear—and accelerating."

The chart showed a steadily rising curve with periodic spikes.

"Each spike represents a major temporal bleeding event," Santos explained. "They're growing more frequent and more intense. The most recent—which I'm guessing correlates with your discovery in the underground chamber—was nearly double the strength of its predecessor."

"Can you project the progression?" Dr. Mackie asked.

Santos nodded grimly, extending the curve forward. It rose exponentially, reaching a critical threshold precisely at midnight the following day.

"After that point, the disruption becomes self-sustaining," he explained. "Even if the cosmic lens of the alignment dissipates, the temporal fracture would continue to widen."

"Like a runaway nuclear reaction," Dr. Mackie analogized.

"Similar, yes. Once critical mass is achieved, the process becomes irreversible."

Tobias had been quietly absorbing this information, connecting it with what they'd already discovered. Now he spoke up. "The synchronized clocks in my shop—they've been counting down to this moment all along."

"Quite likely," Santos agreed. "Timepieces are naturally sensitive to chronometric disturbances. The more precisely crafted, the more sensitive they become."

"But they've been showing 11:32 for hours now," Alice noted. "No further movement."

Santos frowned. "That's concerning. It suggests a buildup of temporal potential energy—like water behind a dam that's about to break."

As if triggered by his words, the building shuddered slightly. The holographic projection flickered, momentarily showing different planetary positions before stabilizing.

"Temporal quake," Dr. Mackie identified it, checking her instruments. "Stronger than previous ones."

Santos moved quickly to his computers, examining readings. "It originated beneath the city center—directly under the clocktower. The temporary containment is degrading faster than anticipated."

"We need to retrieve the Anchor Star immediately," Alice decided. "The map indicates it's hidden at Fellwater Dock."

"I know the area well," Santos said. "It's one of the oldest sections of the harbor, dating back to colonial times." He studied the map Tobias had unfolded on a nearby table. "These markings correspond to specific astronomical alignments visible from that location during different historical periods."

"Can you help us interpret them?" Tobias asked.

"Of course." Santos examined the map more closely. "Your grandfather was using celestial navigation principles—essentially creating a star map overlaid on Daybridge's geography." He pointed to specific markings. "These indicate viewing positions, while these show sightlines. Together, they triangulate to... here."

His finger rested on a point near the old stone breakwater. "Beneath the Harbormaster statue, just as you suspected."

"'The Hunter guards what fell from heaven,'" Tobias quoted from his grandfather's notes.

"A fitting description," Santos agreed. "The statue depicts Augustus Fell, the city's first harbormaster, as a hunter. It was erected in 1892, so it would have been there when your grandfather hid the Anchor Star."

Another tremor shook the building, stronger than the first. Outside the windows, the sky briefly darkened to night, stars becoming visible for several seconds before returning to late afternoon.

"The temporal fluctuations are worsening," Santos said, checking his instruments again. "And spreading. This facility's shielding won't hold indefinitely."

Alice's phone rang—Captain Vaughn with an update.

"Chen, we've got major problems downtown," he reported, his voice tight. "The clocktower just ran backward for ten minutes, then skipped ahead three hours. Every digital device in a six-block radius is malfunctioning, and we've got people reporting encounters with themselves from different time periods."

"Temporal doubles," Dr. Mackie murmured. "The bleeding is becoming bidirectional."

"We're heading to Fellwater Dock," Alice informed Vaughn. "We've identified the location of the Anchor Star and confirmed tomorrow at midnight as our deadline."

"Make it fast," Vaughn replied. "Harlow's been demanding to speak with you. Says only he knows how to properly integrate the artifacts without destroying the city."

Alice's expression hardened. "He's manipulating us. He wanted the temporal fracture to happen."

"Maybe, but he's the closest thing we have to an expert on the Pendulum besides Merrick's grandfather, who's inconveniently ninety-eight years in the past."

"We'll consider it if necessary," Alice conceded. "For now, maintain the clocktower security and prepare for potential evacuation of the surrounding blocks."

After ending the call, she turned to the others. "We need to move quickly. Professor Santos, can you provide any equipment that might help us locate or retrieve the Anchor Star?"

"Better than that," Santos replied, moving to a cabinet along the wall. "I can provide the astronomical calculations necessary for proper alignment during tomorrow's ritual."

He extracted several rolled charts and a small device resembling an astrolabe but with digital components. "This chronometric sextant can measure temporal fluctuations relative to stellar positions. You'll need it to calibrate the Pendulum and Anchor Star during integration."

"Thank you," Tobias said, carefully accepting the instruments. "Do you want to join us for the retrieval?"

Santos shook his head regretfully. "I must remain here to monitor the celestial progression. As we approach the alignment, I can provide real-time data on the cosmic lens formation." He handed Dr. Mackie a small communication device. "This links directly to our systems. I'll stay in contact."

As they prepared to depart, Santos moved to a smaller display console. "Before you go, there's something else you should see."

The screen showed a composite image of the night sky with a simulation of how it would appear during the alignment. The three planets formed their triangular configuration, with Comet Bennett-Zhao passing through the center.

"Watch what happens when I overlay the temporal distortion field."

A blue-hued pattern appeared on the display, showing energy waves emanating from the cosmic configuration and converging directly over Daybridge.

"The alignment creates a temporal lens that focuses chronometric energy onto this specific geographic location," Santos explained. "But the question has always been: why here? Why Daybridge specifically?"

He adjusted the display, adding a geological overlay of the region. Five glowing lines converged beneath the city center—the ley lines they already knew about.

"Natural energy conduits, yes," Santos acknowledged. "But there's something more fundamental."

With another command, he zoomed out to a wider geological view, revealing a circular pattern around Daybridge that had been invisible at street level.

"The city sits in an impact crater," he said simply. "Very ancient, largely eroded and obscured by later geological processes, but unmistakable when viewed from this perspective."

"An impact crater," Tobias repeated. "From what?"

"From the original Anchor Star," Santos said quietly. "Or rather, the larger celestial body that contained it. This area was struck by a meteor approximately twelve thousand years ago—well before human settlement but leaving a permanent mark on the landscape."

"The ley lines follow the stress fractures from the impact," Dr. Mackie realized, studying the pattern.

"Exactly. And the clocktower stands precisely at the impact center." Santos looked at them gravely. "Daybridge exists because of the Anchor Star. The original settlers were drawn to this location due to its unusual properties—the abundance of fresh water, the natural harbor formation, the inexplicable sense of 'rightness' many founders reported in their journals."

"The temporal energy has been influencing this area for millennia," Madame Winters murmured. "No wonder the supernatural community congregated here."

"And now the cosmic lens is reforming," Santos continued, "focusing energy back onto the original impact point during the same comet's return. It's not just an astronomical coincidence—it's a cycle that's been repeating since before recorded history."

Another tremor shook the building, stronger than the previous ones. The lights flickered, and several instruments issued warning tones.

"You need to go," Santos urged them. "Find the Anchor Star. Complete what your ancestors began in 1927. This cycle doesn't have to end in catastrophe if you can establish permanent containment."

As they hurried to the vehicles, the sky above Daybridge rippled with intensifying auroral patterns—curtains of blue-green light dancing even in daylight. In the distance, the clocktower was visible on the city skyline, occasionally appearing to shift position or change architectural styles as temporal bleeding affected it.

"The underground chamber, the clocktower's location, the celestial alignment," Tobias said as they drove away from the observatory. "My grandfather understood it all—the connections between time, space, and cosmic cycles."

"Not just your grandfather," Madame Winters corrected gently. "The Winters Coven, the Ravencroft vampire line, the Reeves pack—all were part of this effort. Just as we are now."

Ethan, who had been unusually quiet during the observatory visit, finally spoke. "The pattern keeps repeating. Same families, same crisis, different generation."

"Let's hope for a different outcome this time," Alice said, eyes fixed on the road as they navigated around patches of temporal distortion. "Permanent containment instead of another temporary patch."

As they descended from Crescent Hill, the city below presented a troubling sight. Sections of Daybridge flickered between time periods—modern buildings momentarily replaced by their historical predecessors or futuristic versions not yet built. People on the streets moved with confusion, some appearing disoriented as they experienced temporal slippage.

"It's affecting more than just structures now," Dr. Mackie observed. "People are experiencing personal temporal displacement—consciousness shifting slightly out of sync with their physical timeline."

"What does that mean for us?" Alice asked, swerving to avoid a section of road that had temporarily become a streetcar track from the 1930s.

"It means we're all vulnerable to temporal effects," Dr. Mackie replied. "Our perceptions, memories, even physical locations could shift unexpectedly. We need to stay grounded in our present purpose."

Tobias clutched his grandfather's journal, feeling it like an anchor to his own timeline. Inside its pages, Harold Merrick had documented his confrontation with the same forces they now faced—a connection across generations that transcended the failing boundaries of time itself.

As they approached the harbor district, the temporal bleeding grew more pronounced. The modern redeveloped waterfront repeatedly shifted to show its previous incarnations—the industrial port of the mid-20th century, the busy commercial harbor of the 1800s, even glimpses of the original colonial settlement.

Through these fluctuating visions of Daybridge's past and potential futures, they made their way toward Fellwater Dock—and the Anchor Star that waited beneath the hunter's shadow, hidden for nearly a century by a man who had glimpsed the future and prepared for this very moment.

The synchronized clocks might be paused at 11:32, but the true countdown continued inexorably—not in minutes but in cosmic movement, as planets aligned and a comet approached to recreate a configuration that had occurred only once before in living memory.

By this time tomorrow, they would either have contained the fracture permanently or lost Daybridge to temporal chaos. The third toll of midnight would mark either their success or failure.

And time itself hung in the balance.

The journey to Fellwater Dock took them through increasingly unstable parts of Daybridge. They traveled in two vehicles—Alice driving with Ethan and Tobias, while Dr. Mackie followed with Madame Winters and a PIU technician carrying specialized equipment.

As they approached the harbor district, the temporal bleeding intensified. Entire blocks flickered between centuries—modern buildings giving way to colonial structures, then futuristic architecture, before snapping back to present day. Pedestrians moved cautiously, some wearing the dazed expressions that indicated temporal disorientation.

"The PIU has established containment zones around the worst affected areas," Alice explained, navigating around a barricade. "People experiencing severe temporal displacement are being relocated to the university's sports complex. It's built on a minor ley line intersection that's providing some stability."

"What about the werewolf population?" Ethan asked, still looking exhausted from his earlier transformation. "If another temporal moon appears..."

"Pack leaders have established secure transformation spaces," Alice replied. "Captain Vaughn coordinated with them after your incident."

Tobias studied his grandfather's map as they drove. "According to this, we need to approach Fellwater Dock via the old canal towpath. It's been converted to a riverwalk now, but the original route still exists."

They parked near Harbormaster Plaza, an open square facing the river where commerce had once flourished in Daybridge's early days. At its center stood a bronze statue of the city's founder, Jeremiah Day, depicted as a frontiersman with rifle in hand and game at his feet. Though weathered by time, the statue maintained a commanding presence overlooking the harbor.

"The hunter," Ethan identified immediately.

Dr. Mackie's vehicle pulled up beside them. The professor emerged carrying a field kit of scientific instruments, while Madame Winters brought a worn leather satchel that clinked with glass vials and metal implements.

"Temporal distortion is severe here," Dr. Mackie announced, consulting her equipment. "Multiple time streams converging."

"Can you locate the strongest point?" Alice asked.

"I'm trying, but there's interference." She adjusted her instruments. "The ley line beneath us is fluctuating wildly."

Madame Winters closed her eyes, extending her hands. "This way," she said after a moment, pointing toward the riverwalk that curved around the harbor. "The energy flows strongest along the old towpath."

They followed her lead, walking along the brick-paved path that bordered the Daybridge River. Modern lamps and benches lined the route, though these occasionally flickered into their historical predecessors—gas lamps and wooden seats worn by decades of use.

The late afternoon sun cast long shadows across the water, including that of Jeremiah Day's statue extending out over the riverwalk.

"The hunter's shadow," Tobias murmured, watching where the bronze silhouette fell. "During certain times of day, it would point to specific locations."

Dr. Mackie consulted an astronomical app on her tablet. "At sunset on the day of the alignment—tomorrow—the shadow would point directly..." She calculated briefly. "There," she indicated a section of the old stone embankment where river met the constructed harbor wall.

"'Where water meets stone,'" Alice quoted from the clue.

They approached the spot—an unremarkable section of the embankment that appeared identical to the stretches on either side. The stone blocks were moss-covered and weathered, showing at least a century of exposure to river water.

Ethan knelt, examining the stones closely. "There's something here." He brushed away moss from one particular block, revealing a faint engraving—the same stylized 'M' they had seen in the underground chamber.

"Another Merrick marker," Tobias confirmed. He ran his fingers over the symbol, feeling a slight depression in the center. "It's different from the others. This indent in the middle..."

He extracted his chronometer from his pocket, studying it thoughtfully. "Time is one of the three keys mentioned in the clue."

"Try it," Alice suggested.

Tobias carefully positioned the chronometer against the depression. It fit perfectly, like a key in a lock. The moment it seated fully, a low hum emanated from the stone wall. Blue light seeped from the edges of several blocks, outlining a door-shaped section approximately three feet wide.

"The first key works," Dr. Mackie observed, recording the phenomenon with her instruments. "Time unlocks the physical entrance."

"Blood and light remain," Madame Winters said. She approached the illuminated outline, studying it carefully. "There." She pointed to a small channel carved into the bottom edge of the outlined door. "A blood offering is required here."

"Whose blood?" Alice asked.

"Logically, it would need to be someone connected to the original concealment," the witch replied. "A Merrick, a Winters, a Ravencroft, or a Reeves."

Tobias and Ethan exchanged glances.

"I'll do it," Ethan volunteered. "Werewolf healing means it's a temporary inconvenience for me."

Madame Winters extracted a silver blade from her satchel. "This was my grandmother's ritual knife. It should satisfy the magical requirements."

Ethan accepted the knife, making a shallow cut across his palm. He held his bleeding hand over the channel, allowing several drops to fall into the carved groove. The blood didn't pool as expected but instead seemed to be absorbed by the stone itself.

The blue light intensified, spreading further through the outlined door. A clicking sound came from within the wall, like tumblers falling into place.

"Two keys engaged," Dr. Mackie confirmed. "Only light remains."

"But what form of light?" Alice wondered. "Sunlight is fading as evening approaches."

Tobias examined the door outline more carefully. "There's another depression here, at the center of the door." He pointed to a small circular indentation about the size of a quarter. "It's perfectly round, like it's meant to focus something."

Dr. Mackie approached with a specialized flashlight from her kit. "Try concentrated light. This outputs at specific frequencies that often trigger paranormal phenomena."

She directed the beam at the circular depression. Nothing happened.

"Not artificial light, then," Tobias mused. He looked up at the darkening sky, where the first stars were becoming visible. "Starlight, perhaps? The Anchor Star fell from the heavens, after all."

Madame Winters nodded thoughtfully. "The map referenced Orion specifically. Perhaps light from Rigel—the blue giant star—is required."

"But how would we channel starlight from a specific star?" Alice asked.

Tobias's expression changed as realization struck him. "My chronometer. It's not just a timepiece—it's an astronomical instrument." He opened the case, revealing the complex face with its celestial tracking functions. "There's a lens built into the observatory dial that can be aligned to specific stars."

He adjusted several tiny dials on the chronometer's face, configuring it to Rigel's position. "If I'm right, this should capture and focus starlight from Rigel specifically."

As Rigel brightened in the evening sky, Tobias positioned the chronometer, so its lens aligned with the star and the circular depression in the stone. For several moments, nothing happened. Then, as the star reached a specific angle, a thin beam of blue-white light projected from the chronometer onto the stone.

The effect was immediate and dramatic. The entire outlined section of wall glowed brilliantly, then swung inward without a sound, revealing a narrow passage beyond.

"All three keys," Dr. Mackie whispered. "Time, blood, and light."

Ethan's enhanced senses detected it first—the same distinctive scent of ozone and old books that had marked other temporal phenomena. "It's in there. Something powerful."

Alice switched on her flashlight, illuminating rough-hewn steps descending beneath the embankment. "I'll go first. Stay close together."

The passage led them steeply downward, soon reaching the water table. Unlike the dry tunnel beneath Merrick's Chronometry, this one showed signs of regular flooding—water marks on the walls, marine growth in crevices, the distinct smell of river mud.

"The water level must fluctuate with the river," Tobias observed. "During high tide or floods, this entire passage would be submerged."

"Another layer of protection," Dr. Mackie suggested. "The site would be accessible only during specific conditions."

After descending about thirty feet, the passage opened into a small circular chamber carved directly from the bedrock beneath the river. Water covered the floor to a depth of several inches, reflecting their flashlight beams in rippling patterns across the ceiling.

In the center of the chamber stood a stone pedestal rising above the water line. Unlike the grand astronomical observatory they had discovered earlier, this space was utilitarian—designed for concealment rather than celebration.

Atop the pedestal rested a simple wooden box bound with iron bands.

"That's it," Madame Winters said with certainty. "I can feel the temporal energy from here."

They waded through the shallow water to the pedestal. The box was sealed with three locks—one of conventional mechanical design, one with a small basin similar to the blood channel above, and one with a crystalline lens built into its surface.

"The same three keys," Tobias noted. "Consistent security protocol."

They repeated the process—chronometer in the mechanical lock, Ethan's blood in the basin, and focused starlight through the lens. The locks disengaged with a synchronized click.

Tobias carefully lifted the lid.

Inside, nestled on a bed of dark velvet, lay a crystalline object approximately the size of a tennis ball. Unlike the blue glow of the Pendulum, this crystal emanated a pure white light with subtle rainbow refractions where the beams hit the chamber walls. Its surface was smooth but not polished, with the slightly melted appearance characteristic of meteorites that have survived atmospheric entry.

"The Anchor Star," Dr. Mackie whispered, her scientific detachment momentarily overcome by wonder. "A temporally active meteorite."

As they stared at the artifact, Alice experienced another sharp pain behind her eyes. The surrounding chamber wavered, and once again she found herself witnessing a scene from the past.

Harold Merrick stood in this very chamber, carefully placing the Anchor Star in its box. He worked by lantern light, his movements precise despite obvious exhaustion. A younger version of Madame Winters' grandmother assisted him, inscribing protective symbols on the inside of the box lid.

"Are you certain this is necessary, Harold?" the witch asked. "Separating the Star from the Pendulum weakens the containment significantly."

"We have no choice," Harold replied grimly. "Harlow's allies are searching for both artifacts. Together, they enable complete temporal manipulation—the power to rewrite time itself. Separated, they can only maintain the boundary between time streams."

"But the fracture will return when the alignment recurs," she pointed out.

"Yes, in ninety-eight years." Harold secured the first lock. "By then, Harlow and his Chronos Society will be long dead. Future guardians can determine whether reuniting the artifacts is worth the risk."

"And if they choose wrongly?"

Harold paused, looking directly at where Alice stood—or would stand, a century later. "Then they must live with the consequences of unbound time. Past bleeding into present, present into future. Causality itself unraveled."

The witch completed her protective inscriptions. "The Chronos Society believes such unraveling is desirable—that linear time is a prison from which humanity must be freed."

"Because they haven't witnessed true temporal chaos," Harold said bitterly. "They speak of liberation while seeking control. They don't understand that some forces were never meant to be mastered."

As he spoke these words, the vision began to fade. The last thing Alice saw was Harold Merrick looking again in her direction, his expression communicating both warning and hope across the decades that separated them.

"—Detective Chen? Alice?"

She blinked, finding Ethan gripping her arm supportively. "Another temporal echo," she explained, steadying herself. "Harold

Merrick again. He mentioned something called the Chronos Society—apparently what Harlow belonged to."

"That matches what Lord Ravencroft discovered in his archives," Dr. Mackie said. "The Chronos Society was a secret organization dedicated to 'liberating humanity from temporal constraints.' They believed linear time was artificially imposed on a naturally simultaneous universe."

"The same philosophy Professor Harlow expressed in the clocktower," Tobias noted. "Not just an individual obsession, but an organized movement passing through generations."

"And potentially still active," Alice added. "If Harlow is connected to this original society, there may be others."

A distant rumbling interrupted their discussion, followed by the distinct sensation of the chamber shaking. Water sloshed around their feet as dust and small stones fell from the ceiling.

"Another temporal quake," Dr. Mackie warned, checking her instruments. "More severe than the previous ones. The stabilization is failing rapidly."

"We need to get the Anchor Star to the clocktower immediately," Alice decided.

Tobias carefully lifted the artifact from its box. The moment his fingers touched the crystalline surface, he gasped, nearly dropping it.

"What is it?" Ethan asked.

"It's... communicating somehow," Tobias said, his expression one of wonder and confusion. "Not in words, but in... sensations. Possibilities. Like viewing multiple timelines simultaneously."

"The Star exists partially outside normal time," Madame Winters explained. "Those with temporal sensitivity can perceive fragments of its awareness."

Tobias secured the Star in a protective case from his toolkit. "We should hurry. I'm not sure how long the tunnel will remain stable during these quakes."

They retraced their steps up the passage, emerging onto the riverwalk just as another temporal quake shook the city. Across the harbor, buildings flickered between time periods more dramatically than before—entire blocks transforming from present-day structures to historical or even futuristic configurations before reverting.

The sky above had taken on an impossible quality—sunset colors blending with midnight darkness and dawn light simultaneously, as if multiple times of day were competing for dominance. The auroral lights had formed into distinct patterns that resembled enormous clockfaces spanning the horizon.

"The temporal boundaries are collapsing faster than anticipated," Dr. Mackie announced, studying her readings. "The countdown must have accelerated."

As if in response to her observation, the bells of the distant clocktower began to toll—not marking the hour, but sounding a chaotic, discordant sequence that echoed across the city.

Their phones buzzed simultaneously with an emergency alert: *CITYWIDE EVACUATION ORDER IN EFFECT. PROCEED TO DESIGNATED TEMPORAL STABILITY ZONES. THIS IS NOT A DRILL.*

"Vaughn's implementing the contingency plan," Alice explained. "They're moving civilians to the areas least affected by temporal bleeding."

"Which won't matter if we don't get the Anchor Star to the Pendulum before midnight," Tobias said, securing the case containing the artifact.

As they hurried back to their vehicles, Ethan suddenly staggered, clutching his abdomen. "No—not again—" he gasped.

Alice looked up to see the impossible sight of multiple moons visible in the early evening sky—a full moon, a crescent, and a half moon all occupying different positions simultaneously.

"Temporal overlay of multiple lunar phases," Dr. Mackie identified. "The fracture is affecting celestial bodies now."

Ethan fought against the transformation, his features already beginning to shift. "I can't—control it—"

"Don't fight it," Madame Winters advised him. "Your werewolf form may be better equipped to navigate temporal instability."

With a growl of pain and frustration, Ethan surrendered to the change. His transformation was faster this time, his body having already gone through the process earlier. Within moments, he stood before them in full werewolf form, amber eyes gleaming with awareness.

"Can you maintain control?" Alice asked him.

The werewolf nodded once, decisively.

"Then we proceed as planned. Ethan's senses may help us navigate the increasing distortions."

They split between the two vehicles, Ethan joining Alice and Tobias despite the cramped quarters his transformed state created. As they drove toward the Municipal Building, the surrounding city descended further into temporal chaos.

Streets rearranged themselves mid-journey, forcing detours around areas where the road simply ceased to exist in their timestream. Pedestrians shared sidewalks with ghostly figures from other eras, some interacting in confused encounters. Above, the impossible sky continued its kaleidoscopic display of competing dayparts.

Tobias clutched the case containing the Anchor Star, feeling its energy pulse in response to the surrounding chaos. In his pocket, the chronometer with its Pendulum fragment vibrated subtly, as if recognizing the proximity of its counterpart.

"They're resonating with each other," he observed. "And with the temporal distortions."

Alice navigated carefully around a section of road that had transformed into a cobblestone street complete with a horse-drawn trolley. "How much time do we have?"

Tobias checked his watch—one of the few timepieces unaffected by the synchronization. "It's 7:42 PM. The alignment reaches its peak at midnight."

"The third toll," Alice remembered. "We have until the third stroke of midnight to reunite the artifacts."

In the back seat, Ethan growled suddenly, pointing toward the Municipal Building now visible in the distance. Its clocktower stood as a fixed point amid the temporal chaos, but something was wrong. Even from here, they could see figures moving on the observation deck near the bells—silhouettes illuminated by unnatural light emanating from within the tower itself.

"Someone's at the clocktower," Alice said, accelerating despite the hazardous conditions. "The Pendulum chamber may be compromised."

She tried to radio Captain Vaughn but received only static in response. "Communications are down," she reported. "The temporal interference must be blocking signals."

As they approached the Municipal Plaza, they could see that the PIU perimeter had been breached. Several officers lay unconscious on the ground, while others engaged in combat with what appeared to be partially transformed werewolves similar to those that had attacked Tobias's home.

"Harlow's allies," Tobias surmised. "They must have freed him somehow."

Alice parked at the edge of the plaza, drawing her weapon. "We need to reach the clocktower mechanism. Ethan, can you clear us a path?"

The werewolf nodded, moving to the front position as they exited the vehicle. Dr. Mackie and Madame Winters arrived moments later, quickly assessing the chaotic scene.

"The Anchor Star is our priority," Alice reminded them. "Whatever happens, it must reach the Pendulum before the third toll."

They advanced across the plaza, Ethan's imposing werewolf form deterring immediate confrontation. Inside the Municipal Building, emergency lights cast eerie shadows through corridors now empty of the usual government workers. Temporal rifts opened randomly along their path, forcing them to navigate around visions of the building in various historical configurations.

When they reached the clocktower access door, they found it torn from its hinges—the work of supernatural strength. The spiral staircase beyond echoed with sounds of activity above.

"They've reached the mechanism chamber," Tobias said grimly. "We may already be too late."

"We proceed regardless," Alice decided. "Ethan takes point. Dr. Mackie and Madame Winters in the middle with the equipment. Tobias and I will guard the rear with the Anchor Star."

They ascended the stairs cautiously, their progress slowed by increasing temporal distortions. Entire sections of the staircase flickered between time periods, forcing them to time their steps carefully to avoid falls when solid stone momentarily became incomplete scaffolding from the tower's construction phase.

As they neared the mechanism chamber, voices became audible—Professor Harlow's academic tones rising above others in what sounded like instruction or ritual incantation.

Ethan paused, signaling for silence. His enhanced hearing allowed him to distinguish the words being spoken:

"... alignment approaches its apex. The Pendulum's containment has been fully disabled. When midnight strikes, the temporal boundaries will dissolve completely. Prepare yourselves for transcendence."

Alice motioned for them to continue, but with increased caution. They reached the chamber door to find it guarded by two transformed werewolves who immediately detected their approach.

Before the guards could raise an alarm, Ethan launched himself forward with supernatural speed. The resulting confrontation was brief but violent—a blur of fur and fangs as three massive creatures fought in the confined space.

Ethan emerged victorious, though sporting several deep gashes across his chest and arms. He gestured for them to proceed while the guards lay unconscious.

Inside the mechanism chamber, they found a scene of calculated desecration. The great clockworks had been partially disassembled, key components removed or repositioned. The protective sigils Madame Winters had identified earlier had been deliberately scratched away. In the center, the Pendulum chamber stood open, the crystalline artifact pulsing with unstable blue energy that sent arcs of temporal lightning throughout the space.

Professor Harlow stood on the maintenance platform before the exposed Pendulum, surrounded by a dozen figures in dark robes embroidered with chronometric symbols. Among them were both humans and supernaturals—including Diana Blackwood, the vampire representative who had earlier claimed to support their efforts.

"Ah, right on schedule," Harlow greeted them without turning. "The universe does appreciate temporal symmetry. The descendants of those who imprisoned the Pendulum, arriving just in time to witness its liberation."

Alice raised her weapon. "Step away from the mechanism, Harlow. You're still under arrest."

"Detective Chen, your jurisdiction extends to Daybridge's current timestream only," Harlow replied, finally turning to face them. His eyes glowed with the same blue energy emanating from the Pendulum. "In approximately four hours, all time streams will converge. Your authority—indeed, the entire concept of linear authority—will become meaningless."

"You've disabled the containment," Tobias observed, noting the dismantled armatures that had held the Pendulum in alignment. "You've doomed everyone in the city."

"I've freed them," Harlow corrected. "When the alignment peaks at midnight, the Pendulum's full power will be unleashed. Temporal boundaries will dissolve. Past, present, and future will exist simultaneously—as they were always meant to."

"The human mind can't process multiple time streams," Dr. Mackie argued. "You'll drive the entire population insane."

"Initially, perhaps," Diana Blackwood interjected smoothly. "But those with sufficient mental fortitude will adapt. Evolution requires pressure, Doctor. The weak-minded will fall; the strong will transcend."

"The Chronos Society lives," Madame Winters identified the robed figures. "After all these years."

"For nearly two centuries," Harlow confirmed. "Patiently working toward this moment—when the stars align and the Pendulum can fulfill its true purpose."

His gaze fixed on the case in Tobias's hands. "And you've brought us the final component. How thoughtful."

Ethan growled, positioning himself protectively before Tobias.

"Your werewolf can't stop what's already begun," Harlow said dismissively. "The containment is disabled. The clocktower mechanism is modified to amplify rather than restrict the Pendulum's energy. In precisely three hours and forty-two minutes, temporal liberation begins."

"Unless we repair the containment," Tobias challenged. "With the Anchor Star, we can establish permanent stability—what my grandfather couldn't accomplish in 1927."

"Ah yes, Harold Merrick." Harlow's expression darkened. "A brilliant mind tragically limited by conventional thinking. He saw only the danger in temporal fluidity, not the opportunity."

"He saw reality," Tobias countered. "He understood that actions need consequences, that cause must precede effect. Without that framework, existence itself becomes meaningless."

"A clockmaker's perspective," Diana Blackwood commented with aristocratic disdain. "Always concerned with orderly progression. How tediously human."

Alice had been carefully assessing the situation—counting opponents, identifying potential cover, planning engagement tactics. Now she spoke calmly but firmly: "Ethan, Plan Chimera."

The werewolf immediately understood the coded instruction. With a deafening roar that disoriented everyone in the chamber, he charged not at the Chronos Society members but at the massive clock mechanism itself. His supernatural strength enabled him to dislodge a critical gear, sending it rolling across the floor and disrupting the modified configuration.

In the moment of confusion, Alice fired three precisely aimed shots—not at people, but at the support structure holding the maintenance platform. The aged wood splintered, causing Harlow and several society members to lose their balance.

"Now!" Alice shouted.

Dr. Mackie activated a device from her equipment bag—a compact temporal disruptor that created a localized stasis field around the Pendulum chamber. "I can hold it stable for ninety seconds at most!"

Madame Winters began a rapid incantation, her hands weaving protective patterns in the air. The remaining sigils on the mechanism glowed in response, temporarily strengthening despite their damaged state.

Tobias raced toward the Pendulum, the case containing the Anchor Star clutched tightly against his chest. Society members moved to intercept him, but found themselves impeded by furniture and tools that seemed to shift position of their own accord—Madame Winters' magic manipulating the environment to clear a path.

He reached the Pendulum chamber just as Harlow recovered his footing. The professor lunged toward him, hands outstretched to seize the Anchor Star.

"You don't understand what you're doing!" Harlow shouted. "The containment doesn't just restrict the Pendulum—it blinds humanity to temporal truth!"

Tobias dodged his grasp, sliding the last few feet to the open chamber. "I understand exactly what I'm doing," he replied. "Finishing what my grandfather started."

He opened the case, revealing the brilliantly glowing Anchor Star. The moment it was exposed in proximity to the Pendulum, both artifacts pulsed with increased energy—the Pendulum's blue light and the Star's white radiance interacting in complex patterns.

"The resonance is perfect," Dr. Mackie observed through gritted teeth, struggling to maintain the stasis field. "They recognize each other."

"How do I integrate them?" Tobias asked urgently.

"The armatures," Madame Winters called out, still maintaining her protective spell. "They're designed to hold both artifacts in specific alignment."

Tobias examined the dismantled mechanism. His watchmaker's mind quickly comprehended the engineering principles involved, seeing how the separate pieces should fit together. Working rapidly, he began reassembling the armatures while keeping both artifacts within the chamber.

Around them, chaos erupted as Alice and Ethan engaged the Chronos Society members. Supernatural strength and trained combat skills kept the cultists at bay, but they were outnumbered significantly.

"Thirty seconds remaining on the stasis field," Dr. Mackie warned.

Harlow made another attempt to reach the chamber, but Diana Blackwood unexpectedly intercepted him.

"What are you doing?" he demanded. "We agreed—"

"The Council reconsidered," she said coldly. "Temporal chaos serves no one's interests—not even immortals. The vampires withdraw their support."

With that, she used her supernatural strength to hurl Harlow across the chamber, buying Tobias precious additional seconds.

Working with the precision his profession demanded, Tobias completed the armature assembly. The structure now cradled both the Pendulum and the Anchor Star in perfect opposition, their energies visibly interacting across the space between them.

"The integration is aligned," he announced. "But the sigils—they're still damaged."

"I can reinforce them temporarily," Madame Winters said. "But they need physical restoration to maintain permanent containment."

"My watchmaker's tools," Tobias said. "In my bag. I can re-engrave them once the initial integration is stable."

Dr. Mackie's stasis field flickered and failed, allowing the full energy of both artifacts to engage with the reintegrated mechanism. The effect was immediate and dramatic. A shock wave of temporal energy exploded outward from the chamber, passing harmlessly through humans but sending the partially transformed werewolves to their knees.

The clocktower bells began to toll, though it was only 8:17 PM. Each massive peal sent visible ripples through the air, but unlike before, these ripples seemed to stabilize the surrounding reality rather than disrupt it.

"It's working," Dr. Mackie exclaimed, checking her instruments. "The artifacts are synchronizing. The temporal field is stabilizing."

Harlow struggled to his feet, his expression contorted with rage and desperation. "No! You're imprisoning humanity in linear time! You're blinding them to infinite possibility!"

"I'm preventing temporal chaos," Tobias corrected, carefully closing the chamber door once the integration was complete. "The possibilities remain—they just occur in their proper sequence."

The bells continued their unscheduled tolling as the mechanism resumed its normal operation. Throughout the chamber, temporal rifts that had been constantly opening and closing began to shrink and disappear. The multiple moons visible through the tower windows merged into a single crescent in its proper phase.

Alice and the PIU team secured the remaining Chronos Society members, many of whom seemed disoriented as the Pendulum's influence over them faded. Ethan, still in werewolf form but clearly exhausted, slumped against a wall as his wounds began their accelerated healing.

"Is it over?" Alice asked Dr. Mackie, who was reviewing data on her tablet.

"The immediate crisis, yes," the professor confirmed. "The Anchor Star has established a stable containment field around the Pendulum. Temporal bleeding throughout the city should recede within hours."

"But?" Alice sensed the reservation in her tone.

"But the permanent solution requires more than just placing the artifacts in proximity," Dr. Mackie explained. "The protective sigils need complete restoration, and a proper ritual must be performed during the alignment at midnight."

"So we've bought time, but not completed the task," Tobias summarized, already examining the damaged sigils with his watchmaker's precision.

"Exactly. The containment will hold temporarily, but without the ritual at midnight, it will eventually degrade again—perhaps not for decades, but inevitably."

Madame Winters approached, her elderly face showing the strain of her magical exertions. "My grandmother's grimoire contains the ritual requirements. With the Anchor Star now recovered, we can perform the complete ceremony that wasn't possible in 1927."

"And permanently contain the Pendulum?" Alice asked.

"Yes, though 'permanent' in temporal matters is always relative," the witch replied with a small smile. "Let us say rather that the containment would be self-sustaining for centuries rather than decades."

As they discussed next steps, Captain Vaughn arrived with reinforcements, securing the chamber and the captured society members.

"Harlow?" he asked, noting the professor's absence among the detainees.

"Escaped during the confrontation," Alice reported. "Diana Blackwood's intervention gave us the time we needed, but Harlow used the chaos to slip away."

"The vampire turned on her allies?"

"The Vampire Council apparently reconsidered the wisdom of temporal chaos," Alice explained. "Even immortals prefer predictability to absolute uncertainty."

Vaughn surveyed the secured artifacts and the clocktower mechanism now operating with restored stability. "So, we've averted the crisis?"

"Temporarily," Tobias answered, already at work re-engraving the first of the damaged sigils. "We still need to perform the complete ritual at midnight during the alignment. Until then, the containment remains vulnerable."

"And Harlow knows it," Alice added grimly. "He won't give up easily. The Chronos Society has waited nearly two centuries for this opportunity."

"I'll establish a security perimeter," Vaughn decided. "No one enters this tower without direct authorization."

As the PIU team organized the chamber's security, Tobias continued his meticulous work on the protective sigils. Each engraving required watchmaker's precision, recreating the complex patterns that channeled and contained the Pendulum's temporal energy.

Ethan, gradually recovering his strength, managed to shift partially back toward human form—enough to speak, though his appearance remained largely lupine.

"You should rest," Alice told him, bringing water and a protein bar from emergency supplies.

"No time," he replied, his voice a gravelly approximation of his normal tone. "Full moon rising for real tonight. Need to be ready."

"The temporal disruption is subsiding," she assured him. "The moon should return to its proper phase and influence."

"Should," he emphasized. "But after what we've seen today, I'm not taking chances."

Dr. Mackie joined them, her instruments displaying encouraging data. "The temporal bleeding is receding citywide. Stable reality is reasserting itself as the Pendulum's energy is properly channeled."

"And the synchronized clocks?" Alice asked.

"Still showing 11:32 but no longer building potential energy. They've entered a steady state until the final containment is established."

Tobias paused in his engraving work, flexing cramped fingers. "Four hours until midnight. Four hours to prepare for a ritual none of us has performed before, to permanently contain an artifact we barely understand."

"While watching for interference from a fanatical secret society," Alice added.

"Just another day in Daybridge," Ethan rumbled with grim humor.

Outside, the impossible aurora had faded, leaving a normal night sky where stars gradually appeared as true darkness fell. The city below remained partially evacuated, its citizens in designated safe zones until authorities confirmed the temporal emergency had passed.

Temporary stability had been achieved. The greater challenge—permanent containment—still lay ahead.

And somewhere in the city, Professor Harlow and his remaining Chronos Society loyalists plotted their response. Nearly two centuries of preparation wouldn't be abandoned because of one setback. The alignment would still occur at midnight, and with it, one final opportunity to either secure or unleash the Pendulum's power.

The countdown continued, invisible but inexorable. Four hours to midnight. Four hours until the third toll would signal either success or catastrophic failure.

Time, which had been their enemy throughout this crisis, now offered a brief respite—a chance to prepare for the final confrontation between those who would contain time's power and those who would unleash it upon an unprepared world.

CHAPTER NINE: SEEKING THE COVEN

The clocktower stood sentinel over Daybridge as evening deepened into night. From the mechanism chamber, they could see emergency vehicles moving through the streets below, their lights cutting through darkness as authorities continued evacuating residents from the most affected areas. The temporal bleeding had subsided significantly since the Anchor Star's integration with the Pendulum, but occasional ripples still disturbed reality—brief overlaps of past and present manifesting unpredictably throughout the city.

Captain Vaughn coordinated security from a makeshift command post in the tower's base, while Dr. Mackie and her team established monitoring equipment around the Pendulum chamber. Tobias continued his painstaking work re-engraving the protective sigils, his watchmaker's hands steady despite the pressure of their deadline.

"Three hours until midnight," Alice noted, checking her watch. "How many sigils remain?"

"Seven," Tobias replied without looking up from his intricate work. "I can complete them, but barely in time for the ritual."

Madame Winters shook her head, concern evident in her expression. "The physical sigils are only part of the requirement. The ritual itself needs preparation—specific materials, proper alignment, and most importantly, sufficient magical power."

"Your magic isn't enough?" Ethan asked. He had managed to stabilize his partially transformed state, appearing mostly human though retaining some lupine features—elongated canines, amber eyes, and heightened senses.

"For a temporary containment, perhaps," the elderly witch admitted. "But for a permanent solution? No. My grandmother's grimoire is clear—the original ritual required a full coven of thirteen witches, specifically those with temporal sensitivity."

"And you're just one," Alice observed.

"Precisely. The Winters Coven has dwindled over generations. Most of my relatives have left Daybridge, finding the city's supernatural intensity... challenging."

"Then we need to find more witches," Alice concluded. "Specifically, descendants of the original coven if possible."

"The PIU must have records," Ethan suggested. "Supernatural registration files would show family lineages."

Alice was already contacting Vaughn via radio. After a brief conversation, she turned back to the group. "He's pulling records now, but most are archived. It will take time to compile a complete list."

"Time we don't have," Tobias said, briefly glancing up from his engraving work. "We need another approach."

Madame Winters considered for a moment. "There is someone who might help—Madame Rowan. She's the oldest living witch in Daybridge, even older than myself. She was a junior member of my grandmother's coven in 1927."

"She was present during the original ritual?" Dr. Mackie asked with interest.

"Not as a participant, but as an observer. She would have been just a girl then, perhaps sixteen or seventeen. But her memory is sharp, and she has maintained the old ways more strictly than most."

"Where can we find her?" Alice asked.

"That's the difficulty. Madame Rowan withdrew from public life decades ago. She lives in seclusion somewhere on the outskirts of Daybridge, rarely interacting even with other witches."

"But you know how to contact her?" Alice pressed.

"Not directly. But I know how she might be found." Madame Winters moved to her satchel, extracting a small bundle of dried herbs and a tarnished silver compass. "This is a witch-finder—an old tool used when covens needed to gather quickly. It responds to magical signatures, particularly those of blood relations."

She opened the compass, revealing not cardinal directions but symbols etched into the face. The needle oscillated erratically before settling on a rune that resembled a stylized tree.

"Rowan," the elderly witch identified. "She's alive and within the city limits."

"So this will lead us to her?" Alice asked.

"It will point the way, yes. But Madame Rowan values her privacy. She may have wards and misdirections in place to confuse those seeking her."

Alice made a quick decision. "Ethan and I will find her. We have experience locating people who don't want to be found."

"I should go with you," Madame Winters said. "She's more likely to receive fellow practitioners of the craft."

"And I'll continue the sigil restoration," Tobias confirmed, already returning to his work. "Dr. Mackie can monitor the Pendulum's stability while I complete the engravings."

"We'll need transportation," Ethan noted. "If she's on the outskirts, that could mean Raven's Wood or the North Bluffs."

"Take my PIU vehicle," Dr. Mackie offered, tossing them keys. "It has equipment that might help track temporal anomalies. If Madame Rowan was present in 1927, she may carry temporal echoes herself."

With the plan established, Alice, Ethan, and Madame Winters descended the clocktower stairs, passing through multiple security checkpoints established by Vaughn's team. The Municipal Plaza outside had been transformed into an operational command center, with PIU agents and conventional police working alongside supernatural consultants to manage the ongoing situation.

They found Dr. Mackie's vehicle—a modified SUV equipped with specialized detection equipment—and quickly departed, heading northeast toward the wooded areas that bordered Daybridge's city limits. Madame Winters sat in the passenger seat, holding the witch-finder compass before her like a divining rod. Its needle swung purposefully, guiding their path through increasingly remote neighborhoods.

"This area was all farmland when I was young," Madame Winters remarked as they passed the final suburban developments and entered a region of scattered cottages and overgrown fields. "Daybridge has grown so much, but some places resist change."

The compass led them down progressively narrower roads until they reached a gravel track that wound between ancient oak trees. No streetlights illuminated their way here; only their headlights cut through the darkness.

"This feels deliberate," Ethan observed, his enhanced senses alert to their surroundings. "The increasing isolation, the darkness. It's designed to discourage casual visitors."

"Madame Rowan was always protective of her solitude," Winters agreed. "Even in coven gatherings, she kept to herself."

The gravel track ended abruptly at a small clearing. Beyond, only a footpath continued into the woods. The compass needle now spun in tight circles, as if confused by competing signals.

"We continue on foot," Madame Winters announced. "And be mindful where you step. Rowan would have protective measures in place."

They followed the footpath by flashlight, moving carefully through underbrush that seemed to reach toward them with unusual animation. Twice, Ethan had to untangle Madame Winters from vines that had silently wrapped around her ankles.

"Sentient flora," she explained, thanking him for his assistance. "A specialty of Rowan's. She communicates with plants more fluently than with people."

After twenty minutes of careful navigation, they emerged into another clearing. At its center stood a cottage that defied conventional architecture—its structure seamlessly integrated with living trees, as though the building had grown rather than been constructed. Warm light spilled from windows made of what appeared to be amber rather than glass. No clear boundary existed between garden and home; plants grew through and around the walls in organic harmony.

"Remarkable," Alice murmured. "It's completely off-grid."

"Off more than that," Ethan added, his werewolf senses detecting subtle energies. "This place exists partially outside normal space. It's bigger inside than outside."

"A pocket dimension," Madame Winters confirmed. "Old magic, rarely practiced now. Rowan has essentially folded space around her home, creating a sanctuary that operates under slightly different rules than the outside world."

As they approached the cottage, the door opened before they could knock. In the entrance stood a woman whose age was impossible to determine—her silver hair and lined face suggested great age, yet she moved with the fluid grace of someone much younger. She wore simple gardening clothes stained with soil, and her eyes—a startling violet—regarded them with ancient wisdom.

"Elsbeth Winters," she greeted them, her voice surprisingly melodic. "I wondered when you would come. The stars have aligned once more, have they not?"

"Indeed they have, Madame Rowan," Winters replied respectfully. "The temporal fracture has returned."

"As was foretold." Rowan's gaze shifted to Alice and Ethan. "A detective and a werewolf. Interesting companions for such a night."

"You were expecting us?" Alice asked.

"Not you specifically. But someone, yes. The clocktower's song has changed. The Pendulum calls to those who can hear it." She stepped aside, gesturing for them to enter. "Come. Time grows short, even here where it flows differently."

The cottage's interior defied its external dimensions, extending into multiple rooms filled with plants, books, and magical implements. The central space contained a large wooden table covered with star charts and astronomical calculations. Fresh tea steamed from ceramic mugs that hadn't been there a moment before.

"You know why we've come," Alice said, accepting the offered tea with cautious courtesy.

"The ritual must be completed properly this time," Rowan confirmed, seating herself at the table. "What was postponed in 1927 can no longer be delayed."

"You were there," Ethan said. "You witnessed the original containment."

"I did. A young acolyte, barely initiated into the craft." Rowan's violet eyes grew distant with memory. "I watched my elders channel power beyond their understanding, binding what should perhaps have remained free."

"The Pendulum was causing temporal bleeding then, just as now," Madame Winters reminded her. "Containment was necessary."

"Necessary but incomplete," Rowan corrected. "The solution was always temporary—a postponement rather than a resolution."

"Because the Anchor Star was separated from the Pendulum," Alice suggested.

Rowan smiled thinly. "That was part of it. But there was more—a fundamental component missing from the original ritual."

"What component?" Ethan asked.

Instead of answering directly, Rowan rose and moved to an ancient bookshelf. She extracted a volume bound in what appeared to be pale blue leather but which subtly shifted color as it moved, like the surface of deep water. The book had no visible title or markings.

"This is the true grimoire of the Winters Coven," she explained, placing it reverently on the table. "Not the redacted version passed down through the family line, but the original text as written by Cassandra Winters in 1783."

Madame Winters inhaled sharply. "The First Grimoire? I thought it lost during the Great Fire of 1876."

"Not lost. Protected." Rowan opened the book carefully, its pages emitting a faint luminescence. "Cassandra foresaw the temporal fracture centuries before it occurred. She documented a ritual designed specifically to contain artifacts of chronometric power."

She turned pages until reaching an illustration that made Alice lean forward in surprise—a detailed drawing of the Pendulum, though rendered somewhat differently than its current form.

"The Pendulum of Aeon," Rowan identified. "Its true and complete name. What sits in your clocktower is merely one component of a larger artifact."

"There's more of it?" Alice asked with concern.

"No, less. What you have is a fragment of the original." Rowan turned more pages, revealing diagrams of a more complex device. "The complete Pendulum of Aeon consisted of three harmonized components—the Crystal, which you now possess; the Star, which you have recovered; and the Fulcrum, which remains lost."

"A third component," Ethan mused. "That explains why the containment remains temporary even with both known pieces."

"Precisely. Without the Fulcrum, the energies cannot be perfectly balanced. The Crystal pushes outward, the Star pulls inward, but the Fulcrum is needed to stabilize the oscillation between them."

Alice frowned. "If this Fulcrum is essential, why didn't Harold Merrick or your coven mention it in 1927?"

"Because it was believed destroyed centuries ago," Rowan explained. "The complete Pendulum of Aeon arrived on Earth in

1483, when a meteor shower rained down near what would later become Daybridge. The impact shattered the artifact into its three components."

"Extraterrestrial origin," Dr. Mackie had theorized that, Alice recalled.

"The Crystal was discovered first, in the early 1800s," Rowan continued. "Its temporal properties became apparent when those who handled it experienced visions of past and future. The Star was found later, in 1856, by Tobias Merrick's great-great-grandfather."

"And the Fulcrum?" Ethan pressed.

"Never recovered. Assumed destroyed or lost beyond finding." Rowan touched the illustration with weathered fingers. "But I have reason to believe it survived."

She turned to another page, showing astronomical calculations and star charts remarkably similar to those currently spread across her table. "Cassandra's prophecy speaks of 'three pieces sundered, three times aligned, three tolls sounding' before complete restoration becomes possible."

"Three times aligned," Alice repeated. "This is the third alignment since the Pendulum arrived on Earth?"

"Yes. The first occurred in 1831, passing without incident as the components remained separated and dormant. The second was in 1929, when the temporal fracture first manifested. Now the third alignment approaches—the only opportunity for permanent resolution."

"But we still need this Fulcrum," Ethan pointed out. "If it's been lost for centuries, how can we possibly find it before midnight?"

Rowan's violet eyes fixed on him with unsettling intensity. "Because your bloodline has always known where it rests, Reeves. The werewolf packs have guarded the secret since the Great Fire."

Ethan stiffened. "What? That's impossible. I would know if—"

"Would you?" Rowan challenged. "The Pack keeps many secrets, even from its own members. Your great-grandfather John Reeves was Keeper of the Fulcrum. The knowledge would have passed to his son, and then to your father."

Alice turned to her partner. "Your father never mentioned anything about this?"

Ethan's expression darkened. "My father and I weren't exactly close after I joined the PIU. Pack loyalty above all else was his motto."

"Then we need to speak with him immediately," Alice decided.

"Not possible," Ethan replied grimly. "He died three years ago."

The revelation hung heavily in the air. Their best lead to the Fulcrum's location had vanished with Ethan's father.

"There must be records," Madame Winters suggested. "The Pack keeps histories."

"In the Den," Ethan acknowledged. "But access is restricted to Pack leadership. As a PIU officer, I'm considered... compromised."

"Then we appeal directly to the Alpha," Alice proposed. "This concerns the entire city, not just Pack politics."

Rowan closed the ancient grimoire, her expression grave. "There's something else you should know. The Chronos Society has sought the Fulcrum for centuries. They believe uniting all three components without containment would create a device capable of manipulating time itself—allowing them to rewrite history according to their vision."

"Harlow," Alice said. "He's not just trying to prevent our ritual. He's seeking the final piece."

"And he may already know where to look," Rowan confirmed. "The society has infiltrated many organizations over the centuries, including, possibly, the werewolf packs."

Ethan's eyes flashed amber with sudden concern. "The rogues who attacked us weren't officially Pack-sanctioned. If they're working with Harlow..."

"Then they may be pressuring Pack leadership for information about the Fulcrum," Alice finished his thought.

"We need to move quickly," Madame Winters urged. "Even with the Anchor Star integrated, the containment remains vulnerable until the ritual is completed. If Harlow secures the Fulcrum first, he could potentially override our efforts."

Rowan rose from the table with surprising agility for one of her apparent age. "I will accompany you. The ritual requires a coven leader with direct knowledge of the original text." She gathered several items from around the cottage, placing them in a woven bag. "And I may be able to help convince your Alpha of the urgency."

"How?" Ethan asked skeptically.

"The Rowan and Reeves families share history older than the Pack itself," she replied cryptically. "Some debts transcend generations."

As they prepared to leave, Alice's phone chimed with an incoming message—the first clear signal she'd received since entering Rowan's domain. It was from Tobias:

Sigil restoration progressing but encountering resistance. Pendulum energy fluctuating. Dr. Mackie says containment at 60% and weakening. Need coven ASAP.

"The situation is deteriorating," she informed the others. "We need to divide our efforts. Ethan and I will approach the Pack for information about the Fulcrum. Madame Winters, can you and Rowan begin gathering whatever witches remain in Daybridge?"

"The coven records would be at my shop in Crescent Court," Winters confirmed. "We can start there."

"Meet at the clocktower by 11 PM," Alice instructed. "That gives us one hour before midnight to prepare the ritual, assuming we find the Fulcrum."

They exited the cottage into night significantly darker than when they'd entered. The partial moons had vanished, leaving only natural starlight illuminating the clearing. The witch-finder compass now pointed unerringly southwest—toward the city center where the Pack maintained its primary Den beneath an unassuming office building in the financial district.

As they returned to the vehicle, Ethan paused, inhaling deeply. "Someone else has been here," he said quietly. "Recently. Human, but with... something else. A chemical scent I don't recognize."

Rowan nodded gravely. "My wards alerted me to an intruder yesterday. They left before I could confront them, but they were searching for something."

"The First Grimoire?" Madame Winters suggested.

"Perhaps. Or perhaps they sought me specifically." Rowan extracted a small object from her pocket—a surveillance device disguised as an ordinary stone. "Modern technology combined with ancient intent. Someone is very interested in our activities."

"Harlow," Alice concluded. "He's tracking our progress."

"Which means we're racing him to the Fulcrum," Ethan added grimly.

They reached the vehicle and quickly departed, headlights cutting through darkness that seemed to have deepened around them. The forest pressed close to the narrow road, branches occasionally scraping against the SUV's roof like skeletal fingers.

"The woods are agitated," Rowan observed. "They sense the temporal disturbance. Plants experience time differently than animals—more fluidly, less linearly. The fracture affects them profoundly."

As if in response to her words, a massive oak suddenly materialized in the center of the road—not growing rapidly but simply appearing where no tree had been moments before. Alice swerved sharply to avoid a collision.

"Temporal displacement," Rowan identified calmly. "That tree exists in multiple time streams. In some, it grew here; in others, it was never planted. The boundaries are thinning again."

Alice navigated carefully around the manifestation. "I thought the Anchor Star stabilized the fracture."

"Temporarily," Rowan reminded her. "But as midnight approaches, the alignment strengthens. The containment will continue to weaken until the ritual is completed."

They reached the main road leading back to Daybridge proper, where signs of the temporal crisis became increasingly evident. Emergency vehicles raced past them heading outward—evacuating additional neighborhoods as temporal bleeding intensified. In the distance, the city skyline flickered occasionally, buildings from different eras momentarily superimposing over their modern counterparts.

"We'll drop you and Madame Winters at Crescent Court," Alice told Rowan, accelerating toward the city. "Begin gathering the coven while Ethan and I approach the Pack."

"Be cautious with the Alpha," Rowan advised. "Jerome Blackclaw assumed leadership after your father's passing, correct?" She directed this to Ethan.

He nodded stiffly. "My cousin. Traditional in his views. Skeptical of authority outside the Pack."

"He will resist sharing secrets with the PIU," Rowan predicted. "Especially concerning something as significant as the Fulcrum."

"We don't have time for Pack politics," Alice said firmly. "If necessary, we'll invoke emergency powers under the Supernatural Cooperation Act."

"That would create enemies we don't need," Ethan cautioned. "Let me approach Jerome first, appeal to our blood connection."

As they discussed strategy, the SUV's specialized equipment suddenly activated—lights flashing and sensors beeping urgently. A display screen showed energy readings spiking across multiple frequencies.

"Major temporal event imminent," Alice warned, recognizing the pattern from earlier disturbances.

Before they could take any precautions, reality around them... shifted. The road beneath their wheels transformed from asphalt to packed earth, then to a futuristic composite material, before returning to normal asphalt. Buildings along the roadside flickered between time periods, some disappearing entirely to reveal pristine forest, others advancing to sleek structures of glass and unknown alloys.

More disturbing were the figures that briefly appeared—people from various eras momentarily sharing the same space, unaware of each other's existence. A colonial-era militia marched through the ghostly outline of a future transit station while Victorian ladies promenaded past modern convenience stores.

"The fracture is accelerating," Rowan observed, seemingly unperturbed by the surrounding chaos. "The countdown approaches its final phase."

Alice checked her watch: 9:23 PM. Less than three hours until midnight.

The temporal disturbance subsided enough for them to continue driving, though reality remained unstable around them. They reached Crescent Court—a quaint shopping district specializing in metaphysical and occult businesses—and dropped off the two witches outside Winters' Apothecary & Divination.

"Gather everyone you can find with temporal sensitivity," Alice instructed them. "We'll meet at the clocktower by 11 PM with or without the Fulcrum."

"Without it, the ritual will be incomplete," Rowan reminded her. "A stronger temporary solution, perhaps, but not permanent containment."

"One problem at a time," Alice replied pragmatically. "First, we assemble the coven. Then we secure the Fulcrum—or determine a workable alternative."

As the witches entered the apothecary, Alice and Ethan continued toward the financial district. The streets grew increasingly empty as they approached downtown, most civilians having been evacuated to stability zones outside the temporal hotspots.

The Pack's Den occupied the sublevels of the Ironwood Building—a twelve-story office complex owned by a holding company that served as a legal front for werewolf business interests. During business hours, it housed legitimate financial services; after dark, the underground levels transformed into the heart of Pack operations.

They parked in a reserved space marked with the PIU insignia—one of the few courtesies extended to Ethan despite his complicated status with the Pack. The lobby stood empty of its usual security, though cameras tracked their movement across the marble floor toward a private elevator.

Ethan placed his palm against a scanner disguised as decorative paneling. After a moment's hesitation, the elevator doors slid open.

"They're letting us in," he noted with surprise. "That's either a good sign or a very bad one."

The elevator descended smoothly past the ground floor indicators into unmarked territory. When the doors opened again, they revealed a space that defied conventional urban architecture—a vast cavern hollowed from the limestone beneath Daybridge, illuminated by a combination of modern lighting and traditional fire pits. The space combined primitive and sophisticated elements—stone meeting steel, ancient totems alongside computer terminals.

Several werewolves in human form awaited them, including a tall, powerfully built man with silver streaking his dark hair and a facial scar running from temple to jaw. He wore an expensive suit that did nothing to disguise his predatory nature.

"Cousin," he greeted Ethan without warmth. "The Alpha expected your visit."

"Jerome," Ethan acknowledged with equal reserve. "The city faces extinction. I think that overrides our family disagreements."

Jerome Blackclaw's expression remained impassive. "Follow me. The Alpha will see you in the Council Chamber."

As they walked deeper into the Den, Alice observed Pack members engaged in urgent activity—gathering supplies, securing artifacts, preparing what appeared to be evacuation procedures.

"You're preparing to leave the city," she noted.

"We're preparing for all contingencies," Jerome corrected without looking back. "The Pack has survived worse than temporal fractures."

"Not like this one," Ethan countered. "This isn't just another supernatural crisis. Time itself is unraveling."

"So we've noticed." Jerome led them through an archway carved with ancient werewolf symbols, entering a circular chamber where five individuals sat at a crescent-shaped table. At its center, in a chair slightly elevated above the others, sat an older man whose presence commanded immediate attention despite his unassuming appearance.

Alpha Richard Lowell had led the Daybridge Pack for over forty years. Unlike the stereotypical Alpha portrayed in fiction, he was lean rather than muscular, intellectual rather than aggressive. His wire-rimmed glasses and professor's demeanor concealed a tactical mind that had navigated the Pack through decades of supernatural politics.

"Detective Reeves," the Alpha greeted Ethan. "Detective Chen. I was wondering when the PIU would officially request our assistance."

"We don't have time for diplomatic channels," Alice replied directly. "The temporal fracture is accelerating. We need information only the Pack possesses."

"Regarding the Fulcrum," Lowell stated rather than asked, surprising them both. "Yes, we're aware of your search. News travels quickly in supernatural circles, especially during crises."

Ethan stepped forward. "Then you know we need it to complete the containment ritual by midnight."

"I know that's what you believe," Lowell corrected mildly. "Whether it's true is another matter entirely."

"Madame Rowan provided the information," Alice said, watching the Alpha's reaction closely. "From the First Grimoire of Cassandra Winters."

A subtle shift occurred in Lowell's expression—a flicker of recognition quickly suppressed. "Rowan has emerged from seclusion? Interesting."

"She confirms what your records must already show," Ethan pressed. "That my great-grandfather was Keeper of the Fulcrum after the 1927 incident. That knowledge would have passed to my grandfather, then my father."

"And what makes you think it wasn't passed to you?" Lowell asked quietly.

The question hung in the air, momentarily stunning Ethan. "That's... impossible. My father and I barely spoke after I joined the PIU. He considered it a betrayal of Pack loyalty."

"A necessary pretense," Lowell said. "The knowledge of the Fulcrum's location has always been protected by layers of misdirection—including familial estrangement when necessary."

Alice studied the Alpha carefully. "Are you saying Ethan's father deliberately created distance between them to protect this secret?"

"I'm saying that appearances can be deceiving, Detective Chen. Especially in matters concerning artifacts of such power." Lowell turned his attention back to Ethan. "Your father was a dedicated Keeper, Detective Reeves. He understood that knowledge is safest when it appears not to exist at all."

"Then I have no knowledge of the Fulcrum's location," Ethan said with frustration. "If my father intended to pass this information to me, he failed."

"Did he?" Lowell reached into his jacket, extracting an envelope yellowed with age. "This was entrusted to me three years ago, with instructions to deliver it to you 'when the stars align once more.' Those were your father's exact words."

He placed the envelope on the table between them. Ethan's name was written on it in handwriting he immediately recognized—his father's distinctive script.

"You've had this for three years?" Ethan asked, voice tight with suppressed emotion.

"As instructed," Lowell confirmed. "Your father understood timing, Detective Reeves. Some knowledge is dangerous until the moment it's essential."

Ethan took the envelope with slightly trembling hands. The seal broke easily, revealing a single sheet of paper containing a short message and what appeared to be a safe deposit box key.

He read aloud:

Ethan,

If you're reading this, the fracture has returned as the elders predicted. The Fulcrum awaits where our family began—in the heart that beats beneath the huntsman's moon. The key opens the way to what was always yours to protect.

Trust your blood. It remembers what your mind cannot.

—Father

"Cryptic," Alice commented. "The heart that beats beneath the huntsman's moon?"

"A location known to Pack initiates," Jerome explained reluctantly. "The original Den, established when werewolves first settled in Daybridge."

"The Old North Church crypt," Ethan realized. "Where the first Pack gathered during colonial times."

Lowell nodded. "Specifically, a sealed chamber beneath the crypt itself. Few know of its existence today."

"And this key?" Ethan held up the safe deposit key with its faded tag.

"First Colonial Bank, judging by the insignia," Alice observed. "There's a branch near the Old North Church."

"Your father maintained that box for decades," Lowell confirmed. "Its contents have never been disclosed to Pack leadership—a rare exception to our transparency requirements."

Alice checked her watch: 9:47 PM. "We need to move quickly. The bank first, then the church."

"I'll accompany you," Jerome announced unexpectedly. "Pack interests must be represented when the Fulcrum is recovered."

Lowell nodded approval. "A wise precaution. The Fulcrum has been under Pack protection for generations. We should ensure its proper handling."

Alice wanted to object to the additional oversight but recognized the political necessity. "Fine, but we operate under PIU authority. This is a city-wide emergency."

"Understood," Jerome agreed with surprising ease. "The Pack has no desire to see Daybridge destroyed. Our disagreements can wait until after the crisis is resolved."

As they prepared to depart, a young werewolf burst into the chamber, her expression urgent. "Alpha! Intruders at the North entrance. They're asking for access to the historical archives."

"Who?" Lowell demanded.

"Humans with enhanced capabilities. They claim authority from something called the Chronos Foundation."

Ethan and Alice exchanged alarmed glances.

"Harlow," Alice said. "He's looking for the same information we just received."

"Stall them," Lowell instructed the messenger. "Invoke ceremonial protocols, request formal identification—anything to delay access."

"They're growing insistent," the young werewolf reported nervously. "Their leader threatened consequences if denied."

"Let me speak with them," Ethan suggested. "If they're tracking the same information we are, I might learn what they already know."

Lowell considered this briefly before nodding. "Go, but reveal nothing about the Fulcrum. Jerome and Detective Chen can proceed to the bank and church."

"We stay together," Alice countered firmly. "If Harlow's people are here, they may have others waiting at our destinations."

"Time is against us, Detective," Lowell reminded her. "Divided efforts may be our only option."

A distant rumbling interrupted their debate—not the now-familiar temporal quake, but something different. The Alpha's phone rang immediately.

"Perimeter breach," he reported after a brief conversation. "The north entrance has been compromised. Multiple intruders with supernatural and technological augmentation."

"Decision made," Alice said grimly, drawing her weapon. "We're leaving now all of us. If Harlow's forces have breached Pack security, they're more desperate than we realized."

Lowell pressed a concealed button beneath the table. Alarm systems activated throughout the Den as hidden armories opened in the chamber walls.

"Go," he ordered them. "The Pack will handle this incursion. Complete your mission, Detective Reeves. Honor your father's trust."

They departed through a secondary exit as sounds of conflict echoed from the Den's northern quadrant. Jerome led them through maintenance corridors to a service elevator that ascended to the building's loading dock.

"The Pack has protocols for this," he explained as they emerged into the night air. "We've faced hostile incursions before."

"Not from people who can manipulate time," Alice reminded him. "Be careful what you shoot at—they might be projecting from different temporal locations."

They reached their vehicle and departed quickly, Jerome directing them toward the First Colonial Bank. The surrounding city showed increasing signs of temporal degradation—buildings partially transparent, ghostly figures from different eras walking modern streets, traffic signals cycling through patterns that defied conventional sequence.

The bank itself appeared mostly stable—a colonial-style building with modern additions that had stood on the same corner for nearly two centuries. Its windows were dark, the facility closed hours earlier, but Jerome led them to a side entrance used by employees.

"Pack members maintain positions in key institutions throughout Daybridge," he explained, using a security card to bypass the alarm system. "Practical necessity when one's monthly transformations require discreet accommodation."

The bank's interior was illuminated only by emergency lighting, casting long shadows across the marble floor. Jerome navigated confidently to the safe deposit box section, bypassing additional security with his card.

"Your father's box should be in the historical section," he told Ethan. "Accounts maintained for over fifty years receive special storage conditions."

They located the appropriate vault—a smaller room separated from the main safe deposit area, with additional climate controls and security features. The key Ethan had received opened a medium-sized box near the back wall.

Inside they found a wooden case carved with werewolf pack symbols and secured with a biometric lock disguised as decorative metalwork.

"Blood recognition," Jerome identified. "It will open only for a Reeves."

Ethan pressed his thumb against the carved panel. The lock responded with a soft click, the case opening to reveal its contents—a velvet pouch and a leather-bound journal similar to the one they'd found in the underground observatory.

The journal contained detailed records of the Fulcrum's history, written in multiple hands across generations of Keepers. The most recent entries were in Ethan's father's handwriting, describing the artifact's power and the responsibility of its protection.

But it was the velvet pouch that drew their attention. Ethan carefully emptied its contents into his palm—a small crystalline object approximately the size of a golf ball, hexagonal in shape with a hollow center. Unlike the blue glow of the Pendulum or the white radiance of the Anchor Star, this crystal emanated a deep amber light that pulsed with a rhythm reminiscent of a heartbeat.

"The Fulcrum," Alice breathed.

"It's smaller than I expected," Ethan admitted, studying the artifact carefully.

"Size is irrelevant with temporal artifacts," Jerome said. "Its power comes from its quantum resonance, not its physical dimensions."

As Ethan held the Fulcrum, the amber light intensified, responding to his touch. The pulsing accelerated slightly, synchronizing with his own heartbeat.

"It recognizes you as Keeper," Jerome observed. "The bloodline connection is strong."

Alice checked her watch: 10:18 PM. "We need to get to Old North Church. Your father's note mentioned 'the heart that beats beneath the huntsman's moon'—there must be something else waiting there."

They secured the Fulcrum and journal, returning to their vehicle. As they approached Old North Church—one of Daybridge's oldest structures, dating to 1723—the temporal disruptions around them intensified. The church itself flickered between its current restored state and various historical conditions—sometimes appearing under construction, other times showing battle damage from the Revolutionary War, occasionally manifesting futuristic renovations not yet undertaken.

"The fracture is particularly strong here," Jerome noted as they parked beside the church grounds. "Historical sites often serve as focal points for temporal bleeding."

The church stood dark and empty, evacuated like most of downtown. Jerome again used his security access to bypass the alarm system, leading them through the silent sanctuary toward a door marked "Historical Access Only."

Beyond lay narrow stairs descending into darkness. Their flashlights revealed a colonial-era crypt beneath the church, stone walls lined with ancient tombs and memorial plaques.

"The Pack gathered here during the full moon when Daybridge was still a colonial settlement," Jerome explained as they navigated the crypt. "The stone walls contained the sounds of transformation, and the church's sanctified ground discouraged unwelcome visitors."

He led them to the far corner of the crypt, where a weathered stone bearing the carved image of a wolf lay partially concealed behind a more recent memorial. "The entrance to the original Den should be here."

Ethan approached the stone, studying it carefully. "There's no obvious mechanism."

"Blood will reveal it," Jerome suggested. "As with the case."

Ethan pressed his palm against the carved wolf. For a moment, nothing happened. Then the stone began to glow softly from within, amber light seeping through cracks in its surface. With a low grinding sound, it slid sideways, revealing a narrow passage beyond.

"Trust your blood. It remembers what your mind cannot," Ethan quoted his father's letter. "He meant this literally."

The passage descended steeply into earth, ancient wooden supports giving way to natural limestone as they penetrated deeper beneath the church. The air grew noticeably colder, carrying scents of earth and old magic.

After descending approximately thirty feet, they emerged into a circular chamber reminiscent of the Pack's current Council room but older and more primitive. Stone seating arranged in a circle surrounded a central fire pit, cold now for generations. On the walls, crude pictographs depicted werewolf history—the first transformations, early conflicts with settlers, eventual accommodation with human society.

"The heart of the original Pack," Jerome said with reverence. "Few have seen this place in over a century."

In the center of the fire pit stood a small pedestal carved from a single piece of granite. Its surface featured a hexagonal depression that exactly matched the shape of the Fulcrum.

"'The heart that beats beneath the huntsman's moon,'" Ethan repeated. "This chamber is the heart of Pack territory, and the pedestal awaits the Fulcrum's heartbeat."

He removed the artifact from its pouch, its amber light casting long shadows throughout the ancient chamber. As he placed it into the depression, the fit proved perfect. The moment contact was made, the Fulcrum's pulsing intensified dramatically, sending waves of amber light rippling across the chamber.

The pictographs on the walls responded, glowing with the same amber energy. Previously invisible symbols appeared between the crude drawings, forming continuous patterns around the entire circumference of the room.

"Instructions," Alice realized, examining the newly revealed symbols. "These show how the Fulcrum integrates with the other components."

The glowing pictographs depicted three distinct crystalline shapes—the multifaceted Pendulum, the rounded Anchor Star, and the hexagonal Fulcrum—arranged in a specific triangular configuration. Additional symbols showed energy flows between them, creating a balanced circuit that contained rather than projected power.

"The complete containment design," Ethan confirmed. "What the 1927 ritual couldn't achieve without the Fulcrum."

As they studied the revelations, Alice's phone chimed with an incoming message from Tobias:

Sigil restoration complete. Dr. Mackie reports temporal bleeding accelerating citywide. Madame Winters and Rowan have assembled nine witches with temporal sensitivity—short of the thirteen required but potentially sufficient. Current containment at 42% and failing. Where are you?

She checked the time: 10:47 PM. "We need to move. The coven is assembled and waiting."

Ethan carefully removed the Fulcrum from its pedestal. The moment it lost contact, the glowing pictographs began to fade.

"Wait," Alice said quickly. "We need to document these instructions." She photographed the walls rapidly, capturing the configuration details before they disappeared completely.

As they prepared to depart, a low rumbling vibrated through the chamber—different from the temporal quakes they'd experienced previously. This disturbance felt more... deliberate.

"Someone's breaching the passage," Jerome warned, his eyes flashing amber as werewolf instincts heightened his senses. "Multiple intruders."

"Harlow," Alice concluded. "He must have extracted information from the Pack archives."

"Or followed us," Ethan suggested grimly. "We've been so focused on the Fulcrum, we may have missed surveillance."

The rumbling intensified, dust and small stones falling from the ceiling. The passage through which they'd entered partially collapsed, blocking their exit.

"Is there another way out?" Alice asked Jerome urgently.

"Yes, but it's not been used in generations." He moved to the opposite side of the chamber, locating a seemingly solid wall section. "There should be a secondary escape tunnel here, leading to the river."

As Jerome searched for the hidden exit, Ethan secured the Fulcrum in an inside pocket of his jacket. Its amber glow remained visible even through the fabric, pulsing in rhythm with his heartbeat.

"Found it," Jerome announced, triggering a concealed mechanism that revealed a narrow tunnel even smaller than the one they'd used to enter. "It will be tight, but navigable."

Before they could enter, the collapsed passage behind them exploded outward in a blast of energy that sent them staggering. Through the dust and debris emerged three figures—Professor Harlow flanked by what appeared to be partially transformed werewolves, though something about them seemed wrong.

"Artificially enhanced," Jerome growled, recognizing the unnatural transformation state. "Chemical triggering rather than lunar influence."

"Precisely," Harlow confirmed, stepping into the chamber. "Modern science improves upon nature's inefficient design. These associates enjoy werewolf capabilities without the inconvenient monthly schedule."

"Or the Pack connection," Ethan added, noting their feral, almost mechanical movements. "You've stripped away everything that makes transformation meaningful."

"I've stripped away limitations," Harlow corrected. "Just as the Pendulum of Aeon will strip away the limitations of linear time." His gaze fixed on the glow emanating from Ethan's jacket. "You've found the Fulcrum. Excellent work, Detective. You've saved us considerable effort."

"You're too late," Alice said, weapon raised. "The coven is assembled. The containment ritual will proceed with or without you."

"Without the Fulcrum, your ritual remains incomplete," Harlow reminded her. "A temporary solution at best. History repeating itself."

"Then we'll complete it properly," Ethan declared. "With all three components."

Harlow sighed with theatrical patience. "You still don't understand. Containment is regression. The Pendulum wasn't meant to be contained—it was meant to liberate. To evolve humanity beyond temporal constraints."

"By destroying causality itself," Alice countered. "Collapsing all time streams into chaos."

"Not chaos—simultaneity," Harlow corrected, his eyes gleaming with zealous intensity. "Imagine experiencing all possible versions of yourself at once. Every choice made and unmade. Every path taken and not taken. Pure potential, eternally realized."

"And the millions who can't mentally process such an experience?" Jerome challenged. "Those driven mad by temporal psychosis?"

"Casualties of evolution," Harlow dismissed them. "No significant change comes without cost."

As they spoke, Alice noted the secondary escape tunnel behind her. Jerome stood closest to it, with Ethan positioned between them and Harlow's group. A plan formed quickly in her mind.

"The Fulcrum," she said directly to Ethan, maintaining eye contact meaningfully. "Show him."

Ethan hesitated briefly before understanding her intent. He reached slowly into his jacket, extracting the hexagonal crystal with its pulsing amber light.

"Magnificent," Harlow breathed, his attention completely captured by the artifact. "The final component, after centuries of searching."

"You want to understand its power?" Ethan asked, holding the Fulcrum before him. "Then watch carefully."

In a swift motion, he tossed the Fulcrum—not to Harlow, but to Alice, who caught it deftly. Simultaneously, he transformed partially into werewolf form, the change accelerated by the temporal energy permeating the chamber. His sudden shift into a larger, more powerful form created momentary confusion among Harlow's associates.

"Go!" Ethan roared to Alice and Jerome. "Get it to the tower!"

Alice didn't hesitate, diving into the escape tunnel with the Fulcrum secured. Jerome followed immediately, using his werewolf strength to pull a support beam down behind them, collapsing the tunnel entrance to delay pursuit.

The narrow passage forced them to crawl rapidly through darkness, guided only by Alice's flashlight and Jerome's enhanced senses. Behind them, they heard the sounds of conflict—Ethan engaging Harlow's enhanced werewolves to buy them time.

"He can't hold them long," Jerome said grimly as they navigated the cramped tunnel. "Those chemical hybrids lack Pack restraint. They'll tear him apart if necessary."

"Ethan can handle himself," Alice replied with more confidence than she felt. "Our priority is getting the Fulcrum to the clocktower before midnight."

After several minutes of difficult progress, the tunnel began to slope upward. Eventually, they reached a rusted iron grate partially concealed by vegetation. Jerome forced it open, revealing that they had emerged near the riverbank approximately two blocks from the church.

Alice checked her watch: 11:09 PM. Fifty-one minutes until midnight.

She tried calling for backup but found communications increasingly unreliable as temporal interference intensified across the city. The sky above had taken on an impossible quality—stars visible through what appeared to be daylight, multiple moon phases occupying different sections of the heavens simultaneously.

"The fracture is approaching critical threshold," Jerome observed, looking at the disrupted sky. "We need to hurry."

They ran toward the Municipal Plaza, navigating streets rendered hazardous by temporal bleeding. Buildings flickered between past, present, and potential future configurations. Ghostly figures from multiple eras walked, rode, or drove through spaces they simultaneously occupied.

Most disturbing were the moments when the bleeding affected them directly—brief sensations of existing in multiple versions at once. Alice experienced disorienting flashes of alternate choices:

herself as a lawyer rather than a detective, as a mother with children, as someone who had left Daybridge years ago. Jerome similarly faltered occasionally, momentarily confused by glimpses of other potential selves.

The Fulcrum pulsed in Alice's hand, its amber light seemingly stabilizing their immediate vicinity. The artifact created a bubble of temporal consistency around them, pushing back against the fracture's effects.

They reached Municipal Plaza at 11:23 PM, finding it transformed into a fortified position. PIU agents and conventional police maintained a security perimeter around the clocktower, while emergency vehicles stood ready to respond to temporal incidents throughout the city.

Captain Vaughn met them at the perimeter checkpoint. "Chen! We've been trying to reach you. Where's Reeves?"

"Delayed," she replied, not wanting to explain the full situation. "He secured our objective first." She showed him the Fulcrum, its amber light pulsing steadily.

"The third component," Vaughn recognized it immediately. "Dr. Mackie will want to see this right away. The coven is assembled in the mechanism chamber."

"How many witches did they find?" Alice asked as they hurried toward the tower entrance.

"Eleven, including Madame Winters and Rowan. Short of the ideal thirteen, but it's all we could gather on short notice."

"And Tobias?"

"Completed the sigil restoration about twenty minutes ago. He's exhausted but functional."

They ascended the clocktower stairs rapidly, the temporal disturbances noticeably less severe within the tower itself. The Pendulum's stabilizing influence, even in its currently vulnerable state, provided a bubble of relative normalcy.

The mechanism chamber had been transformed for the ritual. The massive clockworks continued their steady operation, but the surrounding floor had been marked with complex magical symbols drawn in various substances—chalk, ash, salt, and what appeared to be blood. Eleven witches in ceremonial attire stood at specific points around the circular pattern, with Madame Winters and Rowan positioned closest to the Pendulum chamber.

Tobias worked with Dr. Mackie near the exposed Pendulum and Anchor Star, consulting the photographs Alice had sent of the integration instructions. The two artifacts remained in their current configuration, pulsing with blue and white light respectively, creating interference patterns where their energies intersected.

"Detective Chen," Dr. Mackie greeted her with visible relief. "You have it?"

Alice displayed the Fulcrum. "Exactly as described in the First Grimoire."

"And Detective Reeves?" Tobias asked, noting Ethan's absence.

"Covering our escape," she replied grimly. "Harlow found us at Old North Church. Ethan stayed behind to delay them."

"Then we proceed immediately," Rowan decided. "The alignment peaks in thirty-four minutes. We need the Fulcrum integrated before the first toll of midnight."

Tobias examined the hexagonal crystal with professional appreciation. "It's beautiful craftsmanship, if you can call something of extraterrestrial origin 'crafted.' The structure perfectly complements the other components."

"The integration point is here," Dr. Mackie indicated a position between the Pendulum and Anchor Star where the armatures formed a triangular support structure. "Based on your photographs of the ancient diagrams, the three components create a balanced circuit—the Pendulum pushes outward, the Anchor Star pulls inward, and the Fulcrum stabilizes the oscillation between them."

Tobias carefully positioned the Fulcrum within the waiting armature. The moment all three crystals were in proximity, their separate illuminations intensified dramatically—blue, white, and amber energies reaching toward each other in visible currents.

"Perfect resonance," Dr. Mackie confirmed, checking her instruments. "They recognize each other as parts of a whole."

Rowan approached, examining the configuration with ancient eyes. "The Pendulum of Aeon awakens to its true nature. After centuries fragmented, it yearns for reunification."

"Is that dangerous?" Alice asked, noting how the energy flows between components continued to intensify.

"Extremely," Rowan confirmed without sugar-coating. "The fully assembled artifact contains power beyond human comprehension. Without proper containment, it could shatter time itself across this entire region."

"Then we'd better get the containment right," Tobias said, making final adjustments to the armatures to ensure perfect alignment.

Madame Winters directed the witches to their positions around the chamber. "The ritual must begin precisely at 11:45, allowing fifteen minutes to establish the containment field before midnight strikes."

"What about the missing witches?" Alice asked. "You said thirteen were required."

"We'll compensate with increased contributions from those present," Rowan explained. "More demanding, but possible."

As they made final preparations, the door to the chamber burst open. Ethan staggered in, bloodied but alive, supported by—to everyone's surprise—Alpha Lowell.

"Reinforcements," Lowell announced, helping Ethan to a chair. "The Pack stands with Daybridge in this crisis."

"You're injured," Alice hurried to her partner's side.

"I'll heal," Ethan assured her, though his condition suggested otherwise. Deep gashes across his chest and arms still bled freely, and one eye was swollen shut. "Harlow's hybrids fight without restraint or technique, but they're effective."

"Harlow himself?" Alice asked.

"Escaped during the confrontation. He's still out there, likely planning another attempt."

"Which is why the Pack has secured the lower levels," Lowell explained. "No one will reach this chamber without going through my people first."

Rowan approached Ethan, examining his injuries with practiced eyes. "You're needed for the ritual, Detective Reeves. Your blood connection to the Fulcrum makes you an ideal conduit."

"I can barely stand," Ethan objected.

"Your physical condition is irrelevant," she assured him. "It's your essence we require—the bloodline that has protected the Fulcrum for generations."

As they spoke, temporal disturbances intensified throughout the city. Through the mechanism chamber's windows, they could see the impossible sky reaching new levels of disruption—day and night existing simultaneously in patches, multiple weather conditions occupying the same space, the very air seeming to fold into itself in rippling patterns.

Dr. Mackie checked her instruments with growing concern. "Temporal boundary degradation approaching critical threshold. If the containment isn't established before midnight, the fracture will become irreversible."

"Then we begin now," Rowan decided, checking the ornate pocketwatch she carried. "It's 11:43. Close enough."

The witches took their positions, joining hands to form a circle around the clocktower mechanism. Rowan and Madame Winters stood nearest the Pendulum chamber, with Ethan positioned between them despite his injuries. Tobias remained at the mechanism itself, ready to make any necessary adjustments to the armatures, while Alice and the others withdrew to the chamber's perimeter.

Rowan began the ritual, her voice carrying unexpected power as she recited words in a language Alice didn't recognize—older than Latin, with cadences that seemed to resonate with the clocktower's ticking. The other witches joined in, creating a harmonic pattern that vibrated through the air itself.

The three components of the Pendulum of Aeon responded immediately, their separate illuminations intensifying and beginning to synchronize. The blue, white, and amber energies pulsed in complex patterns, gradually aligning into a single rhythm.

As the ritual progressed, the protective sigils Tobias had restored began to glow with the same combined light, creating a network of illuminated patterns across the entire mechanism. The massive gears and wheels of the clocktower seemed to catch the light, reflecting and amplifying it throughout the chamber.

Outside, the temporal disturbances visibly responded. The chaotic bleeding between time periods began to organize itself, ripples becoming more regular and controlled. The impossible sky started separating into distinct layers, like reality attempting to sort itself into proper sequence.

At precisely 11:55, Rowan called Ethan forward. Despite his injuries, he approached the Pendulum chamber, guided by the two elder witches.

"Your blood completes the connection," Rowan instructed him. "As Keeper of the Fulcrum, you authorize its integration."

Ethan placed his wounded hand against the chamber, allowing his blood to contact the metal surface near where the three components pulsed with increasing synchronization. The effect was immediate—the amber light of the Fulcrum intensified dramatically, reaching out to envelop both the Pendulum and the Anchor Star in its glow.

"The balance establishes," Rowan announced with satisfaction. "The Keeper acknowledges the reunification."

For a moment, everything seemed to be proceeding perfectly. The witches' chanting grew more confident, the components' synchronization more complete, the protective sigils brighter and more defined.

Then, at 11:58, disaster struck.

A massive temporal quake—far stronger than any previous disturbance—shook the entire tower. The clocktower bells above them began tolling chaotically, out of sequence and with unnatural resonance. The witches' circle wavered but held, their chanting intensifying to compensate.

"What's happening?" Alice shouted to Dr. Mackie over the disruptive noise.

"Temporal backlash," the professor explained, checking her wildly fluctuating instruments. "The fracture is fighting the containment, like an immune response!"

Through the windows, they saw the sky tear open—not in random bleeding but in a deliberate, almost surgical pattern. A perfect circle appeared in the fabric of reality directly above the clocktower, revealing... something beyond. Not another time period, but what appeared to be the absence of time itself—a void where causality had no meaning.

"The Eye opens," Rowan called out, her voice somehow cutting through the chaos. "Stand firm! The final challenge approaches!"

The circular tear widened, its edges radiating temporal energy that lashed down toward the tower like lightning. Where these bolts struck, reality itself seemed to unravel—brick becoming wood becoming steel becoming something unidentifiable, all in rapid sequence.

"One minute to midnight," Dr. Mackie announced, her voice tight with tension. "The alignment peaks with the first toll."

The three components of the Pendulum of Aeon now pulsed in perfect unison, their separate colors merging into a single luminescence that defied description—simultaneously blue, white, and amber while being something else entirely. The clocktower mechanism responded, its massive gears moving with supernatural precision as the protective sigils channeled and directed the growing energy.

At thirty seconds to midnight, the chamber door burst open once more. Professor Harlow staggered in; clothes torn and face bloodied but eyes burning with fanatical intensity.

"Stop!" he commanded, though no one moved to obey. "You're making a terrible mistake! The Pendulum wants to be free!"

Alpha Lowell moved to intercept him, but Harlow revealed a device in his hand—something cobbled together from both technological and magical components.

"Temporal disruptor," Dr. Mackie identified it with alarm. "It could shatter the ritual's energy pattern!"

Before Harlow could activate the device, Alice drew her weapon and fired with practiced precision. The bullet struck his hand, sending the disruptor flying across the chamber where it shattered against the wall.

Harlow screamed—not in pain, but in frustrated rage. "You fools! You blind, limited fools! You're imprisoning humanity in linear time!"

"We're saving them from temporal chaos," Tobias countered, never looking away from the delicate adjustments he continued making to the integration armatures.

"Ten seconds," Dr. Mackie announced.

The witches' chanting reached its crescendo as the clocktower mechanism aligned perfectly with the midnight configuration. Above them, the bells prepared for their twelve solemn tolls.

"Three... two... one..."

The first toll of midnight resonated through the chamber with physical force. The sound carried impossible weight, as though the bell had been cast from time itself rather than metal. The circular tear above the tower responded, contracting slightly as the ritual's containment effect began to assert itself.

"It's working!" Dr. Mackie confirmed, watching her instruments. "The temporal boundaries are reinforcing!"

The second toll followed, deeper and more resonant than the first. The three components of the Pendulum of Aeon pulsed in perfect synchronization with the sound, their combined light flowing through the sigil network across the entire mechanism.

Harlow made a final, desperate lunge toward the Pendulum chamber. "No! You don't understand what you're sacrificing!"

Alice intercepted him, using her combat training to redirect his momentum away from the critical components. They grappled briefly before Lowell joined her, his werewolf strength easily subduing the professor.

The third toll began—the critical moment identified in Harold Merrick's notes and Cassandra Winters' prophecy. "The third toll of midnight during the alignment" would determine success or failure.

As the massive sound reverberated through the chamber, the three components of the Pendulum of Aeon reached their peak luminescence. For a moment so brief it might have been imagined, time itself seemed to pause—a perfect stillness in which all possibilities existed simultaneously.

Then, like a wave receding from shore, the temporal chaos began to withdraw. The circular tear above the tower contracted rapidly, sealing itself with a final flash of energy. The impossible sky separated into proper layers, night asserting itself as the natural condition for this moment in time.

The witches' chanting softened but continued, maintaining the energy flow as the remaining nine tolls sounded. Each bell reinforced the containment, strengthening the boundaries between time streams, restoring proper temporal sequence to Daybridge and its surroundings.

After the final toll faded, a new sound emerged from the Pendulum chamber—a crystalline hum of perfect harmony as the three components settled into stable resonance. The protective sigils continued to glow, but now with a steady, sustainable luminescence rather than the intense flaring of active ritual.

"Containment established," Dr. Mackie announced, reviewing her instruments with visible relief. "Temporal boundaries restored to 99.7% integrity and stabilizing further."

"The Pendulum of Aeon rests in balance," Rowan confirmed, her ancient eyes studying the now-unified artifact with satisfaction. "Push and pull perfectly counteracted, oscillation stabilized."

The witches released their circle, many collapsing in exhaustion after the intense magical exertion. Ethan slumped against the wall, his injuries finally demanding attention as the emergency faded.

"Is it truly permanent this time?" Alice asked, watching as Tobias carefully closed and locked the Pendulum chamber.

"As permanent as anything can be in an ever-changing universe," Rowan replied with the wisdom of her years. "The containment is self-sustaining now, drawing power from the ley line convergence beneath the tower. Barring deliberate interference, it should maintain stability indefinitely."

"And the synchronized clocks?" Tobias asked, thinking of his shop full of timepieces frozen at 11:32.

"Should return to normal function," Dr. Mackie predicted. "The temporal resonance that affected them has been contained."

Harlow, now securely restrained by Lowell and a PIU agent, laughed bitterly. "You've accomplished nothing but delay. The Chronos Society has waited centuries—we can wait centuries more. Time is on our side, after all."

"Perhaps," Rowan acknowledged with surprising candor. "But today, at least, time continues to flow as it should—one moment following another in proper sequence. The future arriving in its own time, not all at once."

Outside, the city began to calm. The temporal bleeding receded completely, buildings and streets settling into their proper configurations. Emergency vehicles moved through the downtown area, assisting those disoriented by the crisis. Evacuated citizens would soon be allowed to return to their homes, likely remembering the event as an "unprecedented meteorological phenomenon" rather than a tear in the fabric of time itself—the human mind's remarkable ability to rationalize the supernatural asserting itself once more.

In the mechanism chamber, Tobias completed a final inspection of the restored clockworks. The massive gears and wheels continued their steady movement, now augmented by the balanced energy of the complete Pendulum of Aeon at their core.

"My grandfather would be proud," he said quietly. "The work he began is finally finished."

"Not finished," Rowan corrected gently. "Merely continuing. Time is never truly finished, Mr. Merrick. It flows onward, carrying all things with it—even those who study its mysteries."

Alice joined her exhausted partner, helping him to a more comfortable position as medical personnel arrived to treat his injuries. "You did good, Reeves. Your father would be proud too."

Ethan smiled weakly through his pain. "Family tradition, apparently. Saving the world from temporal disaster."

"Speaking of tradition," she replied with a slight smile, "I believe this qualifies as another successfully closed Paranormal Investigation Unit case. Though the paperwork is going to be a nightmare."

"Some things," Ethan agreed, "remain constant across all possible time streams."

As dawn approached, the clocktower's eastern face caught the first rays of sunlight. Time moved forward once more in its proper sequence—moment following moment, cause preceding effect, the future arriving precisely when it should.

In Merrick's Chronometry, dozens of antique timepieces resumed their individual rhythms, no longer synchronized to an apocalyptic countdown but ticking with their characteristic unique voices—a chorus of time measurement rather than a unified warning.

The Pendulum of Aeon, reunited after centuries of fragmentation, rested in balanced containment at the heart of Daybridge's clocktower. Push and pull, past and future, possibility and actuality—all held in perfect equilibrium by the Fulcrum between them.

Time flowed on, as it always had and always would.

One measured tick at a time.

CHAPTER TEN: THE MUSEUM HEIST

Three days had passed since the containment ritual stabilized Daybridge's temporal fracture. The city was returning to normal—streets cleared of emergency vehicles, evacuated residents back in their homes, and the bizarre auroral lights no longer painting the sky with impossible colors. Official reports attributed the disturbances to an unprecedented convergence of meteorological phenomena, supplemented by mass hallucination triggered by unidentified airborne compounds from a chemical spill—a cover story crafted by the PIU's public relations team and eagerly embraced by those whose minds couldn't process the truth.

For those directly involved, however, normalcy remained elusive.

Merrick's Chronometry was closed for "renovations," the front window bearing a handwritten sign promising to reopen the following week. Inside, Tobias worked methodically, recalibrating the dozens of timepieces affected by the temporal resonance. Each required individual attention, their delicate mechanisms subtly altered by exposure to the Pendulum's energy.

Alice sat at his workbench, reviewing a case file while occasionally glancing at her partner. Ethan occupied a chair by the window, his injuries from the confrontation with Harlow's enhanced werewolves healing with supernatural speed but still requiring bandages across his chest and left arm.

"Professor Harlow isn't talking," Alice reported, closing the file with frustration. "He's invoked some obscure metaphysical protection clause that even our supernatural legal counsel hasn't encountered before."

"The Chronos Society likely has contingencies for capture," Ethan suggested. "They've operated in secret for centuries. I doubt they'd leave their members vulnerable to conventional interrogation."

"Which leaves us with an incomplete picture," Alice said. "We contained the immediate crisis, but we still don't understand what caused it in the first place."

Tobias carefully adjusted the escapement on a particularly valuable pocket watch. "The alignment created conditions for temporal bleeding, but something had to trigger the initial fracture."

"And prevent my grandfather from implementing permanent containment in 1927," he continued. "The Fulcrum was available then—the Pack had it secured. Why use a temporary solution when a permanent one was possible?"

Dr. Mackie entered from the back room, where she'd been conferring with Madame Winters and Rowan about the magical aspects of the containment. "I've been wondering the same thing," she admitted. "The journals and grimoires describe the 1927 incident but never explicitly state what initiated it."

"Or why they separated the components afterward," Alice added. "If the complete Pendulum of Aeon is stable when properly contained, why disassemble it?"

"Safety through separation," Ethan suggested. "If one component was compromised, the others remained secure."

"Perhaps," Tobias acknowledged. "But my grandfather's notes suggest something more specific—a concern about 'resonance with its origin.'"

"Origin?" Alice's attention sharpened. "You mean where it came from?"

"Presumably. The meteorite that brought the Pendulum to Earth in 1483." Tobias set down his tools, turning to face them. "But here's what's been bothering me—if the Pendulum was extraterrestrial and arrived in the 15th century, how did it end up integrated into a clocktower mechanism built in 1876?"

"And how did it cause a temporal fracture in 1927?" Dr. Mackie added. "Something must have activated it."

Madame Winters joined them from the back room, her elderly face showing the fatigue of recent magical exertions. "The First Grimoire mentions a 'calling stone' that awakens temporal artifacts. Cassandra believed the original meteorite contained more than just the Pendulum components."

"A fourth piece?" Alice asked.

"Not a piece of the Pendulum itself, but something that resonates with it—something that could trigger its active state rather than dormancy."

Ethan shifted in his chair, wincing slightly as the movement pulled at his healing wounds. "We should check Harlow's personal effects. The PIU seized everything from his university office and home."

"Already did," Alice replied. "Nothing obviously related to the Pendulum or temporal manipulation. Just academic materials and personal items."

"What about historical records?" Tobias suggested. "If there was another artifact from the same meteorite, it might have been documented somewhere."

Dr. Mackie nodded thoughtfully. "The university archives contain documents from Daybridge's founding through the present. If something was recovered in 1483, there might be a record."

"The Supernatural Artifacts Museum would be another resource," Ethan added. "They maintain collections dating back to the city's earliest days."

Alice's phone chimed with an incoming message. She checked it, her expression growing serious. "Captain Vaughn says there's been a development. Professor Harlow was found unconscious in his cell an hour ago. Medically he's fine, but he appears to have no memory of the past month—including everything related to the Pendulum."

"Memory extraction?" Madame Winters suggested. "A powerful witch or vampire could selectively remove specific memories."

"Or a failsafe implanted by the Chronos Society," Ethan proposed. "Triggered when he was captured."

"Either way, we've lost our primary source of information," Alice concluded. "We need to pursue alternative avenues quickly."

Dr. Mackie was already typing on her tablet. "I'll request access to the university's restricted archives. As department chair, I have clearance for historical research."

"I'll contact the museum," Ethan volunteered. "My cousin Jerome sits on their board of directors. Pack connections have some benefits."

"I need to finish these repairs first," Tobias gestured to the disassembled timepieces, "but I can review my grandfather's journals more thoroughly afterward. There might be clues I missed."

Alice stood, decision made. "We'll reconvene here tomorrow morning to share findings. If there is another component that could reactivate the Pendulum, we need to locate and secure it before anyone else does."

The following morning found them gathered around Tobias's largest workbench, now cleared of clockwork components and covered with research materials. Dr. Mackie had brought printouts from the university archives, while Ethan contributed museum catalogs and inventory listings. Tobias's grandfather's journals lay open alongside Madame Winters' family grimoires.

"I'll start," Dr. Mackie offered, organizing her materials. "The university archives contained several references to a 'star-stone' that fell near what would become Daybridge in 1483. Indigenous accounts describe it as 'a piece of night sky that burned with inner light.'"

She displayed a reproduction of a crude drawing showing a fragmented object surrounded by figures wearing what appeared to be protective talismans. "The native population considered it sacred but dangerous. They built a containment circle around the impact site and appointed guardians to prevent anyone from touching the fragments directly."

"When European settlers arrived in the 1600s, they documented the site as a 'heathen shrine' but noted the unusual properties of the stones," she continued. "Several missionaries reported experiencing 'visions of times yet to come' when approaching the circle."

"Temporal sensitivity," Madame Winters identified. "The artifacts were active even then."

Dr. Mackie nodded. "By the early 1800s, most fragments had been collected by various parties. The historical record becomes fragmented itself, but we can trace the Crystal component to a natural philosopher named Everett who studied its properties before it eventually passed to the Merrick family."

"The Anchor Star appears in Pack records around 1856," Ethan continued the timeline. "Initially held by a werewolf shaman who used it for divination purposes. The Fulcrum entered Pack possession during the same period, though through a different finder."

"But there's mention of a fourth component," Dr. Mackie highlighted a passage from an 1887 journal. "Described as 'a perfect sphere of deepest black that draws light into itself rather than reflecting it.' This object was apparently separated from the others intentionally, as it caused the other fragments to 'awaken from dormancy' when brought into proximity."

"The calling stone," Madame Winters confirmed. "Cassandra's grimoire described it similarly."

"So, what happened to it?" Alice asked.

Ethan spread out a museum catalog dated 1923. "According to this, an 'unusual sphere of unknown origin, possibly meteoric' was donated to Daybridge's Supernatural Artifacts Museum by the Harlow family." He pointed to a black-and-white photograph showing a perfectly round stone displayed on a pedestal. "The accompanying text describes it as 'absorbing light to an unusual degree' and 'causing chronometric instruments to behave erratically when in proximity.'"

"Harlow family," Alice repeated. "As in Professor Harlow?"

"His grandfather, according to the donor information," Ethan confirmed. "Archibald Harlow, founding member of what was then called the 'Society for Temporal Research'—likely an early incarnation of the Chronos Society."

"That can't be a coincidence," Tobias said, examining the photograph closely. "If the Harlow family donated this object to the museum in 1923, and the temporal fracture occurred in 1927..."

"They placed it there deliberately," Alice concluded. "But why donate it to a public museum if it was valuable to their cause?"

"Perhaps they couldn't activate it themselves," Dr. Mackie suggested. "The grimoire indicates that temporal artifacts often require specific conditions or individuals to function properly."

"Or perhaps the museum itself was significant," Madame Winters added. "Its location, its relation to ley lines or other supernatural influences."

Tobias was consulting a modern city map. "The Supernatural Artifacts Museum stands at what was originally the impact site of the 1483 meteorite. The building was constructed directly over the containment circle created by the indigenous population."

"Perfect resonance," Dr. Mackie breathed. "By placing the calling stone in the museum, they positioned it at the exact spot where the Pendulum originally arrived on Earth."

"And four years later, in 1927, the alignment created conditions for that resonance to activate all components simultaneously," Ethan continued the theory. "Triggering the first temporal fracture."

"Which my grandfather and the coven contained by separating the components and implementing the ritual," Tobias finished. "But they didn't know about or couldn't access the calling stone in the museum, so their solution was necessarily temporary."

Alice was already on her phone, contacting the PIU. After a brief conversation, she turned back to the group with a grim expression. "The Supernatural Artifacts Museum reported a break-in attempt last night. Nothing was stolen, but their security system detected multiple intruders near the Pre-Colonial Exhibition Hall."

"Where the meteorite artifacts would be displayed," Ethan surmised.

"The Chronos Society is still active," Alice concluded. "With Harlow neutralized, other members are continuing their work."

"We need to secure that calling stone immediately," Tobias decided.

"Not so simple," Ethan cautioned. "The museum has extensive supernatural security measures. Magical wards, spectral guardians, and recognition enchantments that allow only authorized personnel to handle certain artifacts."

"Plus conventional security," Alice added. "Guards, cameras, motion sensors."

"We can't just walk in and request access?" Dr. Mackie asked.

"The calling stone isn't cataloged under that name," Ethan explained. "It's listed as 'Ceremonial Object of Unknown Origin, Possibly Astronomical.' Without revealing everything about the Pendulum and the temporal fracture, we'd have no official justification for removing it."

"And revealing everything could cause panic," Alice noted. "Not to mention potentially alerting other Chronos Society members to our interest."

"So, we need to retrieve it unofficially," Tobias concluded.

"You mean steal it," Alice corrected.

"Temporarily relocate it to proper containment," he countered with a slight smile. "Given the circumstances, I think the potential destruction of Daybridge's temporal integrity justifies some creative acquisition methods."

"A heist," Ethan said flatly. "You're proposing we rob the Supernatural Artifacts Museum."

"I'm proposing we prevent another temporal fracture by securing all components of an extraterrestrial artifact that nearly destroyed the city last week," Tobias clarified. "The method is unfortunate but necessary."

Alice considered this, her law enforcement instincts warring with pragmatic necessity. "Captain Vaughn would never authorize this officially."

"So we don't ask for official authorization," Tobias suggested. "We present him with a successfully contained threat after the fact."

"Easier to ask forgiveness than permission," Dr. Mackie translated.

"Precisely."

Alice sighed, decision visibly forming. "If—and I emphasize if—we were to consider this approach, we would need a detailed plan accounting for both conventional and supernatural security measures."

"I can provide information about the museum's protective systems," Ethan offered reluctantly. "Jerome shared details during the security upgrade last year, hoping for PIU consultation."

"I can address the magical protections," Madame Winters said. "Many were implemented by my coven in the 1950s. I know their weaknesses."

"And I understand mechanical systems better than most," Tobias added. "Clock mechanisms and security systems share many principles."

Dr. Mackie looked between them with growing concern. "You're actually considering this? Breaking into a museum?"

"We're considering protecting Daybridge from another temporal disaster," Alice corrected. "If there's a legitimate way to acquire the calling stone, I'm all for it. But given the urgency and secrecy required..."

"A specialized extraction operation," Ethan supplied.

"Exactly."

Dr. Mackie relented. "I suppose my expertise would be valuable in identifying the correct artifact with certainty. The photograph is nearly a century old, and the museum has reclassified many exhibits since then."

"Then we develop a plan," Alice decided. "Tonight we'll conduct a reconnaissance of the museum during public hours to familiarize ourselves with the layout and visible security. Tomorrow night, we execute the extraction."

"That's... very rapid," Dr. Mackie noted.

"The Chronos Society has already made one attempt," Ethan reminded her. "They'll try again, likely with better preparation. We need to move before they do."

With reluctant consensus reached, they turned to planning. Ethan sketched the museum's layout from memory while describing security systems. Madame Winters explained the magical protections and how they might be temporarily circumvented. Tobias considered mechanical aspects of locks and display cases.

Alice watched them work with mixed emotions—pride in their dedication and expertise, concern about the legal and ethical boundaries they were crossing, and underlying everything, a sense that this mission was merely the beginning of a larger confrontation with the Chronos Society.

The temporal fracture had been contained, but its cause—and those who sought to exploit it—remained very much active.

The Supernatural Artifacts Museum occupied a Victorian-era building in Daybridge's historic district, its Gothic architecture featuring gargoyles that weren't merely decorative but actual guardians animated by old magic. Originally constructed as a natural history museum in 1879, it had been repurposed in the 1920s to house the city's growing collection of supernatural artifacts—items too significant to destroy but too dangerous for casual access.

That evening found them wandering its halls as ordinary visitors, separating to cover different sections while maintaining communication via text messages. Alice and Ethan focused on security measures, Dr. Mackie and Madame Winters sought the calling stone itself, while Tobias examined locks and display mechanisms.

The Pre-Colonial Exhibition occupied the museum's east wing, a spacious gallery displaying artifacts from indigenous cultures and early European settlement. Glass cases lined the walls and freestanding displays occupied the center floor, each containing objects ranging from mundane tools to items of significant magical power.

"Located it," Dr. Mackie texted the group. "Section 4B, Case 17. 'Ceremonial Sphere, Possible Astronomical Significance, c. 1400-1500 CE.'"

Alice casually made her way to the indicated location, finding Dr. Mackie studying a display case containing several dark objects on velvet backing. The central item matched the photograph from the 1923 catalog—a perfect sphere approximately four inches in diameter, so deeply black it appeared to create a void in the surrounding space. Even the museum lighting seemed unable to illuminate it properly, light bending strangely around its surface.

"That's definitely it," Alice confirmed via text. "How's it secured?"

Tobias joined them, appearing to casual observers as just another museum patron admiring the exhibits. He examined the case with a watchmaker's attention to detail.

"Standard museum case with supernatural enhancements," he texted. "Primary lock is mechanical with magical reinforcement. Secondary containment field around the object itself—likely responds to unauthorized contact with an alarm."

From across the gallery, Ethan noted the security cameras—two visible, covering the case from different angles, plus a third concealed in a decorative ceiling medallion directly above. He also identified pressure sensors in the floor around the display and motion detectors covering the approach.

Madame Winters, appearing to all observers as simply an elderly woman enjoying cultural exhibits, subtly traced patterns in the air with her fingers while muttering what sounded like appreciation of the artifacts. In reality, she was probing the magical protections surrounding the case.

"Triple-warded," she reported via text. "Identity verification, intention detection, and temporal stabilization. The last is particularly troublesome—it's designed specifically to prevent time-altering magic near the artifacts."

"Can you bypass them?" Alice asked when they reconvened in the museum cafe after completing their reconnaissance.

"Not neutralize, but temporarily redirect," the elderly witch clarified. "The wards are anchored to focal points in the gallery. If those anchors were... adjusted... the protective field would ripple, creating a brief window of opportunity."

"How brief?" Tobias asked.

"Thirty seconds at most before the secondary systems detect the anomaly."

Ethan added his observations. "Guards rotate through the Pre-Colonial gallery every fifteen minutes. Two night security staff total, plus a supernatural consultant on call for emergencies."

"The display case itself is high-quality but not exceptional," Tobias noted. "Without the magical reinforcement, I could open it in under a minute."

"So we need a way in after hours, a method to temporarily disrupt the magical protections, and a plan to avoid both human guards and electronic surveillance," Alice summarized. "All while retrieving an object that may trigger temporal distortions when moved."

"The artifact should remain dormant without proximity to the Pendulum components," Dr. Mackie offered. "But I'd recommend a containment case, regardless." She patted her bag. "I've brought shielding materials that can be fashioned into temporary protection."

They finalized their plan over coffee, speaking in measured tones that would appear to casual observers as nothing more than friends discussing museum exhibits they'd enjoyed.

"Tomorrow night, then," Alice confirmed. "We enter at 1:30 AM during the guard rotation, neutralize the security systems, retrieve the artifact, and exit through the loading dock. Total operation time: twelve minutes if all goes according to plan."

"And if it doesn't?" Dr. Mackie asked nervously.

"Then we improvise," Ethan replied with the calm of someone who'd handled numerous operations gone sideways. "But let's aim for the twelve-minute plan."

The following night, clouds obscured the moon and stars as they assembled in the alley behind the Supernatural Artifacts Museum. Alice and Ethan wore black tactical gear bearing PIU insignia—not for deception but for plausible deniability if discovered. Dr. Mackie and Madame Winters were dressed inconspicuously in dark clothing, while Tobias carried a small case of specialized tools disguised as maintenance equipment.

"Guard rotation begins in three minutes," Ethan reported, checking his watch. "Northeast entrance will be unmonitored for approximately forty seconds during the handoff."

Alice activated her radio. "Tobias, you're up first. Cameras in the service corridor need to be looped before we can proceed."

Tobias approached the service entrance, his expression showing none of the anxiety Alice knew he must be feeling. This was far outside his usual expertise as a clockmaker, yet his understanding of mechanical systems made him uniquely qualified for the first stage.

He located the junction box controlling the service area's surveillance system and applied a device of his own creation—a specialized bypass that would insert a continuous loop of empty corridor footage into the security feed. His watchmaker's precision served him well as he connected delicate wiring without triggering tamper alarms.

"Camera loop active," he confirmed after ninety seconds of careful work. "We have a clean corridor for the next eight minutes before the system runs its integrity check."

Alice led the group through the now-unmonitored service entrance, using a keycard Ethan had programmed with temporary access codes. The service corridor beyond was dimly lit by emergency lighting, leading past storage rooms toward the main exhibition spaces.

"Motion sensors begin in the next section," Ethan warned as they approached a security checkpoint. "Dr. Mackie?"

The professor removed a small device from her bag—a prototype temporal field generator developed for PIU research. "This creates a microsecond delay between movement and detection. To the sensors, we'll appear as nothing more than data ghosting."

She activated the device, producing a subtle vibration that made Alice's teeth ache slightly. "Move at exactly the pace I do," Dr. Mackie instructed. "Too fast or slow will break the field coherence."

They proceeded through the checkpoint in careful synchronization, watching as the motion detector lights remained green despite their passage. Beyond lay the main gallery complex, its vast spaces filled with shadowy displays of supernatural artifacts from throughout history.

"The Pre-Colonial Exhibition is through the central hall and left," Ethan directed. "Two cameras cover the approach, plus a spectral guardian that activates after midnight."

"I'll handle the guardian," Madame Winters said confidently. From her bag, she produced a small pouch of herbs and powders. "A sleeping charm. Even supernatural entities require rest occasionally."

They paused at the entrance to the central hall while the elderly witch performed a brief ritual, sprinkling the mixture in a specific pattern while whispering words that seemed to bend around Alice's ears rather than entering them directly.

"Done," Winters announced. "The guardian will experience what amounts to a coffee break—a compelling urge to patrol the opposite wing for the next ten minutes."

With the spectral entity diverted, they crossed the central hall quickly, maintaining the careful pace required by Dr. Mackie's temporal field generator. The Pre-Colonial Exhibition gallery loomed ahead, its entrance flanked by totemic figures whose carved eyes seemed to track their movement despite being inanimate.

"We have seven minutes remaining before the camera loop resets," Tobias reminded them as they entered the gallery.

The calling stone's display case stood where they'd seen it the previous day, illuminated by subtle spotlighting that enhanced the artifact's light-absorbing properties. Even in the darkened museum, the sphere appeared as an absence rather than a presence—a perfect void among solid objects.

"Magical wards first," Alice directed. "Then electronic, then physical access."

Madame Winters approached the display case cautiously, her hands weaving complex patterns in the air as she identified the anchors of the protective enchantments. "There," she indicated points near the ceiling corners. "The ward triangle centers directly above the case. If all three anchors are adjusted simultaneously, the field will ripple for approximately twenty seconds."

Dr. Mackie positioned herself beneath one anchor point, while Ethan took another. Winters maintained position at the third. Each held a small crystal provided by the witch—focal tools that would allow coordinated manipulation of the magical energies.

"On my count," Winters instructed. "Three, two, one..."

They raised their crystals simultaneously, each focusing on their designated anchor point. The air around the display case shimmered briefly, like heat rising from summer pavement. A subtle tone—just at the edge of human hearing—indicated the ward field entering flux state.

"Now, Tobias," Alice directed. "Twenty seconds."

The clockmaker approached the case with practiced efficiency, applying a specialized tool to the mechanical lock while whispering something to the magical reinforcement—a phrase Madame Winters had provided that essentially asked the protection to "look away momentarily."

The case opened with a soft click, the magical alarms remaining dormant during the ward ripple. Tobias carefully lifted the glass top, exposing the calling stone to direct access.

"Twelve seconds," Madame Winters warned, her voice strained from maintaining the ward displacement.

Dr. Mackie quickly positioned a containment box lined with specialized materials beside the artifact. "Don't touch it directly," she cautioned Alice. "Use the tongs."

Alice extracted a pair of silver tongs from Dr. Mackie's kit and carefully lifted the calling stone. Despite its apparent solidity, it felt strangely insubstantial—as though it existed partially in another dimension. She placed it gently in the containment box, which Dr. Mackie immediately sealed.

"Five seconds," Winters counted down.

Tobias closed the display case and reset the lock with remarkable speed, his fingers moving with the precision that made him an exceptional clockmaker. The case secured with moments to spare before the ward field restabilized with an audible snap.

"Target secured," Alice confirmed. "Let's move."

They had turned to leave when a sudden crash echoed from the central hall—the unmistakable sound of breaking glass followed by an alarm that cut off almost immediately.

"Someone else is here," Ethan realized, his enhanced senses detecting multiple heartbeats approaching rapidly. "At least four individuals, moving with purpose."

"The Chronos Society," Alice concluded. "They must have been monitoring the museum as well."

"Two minutes until our camera loop resets," Tobias warned. "We need an alternative exit."

Ethan quickly assessed their options. "Service corridor to the west. It bypasses the central hall and leads to the loading dock."

"Go," Alice directed. "Dr. Mackie, keep that containment box secure at all costs."

They moved quickly toward the western exit, abandoning the careful pace previously required. Dr. Mackie's temporal field generator had depleted its power source, leaving them vulnerable to conventional security measures.

As they reached the gallery's western door, it burst open. Three figures dressed in dark tactical gear similar to their own entered, led by a woman Alice recognized with shock—Diana Blackwood, the vampire representative who had allegedly supported their containment efforts at the clocktower.

"Detective Chen," Blackwood greeted her with aristocratic composure. "I thought I recognized the PIU's tactical approach. Efficient as always."

"Blackwood," Alice responded coldly, positioning herself between the vampire and Dr. Mackie with her contained artifact. "I thought the Vampire Council had 'reconsidered' their position on temporal manipulation."

"The Council reconsiders many things as new information emerges," Blackwood replied smoothly. "The potential of the complete Pendulum assembly, properly directed rather than merely contained, offers opportunities that transcend conventional power structures."

"You're working with the Chronos Society," Ethan realized.

"An oversimplification, but essentially correct. Our interests temporarily align." Blackwood's gaze fixed on the containment box in Dr. Mackie's hands. "You've saved us considerable effort by locating and retrieving the activator. We'll relieve you of it now."

"That's not happening," Alice stated firmly, drawing her weapon. "This artifact nearly destroyed Daybridge once. We're placing it in secure containment."

"Secure containment," Blackwood repeated with a slight smile. "Like the clocktower? Impressive work, truly. But ultimately a waste of the Pendulum's potential."

While she spoke, her associates spread out to flank the group. Alice noted with concern that they moved with supernatural speed and coordination—enhanced humans or lesser vampires under Blackwood's control.

"We don't want conflict, Detective," Blackwood continued reasonably. "Simply hand over the activator, and you can leave without incident. The Council will ensure it's used responsibly."

"Define 'responsibly,'" Tobias challenged. "Because deliberately creating temporal fractures seems rather irresponsible from where I stand."

"Control, not chaos," Blackwood corrected. "The Chronos Society's approach was crude—they sought to shatter temporal boundaries completely. The Vampire Council envisions more... selective adjustments."

"Rewriting history to benefit immortals," Ethan translated. "How original."

Blackwood's pleasant expression hardened slightly. "Time is the only enemy immortals cannot defeat through conventional means. Can you blame us for seeking alternatives?"

"When those alternatives threaten the entire city? Yes," Alice replied simply. She assessed their tactical position—outnumbered, in a confined space, with civilians to protect. Not ideal.

Madame Winters stepped forward, her elderly frame somehow projecting formidable presence. "The wards are restabilizing, Ms. Blackwood. In approximately thirty seconds, the museum's full magical defenses will reactivate. Are you prepared to explain your presence to the spectral guardians?"

Uncertainty flickered across Blackwood's perfect features—the first genuine emotion Alice had seen from the vampire. "You're bluffing. The sleeping charm you used on the guardian would affect all supernatural security equally."

"A reasonable assumption," Winters acknowledged with a slight smile. "But incorrect. I've been maintaining these protections since the 1950s. I know their rhythms intimately—including how to trigger a premature activation."

To demonstrate, she made a subtle gesture with her left hand. The totemic figures flanking the gallery entrance shuddered slightly, their carved eyes beginning to glow with internal light.

"Fifteen seconds," Winters counted calmly.

Blackwood visibly calculated her options. "This isn't over," she decided, gesturing for her associates to withdraw. "The Council has patience Detective Chen. We've waited centuries for the right opportunity—we can wait a while longer."

"Next time, just submit a formal request to examine the artifact," Alice suggested dryly. "Much less dramatic."

With a final cold smile, Blackwood and her team retreated through the door they'd entered, moving with vampire speed that left only a displaced air current to mark their passing.

"Were you really controlling the totems?" Ethan asked Madame Winters once they were gone.

"No," the elderly witch admitted with a mischievous smile. "But they weren't certain, and uncertainty is anathema to creatures like Blackwood who base their existence on absolute control."

"The camera loop has reset," Tobias warned. "Security systems will detect us now."

"Then we move immediately," Alice decided. "Original exit plan through the loading dock. Double-time."

They navigated the remaining distance through the museum with urgent haste, no longer attempting to avoid detection but simply outpacing the security response. Alarms activated behind them as motion sensors detected their movement, but they reached the loading dock before the human guards could intercept them.

Ethan disabled the dock's external lock, allowing them to escape into the alley where they'd started. Their vehicle waited with engine running, courtesy of preparations Alice had made earlier. Within moments, they were driving away from the museum, the containment box with its precious cargo secured between Dr. Mackie and Madame Winters in the back seat.

"That was... not according to plan," Tobias observed once they'd put several blocks between themselves and the museum.

"Plans rarely survive contact with the enemy," Alice replied, her tactical training asserting itself. "But we achieved the primary objective."

"And confirmed that the Chronos Society has powerful allies," Ethan added grimly. "The Vampire Council isn't known for involving itself in temporary problems. If they're interested in the Pendulum..."

"Then its potential extends beyond what we've witnessed," Dr. Mackie finished. "The temporal fracture may have been merely a side effect of its true capabilities."

"Which makes proper containment even more critical," Tobias said.

They drove to Merrick's Chronometry, entering through the reinforced back entrance Tobias had installed after the previous week's events. The shop's interior remained closed to the public, workbenches cleared to make space for their supernatural research.

Dr. Mackie carefully placed the containment box on the central table. "We should transfer it to more permanent protection before opening it. The temporal energy readings are already increasing, even through the shielding."

"I prepared a dedicated containment vessel," Tobias said, retrieving an ornate wooden box from beneath his workbench. Its interior was lined with a combination of materials—lead, silver, crystal, and inscribed copper—creating a multi-layered barrier against various energy types.

"The inscriptions are from Cassandra's grimoire," Madame Winters confirmed, examining the box. "Specifically designed to contain temporal artifacts. Well done, Mr. Merrick."

With careful precision, they transferred the calling stone from Dr. Mackie's temporary container to Tobias's permanent one. Even during the brief moment of transition, Alice felt a strange sensation—as though time briefly hesitated around them, multiple possibilities overlapping before settling back into normal flow.

"Did you feel that?" she asked the others.

"Temporal resonance," Dr. Mackie confirmed. "Even here, miles from the clocktower, it seeks connection with the other components."

"Which raises the critical question," Ethan said as Tobias secured the box. "What do we do with it now? If it can activate the Pendulum even at a distance..."

"We need a location both secure and isolated," Alice determined. "Somewhere the Chronos Society and Vampire Council can't easily access."

"I have a suggestion," Madame Winters offered. "The underground observatory beneath Merrick's Chronometry—where you found the first clues to the Anchor Star. It's directly connected to the ley line network but exists in a pocket of stability. With additional protections, it could serve as a permanent containment site."

"The opposite approach from the museum," Tobias realized. "Instead of displaying it prominently, we conceal it completely."

"And instead of placing it at the meteorite's impact site to maximize resonance, we position it at a stabilization point to minimize connection," Dr. Mackie added, understanding the concept. "Elegant."

"Then that's our next step," Alice decided. "Tomorrow we'll prepare the observatory and transfer the calling stone to permanent containment."

As they finalized plans for the artifact's security, Alice's phone rang—Captain Vaughn calling at nearly 3 AM could only mean trouble.

"Chen," she answered, listening intently to his report before responding. "Understood. We'll be right there."

She ended the call, her expression grave. "There's been a security breach at the Municipal Building. Someone attempted to access the clocktower mechanism chamber."

"Blackwood?" Ethan suggested.

"Unknown. The attempt failed—our additional security measures held—but it confirms our suspicions. The Pendulum remains a target."

"Even properly contained and with the components integrated?" Tobias asked with concern.

"Apparently so," Alice confirmed. "Which means our work isn't finished. The immediate crisis has passed, but the longer game is just beginning."

Dr. Mackie glanced at the wooden box containing the calling stone. "We've recovered all known components now. What else could they possibly want with the Pendulum?"

"Control," Madame Winters said simply. "What beings like Diana Blackwood always want. Not just containment of temporal energy, but the ability to direct it. To harness time itself as a tool—or a weapon."

"Can that be done?" Tobias asked. "Could the Pendulum actually be used to manipulate time deliberately, rather than simply causing random fractures?"

"Theoretically," Dr. Mackie acknowledged. "The complete assembly, with all components including the activator, could potentially be reconfigured from a containment system to a directional one. It would require extraordinary expertise in both temporal physics and supernatural manipulation, but..."

"But not impossible," Alice concluded grimly. "Especially for organizations with centuries of research and unlimited resources."

"So we've won the battle but not the war," Ethan summarized.

"Precisely." Alice regarded the containment box with newfound concern. "We've prevented immediate disaster, but we've also confirmed that the Pendulum is more significant than we initially believed. This was never just about stopping a temporal fracture."

"It was about who controls time itself," Tobias realized.

The implications hung heavily in the air as dawn approached. They had successfully retrieved the calling stone—the final component needed to understand the Pendulum of Aeon's full capabilities. But in doing so, they had also confirmed that far more powerful forces than Professor Harlow were interested in its potential.

The clocktower stood secure for now, the integrated components safely contained. The calling stone would soon be hidden where its activating influence couldn't trigger another fracture. Daybridge had returned to normal, its citizens blissfully unaware of how close they'd come to temporal dissolution.

Yet as Alice surveyed her unlikely team—a clockmaker, a werewolf detective, an elderly witch, and a temporal physicist—she knew their work was just beginning. The Chronos Society and Vampire Council wouldn't abandon their pursuits easily. Other factions might emerge, drawn by rumors of an artifact capable of manipulating time itself.

The Pendulum's story wasn't ending. In many ways, it was just beginning to unfold.

And in Daybridge, where supernatural and mundane had coexisted for centuries, time remained the most mysterious force of all—flowing forward relentlessly, yet harboring secrets that transcended simple progression from past to future.

The clocks in Merrick's Chronometry ticked onward, each marking time in its unique voice. And beneath their mechanical certainty lay a deeper truth: time itself might be more malleable than anyone had imagined.

For now, at least, it remained securely contained.

Tick by measured tick.

CHAPTER ELEVEN:
DECIPHERING THE RITUAL

The early morning sun spilled through the newly repaired windows of Merrick's Chronometry, illuminating the organized chaos of Tobias's workshop. Four days had passed since they'd retrieved the calling stone from the Supernatural Artifacts Museum, days filled with intensive research and preparation. The artifact now rested in specially designed containment within the underground observatory beneath the shop, surrounded by protective sigils and isolation barriers.

Alice sat at a cleared workspace, surrounded by reports documenting the attempted breach at the Municipal Building. Security footage showed three figures in dark clothing approaching the clocktower entrance, only to be repelled by the enhanced protective measures installed after the containment ritual. Their faces remained obscured by both conventional masks and what appeared to be magical concealment—blurring effects that prevented clear identification.

"Definitely supernatural," she concluded, sliding the images across the table to Ethan. "The distortion pattern matches vampire glamour techniques."

"Blackwood's associates," Ethan agreed, examining the photos with his enhanced perception. "The movement patterns are consistent with what we saw at the museum. Enhanced humans under vampire control."

Tobias looked up from the antique pocket watch he was servicing—his first return to normal work since the crisis began. "They're persistent. Why continue pursuing the Pendulum when it's already contained and the fracture is sealed?"

"Because containment and control are different objectives," Madame Winters answered from her position near the window. The elderly witch had been a regular presence at the shop since their museum operation, dividing her time between Merrick's Chronometry and consultations with Madame Rowan.

"The Vampire Council sees the Pendulum as a potential tool," she continued, "not merely a threat to be neutralized. They believe its temporal properties could be harnessed rather than simply contained."

"To what end?" Alice asked, though she suspected she knew the answer.

"Immortality has its limitations," Ethan explained. "Vampires can live indefinitely but remain bound by linear time's progression. They can't return to the past or experience alternate timelines."

"An immortal existence becomes predictable after centuries," Madame Winters added. "The Council likely sees the Pendulum as a means to expand their experience—to access multiple versions of reality rather than just one unending timeline."

Dr. Mackie entered from the back room, carrying several ancient texts borrowed from university archives. "It's not just vampires who might benefit," she noted, setting down her burden. "Any being with extended lifespan would value temporal manipulation—elder witches, ancient werewolf bloodlines, even certain fae entities."

"Which explains why the Chronos Society has survived for centuries despite setbacks," Alice concluded. "They've always had powerful supernatural patrons supporting their research."

The bell above the shop door chimed, announcing Madame Rowan's arrival. The ancient witch entered with surprising grace for one of her apparent age, carrying a leather satchel whose contents clinked softly with each step. Her silver hair was bound in an intricate braid, and her violet eyes surveyed the assembled group with calm assessment.

"Progress, I see," she commented, noting the organized research materials. "But insufficient preparation for what comes next."

"Next?" Tobias inquired, setting aside his watchmaker's tools. "The fracture is contained, the calling stone secured. What remains?"

"Permanence," Rowan replied simply, opening her satchel to extract a bundle wrapped in midnight-blue silk. "What we achieved at the clocktower was comprehensive but not complete. The containment requires reinforcement through proper ritual during the next lunar apex."

She unwrapped the silk to reveal fragmented pages of what appeared to be the First Grimoire—the original text written by Cassandra Winters in 1783. The pages were brittle with age, their edges charred as though rescued from fire.

"I've been reconstructing the complete ritual from these fragments," she explained. "The ceremony performed during the alignment was effective but improvised. Cassandra's original design was more elegant—and more permanent."

"The full moon is in three days," Ethan noted. "Is that the lunar apex you mentioned?"

"Indeed. When the moon reaches its zenith directly above the clocktower, a window opens for reinforcing temporal workings." Rowan carefully arranged the fragments on the table. "The tower itself was positioned with this astronomical alignment in mind. Harold Merrick and the original architect were both members of an esoteric architectural society that understood celestial influences."

Alice studied the ancient text with interest, noting symbols that resembled those engraved on the clocktower mechanism. "These appear to be instructions for a more complex integration than what we implemented."

"Precisely," Rowan confirmed. "The current configuration stabilizes the temporal fracture but doesn't fully harmonize the components. They coexist rather than truly unifying."

"Like gears that mesh but don't optimize power transfer," Tobias suggested, his clockmaker's perspective providing an apt metaphor.

"Exactly so, Mr. Merrick. The Pendulum, Anchor Star, and Fulcrum are positioned correctly but not resonating at their optimal frequency." Rowan indicated illustrations on the grimoire pages showing a more complex arrangement than their current setup. "This configuration would create true harmonic balance—not just containment but synthesis."

Dr. Mackie examined the diagrams with scientific interest. "These indicate physical modifications to the clocktower mechanism itself—integration rather than simply housing the components."

"Yes," Rowan confirmed. "The Pendulum wasn't meant to be merely contained within the clockworks but to become an integral part of them—the literal heart of the tower's operation."

Tobias leaned closer, his expertise immediately recognizing the mechanical implications. "This would require recalibrating the entire mechanism—adjusting every gear, weight, and spring to accommodate the Pendulum's natural oscillation instead of forcing it to conform to our predetermined rhythm."

"A fundamental reversal of our approach," Dr. Mackie realized. "Instead of imposing our timeflow on the Pendulum—"

"We allow it to establish the base rhythm, then build our measurement around it," Tobias finished. "Brilliant, actually. Like designing a clock around the natural swing of a pendulum rather than forcing an artificial period."

"My grandfather must have understood this," he continued, retrieving his family journals from a nearby shelf. "There are references here to 'harmonic integration' and 'natural periodicity' that never made sense before."

"Harold Merrick understood the concept but lacked the complete Pendulum assembly," Rowan explained. "Without all components, true integration was impossible."

"So we need to modify the clocktower mechanism," Alice summarized. "Essentially rebuilding it around the Pendulum assembly rather than simply housing it."

"An engineering challenge of considerable complexity," Tobias acknowledged, already sketching preliminary designs based on the grimoire illustrations. "The existing mechanism has operated continuously for nearly 150 years. Modifying it without stopping the tower completely would be..."

"Necessary," Rowan interjected firmly. "The clocktower must not stop. Its continuous operation maintains the current containment field. Modifications must be implemented while it continues functioning."

"Like performing heart surgery on a patient without stopping the heart," Ethan observed.

"An apt analogy," Rowan agreed. "And equally delicate."

Alice considered the practical challenges. "We'd need unrestricted access to the clocktower for several days, specialized tools, and expertise in both mechanical engineering and temporal magic."

"The PIU can secure access," Ethan assured her. "Captain Vaughn will authorize it given the potential security implications."

"I can design the necessary modifications," Tobias said, his sketches already taking detailed form. "But implementation will require precision I can't guarantee while the mechanism remains in motion."

"I might have a solution for that," Dr. Mackie offered. "My department has been developing temporal manipulation technology—nothing on the scale of the Pendulum, but potentially capable of creating localized stasis fields. We could essentially freeze small sections of the mechanism temporarily while modifications are implemented."

"Dangerous," Madame Winters cautioned. "Temporal technology near an already sensitive artifact could trigger unforeseen reactions."

"Which is why we'll need magical stabilization concurrent with the technological approach," Rowan determined. "A balancing of methodologies."

As they discussed technical details, Alice felt a familiar pressure building behind her eyes—the precursor to what she now recognized as a temporal echo. These experiences had grown more frequent since her initial exposure to the Pendulum, as though her natural sensitivity had been enhanced by proximity to the artifact.

She gripped the edge of the table, bracing herself as reality around her began to waver. The shop interior blurred, colors bleeding into one another before reforming into the same space but in a different era.

The year was 1876, based on the calendar visible on the wall. The workshop looked remarkably similar to its present configuration, though the tools were period-appropriate and gas lamps provided illumination instead of electric lights. A man who strongly resembled Tobias—his great-grandfather, she presumed—stood before technical drawings of the Municipal Building clocktower, then under construction.

"The timing mechanism must accommodate future modifications," he was explaining to a bearded man in formal attire who could only be the architect. "The central chamber requires specific dimensions and access points."

"Highly irregular, Mr. Merrick," the architect replied with visible frustration. "The structural integrity—"

"Is not compromised by these specifications," Merrick interrupted firmly. "The tower's function transcends mere timekeeping or architectural statement. You know this, Whitmore."

The architect—Whitmore—sighed in resignation. "The Society has authorized your requirements. I simply question the wisdom of designing such a prominent structure around speculative future needs."

"Not speculative," Merrick corrected, tapping a leather-bound journal similar to those Tobias still used. "Prophesied. Cassandra Winters' visions have never proven false."

"Witchcraft," Whitmore muttered, though without genuine malice. "Very well. The chamber will be constructed to your specifications, and the mechanism designed to accommodate your... anticipated modifications."

"Good." Merrick rolled up the technical drawings. "When completed, the tower will stand for centuries—a guardian against what approaches."

"This obsession with future calamity," Whitmore said, shaking his head. "Perhaps it will never come to pass."

"It will," Merrick replied with absolute certainty. "The stars align in cycles, Whitmore. What has happened will happen again. Our duty is to prepare the way for those who will face it."

The vision began to fade, the figures becoming translucent as present reality reasserted itself. Just before it disappeared completely, Alice noticed something she'd missed initially—a small model on Merrick's workbench representing the Pendulum components in precisely the configuration Rowan had just shown them from the grimoire fragments.

They had known all along what would be needed.

"—Detective Chen? Alice?"

She blinked, finding Ethan gripping her arm supportively while the others watched with concern.

"Another temporal echo," she explained, reorienting herself. "1876, during the clocktower's design phase. Tobias's great-grandfather was instructing the architect on specific requirements for the mechanism chamber."

"What requirements?" Tobias asked intently.

"Dimensions and access points designed to accommodate future modifications—specifically, the integration we're now considering." Alice looked at Rowan. "They built the tower with this eventuality in mind. Your Cassandra Winters had prophesied it."

Rowan nodded, unsurprised. "Cassandra's gift of foresight was exceptional, even among temporal sensitives. She glimpsed fragments of future events, particularly those concerning the Pendulum's return."

"So, the clocktower was designed from the beginning to house the Pendulum," Dr. Mackie realized. "Not simply as a convenient location chosen in 1927, but as its intended purpose from inception."

"The Municipal Building itself was positioned at a ley line convergence point," Madame Winters added. "City planning documents from that era show several proposed locations, but this one was selected despite higher construction costs and engineering challenges."

"A century and a half of preparation," Ethan marveled. "Generations working toward a single purpose."

"Like the Chronos Society," Alice noted. "But with opposing objectives."

"Not opposing—complementary," Rowan corrected. "The Society seeks liberation; the Guardians seek stability. Both recognize the Pendulum's significance but differ in their approach to its power."

"Guardians?" Tobias questioned. "You mean my family?"

"Your family, the Winters coven, the Reeves pack, and others who understood the cosmic balance." Rowan gestured to the assembled group. "Just as you five have been drawn together in this generation—a clockmaker, a temporal physicist, a werewolf, a witch, and a sensitive with law enforcement training. The pattern repeats."

Alice felt a chill at this observation. "You're suggesting we were... predetermined for these roles?"

"Not predetermined," Rowan replied carefully. "Aligned by probability. The universe has patterns, Detective Chen. Where temporal power gathers, certain archetypes naturally converge to address it."

"That sounds uncomfortably like destiny," Ethan remarked skeptically.

"Call it statistical inevitability if you prefer," Dr. Mackie suggested. "From a quantum perspective, certain configurations of events and individuals become highly probable under specific conditions."

"Regardless of cosmic patterns," Tobias interjected practically, "we have a concrete task before us. Modifying the clocktower mechanism requires detailed planning." He indicated his sketches, which had evolved into preliminary engineering drawings. "I'll need complete schematics of the current configuration to develop a proper integration design."

"The city archives should have the original plans," Alice noted. "I'll request access through official channels."

"And I'll begin gathering the necessary materials for the ritual component," Madame Winters offered. "Some ingredients require specific preparation that should start immediately."

"I'll coordinate with my department for the temporal manipulation technology," Dr. Mackie added. "Though I'll need clearance for removing it from university facilities."

"I can arrange that," Ethan assured her. "The PIU has requisition authority for supernatural crisis prevention."

As they organized their respective tasks, Alice experienced another wave of pressure behind her eyes—milder than before but unmistakable. This time, however, she wasn't pulled into a full temporal echo. Instead, brief flashes of images appeared in her mind like fragmented memories: the clocktower under moonlight, the mechanism chamber filled with figures in ceremonial attire, the Pendulum assembly emitting harmonized light that seemed to pulse in rhythm with the tower's massive bells.

"The full moon ritual," she murmured, recognizing what she was seeing. "I'm getting glimpses of what's to come."

Rowan regarded her with heightened interest. "Forward echoes are rare, even among natural sensitives. Your connection to the timestream is evolving, Detective Chen."

"Is that... safe?" Alice asked, concerned by this development.

"Temporal sensitivity is neither safe nor dangerous inherently," Rowan replied. "It simply is. How you navigate it determines its impact on you."

"These experiences have been increasing in frequency," Alice noted. "At first, they were triggered by proximity to the Pendulum, but now they seem to occur spontaneously."

"Like a muscle that strengthens with use," Dr. Mackie suggested. "Your natural ability is developing through exposure and practice."

"Can it be controlled?" Alice asked Rowan directly. "Directed rather than simply experienced?"

"With training, yes." The ancient witch studied her thoughtfully. "Your sensitivity appears to be focusing on events relevant to our current situation—a useful alignment. With proper techniques, you could potentially access specific time streams intentionally."

"That would be advantageous," Ethan acknowledged. "Targeted information gathering rather than random insights."

"I can begin instruction, if you wish," Rowan offered. "Though developing true control typically requires months of practice."

"We have three days until the full moon," Alice reminded her. "Let's focus on what's immediately necessary for the ritual."

Tobias had been quiet, continuing his design work while they discussed Alice's developing sensitivity. Now he looked up, his expression showing the satisfaction of a problem solver who had found an elegant solution.

"I think I've identified the core integration approach," he announced, turning his sketches for the others to see. "The Pendulum assembly needs to connect with the clocktower mechanism at eight specific points—what horologists call 'escapement interfaces.' These regulate the transfer of energy throughout the system."

Dr. Mackie examined the design with professional appreciation. "Fascinating. You're essentially creating a mechanical translation system between the Pendulum's natural oscillation and the tower's conventional timekeeping."

"Exactly," Tobias confirmed. "Rather than forcing the Pendulum to conform to our time measurement, we're allowing it to establish the base rhythm while the translation system converts that to conventional hours and minutes."

"Will the clock still keep accurate time?" Ethan asked practically.

"Yes, though its definition of 'accurate' will be more fundamental," Tobias explained. "The Pendulum oscillates at what appears to be quantum frequency—essentially measuring the actual passage of time rather than our arbitrary divisions of it."

"So the tower would display conventional time but operate on true cosmic time," Alice summarized.

"Precisely. And in doing so, it would not merely contain the Pendulum's energy but channel it constructively." Tobias indicated a section of his design showing energy flow throughout the mechanism. "The temporal energy that previously caused fractures would instead power the harmonization of local timeflow."

"This is consistent with Cassandra's vision," Rowan confirmed, examining the sketches. "The Pendulum was never meant to be merely contained—it was meant to be integrated. To serve as Daybridge's cosmic heartbeat."

"Which explains why the Chronos Society and Vampire Council remain interested despite our containment success," Ethan realized. "They understand there's more potential in the Pendulum than we've activated."

"Potential they wish to direct toward their own purposes rather than universal stability," Madame Winters added grimly.

Alice consulted her notes from the previous temporal echo. "According to what I witnessed, the original clocktower design includes specific access points for these modifications. If we locate those, implementation should be more straightforward than attempting to adapt a completely conventional mechanism."

"We should also consider security implications," Ethan cautioned. "If the Council knows we're planning these modifications..."

"They'll almost certainly attempt to interfere," Alice agreed. "We'll need continuous protection during both preparation and implementation."

"The Pack can provide security," Ethan volunteered. "After witnessing the temporal fracture's effects, Alpha Lowell understands the stakes. He'll assign reliable members."

"And I'll request additional PIU protection," Alice added. "Between supernatural and conventional security, we should have adequate coverage."

As their planning continued, Tobias remained focused on his technical designs, adding increasingly detailed specifications for each modification. His expression showed both concentration and a deeper emotion Alice recognized as family pride—continuing the work his ancestors had begun generations earlier.

"There's a personal element to this for all of us," she observed quietly to Ethan. "Tobias continuing his family's legacy, you reconnecting with Pack tradition, Madame Winters and Rowan preserving their coven's purpose."

"And you?" Ethan asked, studying his partner thoughtfully.

Alice considered this. "I'm not sure yet. My sensitivity doesn't connect to any family tradition I'm aware of. My parents were practical people—my father a conventional police officer, my mother an accountant."

"Perhaps your role is to bring a new perspective," Ethan suggested. "Traditions need fresh viewpoints to remain relevant."

"Or perhaps your lineage contains more than you know," Rowan interjected, having overheard their conversation. "Temporal sensitivity often skips generations, remaining dormant until circumstances awaken it."

The idea that her newfound abilities might connect to an unknown family history was both intriguing and unsettling. Alice had always defined herself through deliberate choices rather than inherited traits or predestination. The suggestion that some aspects of her current situation might have been influenced by factors beyond her control challenged her self-perception.

"Regardless of its origin," she said firmly, "my priority is using this sensitivity effectively for our current task. If it helps us implement a permanent solution for the Pendulum, that's what matters."

"Well said," Madame Winters approved. "Intent matters more than inheritance in magical matters."

Their planning session continued into the afternoon, with responsibilities divided according to expertise. Tobias would focus on the mechanical modifications, Dr. Mackie on the temporal stasis technology, Madame Winters and Rowan on ritual preparations, and Alice and Ethan on security arrangements and official authorization.

As evening approached, they dispersed to begin their respective tasks, agreeing to reconvene the following morning at the clocktower for initial assessment. Alice remained behind briefly, helping Tobias organize his workshop for the complex manufacturing ahead.

"Your great-grandfather would be proud," she told him as he carefully packed specialized tools into a leather case. "Seeing his preparations finally fulfilled."

"I hope so," Tobias replied, his expression thoughtful. "Though I wonder if he anticipated how the knowledge would pass down. My grandfather's journals are deliberately obscure on certain points—as though he wanted to ensure the information reached the right person at the right time, but not before."

"A time-release family secret," Alice observed. "Appropriate for clockmakers."

"Indeed." Tobias closed his tool case, securing its ornate brass latches. "There's a phrase repeated throughout the journals: 'The clock reveals its secrets only when time is right.' I always thought it was merely a philosophical observation about patience in craftsmanship."

"And now?"

"Now I wonder if it was literal instruction—that certain aspects of the clocktower's design would only become apparent when specifically needed." He extracted a small pocket watch from his waistcoat—the chronometer containing the Pendulum fragment that had helped them locate the Anchor Star. "This has been passed down through generations of Merricks, always to the family member who showed the greatest aptitude for chronometry."

"A key as well as a timepiece," Alice noted, recalling how it had opened multiple locks during their investigation.

"Yes, and perhaps more than we've yet discovered." Tobias examined the watch thoughtfully. "If my ancestors built hidden access points into the clocktower, this may interact with them in ways we haven't anticipated."

"Another aspect to explore during tomorrow's assessment," Alice said. She gathered her notes, preparing to leave. "Get some rest, Tobias. The next few days will be demanding."

"You as well, Detective Chen. And..." he hesitated briefly, "perhaps be prepared for additional temporal echoes. If your sensitivity is increasing as Rowan suggests, proximity to the clocktower might trigger stronger experiences."

"I'll be ready," she assured him, though privately she wondered if one could ever truly be prepared for experiencing multiple time streams simultaneously.

As she left the shop, the evening sky above Daybridge showed no sign of the temporal distortions that had manifested during the fracture crisis. Stars appeared in their expected positions, the waxing moon—approaching full but not yet there—cast normal illumination across the city streets. To casual observers, everything had returned to normal.

Yet beneath this apparent stability, Alice knew preparations were underway on multiple fronts. The Guardians worked to reinforce the Pendulum's containment, while the Chronos Society and Vampire Council undoubtedly planned their own interventions. The clocktower stood at the center of these competing interests—a nexus point where time streams converged and temporal power concentrated.

In three days, the full moon would reach its zenith above that tower. Whatever happened then would determine whether the Pendulum of Aeon remained a contained artifact or became something more—either the stabilizing cosmic heartbeat Tobias envisioned or a tool for those who sought to manipulate time itself.

The countdown had begun once more.

The Municipal Building's grand facade gleamed in morning sunlight as Alice approached, official authorization documents secured in her shoulder bag. Captain Vaughn had approved their request for extended access with minimal questions—the recent security breach providing sufficient justification for a "comprehensive system review and upgrade."

Ethan waited at the main entrance, accompanied by two uniformed PIU officers who would establish the initial security perimeter. "Maintenance access has been cleared," he informed her as they entered. "The regular clocktower technician has been temporarily reassigned to 'specialized training.'"

"And our cover story?" Alice asked as they passed through security.

"Historical preservation assessment combined with security system upgrade," Ethan replied. "Plausible enough that most municipal employees won't question our presence, while giving us unrestricted access to the tower itself."

They took the dedicated elevator to the clocktower's base level, where they found Dr. Mackie already setting up monitoring equipment. The professor had arrived early to establish baseline readings of the Pendulum's current energy output and stability metrics.

"Temporal field is consistent with our last measurements," she reported, studying data on her tablet. "Containment holding at 97.8% efficiency. Minor fluctuations within expected parameters."

"The integration should improve that to near-perfect stability," Ethan noted.

"Theoretically," Dr. Mackie agreed cautiously. "Though any modification introduces variables."

They ascended the spiral staircase to the mechanism chamber, where the massive clockworks continued their steady operation. The Pendulum assembly remained secured in its central chamber, the three components—Crystal, Star, and Fulcrum—arranged in the triangular configuration they had established during the containment ritual.

Tobias arrived minutes later, accompanied by a young assistant carrying additional equipment. "Marcus is my apprentice," he explained as he made introductions. "His assistance with the mechanical aspects will be invaluable, and he's already aware of the supernatural elements involved."

"Werewolf sensitivity runs in my family," Marcus explained with a slightly awkward smile. "I've been seeing things others can't since childhood. Working for Mr. Merrick has been the first job where that's considered an asset rather than a liability."

Alice appreciated Tobias's practical approach to staffing—they needed trusted individuals with relevant skills, and supernatural awareness was certainly relevant in this context.

With the initial team assembled, they began a comprehensive assessment of the clocktower mechanism. Tobias and Marcus examined the massive gears, weights, and structural elements with horologist precision, identifying the eight "escapement interfaces" where the Pendulum's integration would occur.

"Look at this," Tobias called from behind a particularly large gear assembly. "The access point is already here—concealed but definitely intentional."

The others joined him, observing what appeared to be a specially designed connection point hidden within the conventional mechanism. A small panel bearing the same maker's mark they had seen in the underground observatory could be rotated to reveal an interface precisely matching the specifications in Tobias's design.

"They built it ready for this moment," Marcus observed with wonder.

"Seven more to locate," Tobias noted, already moving to the next potential position. "If they follow the pattern I'm anticipating, they should form an octagonal arrangement surrounding the Pendulum chamber."

Alice followed, helping to document each discovery while Ethan established security protocols with the PIU officers. Dr. Mackie continued her monitoring, correlating energy fluctuations with their examination of the mechanism.

By midday, they had identified six of the eight integration points, confirming Tobias's theory about their deliberate inclusion in the original design. Each revealed connection point showed remarkable craftsmanship—precision engineering concealed within conventional clockwork, waiting nearly 150 years to fulfill its purpose.

Madame Winters and Rowan arrived as they located the seventh interface, bringing ritual materials and additional insights from their examination of the grimoire fragments.

"The integration points form a ceremonial octagram," Rowan observed, studying their documented positions. "A powerful configuration for harmonic stabilization."

"The eighth point should be here," Tobias indicated a position opposite the first discovery. "But this section appears to have been modified at some point—the original access panel is missing."

"During the 1927 containment," Madame Winters suggested. "My grandmother's records mention emergency modifications to the mechanism when they implemented the temporary solution."

"Which means we'll need to fabricate a replacement interface," Tobias concluded, already taking measurements. "Challenging but feasible with the original as reference."

While they continued the technical assessment, Rowan established a ritual perimeter around the chamber's edges—subtle protections that would help stabilize their work and provide early warning of supernatural interference.

"I sense remnants of the original wardcraft," she noted as she worked. "Layers of protection accumulated over decades, some still active though faded."

"Can they be reinforced?" Alice asked.

"Better to integrate them into our new protections," Rowan replied. "Acknowledging what came before while establishing what comes next—a fundamental principle of temporal magic."

By late afternoon, they had completed their initial assessment and developed a comprehensive implementation plan. Tobias would fabricate the necessary mechanical components at his workshop, Dr. Mackie would prepare the temporal stasis technology, and the witches would continue ritual preparations. Actual implementation would begin the following day, with the final integration culminating during the full moon ritual.

As the others packed their equipment, Alice approached the Pendulum chamber, studying the contained artifacts through its crystal viewing panel. The three components continued their synchronized pulsing—blue, white, and amber energies flowing between them in complex patterns. The sight triggered an unexpected temporal echo.

This time, instead of being pulled fully into another era, Alice experienced what felt like an overlay—present reality remaining visible while another timestream appeared simultaneously, like a double exposure photograph. She saw the mechanism chamber as it currently existed, but also as it would appear during the full moon ritual—figures in ceremonial attire surrounding the Pendulum, modified mechanism fully integrated, energies flowing through the octagonal connection points to create a harmonic field throughout the tower.

Most strikingly, she saw herself in this future vision—standing at a specific position near the Pendulum chamber, hands extended in a gesture she didn't recognize, eyes glowing with the same combined light emitted by the three artifacts.

The overlaid vision lasted only seconds before fading, leaving Alice momentarily disoriented but with crystal-clear recall of what she'd witnessed.

"You saw something," Rowan observed, approaching quietly.

"The ritual," Alice confirmed. "But not as an observer this time. I was participating—actively channeling energy from the Pendulum."

Rowan nodded, unsurprised. "Your role becomes clearer. The sensitive often serves as a conduit during temporal workings—a living bridge between time streams."

"I have no training for such a role," Alice pointed out.

"Yet your ability develops rapidly," Rowan countered. "The Pendulum recognizes your natural affinity. It would not show you this future if you were incapable of fulfilling it."

"What exactly would this 'conduit' role involve?" Alice asked, practical concerns overriding metaphysical uncertainty.

"Directing the harmonized energy throughout the tower's structure," Rowan explained. "The mechanical integration Tobias designs will establish the physical connections, but living consciousness must guide the initial energy flow—setting the pattern that the system will then maintain autonomously."

"And if something goes wrong?"

"Temporal backlash," Rowan acknowledged candidly. "Potentially severe for the conduit, whose consciousness intersects directly with the energy flow."

"You mean I could be hurt," Alice translated the euphemism.

"Or displaced," Rowan clarified. "Consciousness separated from proper temporal position—experiencing multiple time streams simultaneously without the anchoring of physical form."

"That sounds worse than physical injury," Alice observed grimly.

"It would be challenging," Rowan agreed. "Though not necessarily permanent. With proper training before the ritual, you can establish mental techniques to maintain your temporal cohesion regardless of energy fluctuations."

"And this training?"

"Would need to begin immediately and continue intensively until the full moon."

Alice considered her options. The vision had shown her participating successfully, suggesting the training would be effective.

However, visions showed possibilities, not certainties—futures that could be, not necessarily would be.

"If not me, who else could serve as a conduit?" she asked practically.

"Another sensitive with sufficient natural ability and connection to the Pendulum," Rowan replied. "Though none I've encountered in Daybridge possess your particular resonance with this artifact."

"So I'm the logical choice, if not the only one."

"You are the aligned choice," Rowan corrected. "The pattern continues to form around specific individuals in specific roles. You may decline, of course—free will remains paramount—but doing so would necessitate finding an alternative approach with less optimal probability of success."

Put that way, the decision seemed clear despite the risks. Alice had never shirked difficult assignments, and the stakes—Daybridge's continued temporal stability—certainly warranted personal risk.

"I'll do it," she decided. "But I want to understand exactly what I'm agreeing to. No mystical vagueness or partial explanations."

Rowan smiled slightly. "A reasonable condition. Let us begin this evening. My cottage provides an ideal environment for the initial training—free from temporal distraction and other energetic interference."

As they rejoined the others, Alice shared her decision and the additional role she would play in the upcoming ritual. Ethan reacted with predictable concern for his partner's safety, while Tobias and Dr. Mackie immediately considered technical implications.

"If you'll be channeling energy through the integration points," Tobias noted, "I should modify their configurations to include additional stabilization features. Essentially creating surge protection for the human component in the system."

"And I can calibrate the temporal stasis fields to create a protective buffer around your position," Dr. Mackie added. "Not interfering with the energy flow but providing a safety margin if fluctuations occur."

Their practical responses reinforced Alice's confidence in the decision. This team had already faced and overcome significant challenges together—each contributing their unique expertise toward a shared purpose. This next phase would follow the same pattern, with her sensitivity serving as one component in their collective approach.

As they departed the clocktower, Ethan pulled her aside briefly. "Are you sure about this? Rowan's cottage is... not entirely in this dimension from what I understand. And temporal consciousness manipulation isn't exactly standard PIU training."

"I'm sure," Alice confirmed. "My sensitivity has been developing whether I wanted it to or not. Better to gain control and direction than continue experiencing random echoes."

"Just... be careful," he advised. "Witches tend to see individuals as components in cosmic patterns. Don't let Rowan's perspective override your own agency."

"Never," Alice assured him with a slight smile. "I'm approaching this as I would any specialized training—a skill to be learned and applied appropriately, not a mystical destiny to surrender to."

"That's my partner," Ethan approved. "Practical even when dealing with cosmic forces."

They separated outside the Municipal Building, each heading to their assigned preparations. Alice accompanied Rowan toward the outskirts of Daybridge, where the ancient witch's integrated cottage awaited—a space existing partially outside conventional space-time, ideal for the sensitive training to come.

As they traveled, Alice reflected on the rapid evolution of her understanding since the temporal fracture first manifested. From initial skepticism about supernatural elements beyond those officially documented by the PIU, she had progressed to accepting her own developing temporal sensitivity and now preparing to serve as a conscious conduit for energies that transcended conventional physics.

The practical detective still remained—analyzing, questioning, seeking evidence and verification. But that pragmatic core now existed alongside expanded awareness of realities beyond ordinary perception. Not replacement but integration—much like the approach they were taking with the Pendulum itself.

When they reached the forest path leading to Rowan's cottage, the ancient witch paused, studying Alice with her unnervingly perceptive violet eyes.

"Before we begin," she said, "understand that temporal sensitivity, once fully awakened, never truly recedes. The training we undertake will permanently alter your perception of reality—allowing you to recognize the multiplicity of time streams that constantly surround us."

"Is that a warning or a promise?" Alice asked.

"Both," Rowan replied simply. "Knowledge transforms the knower, Detective Chen. Perceiving time's true nature changes one's relationship with it. Many find this liberating; others find it disorienting."

"And you think I'll find it...?"

"Clarifying," Rowan predicted with quiet certainty. "You have always sought to understand the underlying patterns of events—it's what makes you an exceptional detective. Temporal sensitivity will reveal patterns previously invisible to you, connecting seemingly unrelated occurrences across different timeframes."

The assessment was surprisingly accurate. Throughout her career, Alice had indeed excelled at pattern recognition—identifying connections others missed in criminal investigations. The prospect of extending that ability across temporal dimensions was professionally intriguing despite the personal adjustments it might require.

"Then let's proceed," she decided. "Three days isn't much time to master a new perceptual framework."

"Time," Rowan noted with a slight smile as they continued down the forest path, "is precisely what we'll be working with. And in the right circumstances, three days can contain multitudes."

The cottage appeared ahead, its structure still seamlessly integrated with living trees and vegetation. As they approached, Alice felt a subtle shift in her perception—as though crossing an invisible boundary into slightly different physical laws. The air felt thicker, colors more vibrant, and time itself seemed to flow at an altered rhythm.

"Welcome to my temporal sanctuary," Rowan said, opening the amber-glass door. "Where an hour outside might contain a day within, and where the boundaries between time streams grow thin enough to perceive and eventually traverse."

Alice stepped across the threshold, accepting both the invitation and the transformation it represented—another boundary crossed in her expanding understanding of time's true nature.

Behind them, in Daybridge proper, the clocktower continued its steady operation, marking conventional hours and minutes while concealing the extraordinary Pendulum at its heart. In workshops and laboratories across the city, her colleagues prepared components for the integration that would transform that ordinary timekeeping device into something far more significant—a stabilizing influence for the entire region's temporal integrity.

And beneath the city, in boardrooms and secret chambers, others made their own preparations—those who saw the Pendulum not as something to be contained and harmonized, but as a tool to be controlled and directed. The Vampire Council, the remaining

Chronos Society members, perhaps others yet unidentified—all anticipating the full moon and the opportunity it represented.

Three days until temporal forces converged.

Three days to prepare for whatever might emerge from that convergence.

Time enough, Alice hoped, to learn how to navigate between the moments that constituted reality itself.

CHAPTER TWELVE: THE APPROACHING STORM

Time moved strangely in Madame Rowan's cottage. What felt like several days of intensive training to Alice had consumed only eight hours in the outside world. Within that peculiar pocket of altered temporal flow, she had begun to understand her sensitivity not merely as random visions but as a perceptual framework that could be directed and controlled.

"Time is not a river but an ocean," Rowan had explained as they sat in her circular study, surrounded by artifacts that seemed to shimmer between different states of existence. "Events don't simply flow from past to future but exist simultaneously across a vast expanse. Your sensitivity allows you to perceive ripples in that ocean—places where time streams intersect or events resonate across different periods."

Under the ancient witch's guidance, Alice had learned to recognize the subtle pressure behind her eyes not as the precursor to disorienting visions but as an indication of temporal thinning—moments when her consciousness could deliberately reach across time streams rather than being involuntarily pulled into them.

She emerged from the cottage into early morning light, her perception fundamentally altered. The surrounding forest seemed overlaid with ghostly impressions—trees as they had appeared decades earlier, paths that once existed, animals that had passed through moments or centuries ago. Not hallucinations but actual glimpses of time's persistence.

"You're seeing temporal residue," Rowan noted, observing her reaction to the transformed landscape. "All places retain impressions of what they have been and suggestions of what they might become.

Most humans filter these impressions automatically; sensitives perceive them naturally."

"It's... beautiful," Alice admitted, watching the layered reality around her. "Complex in a way I never imagined."

"Beauty and complexity, yes," Rowan agreed. "But also practical value for your upcoming role. The integration ritual requires you to perceive the clocktower's temporal structure—past configurations, present state, and potential futures—to properly channel the Pendulum's energy."

They made their way toward the city, taking Rowan's ancient but well-maintained automobile. As they approached Daybridge proper, Alice noticed something concerning—distortions in the temporal residue that appeared not as natural layers but as jagged disruptions, like tears in the fabric of reality itself.

"Something's wrong," she observed, indicating an area where the overlapping time streams seemed particularly fractured. "The residue is unstable."

Rowan nodded grimly. "The approaching alignment is affecting temporal integrity even with the Pendulum contained. This is why the integration is essential—the current configuration maintains boundaries but doesn't harmonize them."

They passed a neighborhood park where the distortions manifested physically—a cherry tree cycling rapidly through seasons, blossoms appearing, withering, and regenerating in minutes rather than months. Nearby, a fountain's water flowed upward against gravity before resuming normal behavior. Pedestrians hurried past these anomalies, some staring in confusion while others seemed not to notice at all.

"Perception filtering," Rowan explained, noting Alice's observation of the varied reactions. "Many minds cannot process temporal inconsistencies and simply refuse to acknowledge them. Others perceive but rationalize. Only a few truly see."

"And these anomalies—are they spreading?"

"Yes. The celestial alignment amplifies the Pendulum's energy beyond current containment capabilities. The integration must be completed before the full moon reaches zenith, or these disturbances will escalate dramatically."

They arrived at Merrick's Chronometry to find the shop transformed into a manufacturing workshop. Tobias and his apprentice Marcus worked with focused intensity at multiple stations, crafting specialized components for the clocktower integration. The back room had been converted to a testing area where Dr. Mackie calibrated equipment alongside university assistants cleared for limited information about the project.

Most striking to Alice's enhanced perception was the temporal residue throughout the shop—layers upon layers of watchmaking activities spanning generations, as though every Merrick who had ever worked in this space had left impressions that continued to exist simultaneously with the present.

"You see them," Tobias noted, observing her gaze tracking invisible figures. "My ancestors."

"Yes," Alice confirmed. "They're... everywhere. Working, designing, planning." She focused on a particularly clear impression near the main workbench—a man resembling Tobias but older, hunched over technical drawings that matched those currently spread across the same surface. "Your grandfather, I think. He's working on the same integration components you are."

"Harold Merrick," Tobias identified with quiet pride. "The temporal echo of his work persists because it remains unfinished—a task handed down through generations."

"Your sensitivity has developed considerably," Rowan observed approvingly. "Yesterday you experienced involuntary echoes; now you perceive time streams consciously."

"The cottage training was effective," Alice acknowledged, though she suspected her rapid progress reflected something inherent in her nature rather than merely Rowan's techniques. Her sensitivity had been there all along, merely awaiting awakening.

Ethan arrived minutes later, his appearance immediately concerning to Alice. Her partner looked haggard—dark circles beneath eyes that held a continuous amber tinge rather than their usual brown. His movements seemed slightly uncoordinated, as though fighting against unpredictable impulses.

"The moon," he explained before she could ask, noting her worried expression. "Its pull is... distorted. The approaching alignment is affecting werewolf physiology."

"The transformation impulse is occurring at unexpected intervals," Rowan identified, studying him with professional interest. "The lunar influence is bleeding across time streams rather than following its normal cycle."

"Exactly," Ethan confirmed with obvious frustration. "I'll feel the change beginning, suppress it through training and focus, then suddenly it's gone—only to return hours later with no warning. The entire Pack is experiencing similar effects."

"Is it dangerous?" Alice asked, concerned both personally for her partner and professionally for public safety if an entire werewolf population faced unpredictable transformations.

"Not immediately," Ethan assured her. "Alpha Lowell has implemented emergency protocols. Pack members with less control are sequestered at the Den with support staff. Those of us with stronger discipline are maintaining normal duties but with contingency plans."

"This actually confirms our theory about the Pendulum's current state," Dr. Mackie noted, joining them from the testing area. "Its energy is affecting natural cycles throughout the region—lunar influence, tidal patterns, even plant growth rates. The containment maintains boundaries between time streams but doesn't regulate the flow between them."

"Like a dam with inconsistent pressure release," Tobias suggested, looking up from his work. "It prevents catastrophic flooding but creates turbulence downstream."

"And the integration will correct this?" Alice asked.

"Transform turbulence into laminar flow," Dr. Mackie confirmed. "At least theoretically. The octagonal connection points should create a balanced energy distribution rather than mere containment."

Tobias displayed the components they'd fabricated so far—precision-crafted interfaces that would connect the Pendulum assembly to the clocktower mechanism at the eight points they'd identified. Each incorporated elements that seemed to Alice's enhanced perception to exist partially outside normal matter—materials that shimmered with peculiar resonance.

"Temporal alloys," he explained, noting her attention to these sections. "Metals exposed to the Pendulum during previous activations, recovered from my family's archives. They retain harmonic properties that facilitate energy transfer between the artifact and conventional mechanisms."

"We've completed six of the eight interface components," Marcus reported. "The remaining two are more complex due to their positioning within the mechanism, but should be finished by this evening."

"Which keeps us on schedule for beginning installation tomorrow," Tobias concluded. "Final integration to occur during the full moon ritual the following night."

Alice nodded, mentally reviewing the timeline. Today for completion of components, tomorrow for initial installation and testing, the third day for final integration during the lunar zenith. Ambitious but necessary given the escalating anomalies.

"What about security?" she asked Ethan. "Has Captain Vaughn approved the additional measures?"

"Full PIU coverage plus Pack auxiliaries," he confirmed. "The official justification is 'prevention of vandalism to historical infrastructure' following the previous breach attempt. Vaughn knows the actual stakes but is keeping operational details compartmentalized."

"A wise precaution," Rowan commented. "The fewer who understand the Pendulum's true significance, the less risk of interference."

As they discussed security arrangements, a sharp crystalline tone emanated from the back room—one of Dr. Mackie's monitoring devices triggering an alert. The professor hurried to check the reading, her expression growing concerned as she studied the data.

"Significant temporal distortion detected downtown," she reported. "Centered on the Financial District, approximately half-a-mile radius. Readings suggest a Class Three anomaly."

"Class Three?" Alice questioned.

"Localized temporal acceleration or deceleration," Dr. Mackie clarified. "Time flowing at a measurably different rate than surrounding areas. Potentially hazardous to anyone entering or leaving the affected zone without proper transition."

"We need to establish a containment perimeter," Ethan decided, already reaching for his phone to contact PIU dispatch. "Prevent civilian exposure until the effect dissipates."

"I'll come with you," Alice offered. "My sensitivity might help identify the anomaly's boundaries more precisely than equipment alone."

Ethan nodded agreement as he coordinated with dispatch. After completing the call, he turned to the others. "PIU response teams are en route. Dr. Mackie, can you provide remote monitoring support?"

"Of course. The portable units can transmit data to my systems here." She quickly assembled equipment for them to take, including hand-held sensors and protective amulets designed to maintain temporal stability for the wearer.

"Be cautious," Rowan advised as they prepared to depart. "These anomalies may manifest unpredictably. What appears as simple acceleration or deceleration could involve more complex temporal effects."

With equipment secured and protective measures in place, Alice and Ethan departed for the Financial District while the others continued their preparation work. The drive downtown revealed additional anomalies throughout the city—subtle distortions visible to Alice's enhanced perception but increasingly apparent even to conventional observation.

At a major intersection, traffic lights cycled through their sequence at irregular intervals, causing confusion and minor accidents. In a cafe courtyard, conversations seemed to echo before being spoken, patrons reacting to words not yet uttered. Most disturbing was a small garden where flowers bloomed and wilted repeatedly in rapid cycles, their natural lifespan compressed into minutes.

"It's getting worse," Ethan observed grimly. "And most people still don't fully register what they're seeing. They look confused but not panicked."

"Perception filtering," Alice repeated Rowan's earlier explanation. "Their minds protect them from what they can't integrate into their understanding of reality."

"Convenient evolutionary adaptation," Ethan noted. "Though I wonder if it ultimately helps or hinders us as a species."

They reached the perimeter of the Financial District to find PIU vehicles establishing blockades at major access points. Agent Torres, a supernatural specialist who had worked with them on previous cases, approached as they parked.

"Glad you're here," she greeted them. "This one's unusual even by our standards. Time inside the affected zone is running approximately 1.7 times faster than normal, according to initial readings."

"Anyone trapped inside?" Alice asked.

"About two hundred office workers in various buildings. We're advising them to shelter in place rather than attempt to cross the boundary. Medical's concerned about physiological effects of transitioning between different timeflows without proper protection."

Alice extended her newfound perceptual abilities, studying the anomaly before them. To her enhanced senses, the boundary appeared as a shimmering curtain separating normal timeflow from the accelerated zone beyond. More concerning were the fracture lines radiating outward from the central distortion—indications that the anomaly was growing.

"It's expanding," she reported. "Slowly but steadily. And it's not uniform—there are... nodes, points where the acceleration is more pronounced."

Ethan consulted Dr. Mackie's sensor equipment, which confirmed Alice's assessment. "Expansion rate approximately three meters per hour. At this pace, it could encompass the entire downtown area by tomorrow morning."

"We need to establish whether this is a natural manifestation of the approaching alignment or deliberate interference," Alice decided. "Dr. Mackie's equipment can measure the effect but not necessarily its cause."

"I can help with that," Ethan said. "Werewolf senses can detect magical signatures, especially with the enhanced perception I'm experiencing due to the lunar distortion."

They donned the protective amulets—simple pendants inscribed with stabilization sigils designed by Madame Winters—and approached the boundary cautiously. Even with protection, the transition felt disorienting—a momentary sensation of being stretched and compressed simultaneously as their bodies adjusted to the altered temporal rate.

Inside the anomaly, the environment appeared normal except for accelerated movement—people walking slightly faster than natural, flags waving at increased speed, even clouds visibly racing across the visible sky above the street canyon of buildings. Most striking was the auditory effect—voices and ambient sounds shifted higher in pitch, creating an unsettling soundtrack to the accelerated scene.

"Definitely unnatural," Ethan confirmed after sampling the air with enhanced senses. "There's a magical signature—subtle but distinct. Similar to what we encountered at the museum during the Chronos Society confrontation."

"Deliberate, then," Alice concluded. "Someone testing the Pendulum's growing instability, perhaps? Or creating a distraction?"

"Or conducting an experiment," Ethan suggested. "Learning how temporal manipulation can be directed and controlled on a localized scale."

They proceeded toward the center of the anomaly, following both sensor readings and Alice's perceptual guidance. The accelerated timeflow became more pronounced as they approached what appeared to be the origin point—the elegant art deco lobby of the Blackwood Financial Tower.

"Of course," Alice said with grim recognition. "Diana Blackwood's corporate headquarters."

"The vampire who claimed to support our containment efforts while actually working with the Chronos Society," Ethan recalled. "This confirms her continued interest in temporal manipulation."

The tower's lobby appeared normal except for the accelerated movement of security personnel and visitors. Alice's enhanced perception, however, revealed something more significant—a subtle energy pattern emanating from the building's core, pulsing in a rhythm that seemed disturbingly familiar.

"It's resonating with the Pendulum," she realized. "Not directly connected but... harmonized somehow. Like they're communicating across a distance."

Ethan consulted the sensor equipment. "Dr. Mackie's readings confirm energy patterns similar to the Pendulum's signature but at a fraction of the intensity. Some kind of echo or induced resonance."

"We need to see what's generating it," Alice decided. "Security will recognize us as PIU, but given Blackwood's involvement, we should expect resistance."

They approached the security desk, badges displayed. The guards—who Alice immediately recognized as vampiric through their slightly too-perfect appearance and complete lack of temporal residue—regarded them with professional suspicion.

"Paranormal Investigation Unit," Ethan identified them formally. "We're responding to reports of unusual phenomena originating from this location."

"No unusual phenomena here, Detectives," the head security officer replied with practiced smoothness. "Perhaps you've been misdirected."

"The entire Financial District is experiencing accelerated timeflow," Alice stated directly. "Centered on this building. Our equipment confirms the source is within this structure."

"Ms. Blackwood is not currently available to address PIU concerns," the guard responded, unmoved. "I suggest scheduling an appointment through proper channels."

Before Alice could respond, her enhanced perception detected a significant shift in the energy pattern—a sudden intensification followed by a pulse that rippled outward from the building's core. The effect manifested physically seconds later as the acceleration rate within the anomaly visibly increased—people now moving at nearly twice normal speed, digital displays flickering as they struggled to maintain normal function in accelerated time.

"That wasn't a natural fluctuation," Ethan noted urgently. "Someone's actively modifying the effect."

Alice made a rapid decision. "Emergency override protocol," she announced formally, producing the special authorization Captain Vaughn had provided for extreme supernatural incidents. "This building is now under PIU jurisdiction pending resolution of an active Class Three temporal anomaly. Interference with our investigation constitutes a violation of the Supernatural Cooperation Act, Section 7."

The security team exchanged glances, clearly receiving instructions through concealed communication devices. After a tense moment, the head officer nodded reluctantly.

"Fifteenth floor research division only," he specified. "Escorted access. Ms. Blackwood's private executive levels remain restricted regardless of your authorization."

"Acceptable for initial assessment," Alice agreed, recognizing the value of cooperation over confrontation at this stage. "Lead the way."

As they entered the elevator, Alice extended her perceptual abilities throughout the building, attempting to map the energy pattern more completely. The source definitely centered on the research division they were approaching, but she detected tendrils extending both upward to the executive levels and downward to what appeared to be sub-basements not shown on the building's public plans.

"Multiple components to whatever they're doing," she murmured to Ethan. "The research division is just one element."

The elevator moved with unsettling speed due to the accelerated timeflow, reaching the fifteenth floor in seconds rather than the normal half-minute ascent. When the doors opened, they revealed a sophisticated laboratory space occupied by both human and vampire researchers working with equipment that appeared to combine conventional technology with supernatural elements.

At the center of the main research area stood a device that immediately captured Alice's attention—a scaled-down version of the clocktower mechanism, complete with a crystalline component that pulsed with energy remarkably similar to the Pendulum's signature.

"A resonator," Ethan identified it, consulting Dr. Mackie's equipment. "It's creating a harmonic frequency that interacts with the Pendulum's energy field."

Dr. Elias Montrose, a thin man with wire-rimmed glasses whom Alice recognized from university faculty directories as a theoretical physicist specializing in quantum mechanics, approached them with obvious reluctance.

"Detectives," he greeted them stiffly. "I understand you have questions about our research."

"Starting with what exactly you're researching, Dr. Montrose," Alice replied. "Your device is generating a temporal anomaly affecting half a mile of downtown Daybridge."

"A regrettable but anticipated side effect," Montrose acknowledged without apparent concern. "The resonance field requires calibration through practical testing. We've contained the effect to non-residential areas specifically to minimize disruption."

"'Contained' is generous terminology for an expanding temporal acceleration zone," Ethan observed dryly. "Your 'side effect' has trapped two hundred people in accelerated time and is growing by the hour."

"A temporary condition," Montrose assured them. "Once calibration is complete, the field will stabilize and eventually dissipate. Blackwood Financial has already prepared compensation packages for any inconvenienced parties."

Alice studied the physicist more carefully, noting subtle indications of vampire influence—the slightly unfocused gaze and unnatural calm suggesting partial enthrallment. Not fully controlled but certainly compromised in his decision-making.

"What exactly are you calibrating for?" she asked directly, gesturing toward the resonator. "This device clearly mimics aspects of the Municipal Building clocktower."

Montrose hesitated, the enthrallment influence visibly conflicting with scientific integrity. "We're developing temporal stabilization technology," he finally answered. "Ms. Blackwood believes the recent atmospheric disturbances indicate underlying temporal instability that could affect financial markets. Our research aims to create protective fields around key infrastructure."

"A convenient explanation," Ethan noted skeptically. "Though it doesn't account for the resonance pattern deliberately synchronized with the Pendulum."

At the mention of the Pendulum, Montrose's expression flickered with genuine surprise. "You know about—" He stopped himself abruptly. "I'm not authorized to discuss proprietary research details without Ms. Blackwood's approval."

The resonator's pulsing suddenly intensified, its crystalline component shifting from blue to purple as the energy output increased. Throughout the laboratory, equipment readings spiked dramatically.

"Phase transition initiating," announced an automated system. "Temporal acceleration approaching factor three. Stabilization fields holding at 87% efficiency."

"Shut it down," Alice ordered immediately. "Whatever calibration you're attempting is destabilizing rapidly."

"We can't interrupt mid-phase," Montrose objected. "The resonance cascade would—"

He was interrupted by a building-wide announcement system. "Security alert. Unauthorized energy signature detected in the research division. All personnel implement containment protocol immediately."

Laboratory staff responded with practiced efficiency, activating additional equipment and defensive measures. The security officer who had escorted them reached for his weapon, but Ethan moved faster, disarming him with supernatural speed enhanced by the accelerated timeflow environment.

"This isn't a negotiation," Alice stated firmly, drawing her own weapon. "That device is creating a dangerous temporal anomaly in violation of at least six supernatural regulatory statutes. Deactivate it immediately or we'll implement emergency containment measures."

Montrose appeared genuinely conflicted, glancing between the resonator and the increasingly unstable readings on surrounding monitors. "Ms. Blackwood specifically instructed—"

"Ms. Blackwood isn't experiencing accelerated cellular degradation," Ethan interrupted sharply. "Every human in this zone is aging faster than normal. Including you, Doctor."

This practical consideration appeared to penetrate the enthrallment influence. Montrose made a decision, moving to the resonator's control console.

"I can initiate a controlled shutdown sequence," he offered. "It will take approximately twelve minutes to safely power down the resonance field without creating feedback distortions."

"Do it," Alice authorized, maintaining her position while Ethan secured the security officer and established a perimeter around the resonator.

As Montrose began the shutdown procedure, Alice extended her perceptual abilities throughout the building once more, attempting to identify any secondary systems that might interfere with their intervention. What she detected was concerning—energy patterns in the sub-basement levels shifting in response to the resonator's changing output, suggesting coordinated components of a larger system.

"There's more to this than just the resonator," she informed Ethan quietly. "Whatever they're doing involves multiple locations within the building. The research division is just the visible element."

Before Ethan could respond, the elevator doors opened to admit Diana Blackwood herself, accompanied by two associates whose supernatural auras identified them as elder vampires of considerable power. Unlike the security team's professional neutrality, Blackwood made no effort to conceal her irritation at their presence.

"Detectives Chen and Reeves," she greeted them with cold precision. "I don't recall scheduling an inspection of my private research facilities."

"The PIU doesn't require appointments to investigate active supernatural threats," Alice replied evenly. "Your resonator has created a temporal anomaly affecting hundreds of people and expanding by the hour."

"A minor calibration issue," Blackwood dismissed the concern. "Which Dr. Montrose appears to be addressing quite adequately without armed intervention."

"This goes beyond calibration problems," Ethan countered. "You're deliberately creating a resonance pattern synchronized with the Pendulum. For what purpose?"

Blackwood's perfect features revealed nothing, but Alice's enhanced perception detected a subtle shift in her temporal signature—a flickering that suggested agitation despite the vampire's outward composure.

"My corporation invests in diverse research areas, Detective Reeves. Temporal stabilization technology has significant potential applications in finance, communications, and security sectors."

"And in manipulating artifacts of considerable power," Alice added pointedly. "Like the Pendulum of Aeon."

At this direct reference, Blackwood's facade cracked slightly. "You continue to impress, Detective Chen. Most humans would never connect experimental resonance technology to a contained artifact across town."

"Most humans aren't temporal sensitives who've helped contain a fracture your allies tried to exploit," Alice replied.

Blackwood smiled thinly. "Contained but not completed. Your makeshift ritual during the alignment was admirable improvisation, but hardly the optimal configuration for the Pendulum's capabilities."

"Which you're hoping to influence remotely through harmonic resonance," Ethan concluded. "Using this device to establish a connection that bypasses the physical protections around the clocktower."

"Theoretical research only," Blackwood maintained smoothly. "The Vampire Council has a legitimate interest in temporal stability given our extended lifespans. Surely that justifies academic exploration of relevant phenomena."

The resonator's pulsing had begun to slow as Montrose continued the shutdown sequence, its color shifting gradually from purple back toward blue. Throughout the laboratory, equipment readings showed decreasing intensity in the temporal field.

"Theoretical research doesn't typically create expanding temporal anomalies in populated areas," Alice observed. "Nor does it require sub-basement installations connected to ley line access points."

Blackwood's expression registered genuine surprise at this specific knowledge. "Your sensitivity has developed considerably, Detective. Perhaps we should discuss potential collaboration rather than this adversarial approach. The Vampire Council recognizes valuable talents across species boundaries."

"I'm not interested in helping you weaponize time," Alice replied directly.

"Weaponize? Such dramatic terminology." Blackwood shook her head with apparent disappointment. "We seek understanding and controlled application of natural forces. The approaching celestial alignment presents rare research opportunities that benefit multiple communities, not merely vampiric interests."

As they spoke, Alice maintained her perceptual awareness of the building's energy patterns. The resonator continued its controlled shutdown, but the sub-basement activities were increasing rather than diminishing—suggesting Blackwood's apparent cooperation might be misdirection rather than genuine compliance.

"The resonator shutdown is at 60%," Montrose reported. "Temporal field contraction beginning at the anomaly boundaries. Estimated return to normal timeflow in approximately twenty-three minutes."

"You see? No cause for dramatic intervention," Blackwood gestured gracefully toward the readings. "Once the calibration data is collected, normal conditions resume with no lasting effects."

Ethan consulted Dr. Mackie's equipment, which largely confirmed Montrose's assessment. "The acceleration is diminishing at the perimeter, but the core intensity remains concerning."

Alice made a rapid decision. "We'll monitor the complete shutdown and field dissipation. Once normal timeflow is restored throughout the affected zone, Blackwood Financial will submit complete research documentation to PIU supernatural oversight for compliance review."

"Such regulatory cooperation might be negotiable," Blackwood countered smoothly, "in exchange for certain information sharing regarding the Pendulum's current configuration. Mutual benefit rather than one-sided demands."

"Not open for negotiation," Alice stated firmly. "Compliance with supernatural regulations isn't optional, Ms. Blackwood, regardless of your Council's influence."

The vampire's perfect features hardened almost imperceptibly. "The Council has maintained peaceful relations with human authorities for centuries, Detective Chen. That relationship benefits from flexibility on both sides."

"And from adherence to established boundaries," Ethan added. "Temporal manipulation crosses several of those boundaries."

Before Blackwood could respond, Alice's enhanced perception detected a significant shift in the building's energy pattern—a sudden surge from the sub-basement levels followed by a pulse that rippled upward through the structure. Simultaneously, the resonator's shutdown sequence interrupted, its crystalline component flaring with renewed intensity.

"System override initiated," announced the automated monitoring system. "Remote synchronization protocol activated."

"What are you doing?" Alice demanded, noting Blackwood's lack of surprise at this development.

"Not my doing, Detective," the vampire replied with seemingly genuine concern. "The secondary systems shouldn't activate until—" She stopped herself, turning to Montrose. "Status report."

The physicist frantically reviewed rapidly changing data across multiple screens. "The resonance field has established a direct harmonic connection with the target artifact. Energy transfer occurring at exponentially increasing rates. The containment protocol is failing."

"Target artifact meaning the Pendulum," Ethan translated grimly. "You're attempting to siphon energy from it."

"Not siphon—synchronize," Blackwood corrected, her calm demeanor slipping as she reviewed the escalating readings. "But the process should be gradual, controlled. This acceleration is premature."

Alice's perception extended beyond the building, sensing ripples spreading throughout the city's temporal fabric. The resonator wasn't merely creating a localized anomaly now—it was establishing a direct connection with the Pendulum, potentially disrupting the containment they'd established at the clocktower.

"Shut it down completely," she ordered. "Emergency termination, not controlled deceleration."

"That would create a temporal backlash throughout the affected zone," Montrose objected. "Potentially harmful to anyone within the field boundaries."

"Less harmful than what happens if you destabilize the Pendulum's containment," Ethan countered.

Blackwood appeared to make a calculation, possibly weighing corporate research against broader consequences. "Implement emergency shutdown," she finally instructed Montrose. "Priority one."

The physicist hesitated only briefly before entering override commands into the system. The resonator's brilliance dimmed significantly, though its core continued to pulse with stubborn energy.

"Shutdown initiated but incomplete," Montrose reported. "The harmonic connection is self-sustaining at this point. The resonance field has achieved quantum entanglement with the target artifact."

"In plain language," Alice demanded.

"It's linked directly to the Pendulum now," Montrose explained. "Each affecting the other regardless of distance or conventional barriers. We can diminish our side of the equation but can't sever the connection entirely without corresponding action at the clocktower."

Alice immediately contacted Tobias via their secure communication channel, briefly explaining the situation and the need for countermeasures at the Pendulum itself.

"He's already detected the interference," she reported after ending the call. "The Pendulum's energy signature changed approximately three minutes ago—corresponding to when your resonator established connection. They're implementing protective measures now."

"The shutdown is progressing but meeting resistance," Montrose updated them. "Estimated complete deactivation in seven minutes at current rates."

"And the temporal anomaly?" Ethan asked.

"Contracting from the boundaries inward but more slowly than anticipated. The acceleration effect has diminished to approximately 1.3 times normal rather than the previous 1.7."

Alice maintained her perceptual monitoring of both the local effects and the broader ripples throughout the city. Something felt wrong about the situation—the energy patterns suggested more than a simple unexpected acceleration of an experimental process.

"This wasn't an accident," she realized, studying Blackwood more carefully. "The resonator was designed to establish this connection all along. The 'calibration' story was cover for a deliberate attempt to influence the Pendulum remotely."

"An oversimplification," Blackwood replied without directly denying the accusation. "The Council authorized exploration of harmonic resonance as a protective measure given the approaching celestial alignment. If the Pendulum's containment were to fail naturally, having an established connection could help mitigate widespread temporal disruption."

"By redirecting that energy here," Ethan concluded. "Giving you control over how and where temporal effects manifest."

"Control is preferable to chaos," Blackwood stated simply. "As you demonstrated with your own containment efforts."

The resonator continued its shutdown sequence, its brilliance now significantly diminished though still active. Throughout the laboratory, monitoring equipment showed the temporal anomaly gradually normalizing, the accelerated timeflow slowly returning to standard rates.

"Five minutes to complete deactivation," Montrose reported. "Field contraction proceeding as expected."

Alice's phone chimed with an update from Tobias: *Pendulum stabilizing. Implementing additional protection through sigil reinforcement. Dr. Mackie confirms harmonic interference diminishing.*

"Your colleagues are quite efficient," Blackwood observed, noting Alice's slight relaxation after reading the message. "Harold Merrick would be proud of his grandson's dedication to family tradition."

The casual reference to Tobias's grandfather—information not publicly connected to the recent temporal events—confirmed Alice's suspicion that Blackwood's knowledge went far beyond what she had officially acknowledged.

"The Vampire Council has been monitoring the Pendulum situation for generations, haven't they?" she asked directly.

"The Council monitors all significant supernatural phenomena," Blackwood replied carefully. "Artifacts of the Pendulum's power naturally warrant attention, particularly when they affect temporal stability—a matter of existential importance to immortals."

"And the Chronos Society? Are they still your partners in this research?"

"The Society has always been more revolutionary than the Council prefers," Blackwood answered with diplomatic precision.

"Their goal of complete temporal liberation contradicts our interest in a controlled, predictable timeflow. Recent events have... strained that relationship."

The resonator's energy had diminished to a faint pulse, its connection with the Pendulum now barely perceptible to Alice's enhanced senses. Throughout the laboratory, staff began powering down additional equipment as the emergency shutdown neared completion.

"Two minutes to full deactivation," Montrose confirmed. "Temporal field now at 1.1 times normal rate and decreasing. Boundary contraction accelerating as resonance diminishes."

"Once normal conditions are restored," Alice informed Blackwood formally, "this facility will be subject to a complete PIU inspection. All research materials related to temporal manipulation technology will be secured pending regulatory review."

"My legal department will have significant objections to such overreach," Blackwood noted with perfect composure. "Proprietary corporate research enjoys certain protections even under supernatural regulations."

"Not when it creates public safety hazards," Ethan countered. "The Supernatural Cooperation Act includes specific provisions regarding experimental technologies with wide-area effects."

Their discussion was interrupted by a building-wide alert system: "Attention all personnel. Temporal normalization procedures in progress. Please remain at your stations until standard timeflow is confirmed. Medical monitoring available on levels three and eleven for those experiencing transition symptoms."

Alice's enhanced perception detected the final contraction of the accelerated field, temporal normality reasserting itself throughout the Financial District as the resonator completed its shutdown sequence. The ripples she had sensed spreading throughout the city's temporal fabric were subsiding, though not disappearing entirely—the approaching celestial alignment continued to create underlying instability regardless of this specific incident.

"Deactivation complete," Montrose announced with evident relief. "Resonator in dormant state. Temporal field fully normalized throughout the affected zone."

"Excellent work, Doctor," Blackwood acknowledged smoothly. "Please prepare a complete data analysis for my review." She turned to Alice and Ethan with practiced corporate diplomacy. "Detectives, I believe your immediate concerns have been addressed. My staff will cooperate fully with any formal information requests submitted through appropriate channels."

The dismissal was polite but unmistakable—Blackwood clearly considered the immediate crisis resolved and expected them to depart without further intervention. Alice, however, had no intention of leaving without ensuring the situation was truly contained.

"Dr. Montrose," she addressed the physicist directly, "please confirm that all related systems throughout the building have also been deactivated—including those in the sub-basement levels."

Montrose glanced uncertainly at Blackwood, whose perfect composure showed the barest flicker of annoyance at this specific knowledge.

"The ancillary systems are automatically linked to the primary resonator," he finally answered. "They deactivate in synchronized sequence when the main system shuts down."

"I'd like confirmation, not assurance," Alice insisted. "Please check the monitoring systems."

After another hesitant glance at Blackwood, who provided a nearly imperceptible nod, Montrose accessed additional controls. "Sub-level systems showing dormant status," he reported after reviewing the data. "All energy signatures within baseline parameters."

Alice extended her perceptual abilities once more, verifying this assessment through her sensitivity rather than relying solely on potentially manipulated instrument readings. The building's energy pattern had indeed stabilized, the unusual configurations she had detected earlier now either dormant or disguised beyond her current ability to perceive.

"We'll be implementing continuous monitoring of this location," she informed Blackwood. "Any attempt to reactivate the resonator or related technology without prior PIU clearance will result in immediate enforcement action."

"Understood, Detective," Blackwood acknowledged with perfect corporate courtesy. "Blackwood Financial values its relationship with regulatory authorities and will ensure complete compliance while our legal department addresses the broader jurisdictional questions."

The practiced response contained neither commitment nor defiance—merely the standard corporate position of superficial cooperation while preparing procedural challenges. Alice had expected nothing more, recognizing that their immediate objective of halting the dangerous resonance experiment had been achieved, even if the longer-term regulatory battle remained to be fought.

They departed after confirming with PIU field teams that the temporal anomaly had fully dissipated throughout the Financial District. Building security escorted them to the lobby with rigid professionalism, clearly relieved to see them leaving without attempting further intervention in restricted areas.

Outside, normal timeflow had resumed completely, though Alice's enhanced perception detected residual distortions in the temporal fabric—aftereffects that would likely persist for hours before fully normalizing. PIU teams were already implementing follow-up protocols, checking affected buildings for any lingering anomalies and coordinating with medical units to evaluate individuals who had experienced prolonged exposure to accelerated time.

"Blackwood wasn't surprised by what happened," Ethan observed as they returned to their vehicle. "The 'accidental' resonance connection was almost certainly their intended outcome all along."

"Agreed," Alice confirmed. "They were attempting to establish a back-door connection to the Pendulum—possibly to influence it during the integration ritual we're planning."

"Or to siphon energy from it once fully activated," Ethan suggested. "Either way, the timing is significant. They're preparing for the same celestial alignment we are."

Alice contacted Tobias for a more detailed update as they drove back toward Merrick's Chronometry. The clockmaker confirmed that the Pendulum had experienced temporary destabilization corresponding exactly with the resonator's activation but had since returned to normal containment parameters.

"The harmonic connection was definitely deliberate," he reported. "Dr. Mackie's analysis shows precisely calibrated frequencies designed to bypass our protective measures. If we hadn't already been monitoring for interference, it might have established a permanent link before we detected it."

"Which means Blackwood will try again," Alice concluded. "Today's attempt was likely a test run—gathering data on our protective measures and response protocols."

"We've implemented additional shielding," Tobias assured her. "Both technological and magical barriers specifically designed to prevent harmonic resonance. Dr. Mackie is adjusting the integration components to include resonance dampening features as well."

"Good. We'll be back shortly to assist with the modified preparations."

As they approached downtown, Alice noticed something concerning—the temporal distortions she had been perceiving throughout the city were intensifying rather than diminishing. Despite the resonator's deactivation, the underlying instability caused by the approaching celestial alignment continued to grow.

In a neighborhood park, the cherry tree that had been cycling through seasons now appeared frozen between states—half in blossom, half in full leaf, the unnatural configuration visible even to conventional perception. Nearby, a public clock displayed different times on each of its four faces, the hands moving at inconsistent speeds despite sharing a single mechanism.

Most disturbing was the whispering—a sound Alice had first encountered during the initial temporal fracture, now returning with increased intensity. The clocks throughout Daybridge had begun to synchronize again, their collective ticking forming patterns that manifested as barely audible voices just at the edge of perception.

"You hear it too," Ethan noted, observing her attention to the sound.

"Yes. The clocks are whispering again—more urgently than before. Warning us."

"About the celestial alignment?"

"I think so. But there's something more specific..." She concentrated on the fragmented phrases carried through the mysterious temporal resonance. "Something about 'the third attempt' and 'the final configuration.' As though this alignment is particularly significant compared to previous occurrences."

"The third alignment since the Pendulum arrived on Earth," Ethan recalled Rowan's explanation. "Each previous cycle featured attempts to either exploit or contain its power."

"And this third cycle represents some kind of culmination," Alice suggested, piecing together the fragmented whispers. "A final opportunity to either permanently stabilize the Pendulum or unleash its full potential."

The implications were sobering. If Blackwood and potentially other factions understood this significance, their efforts to influence or control the Pendulum would intensify dramatically as the full moon approached. The resonator experiment might have been neutralized, but it represented merely one approach among many possible interventions.

They arrived at Merrick's Chronometry to find increased activity—additional PIU personnel establishing security protocols while Tobias and his team accelerated their manufacturing efforts. Dr. Mackie had expanded her monitoring network to cover the entire city, tracking temporal distortions and potential interference attempts.

"The resonator incident confirmed our vulnerabilities," she explained as they entered. "We're implementing comprehensive countermeasures against both technological and magical interference methods."

"Including these," Madame Winters added, displaying protective amulets similar to those they had used at Blackwood Tower but with enhanced design. "Improved temporal stabilization charms that protect against both acceleration and deceleration effects."

Tobias looked up from his work on the integration components. "We've modified our implementation timeline based on the escalating distortions. Initial installation begins tonight rather than tomorrow—enough to establish preliminary connections without waiting for the complete assembly."

"A phased approach," Dr. Mackie elaborated. "Creating incremental stability improvements rather than a single comprehensive implementation during the full moon ritual."

"Wise precaution," Alice approved. "Especially given Blackwood's demonstrated interest and capabilities."

"The Vampire Council rarely acts alone," Rowan noted, joining them from her position near the monitoring equipment. "Today's resonator experiment suggests coordination with other factions, even if the Chronos Society partnership has indeed fractured."

"You think there are more players involved than we've identified?" Ethan asked.

"Temporal power attracts diverse interests," the ancient witch replied. "Some seeking stability, others control, still others liberation from time's constraints entirely. The approaching alignment naturally intensifies these competing agendas."

Alice shared her observations about the increasing temporal distortions throughout the city, particularly the synchronized whispering of clocks that seemed to warn of the alignment's significance as a third and potentially final cycle.

"The pattern completes," Rowan confirmed with solemn recognition. "Cassandra's prophecy spoke of three alignments—discovery, awakening, and resolution. The Pendulum's arrival in 1483, its first activation in 1927, and now its final configuration in our present."

"Final in what sense?" Alice asked, concerned by the terminology.

"Either permanent harmonization through proper integration," Rowan explained, "or irreversible fracture if improperly handled. The third alignment represents a culmination point where the Pendulum's relationship with our timestream becomes fixed rather than fluctuating."

The implications were both encouraging and alarming—suggesting their integration ritual could achieve truly permanent stability, but also that failure would result in consequences far more severe than the temporary fracture they had previously contained.

"Then we proceed as planned, but with heightened caution," Alice decided. "Tonight's partial implementation, tomorrow's continued preparation, and the full integration during the lunar zenith the following night."

"With continuous security and monitoring throughout," Ethan added. "Blackwood's attempt won't be the last interference we face."

As they discussed security arrangements, Alice experienced another perceptual shift—not a full temporal echo but a brief overlay similar to what she had witnessed at the clocktower. For a moment, she saw the shop as it would appear during a future crisis—equipment damaged, protective measures failing, figures struggling against some unseen force emanating from the direction of the Municipal Building.

The vision faded quickly, leaving her with an urgent sense that their current preparations, while necessary, might be insufficient against whatever opposed them. The approaching celestial alignment wasn't merely an astronomical event but a focal point where multiple agendas, powers, and time streams converged.

Daybridge stood at the center of temporal forces beyond conventional understanding—forces that had been building toward this moment for centuries. The whispering clocks, the escalating anomalies, the desperate interventions by various factions—all pointed toward a culmination that would determine not just local stability but potentially the nature of time itself within their region.

The storm was approaching, gathering strength with each passing hour. Their preparations would be tested not just by deliberate interference but by the fundamental instability of a universe where time itself had become unsettled.

In three phases—tonight, tomorrow, and the final ritual beneath the full moon—they would attempt to transform crisis into permanent resolution. The Pendulum of Aeon would either become Daybridge's cosmic heartbeat as Tobias envisioned or remain a focus for those who sought to manipulate time's fundamental nature.

The countdown continued, measured in synchronized whispers and distorted reflections of reality itself.

CHAPTER THIRTEEN: BETRAYAL AT THE TOWER

Darkness settled over Daybridge as the implementation team converged on the Municipal Building clocktower. The night sky above displayed unsettling characteristics—stars appearing in impossible configurations, the waxing moon occasionally showing multiple phases simultaneously before settling back into its proper form. Even to conventional observation, reality seemed increasingly tenuous as the celestial alignment approached.

Alice arrived first, coordinating with PIU security teams to establish a secure perimeter around the tower. Captain Vaughn had authorized exceptional measures following the Blackwood resonator incident, positioning officers at all access points and implementing supernatural detection protocols to identify potential infiltrators.

"Full coverage on all approaches," Agent Torres reported, reviewing security deployments on a tablet. "Conventional and mystical surveillance integrated as you requested. Nothing enters this building without thorough vetting."

"Good," Alice approved. "Be particularly alert for vampire glamour techniques or temporal displacement signatures. After today's incident, we should anticipate sophisticated infiltration attempts."

Her enhanced perception scanned the surrounding area, identifying numerous temporal inconsistencies but no immediate threats. The whispering of synchronized clocks continued in the background of her awareness—urgent, insistent murmurings that seemed to emanate from the tower itself and echo throughout the city.

Ethan arrived next, accompanied by two Pack members whose controlled partial transformation indicated their role as supernatural security specialists. Like her partner, they displayed the amber-eyed alertness and heightened sensory awareness of werewolves operating at peak capability despite the distorted lunar influence.

"Jerome and Lydia will monitor mystical approaches," Ethan explained as they joined her. "The Pack has its own interest in seeing the Pendulum properly integrated. Alpha Lowell considers this official Pack business now."

"The distorted transformation cycles are affecting the entire supernatural community," Jerome added, his voice carrying the slight roughness of partially transformed vocal cords. "Even species not normally influenced by lunar cycles report disrupted natural rhythms."

Tobias arrived with Marcus; their vehicle loaded with specialized equipment for the initial integration phase. Dr. Mackie followed minutes later with university assistants carrying monitoring technology and temporal stabilization devices. Madame Winters and Rowan completed the assembly, bringing ritual components needed for the magical aspects of the implementation.

As they gathered in the tower's base, Alice outlined the evening's objectives. "Tonight, we implement the first phase—establishing four of the eight integration points to create preliminary stabilization. This partial connection should immediately improve temporal integrity throughout the city while preparing for the full integration during the lunar zenith."

"The initial four points form a square configuration," Tobias elaborated, displaying technical drawings. "Connecting the cardinal directions of the mechanism to create a foundational stability framework. Tomorrow we'll add the intercardinal connections to form the complete octagram."

"My monitoring equipment confirms accelerating distortion patterns throughout Daybridge," Dr. Mackie reported, reviewing data on her tablet. "Temporal bleeding between periods is increasing exponentially as the alignment approaches. Without intervention, we can expect critical fracture conditions within thirty-six hours."

"The four-point integration should significantly reduce those distortions," Tobias assured them. "Even partial harmonic connection will improve stability."

"We've prepared protective charms for everyone involved," Madame Winters added, distributing enhanced versions of the amulets they had used during the Blackwood incident. "These will shield against temporal fluctuations during the implementation process."

With roles established and equipment distributed, they proceeded to the mechanism chamber, ascending the spiral staircase with their specialized tools and components. The massive clockworks continued their steady operation, though Alice's sensitivity detected subtle irregularities in the mechanism's rhythm—evidence of growing temporal distortion affecting even this carefully maintained system.

The Pendulum assembly remained secure in its central chamber, the three components—Crystal, Star, and Fulcrum—pulsing with synchronized energy that had noticeably intensified since their last observation. The blue, white, and amber illumination created complex interference patterns that seemed to extend beyond visible light into dimensions Alice could perceive but not fully comprehend.

"The components sense the approaching alignment," Rowan observed, studying the artifacts with ancient eyes. "They prepare for transformation, whether through our guided integration or through more chaotic manifestation if left unaddressed."

Tobias immediately began organizing the implementation process, directing Marcus and Dr. Mackie's assistants in positioning equipment while he prepared the specialized interface components. The first connection point—the northern cardinal position in their octagram configuration—would establish the initial harmonic link between the Pendulum assembly and the clocktower mechanism.

As preparations continued, Alice experienced another perceptual overlay—a momentary glimpse of the same chamber in multiple time streams simultaneously. She saw the current implementation alongside fragments of the 1927 containment ritual and glimpses of what appeared to be the future completion ceremony during the full moon. Most disturbingly, she also perceived a shadow version where the implementation failed catastrophically, the tower itself fracturing as temporal energy escaped containment entirely.

"You see multiple potentials," Rowan noted quietly, observing her reaction. "The junction point where time streams converge or diverge based on our actions here."

"Yes," Alice confirmed. "Including failure scenarios."

"Knowledge of possible failure is valuable," the ancient witch advised. "It shows what must be avoided without determining that it must occur."

With the equipment positioned and preliminary measurements completed, Tobias prepared to install the first integration interface. The specialized component incorporated elements of conventional clockwork precision with the temporal alloys he had described earlier—metals that existed partially outside normal matter, capable of conducting the Pendulum's energy without degradation.

"Initiating first connection sequence," he announced, signaling Dr. Mackie to activate the localized temporal stasis field that would stabilize the selected section of mechanism during modification.

The stasis field shimmered into existence around the northern connection point, creating what appeared to be a bubble of perfect stillness within the otherwise continuously operating clockworks. Within this protected space, Tobias could work without disrupting the mechanism's ongoing function—essential for maintaining the current containment while implementing the enhanced integration.

"Stasis field stable at 99.7% temporal isolation," Dr. Mackie confirmed, monitoring readings on specialized equipment. "You have approximately twenty minutes of optimal working conditions before field degradation begins."

Tobias worked with remarkable precision, his watchmaker's hands steady as he carefully removed the access panel concealing the original integration point his ancestors had built into the clocktower design. The revealed connection matched his technical drawings exactly—confirmation that the tower had indeed been designed from the beginning to accommodate this eventual integration.

"Perfect," he murmured with professional satisfaction. "Exactly as the journals described."

With Marcus assisting, he began installing the specialized interface component, connecting it to both the existing mechanism and the adaptation framework that would ultimately link to the Pendulum assembly. The work required exceptional precision—components that had to align at both physical and temporal levels, creating harmonic resonance rather than merely mechanical connection.

While Tobias implemented the technical aspects, Madame Winters and Rowan prepared the magical reinforcement that would accompany each integration point. Using materials from their ritual components, they created a protective sigil network surrounding the connection—mystical patterns that would help channel and stabilize the Pendulum's energy once the interface was activated.

Alice and Ethan maintained security oversight, with Ethan's enhanced senses continuously monitoring for any indication of interference while Alice extended her temporal perception throughout the tower, alert for disturbances in the surrounding time streams that might indicate approaching threats.

"First interface installation complete," Tobias announced after approximately fifteen minutes of concentrated work. "Ready for initial activation and testing before proceeding to the second connection point."

Dr. Mackie adjusted her equipment to monitor the energy flow as the interface prepared to channel a controlled portion of the Pendulum's output. "Establishing baseline readings for comparison. All monitoring systems active."

"Protective sigils aligned and empowered," Madame Winters confirmed. "Mystical containment ready."

Tobias made a final adjustment to the interface, then nodded to Dr. Mackie. "Deactivate the stasis field. Let's see if it synchronizes properly."

As the temporal stasis field dissipated, the newly installed interface came into contact with the normal timeflow of the surrounding mechanism. For a moment, nothing appeared to happen. Then a subtle resonance began—the interface component emitting a soft harmonic tone as it established a connection with the larger system.

"Initial synchronization successful," Tobias confirmed, monitoring the connection with specialized gauges. "Mechanical integration functioning within optimal parameters."

Dr. Mackie checked her readings with growing excitement. "Energy conductivity established! The interface is successfully channeling a controlled portion of the Pendulum's output into the clocktower mechanism."

Most striking was the visible manifestation of this connection—a thread of combined blue-white-amber light extending from the Pendulum assembly to the northern interface point, flowing through the specialized conduits Tobias had installed. The light didn't merely illuminate but seemed to strengthen the surrounding mechanism, the metal itself appearing more substantive where the energy touched it.

"Temporal reinforcement," Rowan identified the effect. "The mechanism is becoming anchored across multiple time streams simultaneously, increasing its fundamental stability."

Alice extended her perception to assess the broader impact of this initial connection. To her enhanced senses, the thread of energy flowing through the northern interface created a stabilizing effect that extended beyond the tower itself—a pulse of harmonic resonance that rippled outward through Daybridge's temporal fabric, smoothing distortions and strengthening boundaries between periods.

"It's working," she confirmed. "The distortion patterns are already showing measurable improvement, even with just one connection point active."

"The whispers are changing too," Ethan noted, his enhanced hearing detecting the subtle shift in the synchronized clocks throughout the city. "Less urgent, more... rhythmic."

"Exactly as theorized," Tobias said with satisfaction. "Each connection point extends the stabilization field while preparing for the complete octagram configuration. Let's proceed to the eastern position."

They repeated the process for the eastern cardinal point, with Dr. Mackie establishing another temporal stasis field while Tobias and Marcus installed the second interface component. Madame Winters and Rowan created the accompanying sigil network, their magical protections complementing the mechanical integration.

As the second interface activated, a new thread of harmonized light connected it to the Pendulum assembly, creating a partial circuit with the northern point. The stabilizing effect intensified notably, the ripples of harmonic resonance extending farther through Daybridge's temporal fabric.

"Two points active, energy flow stable and balanced," Dr. Mackie reported, reviewing her monitoring data. "Temporal distortion throughout the affected region decreased by approximately 27% from baseline readings."

"The Pendulum responds positively to the integration," Rowan observed, studying the artifacts through the chamber's viewing panel. "The components are aligning more precisely as the connection strengthens."

They proceeded to the southern cardinal point, repeating the now-established procedure with increasing confidence as each successful connection reinforced the growing stability field. With three interface points active, the harmonized energy began forming a more complex pattern—threads of light connecting the Pendulum assembly to the cardinal positions in a triangular configuration that visibly strengthened the surrounding mechanism.

"Temporal distortion reduction now at 43%," Dr. Mackie announced with evident satisfaction. "The stabilization effect is accelerating as predicted."

As they prepared to implement the fourth and final connection for this phase—the western cardinal point that would complete the square configuration—Alice's enhanced perception detected something concerning. A subtle distortion in the temporal fabric near the tower's base, different from the natural anomalies they had been monitoring—more deliberate, more focused.

"Something's approaching," she warned the team. "A temporal signature attempting to bypass our security perimeter."

Ethan immediately contacted the PIU teams at the building's access points, but received confirmation that all entrances remained secure with no detected intrusions. Jerome and Lydia extended their werewolf senses, scanning for supernatural presences that might have evaded conventional detection.

"I sense something too," Jerome confirmed after a moment. "Not physical presence but... influence. Like a projected consciousness rather than a material intrusion."

"Astral approach," Rowan identified immediately. "Someone attempting to access the tower through non-physical means while their body remains elsewhere."

Dr. Mackie consulted her monitoring equipment. "No technological signature detected. Whatever this is, it's purely mystical in nature."

"Continue the implementation," Alice decided after considering their options. "Completing the square configuration will strengthen our position regardless of potential interference. Madame Winters, can you and Rowan establish additional protective measures against astral intrusion?"

"Certainly," the elderly witch confirmed. "Though complete blockage requires knowing the specific approach vector."

While Tobias and his team prepared the western interface component, the witches established a secondary protective circle surrounding the entire mechanism chamber—a mystical barrier designed to repel non-physical intrusions while allowing their legitimate work to continue.

Alice maintained her perceptual monitoring of the approaching disturbance, which appeared to be probing the tower's defenses rather than attempting immediate penetration. The signature felt vaguely familiar, though she couldn't immediately place where she had encountered it before.

"Western interface ready for installation," Tobias announced, drawing her attention back to the implementation process. "Stasis field activated and stable."

They proceeded with the fourth connection point, maintaining heightened awareness of the potential intrusion while completing this critical phase of the integration. Tobias worked with impressive efficiency, his movements economical and precise as he installed the western interface component and connected it to the adaptation framework.

"Installation complete," he reported after twelve minutes of concentrated work. "Ready for activation to complete the square configuration."

As the temporal stasis field dissipated and the western interface prepared to activate, Alice's perception detected a sudden intensification in the approaching disturbance. The probing presence had apparently identified a vulnerability in their protective measures and was now attempting to exploit it.

"Intrusion imminent!" she warned. "Something's breaking through our outer defenses."

Before they could respond, the chamber's atmosphere shimmered with unnatural distortion—a rippling effect like heat haze but moving with a deliberate pattern rather than random fluctuation. Within this distortion, a shadowy figure began to coalesce—translucent at first but gradually gaining definition.

"Astral projection with temporal reinforcement," Rowan identified, immediately strengthening the protective circle with additional incantations. "A sophisticated approach requiring considerable power."

The projection continued materializing despite their countermeasures, eventually forming into a recognizable figure—Diana Blackwood, or rather, her consciousness projected from her physical body elsewhere. The vampire's astral form appeared nearly solid though slightly luminous, her perfect features set in an expression of intense concentration.

"Impressive protective measures," her projected voice acknowledged, sounding distant yet clear. "Though insufficient against techniques refined over centuries."

"Blackwood," Alice identified unnecessarily. "Your resonator experiment failed, so you're trying to direct interference now?"

"Not interference—observation," the vampire's projection corrected. "The Council merely wishes to verify that your implementation proceeds correctly. The Pendulum's stability affects all supernatural beings, after all."

"Observation doesn't require bypassing multiple security layers," Ethan noted skeptically.

"Conventional requests for access seemed unlikely to be approved given our recent... misunderstanding," Blackwood's projection replied smoothly. "And time is of the essence, as you well know."

While they conversed, Alice noticed Tobias and Dr. Mackie exchanging concerned glances before subtly adjusting their equipment—preparing contingencies should Blackwood's "observation" prove more intrusive than claimed.

"Your Council's interest is noted," Alice acknowledged diplomatically. "But this implementation requires focused attention without external distractions. We'll provide a full briefing once the current phase is complete."

"A reasonable offer under normal circumstances," Blackwood's projection conceded. "However, we've detected concerning energy signatures suggesting potential instability in your approach. The northern interface connection appears to be channeling asymmetrical temporal flow—a pattern that could exacerbate rather than reduce distortion if left uncorrected."

The specific technical observation, delivered with such confidence, surprised even Tobias, who quickly glanced at his monitoring gauges before shaking his head slightly to indicate the claim was false.

"Our readings show perfect symmetry across all active connection points," Dr. Mackie stated firmly. "Whatever measurements you're receiving are either inaccurate or deliberately misleading."

Blackwood's projection smiled with perfect composure. "Perhaps our instruments detect subtleties yours cannot. The Council's temporal monitoring technology benefits from centuries of refinement."

The exchange had diverted attention from the western interface, which continued its activation sequence during their conversation. As the final cardinal connection point prepared to complete the square configuration, Alice's enhanced perception detected something alarming—a subtle corruption in the energy flow, seemingly originating from Blackwood's projection itself.

"She's not just observing," Alice realized aloud. "She's attempting to influence the activation pattern!"

Rowan immediately strengthened the protective circle, focusing specific countermeasures toward Blackwood's projection. "Vampire astral forms can carry manipulative energy, especially those of elders who have mastered blood magic."

Blackwood's perfect facade showed momentary irritation at being discovered. "A minor corrective influence only. The Council has experience with temporal artifacts that your makeshift team lacks, despite your admirable efforts thus far."

The western interface reached its activation threshold, the fourth thread of harmonized light extending from the Pendulum assembly to complete the square configuration. As the connection established, a pulse of energy rippled through the entire mechanism—the four cardinal points resonating together to create a strengthened stability field that extended throughout the tower and beyond.

However, where the energy intersected with Blackwood's projection, a visible distortion occurred—the vampire's astral form apparently attempting to redirect a portion of the flow toward purposes unknown. Rowan and Madame Winters immediately reinforced their protective measures, while Dr. Mackie adjusted her equipment to counteract the interference.

"Whatever you're attempting stops now," Alice stated firmly. "Your projection may be difficult to exclude entirely, but we can certainly prevent any manipulation of the energy field."

Blackwood's projection regarded them with calculated assessment before responding. "The Council merely seeks to ensure optimal configuration for all concerned parties. The Pendulum's integration affects supernatural entities differently than humans—a perspective your team may not fully appreciate despite its... diverse composition."

As they confronted the vampire's interference, Alice's enhanced perception detected another approach—a second temporal signature, distinct from Blackwood's but equally deliberate, moving toward the tower from a different vector entirely.

"We have another intrusion attempt," she warned the team. "Different signature, different approach vector."

"The Chronos Society," Blackwood's projection identified immediately, her expression showing genuine concern rather than her usual calculated composure. "They've been monitoring your implementation as well, with considerably less benign intentions than the Council's."

Before they could verify this claim, the chamber's atmosphere distorted again—this time with a harsh, jagged quality unlike the vampire's smoother manifestation. The air seemed to tear rather than ripple, creating a momentary glimpse into what appeared to be another location entirely—a darkened laboratory filled with equipment combining technological and mystical elements.

Through this partial breach appeared another projected consciousness—Professor Harlow, despite his apparent memory loss while in PIU custody. His projection lacked the refined stability of Blackwood's, flickering between solid and transparent states, but carried an intensity that suggested considerable power behind the manifestation.

"The integration must not proceed," Harlow's projected voice declared, sounding distorted and unnatural. "You bind what should be liberated—imprisoning potential within artificial constraints."

"Harlow," Ethan identified with surprise. "Your memory loss was obviously temporary—or fabricated entirely."

"Memory is fluid when one understands temporal mechanics, Detective Reeves," Harlow's projection replied. "A convenient adaptation to circumstances rather than a permanent condition."

The professor's projected form moved toward the Pendulum assembly, seemingly intent on direct interference despite the protective measures surrounding it. Unlike Blackwood's subtle manipulative approach, Harlow appeared prepared for more dramatic intervention.

"The Society grows desperate," Blackwood's projection observed with aristocratic disdain. "Crude methods revealing a limited understanding of true temporal harmony."

"Your Council seeks control rather than harmony," Harlow countered sharply. "Preserving immortal privilege rather than universal liberation."

The conflict between these rival projections created visible distortion in the chamber's atmosphere—competing energies clashing and intensifying the temporal instability their implementation sought to resolve. More concerning was the effect on the newly established connection points, which began fluctuating in response to these external influences.

"The interface stability is compromised," Tobias reported urgently, monitoring his gauges. "These projections are disrupting the harmonic resonance pattern."

"We need to exclude both intrusions immediately," Alice decided. "Rowan, can you and Madame Winters establish a complete barrier rather than merely a protective circle?"

"Possible but challenging with the implementation in progress," the ancient witch confirmed. "We'd need to temporarily suspend energy flow through the connection points to avoid feedback distortion."

"Do it," Alice authorized. "Dr. Mackie, prepare for controlled deactivation of the interface connections. We'll reestablish once the chamber is secured."

As they prepared this protective measure, Harlow's projection made a sudden move toward the western interface—the most recently activated connection point and therefore potentially the most vulnerable. His projected form extended what appeared to be a manipulative energy pattern intended to corrupt or redirect the established flow.

"Stop him!" Blackwood's projection demanded, her own astral form moving to intercept—whether to prevent Harlow's interference or to exploit the opportunity for her own purposes remained unclear.

Tobias reacted instantly, physically positioning himself between Harlow's projection and the vulnerable interface component. Although projections theoretically couldn't interact directly with physical matter, the temporal nature of both the intruder and the implementation created unpredictable conditions where conventional limitations might not apply.

"The interface is stabilizing," he reported, monitoring the gauges while maintaining his protective position. "If we can exclude these projections quickly, the square configuration should self-regulate."

Rowan and Madame Winters accelerated their barrier creation, combining centuries of mystical expertise to establish a complete exclusion field around the mechanism chamber. The air began to shimmer with their implemented protections, the competing projections visibly weakening as the barrier strengthened.

"You cannot exclude us entirely," Harlow's projection insisted, though his form flickered with increasing instability. "The Society's connection to the Pendulum transcends conventional barriers."

"As does the Council's interest," Blackwood's projection added, similarly affected but maintaining greater coherence. "This implementation concerns all who exist within temporal constraints."

As the exclusion barrier neared completion, Alice's enhanced perception detected something alarming—a subtle reconfiguration in the energy pattern emanating from Harlow's projection, shifting from attempted manipulation to what appeared to be deliberate destabilization. The professor wasn't merely trying to influence the implementation now but to actively disrupt it.

"He's attempting to trigger a localized fracture!" she warned the others. "Not control but sabotage!"

Harlow's projection focused intense energy toward the western interface, creating visible distortion in the surrounding mechanism. The harmonized light flowing through the connection point began fluctuating erratically, threatening to break the carefully established pattern maintaining the square configuration.

Tobias responded immediately, physically interposing himself while adjusting the interface controls to counteract the disruption. His expertise with chronometric mechanisms allowed him to make rapid compensatory adjustments, preventing immediate failure but placing himself directly in the path of Harlow's increasingly desperate interference.

"Almost there," Rowan announced as the exclusion barrier strengthened, now visibly constricting both projections despite their resistance. "Maintain positions for thirty more seconds until complete closure."

Harlow's projection, sensing imminent exclusion, appeared to make a final desperate attempt at disruption. His form concentrated into a more focused configuration, directing what seemed to be his remaining projected energy in a single concerted attack on the western interface—and by extension, on Tobias who continued defending it.

"Look out!" Alice warned, her enhanced perception detecting the building energy surge before it manifested physically.

The surge released with unexpected force—not merely magical energy but a temporal distortion that momentarily created a localized fracture point precisely where Tobias stood. The clockmaker had no time to evade as reality around him shimmered and distorted, the boundary between time streams temporarily dissolving.

For a brief, horrifying moment, Tobias existed in multiple states simultaneously—fragmented across several potential time streams as the fracture disrupted his temporal cohesion. Then, as the exclusion barrier finally completed and forcefully ejected both projections from the chamber, the fracture point collapsed back into a singular reality.

Except Tobias was no longer there.

"Tobias!" Marcus cried out, rushing to the spot where his mentor had stood moments earlier. Nothing remained but faintly shimmering air and monitoring equipment now displaying chaotic readings.

"Temporal displacement," Rowan identified immediately, her ancient eyes assessing the residual energy pattern where the clockmaker had vanished. "He's been pushed into the fracture rather than physically harmed."

"Pushed where exactly?" Alice demanded, extending her perceptual abilities to their limit in an attempt to locate him within the surrounding time streams.

"When is perhaps the more relevant question," Dr. Mackie suggested, her scientific perspective providing crucial insight. "The fracture Harlow created was temporal rather than spatial. Tobias has been displaced in time rather than location."

Ethan was already checking the Pendulum assembly, ensuring the artifacts themselves remained secure despite the disruption. "The components are stable, and the interface connections are holding despite the interference. Whatever Harlow attempted failed to compromise the core implementation."

"But succeeded in removing the one person most essential to completing it," Alice noted grimly. "This wasn't random sabotage—it was targeted specifically at Tobias. Harlow knew exactly what he was doing."

"Can we retrieve him?" Marcus asked desperately, still staring at the empty space where his mentor had disappeared. "There must be a way to reverse the displacement."

Rowan and Madame Winters exchanged significant glances before the ancient witch responded. "Possibly. The displacement appears recent enough that his temporal signature remains partially connected to our timestream. With proper techniques, we might establish a retrieval vector."

"What do you need?" Alice asked immediately.

"Something intimately connected to his personal timeline," Rowan specified. "An object carried for years, ideally with emotional significance that strengthens its temporal resonance with his specific pattern."

"His pocket watch," Marcus realized. "The chronometer with the Pendulum fragment—it's been passed through generations of Merricks. He never goes anywhere without it."

"But he was wearing it when he was displaced," Ethan pointed out. "It would have gone with him."

"Not necessarily," Dr. Mackie interjected, reviewing readings from her monitoring equipment. "The displacement event shows unusual energy partitioning—as if something created partial temporal anchoring during the fracture."

She indicated a subtle reading on one of her instruments. "There's a residual signature here consistent with chronometric materials. The watch might have separated during displacement due to its unique properties."

Marcus began carefully searching the area where Tobias had stood, methodically examining the floor and surrounding mechanism components. After several tense moments, he gave a triumphant exclamation.

"Here!" He held up the distinctive pocket watch, its silver case gleaming in the chamber's illumination. "It must have fallen during the displacement."

Rowan took the watch carefully, her ancient eyes studying it with more than physical sight. "This carries strong temporal resonance—not merely with Tobias but with the Merrick bloodline across generations. Excellent for establishing a retrieval connection."

"How long will it take?" Alice asked, acutely aware that their implementation timeline left little room for delays.

"Preparing the retrieval ritual requires specific components," Madame Winters replied. "Some of which we have here among our ritual materials, others we would need to obtain."

"Approximate timeline?" Ethan pressed.

"Several hours for preparation," Rowan estimated. "The ritual itself would be brief but must be precisely timed to align with the displaced individual's temporal signature—which appears to be fluctuating based on these readings."

Alice made a rapid assessment of their situation. The square configuration had been successfully implemented despite the interference, creating a significant improvement in temporal stability throughout Daybridge. The remaining octagram implementation could theoretically proceed without Tobias, though his expertise would be sorely missed, particularly during the final integration ritual.

"We divide efforts," she decided. "Dr. Mackie and Marcus will continue monitoring and maintaining the current implementation. Ethan coordinates security with increased protective measures against further intrusions. Madame Winters and Rowan prepare the retrieval ritual with whatever assistance they require. I'll use my sensitivity to attempt tracking Tobias's temporal signature."

"And if we can't retrieve him before the lunar zenith?" Dr. Mackie asked the question everyone was thinking but hesitant to voice.

"Then we proceed with the final integration regardless," Alice stated firmly. "Tobias would insist on completing the implementation even in his absence. The city's stability must take priority."

As they reorganized to address this unexpected crisis, Alice extended her perceptual abilities throughout the surrounding time streams, searching for any trace of Tobias's distinctive signature. Her enhanced sensitivity, developed through Rowan's intensive training, allowed her to perceive temporal displacements that would remain invisible to conventional observation.

What she detected was concerning—fragmented impressions of Tobias existing across multiple time streams simultaneously, his consciousness apparently shifting between different periods without stabilizing in any single one. The displacement had not simply relocated him to another time but had fractured his temporal cohesion, leaving him adrift between moments.

"I can sense him," she reported to the others. "But he's not stable in any single timestream. He's... shifting, moving between periods without anchoring properly."

"Temporal flux state," Rowan identified with evident concern. "Dangerous for extended duration. Human consciousness isn't designed to process multiple time streams simultaneously without proper protection."

"How long can he survive in such a state?" Ethan asked directly.

"Physically? Perhaps days," the ancient witch replied. "Mentally? Much less. Witnessing too many potential realities simultaneously can overwhelm even the most disciplined mind."

This sobering assessment heightened the urgency of their retrieval efforts. While the implementation remained their primary mission, Tobias's safe return had become a critical secondary objective—both for his personal safety and for the successful completion of the final integration ritual where his expertise would prove invaluable.

As Rowan and Madame Winters began gathering components for the retrieval ritual, Alice continued her perceptual tracking of Tobias's fragmented signature. Among the chaotic impressions, certain patterns emerged—specific periods where his presence appeared stronger, more coherent.

"He seems to be gravitating toward certain time streams," she observed. "Particularly 1927 during the original containment ritual, and 1876 during the clocktower's construction. Periods significant to both the Pendulum and his family history."

"Unconscious temporal affinity," Rowan explained. "Even in flux state, his consciousness seeks familiar patterns—moments connected to his identity and purpose. This actually improves our retrieval chances, as consistent patterns provide stronger connection points."

Dr. Mackie and Marcus focused on maintaining the implemented connections, ensuring the square configuration remained stable despite the disruption. The four cardinal points continued channeling harmonized energy from the Pendulum assembly, creating a balanced stability field that significantly improved temporal conditions throughout Daybridge despite remaining incomplete.

"The interfaces are functioning at 97% efficiency despite the interference," Dr. Mackie reported after thorough diagnostics. "Temporal distortion throughout the affected region remains reduced by approximately 42% from pre-implementation levels."

"And the Pendulum assembly itself?" Alice asked.

"Stable and responsive to the established connections. The components continue their synchronized energy output without interruption."

This confirmation provided some reassurance amid the crisis—their primary mission remained on track despite Harlow's sabotage attempt. The square configuration, while not the complete solution, represented significant progress toward the ultimate goal of permanent integration.

Ethan coordinated with security teams to implement enhanced protective measures throughout the tower, particularly focusing on mystical defenses against further projected intrusions. Jerome and Lydia established a continuous perimeter using werewolf sensory capabilities, while PIU specialists deployed additional technological countermeasures.

"No further approach attempts detected," Ethan reported after these measures were in place. "Though both Blackwood and Harlow likely need recovery time before attempting another projection of that magnitude."

"They won't be the only interested parties," Alice noted. "Now that implementation has begun, others may recognize the opportunity—or threat—it represents."

"The square configuration creates a distinctive energy signature visible to those with appropriate sensitivity," Rowan confirmed. "Many will now realize what we're attempting."

This reality underscored the importance of completing their mission quickly, before additional interference could compromise their progress. The remaining implementation phases—establishing the intercardinal connection points tomorrow and performing the final integration ritual during the lunar zenith—would face increased opposition from various factions with competing agendas regarding the Pendulum's future.

As these protective and monitoring efforts continued, Rowan and Madame Winters completed initial preparations for the retrieval ritual. Using Tobias's pocket watch as a focal point, they established what the ancient witch described as a "temporal tether"—a magical connection that would theoretically allow them to locate and retrieve his consciousness from its fractured state.

"The ritual requires specific timing," Rowan explained as she arranged components in a precise pattern surrounding the watch. "We must conduct it during a moment when his temporal signature achieves maximum coherence in a specific timestream—essentially creating a stable target for extraction."

"How do we identify such a moment?" Alice asked.

"Through your sensitivity," Rowan replied. "You can perceive his shifting patterns more clearly than our instrumental methods. When you detect him stabilizing in a recognizable period, we'll initiate the retrieval sequence."

This responsibility added further weight to Alice's role in their unfolding crisis. Not only would she serve as a conduit during the final integration ritual, but now Tobias's safe return depended on her ability to track and identify his temporal position with sufficient precision for the retrieval to succeed.

As midnight approached, they completed this first phase of their emergency response—establishing enhanced security, maintaining the implemented connections, and preparing for both Tobias's retrieval and the continuation of their implementation schedule. The clocktower mechanism continued its steady operation, the four cardinal connection points glowing with harmonized energy that visibly strengthened the surrounding structure.

Alice took a moment to extend her enhanced perception beyond the tower, assessing conditions throughout Daybridge following their partial implementation. The improvement was immediately apparent—temporal bleeding between periods had significantly decreased, anomalies like the cycling cherry tree had stabilized, and the whispering of synchronized clocks had moderated from urgent warning to steadier rhythm.

However, these improvements remained incomplete. Without the full octagram configuration, distortions continued manifesting in various locations, particularly near ley line intersections where temporal boundaries remained thinnest. The approaching celestial alignment continued intensifying these effects, working against their partial stabilization measures.

"We need to continue implementation tomorrow regardless of whether we've retrieved Tobias," she concluded after sharing these observations. "The square configuration has helped significantly but won't withstand the full alignment without completion to octagram form."

"Marcus and I can handle the mechanical aspects with Dr. Mackie's guidance," Jerome offered. "I've worked with Tobias on clocktower maintenance before—not the same expertise level, but practical knowledge of the mechanism."

"And I can direct the technical integration based on Tobias's designs," Marcus added. "He's been teaching me the principles behind the components, even if I haven't mastered all the implementation details."

This willingness to adapt despite challenging circumstances reinforced Alice's confidence in their team. Each member had stepped forward to address the crisis, offering their respective expertise and support without hesitation.

"Then we proceed as planned," she decided. "Tonight we maintain the current implementation while attempting Tobias's retrieval. Tomorrow we continue with the intercardinal connection points regardless of whether that retrieval succeeds. The final integration ritual proceeds during the lunar zenith as originally scheduled."

As the others acknowledged this directive, Alice experienced another perceptual shift—a momentary glimpse of multiple potential outcomes radiating from their current crisis point. Some showed successful completion, others catastrophic failure, with countless variations between these extremes. The temporal tapestry surrounding the clocktower had become increasingly complex, future possibilities multiplying as the celestial alignment approached.

Most significantly, she perceived something about Tobias's displacement that hadn't been immediately apparent—a pattern suggesting deliberate calculation rather than merely opportunistic sabotage. Harlow's attack had targeted the clockmaker with surprising precision, suggesting foreknowledge of both his importance to the implementation and the specific vulnerability created during interface activation.

"The sabotage was planned," she realized aloud. "Harlow knew exactly when and how to create that localized fracture. He must have had inside information about our implementation schedule and methodology."

"Suggesting a security breach or inside source," Ethan concluded grimly. "Someone with access to our planning or preparation process."

This troubling possibility cast their situation in an even more concerning light. If Harlow had obtained detailed information about their implementation approach, other aspects of their plan might similarly be compromised—including tomorrow's continued installation and the final integration ritual itself.

"We need to identify the source of this breach," Alice decided. "Review everyone with access to implementation details, particularly those who might have connections to either the Chronos Society or competing interests."

As they began this security review, compiling a list of all personnel involved in various aspects of the preparation process, Alice's enhanced perception detected another significant temporal shift in Tobias's fragmentary signature. Among the chaotic impressions of his consciousness shifting between periods, a momentary stability appeared—a clearer image of him apparently interacting with figures in what appeared to be the 1927 containment ritual.

"I have him," she reported urgently to Rowan and Madame Winters. "He's temporarily stabilized in 1927—appears to be observing or possibly participating in the original containment ceremony."

"Perfect opportunity," Rowan confirmed, immediately accelerating her ritual preparations. "If he's achieving coherence in a significant timestream, the retrieval has a higher probability of success."

The ancient witch positioned the pocket watch at the center of an intricate pattern created with specialized materials—crushed crystals, powdered herbs, and what appeared to be actual clock components arranged in a configuration resembling the mechanism chamber's layout in miniature form.

"We need to establish the retrieval vector quickly," she instructed. "Direct your perception toward his signature and maintain focus regardless of surrounding distractions. I'll initiate the connection sequence while Elsbeth reinforces the anchor point here in our timestream."

Alice concentrated on the glimpse of Tobias she had detected, focusing her enhanced perception like a searchlight through the chaotic temporal landscape. His image strengthened as she maintained this focus—the clockmaker appearing more substantial within the 1927 scene, apparently becoming aware of his displaced state as he studied the historical ritual with professional interest.

"He's recognizing his situation," she reported. "Becoming conscious of his displacement rather than merely experiencing it passively."

"Excellent," Rowan approved. "Self-awareness improves retrieval chances significantly. His consciousness can actively participate in returning once we establish a connection."

The ancient witch began the retrieval ritual, her voice taking on resonant qualities that seemed to extend beyond conventional sound—syllables that existed partially outside normal perception, vibrating with temporal significance rather than merely auditory meaning. Madame Winters joined this incantation from her position at the opposite side of the ritual arrangement, their combined expertise creating a harmonized pattern that visibly affected the surrounding atmosphere.

The pocket watch at the center began emitting a subtle illumination—not merely reflecting the chamber's light but generating its own gentle radiance. This luminescence pulsed in a rhythm that matched the Pendulum's energy signature, suggesting a deep connection between the chronometer and the artifacts that had shared its origins.

"Connection establishing," Rowan announced between precisely articulated phrases of the continuing incantation. "Temporal tether forming between anchor point and target signature."

Alice maintained her focused perception, serving as the guidance system for this metaphysical retrieval attempt. Through her sensitivity, she could perceive the forming connection—a thread of concentrated temporal energy extending from their present location toward the 1927 timestream where Tobias had temporarily stabilized.

The connection strengthened gradually, the watch's pulsing illumination intensifying as the tether solidified. Within her perceptual field, Alice could see Tobias becoming aware of this connection—his attention shifting from the historical ritual he was observing toward the tether reaching out to him across decades of separation.

"He sees it," she reported. "He's recognizing the retrieval attempt."

"Guide him," Rowan instructed without interrupting her rhythmic incantation. "Your perception forms the bridge. Help him understand how to follow it back."

Alice had never attempted direct communication across time streams before, but her developing sensitivity suggested possibilities. Focusing her consciousness along the established tether, she projected thoughts toward Tobias's temporal signature—impressions rather than words, intentions rather than specific instructions.

To her surprise, she felt response—acknowledgment and understanding flowing back along the connection. Tobias not only perceived the retrieval attempt but comprehended its purpose and mechanics. His watchmaker's intuitive understanding of temporal principles apparently extended to this metaphysical application as well.

"He's attempting to follow the connection," she reported as his signature began moving along the established tether, gradually shifting from 1927 toward their present timestream.

The ritual's energy intensified visibly, the pattern surrounding the pocket watch glowing with increasing brilliance as the retrieval progressed. Rowan and Madame Winters maintained their harmonized incantation, though Alice could sense the considerable effort this sustained working required from both witches.

As Tobias's signature approached their timestream, resistance manifested—the natural temporal boundaries resisting this unconventional crossing. The connection wavered momentarily, threatening to dissolve before retrieval could complete.

"Resistance at the transition threshold," Rowan identified without breaking rhythm. "Detective Chen, your role as conduit becomes essential here. Channel stabilizing energy through the connection to strengthen his approach vector."

Though uncertain exactly how to accomplish this, Alice instinctively understood the concept. Drawing upon her developing sensitivity, she concentrated on the connection between time streams, visualizing it strengthening and solidifying under her focused attention. Her consciousness extended along this path, meeting Tobias's approaching signature at the point of greatest resistance.

The contact created momentary disorientation as her perception briefly synchronized with his displaced experience—fractured glimpses of multiple time streams, the clocktower existing in various states across decades, faces familiar and unknown moving through overlapping scenes. Within this chaos, Tobias maintained remarkable coherence, his consciousness organized around core principles of chronometric precision despite the temporal distortion surrounding him.

Alice extended stabilizing influence through this contact, her sensitivity providing structure that helped counteract the disruptive resistance at the threshold between time streams. The connection strengthened visibly, the pocket watch's illumination achieving steady brilliance rather than pulsing fluctuation.

"The threshold stabilizes," Rowan confirmed, her ancient voice carrying satisfaction despite evident fatigue. "Final approach vector aligning with present timestream coordinates."

The ritual reached its culmination as the witches' harmonized incantation achieved perfect resonance with the pocket watch's steady illumination. The air above the ritual arrangement shimmered with increasing distortion—not the jagged, disruptive pattern of Harlow's interference but a smoother, more controlled manipulation of temporal boundaries.

Within this controlled distortion, Tobias's form began materializing—translucent at first but gradually gaining substance as his consciousness completed the transition between time streams. Unlike the projected intrusions they had confronted earlier, this manifestation represented actual physical return rather than merely consciousness transmission.

With a final surge of energy that momentarily illuminated the entire chamber, the retrieval completed. The ritual components flared brilliantly before extinguishing, the pocket watch's glow subsiding to normal reflection as Tobias Merrick stood fully materialized in their midst—disoriented but unmistakably present and whole.

"Tobias!" Marcus exclaimed with undisguised relief, moving immediately to support the clockmaker who appeared momentarily unsteady on his feet.

"Fascinating experience," Tobias managed despite obvious exhaustion. "Though not one I'd recommend without proper preparation."

Alice's enhanced perception confirmed his complete return—his temporal signature once again properly anchored in their timestream rather than fragmented across multiple periods. The retrieval had succeeded fully, restoring both his physical presence and temporal cohesion.

"Welcome back," she greeted him simply, though her relief matched Marcus's enthusiasm if expressed more reservedly.

"What did you experience?" Dr. Mackie asked, her scientific curiosity evident despite the serious circumstances.

"Multiple time streams simultaneously," Tobias replied, accepting the chair someone provided as he regained his bearings. "Primarily centered on periods significant to the clocktower and Pendulum—1876 during construction, 1927 during the original containment, even glimpses of potential futures during the approaching alignment."

He focused on Alice with newfound recognition. "I understand your sensitivity much better now. Perceiving multiple time streams simultaneously is... overwhelming without proper contextual framework."

"Did you learn anything useful?" Ethan asked practically. "Anything that might help with our current implementation challenges?"

Tobias nodded thoughtfully, his expression suggesting significant insights despite his fatigued state. "Several critical observations, actually. I witnessed the original 1927 containment ritual from within rather than merely through historical records. Their approach contained elements not documented in the surviving journals—particularly regarding the sigil configuration surrounding the cardinal connection points."

This information immediately captured Rowan's attention. "What specifically about the sigil configuration?"

"They incorporated temporal anchoring elements we haven't included in our current implementation," Tobias explained. "Additional stabilization patterns positioned between the cardinal points rather than merely surrounding them. These appeared to create what I would describe as 'temporal dampening fields' between connection points."

The ancient witch exchanged significant glances with Madame Winters. "This confirms suspicions I've had regarding the original methodology. The surviving grimoire fragments describe anchor points but not the intervening stabilization fields."

"Can we implement these modifications to our existing configuration?" Alice asked.

"Certainly," Rowan confirmed. "Before continuing to the intercardinal connection points tomorrow, we should enhance the existing cardinal implementation with these additional protections."

Tobias had more to share. "I also observed something concerning in glimpses of potential futures—particularly configurations where implementation proceeded without these stabilization fields. In several such futures, the octagram integration created unexpected resonance patterns that amplified rather than contained certain temporal energy frequencies."

"Potential vulnerabilities in our planned approach," Dr. Mackie translated, immediately understanding the implications. "Without these additional stabilization measures, the completed integration might have unintended consequences."

"Precisely," Tobias confirmed. "Most significantly, these vulnerabilities appeared particularly susceptible to external influence—specifically, the kind of harmonic resonance technology Blackwood's organization has been developing."

This revelation cast the vampire's earlier intrusion attempt in a more concerning light. Perhaps her claimed interest in "correcting" their implementation wasn't entirely self-serving manipulation—the Council might genuinely have identified weaknesses in their approach that could be exploited or, from their perspective, improved upon.

"So, Harlow's attack, while certainly destructive in intent, may have inadvertently provided critical information through your displacement," Alice observed. "Information that improves our implementation methodology rather than compromising it."

"Cosmic irony," Tobias acknowledged with a slight smile despite his exhaustion. "Though I wouldn't recommend temporal displacement as a research methodology."

This unexpected positive outcome from what had appeared to be a severe setback reinforced Alice's growing appreciation for temporal complexity—how events that seemed disastrous in immediate context might serve essential purposes within broader patterns. Their implementation plan had been good, but Tobias's displacement had potentially prevented serious flaws from manifesting during final integration.

"We should document these modifications immediately," she decided. "Update our implementation plan for tomorrow's continuation while the observations remain clear."

While Tobias worked with Rowan and Madame Winters to document the enhanced sigil configurations he had observed, Alice returned to her earlier concern regarding the information breach that had enabled Harlow's precisely targeted attack. The clockmaker's displacement and subsequent retrieval had temporarily overshadowed this security issue, but it remained a critical vulnerability that required addressing before they proceeded with further implementation.

"We still need to identify how Harlow obtained such specific information about our implementation methodology," she reminded Ethan as they reviewed security protocols. "The precision of his attack suggests detailed knowledge of both our schedule and technical approach."

"I've compiled a list of everyone with access to implementation details," Ethan reported, displaying the information on a tablet.

"Thirty-seven individuals with varying levels of knowledge about different aspects of the project."

Alice reviewed the list, noting that it included PIU personnel, university staff supporting Dr. Mackie, Pack members providing security, municipal employees with clocktower access, and various consultants who had contributed to specialized components or protective measures.

"Too many to investigate thoroughly before tomorrow's continuation," she observed. "We need to narrow the field based on probable connection to either the Chronos Society or competing interests."

As they began this analysis, eliminating individuals with limited knowledge or strong positive verification, Tobias rejoined them—his documentation of the enhanced implementation methodology temporarily complete and his energy visibly returning after the displacement ordeal.

"I've been considering the sabotage attempt," he informed them. "Something about Harlow's approach suggested familiarity not just with our implementation schedule but with specific vulnerabilities in the western interface component."

"What kind of vulnerabilities?" Alice asked immediately.

"Technical details regarding the temporal alloy configuration," Tobias explained. "The western interface incorporated a slightly different composition than the other three cardinal components—a necessary adaptation to that quadrant's specific mechanical requirements. This difference created a momentary stabilization gap during initial activation—precisely when Harlow attempted to create the localized fracture."

"That level of technical detail wouldn't be included in general briefings," Ethan noted. "It suggests someone with direct access to your manufacturing process or component specifications."

This observation narrowed their focus considerably. Only a handful of individuals had been present during the detailed fabrication of the interface components or had access to the technical specifications describing their composition.

"The museum curator," Alice realized suddenly, remembering a detail that had seemed insignificant at the time. "Dr. Eleanor Whittaker from the Supernatural Artifacts Museum. She visited your shop last week to discuss preservation techniques for temporal artifacts, specifically requesting information about the alloys you were using for the integration components."

"Yes," Tobias confirmed with growing concern. "She expressed scholarly interest in historical metallurgical techniques related to chronometric artifacts. I provided general information but nothing about specific component vulnerabilities."

"Unless she gleaned more than you realized," Ethan suggested. "Her position gives her access to extensive historical documentation about temporal artifacts, possibly including materials related to the Chronos Society's previous work."

"And the timing of her visit coincided with our early implementation planning," Alice added. "Before we had established comprehensive security protocols around the project."

This potential connection warranted immediate investigation. Dr. Eleanor Whittaker had impeccable academic credentials and a respected position at the Supernatural Artifacts Museum—not an obvious Chronos Society affiliate. However, the museum itself had featured prominently in their investigation of the calling stone, and historical records indicated connections between the institution and various esoteric organizations throughout its existence.

"We should review her background more thoroughly," Alice decided. "Particularly any associations or research interests that might suggest Chronos Society connection."

Ethan immediately contacted PIU headquarters to request comprehensive background information on Dr. Whittaker, while Alice considered the implications if this potential infiltration proved accurate. The museum curator had presented herself as a scholarly ally interested in preserving supernatural artifacts rather than exploiting them—a position that had seemed aligned with their own protective approach to the Pendulum.

"If Whittaker is connected to the Chronos Society, we need to reconsider museum security as well," she noted. "The calling stone remains in our containment, but other artifacts with temporal properties might still be accessible in their collection."

"I'll contact Captain Vaughn to authorize enhanced security measures at the museum," Ethan agreed. "Though without definitive evidence of wrongdoing, we'll need to frame it as precautionary rather than accusatory."

While they pursued this investigative angle, Tobias returned to reviewing the implementation status with Marcus and Dr. Mackie. Despite the disruption caused by his displacement, the square configuration remained stable, continuing to channel harmonized energy from the Pendulum assembly through the four cardinal connection points.

"The partial integration is performing even better than anticipated," Dr. Mackie reported after completing thorough diagnostics. "Temporal distortion throughout the affected region has decreased by 46% from baseline readings—slightly better than our earlier measurement."

"The system appears to be self-optimizing," Tobias observed with professional satisfaction. "As the connection points continue channeling the Pendulum's energy, they're establishing more efficient pathways through the mechanism."

This positive development provided some reassurance amid their security concerns. Whatever Harlow's ultimate objective, his sabotage attempt had failed to compromise the implementation's core functionality. The square configuration continued stabilizing Daybridge's temporal fabric, providing essential protection as the celestial alignment approached.

As midnight passed and early morning hours approached, their emergency response transitioned to forward planning. Tobias's retrieval had been successful, and the enhanced implementation methodology he had observed during displacement promised to strengthen their approach. The square configuration remained stable despite the interference attempt, and security measures had been enhanced throughout the tower.

The potential security breach regarding Dr. Whittaker required investigation but wouldn't delay their implementation schedule. Tomorrow they would proceed with the intercardinal connection points, completing the octagram configuration in preparation for the final integration ritual during the lunar zenith.

Alice took a moment to extend her enhanced perception beyond immediate concerns, assessing broader patterns surrounding their unfolding mission. The temporal landscape continued evolving as the celestial alignment approached—time streams converging toward what appeared to be a critical junction point coinciding precisely with the lunar zenith.

Among these converging patterns, she perceived something that hadn't been immediately apparent earlier—a sense of expectation, almost anticipation, emanating from the Pendulum assembly itself. The artifacts weren't merely passive components in their implementation but appeared to be responding to the approaching alignment with something resembling consciousness—not human awareness but a form of intentionality that transcended conventional understanding.

"The Pendulum knows," she murmured, drawing curious glances from those nearby.

"Knows what exactly?" Ethan asked.

"That this alignment is different from previous cycles," Alice attempted to articulate her perception. "That the integration we're implementing represents something beyond mere containment or control. It's... responding to our efforts, not merely being affected by them."

Rowan nodded with understanding beyond the others. "Artifacts of such power often develop what might be termed 'intentional resonance' over time. Not consciousness as we understand it, but patterns of response that transcend their material properties."

"You're suggesting the Pendulum actively participates in its integration?" Dr. Mackie questioned, her scientific perspective challenged by this concept.

"Not with purpose as humans conceive it," Rowan clarified. "But with a form of pattern recognition that aligns with certain configurations and resists others. What we perceive as optimal integration may be what the artifact itself 'prefers' energetically."

This perspective added yet another dimension to their already complex mission. If the Pendulum itself participated in its integration through some form of energetic preference, their implementation approach might benefit from greater adaptability—responding to the artifacts' natural tendencies rather than imposing rigid configuration regardless of energetic feedback.

"We should incorporate response monitoring into tomorrow's implementation," Alice suggested. "Adjust our approach based on how the Pendulum reacts to each connection point rather than following predetermined configurations exclusively."

"Adaptive implementation," Tobias translated this concept into a practical methodology. "We've already observed self-optimization in the square configuration. Expanding this principle to the intercardinal connections makes excellent sense."

As they refined this approach, incorporating both the enhanced sigil configurations Tobias had observed during displacement and this new adaptive methodology, Alice's phone chimed with an incoming message from PIU headquarters—preliminary information regarding Dr. Eleanor Whittaker's background investigation.

The report confirmed her academic credentials and professional history but highlighted several concerning associations—research collaborations with individuals previously identified as Chronos Society affiliates, unexplained funding sources for certain specialized projects, and frequent travel to locations associated with temporal anomalies worldwide.

Most significantly, genealogical research revealed a distant family connection to Professor Harlow himself—a great-uncle who had been among the Chronos Society's founding members in the early 20th century. This relationship had never been publicly acknowledged in her professional biography or museum credentials.

"Definite Chronos Society connection," Alice concluded after reviewing this information. "Not conclusive proof of involvement in the sabotage attempt, but certainly sufficient to warrant heightened scrutiny."

"And consistent with their long-term approach," Ethan noted. "Placing affiliated individuals in positions with access to relevant artifacts and information, often generations in advance of specific operations."

This confirmation of their suspicions highlighted the Chronos Society's patient, multigenerational strategy—positioning resources and assets decades before they might be needed, maintaining a network of influence that extended throughout institutions relevant to their temporal interests.

"We should adjust tomorrow's security protocols accordingly," Alice decided. "Particular focus on preventing further projected intrusions or physical infiltration attempts. If Whittaker provided information about our implementation approach, she likely knows our schedule for completing the octagram configuration."

With this additional security concern addressed, they finalized plans for the night's remaining hours. Most team members would rest in shifts, maintaining essential monitoring and security while recovering from the day's considerable exertions. The square configuration required minimal active management, its self-optimizing nature handling minor fluctuations without intervention.

Tomorrow would bring the next critical phase—implementing the intercardinal connection points to complete the octagram configuration. With an enhanced methodology based on Tobias's displacement observations and adaptive implementation responding to the Pendulum's energetic preferences, they had significantly improved their approach despite Harlow's sabotage attempt.

The betrayal had been identified, if not yet fully confirmed, and their security measures strengthened accordingly. Most importantly, they had successfully retrieved their implementation expert, whose unique insights gained through displacement might ultimately prove more valuable than the undisrupted original approach would have been.

As team members dispersed to their assigned rest or monitoring positions, Alice remained briefly in the mechanism chamber, her enhanced perception studying the harmonized energy flowing through the four cardinal connection points. The square configuration created beautiful patterns in her temporal sensitivity—stabilizing ripples extending throughout Daybridge's fabric, strengthening boundaries between time streams while maintaining essential connections between them.

The whispering of synchronized clocks had evolved further, no longer warning but guiding—rhythmic patterns that seemed to suggest the approaching integration rather than merely anticipating crisis. Throughout the city, temporal anomalies continued stabilizing under the square configuration's influence, though significant distortions remained in areas beyond its current reach.

Tomorrow's implementation would extend this stability field to its full designed coverage. The octagram configuration would prepare the way for the final integration ritual during the lunar zenith—the culmination of work begun generations earlier when the clocktower was first designed to eventually house the Pendulum assembly.

Despite the betrayal and sabotage, they had confronted, their mission continued advancing toward its essential purpose. Time itself seemed to be cooperating with their efforts, patterns converging toward the integration they sought to implement rather than merely resisting their intervention.

The Pendulum of Aeon pulsed steadily at the center of these converging patterns, its three components harmonizing with increasing precision as the alignment approached. Whatever consciousness or intentionality the artifact possessed seemed aligned with their implementation approach—not merely accepting containment but participating in integration.

Tomorrow would bring new challenges, likely including further interference attempts from both the Chronos Society and competing interests like the Vampire Council. But tonight, had demonstrated their team's resilience and adaptability—transforming crisis into opportunity, betrayal into improved methodology.

The clocktower stood as it had for nearly 150 years, measuring time with mechanical precision while concealing far more significant purposes within its architectural design. Soon it would fulfill its ultimate function—not merely containing the Pendulum of Aeon but integrating it into a harmonized system that stabilized temporal integrity throughout Daybridge and beyond.

The countdown continued, each measured tick bringing them closer to either permanent resolution or catastrophic failure. Which outcome awaited remained uncertain, but their path forward had never been clearer.

Time would tell.

And they would help it speak.

CHAPTER FOURTEEN: BETWEEN MOMENTS

Tobias Merrick had never expected to experience time from the outside.

As a watchmaker, he had dedicated his life to measuring time's passage with mechanical precision—creating and maintaining instruments that divided existence into orderly segments of seconds, minutes, and hours. Time had always been something he observed rather than experienced directly.

Until now.

The localized fracture created by Harlow's sabotage had thrust him into a state beyond conventional temporal experience—not simply relocated to another period but suspended between moments, his consciousness fragmenting across multiple time streams simultaneously. The sensation defied description through normal language, which presumed linear progression as its fundamental framework.

In the first disorienting moments following his displacement, Tobias perceived Daybridge's history as overlapping layers—the city existing in all its iterations simultaneously, buildings rising and falling like breath, streets widening and narrowing with the pulse of urban evolution. Human figures moved through these overlapping realities, their lives compressed into streaks of motion and purpose spanning decades in what felt like minutes.

Gradually, his watchmaker's mind—trained to perceive order within complexity—began organizing this chaos. Rather than experiencing all periods simultaneously, he learned to focus on specific temporal layers, directing his attention like adjusting a lens to bring particular moments into clarity while allowing others to fade temporarily into background impressions.

The clocktower became his anchor point—the one structure that maintained relative consistency throughout the chaotic temporal landscape. By focusing on its familiar form, Tobias could stabilize his perception enough to observe specific periods with greater coherence.

His consciousness seemed naturally drawn to moments significant to both the tower and his family's connection to it. The 1876 construction period manifested with particular clarity—he witnessed his great-grandfather consulting with architects, insisting on specific design elements that would accommodate future modifications. These weren't merely aesthetic preferences but deliberate preparations for the clocktower's ultimate purpose as housing for the Pendulum of Aeon.

"The mechanism chamber must maintain these precise dimensions," his ancestor instructed workers with unmistakable authority. "The harmonic resonance requires specific spatial ratios to function properly."

More fascinating was observing how his great-grandfather incorporated hidden features throughout the design—connection points concealed within conventional clockwork elements, access panels disguised as decorative features, even structural reinforcements positioned where temporal energy would eventually flow through implemented interfaces.

The tower had never been merely a timekeeping device or architectural landmark. From its very conception, it had been designed as a temporal stabilization mechanism awaiting its core component—the Pendulum that would eventually provide both its purpose and power.

As Tobias grew more adept at navigating between temporal layers, his perception stabilized on another significant period—1927, when the first temporal fracture had manifested and his grandfather had implemented the initial containment ritual. This moment held particular relevance to their current crisis, potentially offering insights unavailable in surviving documentation.

The mechanism chamber appeared much as it did in Tobias's own time, though lacking modern electrical equipment and safety features. His grandfather—Harold Merrick, whose journals had guided their recent investigations—directed a team combining technical experts and magical practitioners in what was clearly an emergency response rather than planned implementation.

"The fracture expands by the hour," Harold informed his assembled team, his expression showing the same determined focus Tobias recognized from family photographs. "Conventional boundaries between periods are dissolving throughout the downtown district. We must establish containment before midnight or risk complete temporal collapse."

Tobias observed with professional appreciation as his grandfather modified the clocktower mechanism to accommodate the Pendulum Crystal—the only component they possessed at that time. The approach differed significantly from what surviving journals described, incorporating elements that had apparently been deemed too sensitive for written documentation.

Most notably, Harold implemented a sigil configuration surrounding the Pendulum chamber that created what appeared to be temporal dampening fields—mystical barriers that regulated energy flow between the artifact and surrounding mechanism. These dampening fields established precisely calibrated resistance patterns, preventing uncontrolled energy discharge while allowing sufficient flow to maintain stabilization effect.

"The sigils must form interlocking fields," Harold instructed the witches assisting with this aspect of the implementation. "Not merely containing the energy but directing it through specific channels. Think of it as creating temporal circuitry rather than simple barriers."

This approach was considerably more sophisticated than what Tobias had reconstructed from the surviving journals, which described straightforward containment rather than this nuanced energy management system. The discrepancy suggested deliberate omission from written records—perhaps to prevent this methodology from being misapplied by those seeking to manipulate rather than stabilize temporal energy.

As midnight approached in this historical scene, Tobias observed the ritual reaching its culmination. The assembled practitioners formed a circle around the mechanism chamber, their combined efforts creating a powerful stabilization field as Harold activated the modified clocktower mechanism. The Pendulum Crystal pulsed with blue light that gradually synchronized with the tower's mechanical rhythm, establishing harmonized oscillation that extended throughout the structure.

The fracture visibly responded—temporal bleeding between periods diminishing as boundaries reasserted themselves throughout affected areas. The containment appeared successful, though Harold's expression showed concern rather than satisfaction as the ritual concluded.

"It's holding," he confirmed to his anxious team. "But without the companion components, this remains temporary solution rather than permanent resolution. The fracture will eventually reassert itself during future alignments."

This observation aligned with their current understanding, but what followed proved more enlightening. Harold gathered his most trusted associates—two witches from the Winters coven and a werewolf Tobias recognized as an ancestor of Ethan's partner—for private consultation away from the larger group.

"The Society will continue seeking the remaining components," Harold informed them in hushed tones. "They understand now that the Pendulum's power can be accessed through proper implementation. Our temporary containment only increases their determination to achieve complete liberation."

"Then we must prepare for future attempts," one witch—presumably Madame Winters' grandmother—responded with grim determination. "Establish protections that will outlast our individual lifespans."

"Precisely," Harold agreed. "We've contained this crisis, but future generations will face its return. We must leave them the tools and knowledge to implement permanent resolution when all components are finally assembled."

This historical conversation explained much about the deliberate knowledge preservation system that had guided Tobias's recent investigations—the carefully maintained family journals with their strategic omissions, the specialized chronometer passed through generations, the hidden observatory beneath his shop. His ancestors had created an intergenerational response plan, preserving essential knowledge while concealing it from those who might misuse it.

Most significantly, Harold showed his associates a technical drawing depicting the complete octagram configuration they were currently implementing—the eight-point integration system that would harmonize the Pendulum assembly with the clocktower mechanism. This confirmed that their current approach aligned with the original design intent rather than representing a modern interpretation of fragmented historical records.

As Tobias focused on memorizing these technical details, his perception began shifting again—the 1927 scene dissolving as his consciousness drifted toward another significant temporal layer. The disorientation returned briefly before resolving into a new period—the present day, but viewed from outside normal temporal progression.

He could perceive the mechanism chamber where his physical body had been displaced, observing his colleagues responding to the crisis. The scene appeared slightly distorted, as though viewed through rippling water, but he could discern their actions as they assessed the situation and began organizing retrieval efforts.

Most intriguing was observing Alice's developing sensitivity from this external perspective. Her consciousness appeared distinctly different from the others—trailing wisps of temporal energy that extended beyond conventional boundaries, suggesting a capacity to perceive and potentially influence temporal patterns directly. This confirmed what Rowan had suggested about her natural affinity for temporal work—Alice wasn't merely developing sensitivity through exposure but manifesting latent abilities that had always existed beneath conscious awareness.

Tobias attempted communication, trying to project information about the sigil configurations he had observed in 1927, but found himself unable to establish direct contact. His consciousness remained separated from conventional interaction, capable of observation but not participation in events unfolding in normal temporal progression.

As he continued observing their retrieval preparations, his perception shifted once more—but instead of another historical period, he glimpsed what appeared to be potential futures radiating from the present crisis point. These were less distinct than historical scenes, more impression than observation, suggesting multiple possible outcomes rather than predetermined events.

In some potential futures, the integration succeeded brilliantly—the octagram configuration creating perfect harmony between the Pendulum assembly and clocktower mechanism, establishing permanent temporal stability throughout Daybridge and beyond. In others, partial success created improved but incomplete stabilization, requiring ongoing maintenance rather than self-sustaining resolution.

Most concerning were glimpses of failure scenarios—configurations where the integration created unexpected resonance patterns, amplifying rather than containing certain temporal energy frequencies. These potential futures showed catastrophic consequences including expanding temporal fractures that consumed entire districts or even complete disintegration of conventional timeflow throughout the region.

Tobias focused intently on identifying factors that differentiated successful integration from catastrophic failure. The pattern became increasingly clear—implementations incorporating the dampening field sigils he had observed in 1927 consistently achieved better outcomes than those relying solely on the octagram configuration without these additional protective measures.

This critical insight might explain why his grandfather had implemented temporary containment rather than attempting permanent resolution even after the Anchor Star was recovered in 1927. Without the complete Pendulum assembly including the Fulcrum, the dampening fields couldn't achieve proper balance across all energy frequencies—creating risk of amplification rather than stabilization for certain temporal harmonics.

As Tobias assimilated this understanding, he became aware of something unexpected—a retrieval attempt forming around his fragmented consciousness. The sensation manifested as a tether extending from his present timestream, creating what felt like gravitational attraction amid the chaotic temporal landscape he had been navigating.

He recognized Alice's distinctive temporal signature forming the perceptual component of this tether—her developing sensitivity serving as a guidance system for what appeared to be a ritual implemented by Rowan and Madame Winters. The witches had established a retrieval vector using his pocket watch as a focal point, creating a path his consciousness could potentially follow back to proper temporal anchoring.

Understanding the opportunity this presented, Tobias concentrated on the established connection, allowing his fragmented consciousness to be drawn along this metaphysical lifeline toward his home timestream. The journey proved challenging—resistance at temporal boundaries creating disorientation and momentary dissolution of coherent thought—but Alice's focused perception provided crucial stability throughout the transition.

With a sensation resembling physical impact, Tobias found himself suddenly reintegrated with his physical form, standing in the mechanism chamber surrounded by his concerned colleagues. The displacement had ended, his consciousness once again properly anchored within conventional temporal progression.

The experience had been harrowing but tremendously informative. His observations during displacement—particularly regarding the dampening field sigils and their critical role in successful integration—provided essential refinements to their implementation approach. What had appeared to be sabotage might ultimately strengthen their methodology, transforming potential catastrophic failure into improved probability of success.

"Fascinating experience," he managed despite overwhelming exhaustion. "Though not one I'd recommend without proper preparation."

While Tobias remained trapped between time streams, the implementation team confronted both immediate crisis and broader security implications. Alice's enhanced perception had tracked his fragmented temporal signature while simultaneously coordinating with Rowan and Madame Winters to prepare retrieval methodology. This dual focus—maintaining contact with Tobias's displaced consciousness while addressing practical response requirements—tested her developing abilities significantly.

"I can sense him shifting between periods," she reported to the others, maintaining perceptual connection despite the disorientation this created. "Primarily focusing on historically significant moments—the tower's construction, the 1927 containment, occasionally returning to observe our present situation."

"Is he injured?" Marcus asked with evident concern for his mentor.

"Not physically," Alice clarified. "His consciousness remains intact despite fragmentation across time streams. He appears to be actively studying what he observes rather than merely experiencing displacement passively."

This characteristic approach—the watchmaker analyzing temporal mechanics even while personally affected by them—provided some reassurance amid the crisis. Tobias's methodical nature might help him maintain coherence long enough for their retrieval attempt to succeed.

While Rowan and Madame Winters prepared the ritual components required for this retrieval, Ethan focused on the security breach that had enabled Harlow's precisely targeted attack. The werewolf detective's expression showed controlled anger as he reviewed personnel records and access logs, seeking connections that might identify their vulnerability.

"The infiltration was sophisticated," he noted grimly. "Harlow's projected form manifested at precisely the moment of greatest vulnerability during the western interface activation. That level of timing requires inside information about both our schedule and technical specifications."

Alice shared her suspicion regarding Dr. Eleanor Whittaker, the museum curator whose recent interest in Tobias's implementation components now appeared potentially significant. The timing of her visit, combined with her position at an institution historically connected to temporal artifacts, suggested possible Chronos Society affiliation.

"We need confirmation before making accusations," Ethan cautioned, though his expression suggested he found the connection plausible. "Museum curators have a legitimate scholarly interest in historical technologies, and the supernatural community in Daybridge is relatively small. Professional overlap doesn't necessarily indicate malicious intent."

"Agreed," Alice acknowledged. "But her specific interest in the temporal alloy composition of the interface components—precisely where Harlow targeted his attack—warrants investigation regardless of potential Society connection."

While they pursued this investigative angle, Dr. Mackie and Marcus focused on maintaining the implemented square configuration despite the disruption caused by Harlow's interference. The four cardinal connection points continued channeling harmonized energy from the Pendulum assembly, creating a stability field that significantly improved temporal conditions throughout Daybridge even while remaining incomplete.

"The interfaces are functioning within acceptable parameters despite the attack," Dr. Mackie reported after thorough diagnostics. "The square configuration maintains approximately 94% efficiency—lower than optimal but sufficient to prevent critical destabilization until we complete the octagram implementation."

This assessment provided some reassurance amid their security concerns. Whatever Harlow's ultimate objective, his sabotage attempt had failed to compromise the implementation's core functionality. The partial integration continued providing essential protection as they addressed the broader implications of the security breach and worked to retrieve their displaced colleague.

Alice maintained her perceptual connection with Tobias's fragmented signature, noting significant patterns in his movement between time streams. "He appears to be studying the 1927 containment ritual with particular focus," she reported to Rowan. "His signature achieves greater coherence when observing this period than during other temporal shifts."

"Naturally drawn to relevant historical moments," the ancient witch confirmed. "His consciousness seeks information pertinent to our current implementation challenges even while displaced. This focused interest creates a stronger temporal signature than random displacement would produce—improving our retrieval chances significantly."

This observation proved crucial when establishing the retrieval vector during their subsequent ritual attempt. Alice's ability to track Tobias's consciousness as it stabilized within the 1927 timestream provided the precision targeting necessary for successful connection. The pocket watch served as a physical anchor point, its connection to both Tobias personally and the Merrick family lineage creating resonance that transcended conventional temporal boundaries.

The retrieval succeeded despite considerable metaphysical complexity, returning Tobias to proper temporal anchoring with his consciousness intact and his observations preserved. His insights regarding the dampening field sigils used during the original containment ritual provided critical refinements to their implementation methodology—potentially transforming crisis into opportunity by revealing historical techniques that had been deliberately omitted from written records.

Following his recovery and their subsequent revision of implementation plans, the team confronted the security breach more directly. PIU background investigation into Dr. Eleanor Whittaker had revealed concerning associations with known Chronos Society affiliates, including previously undisclosed family connection to

Professor Harlow himself. This confirmation of their suspicions highlighted the Society's patient, multigenerational approach to positioning assets within institutions relevant to their temporal interests.

"We need to confront her directly," Alice decided after reviewing this information. "If she provided Harlow with implementation details, she represents ongoing security vulnerability for tomorrow's continued installation and the final integration ritual."

"Confrontation risks alerting other Society members if she is indeed affiliated," Ethan cautioned. "We could instead implement enhanced security protocols without directly addressing her suspected involvement—essentially closing the vulnerability without confirming we've identified its source."

"Too passive," Alice disagreed. "If Whittaker is actively working with Harlow, she'll continue seeking alternative methods to compromise our implementation. Better to remove the threat directly rather than merely defending against its potential manifestations."

This approach aligned with Alice's law enforcement background—identifying and neutralizing threats proactively rather than establishing defensive perimeters that clever adversaries might eventually circumvent. Ethan recognized the strategic validity despite his initial caution, particularly given the critical importance of tomorrow's continued implementation.

"How do we approach her without creating public incident?" he asked practically. "The museum represents a significant cultural institution within Daybridge, and Whittaker holds a respected academic position regardless of potential Society affiliation."

"Professional pretext," Alice suggested. "We request her consultation regarding temporal artifacts affected by recent disturbances—a plausible reason to bring her to the clocktower given her expertise. Once here, we can address our concerns privately while maintaining public professional courtesy."

This approach balanced security requirements with necessary discretion. A public confrontation risked both alerting other Society members and potentially undermining community confidence in a significant cultural institution during already unsettling period of temporal disturbances.

With this plan established, Ethan contacted Dr. Whittaker early the following morning, extending a formal invitation for consultation regarding "preservation considerations for chronometric artifacts experiencing temporal field distortion." The pretext seemed sufficiently technical and specific to justify urgent consultation while remaining within her professional expertise.

The curator accepted with what Alice perceived as suspicious readiness—expressing immediate availability despite the early hour and minimal explanation provided regarding the consultation's specific purpose. This eagerness to access the clocktower implementation site reinforced their suspicions regarding her potential involvement in Harlow's sabotage attempt.

While awaiting Whittaker's arrival, the implementation team continued preparations for the day's critical work—installing the four intercardinal connection points that would complete the octagram configuration. Tobias had recovered remarkably well from his displacement experience, his natural adaptation to temporal complexities apparently extending to personal exposure as well as theoretical understanding.

"The intercardinal interfaces incorporate enhanced stabilization features based on what I observed during displacement," he explained, displaying modified components that integrated the dampening field technology from the 1927 containment ritual. "These will create balanced resistance patterns between cardinal connection points, preventing uncontrolled energy discharge while maintaining optimal flow characteristics."

These modifications represented a significant improvement over their original design, addressing potential vulnerabilities that might otherwise have created catastrophic resonance during final integration. The temporal dampening fields would prevent external manipulation through harmonic technologies like Blackwood's resonator while ensuring balanced energy distribution throughout the completed octagram configuration.

Dr. Whittaker arrived precisely at the appointed time, presenting professional demeanor that revealed nothing of potential ulterior motives. Her appearance matched her academic reputation—a woman in her late forties with silver-streaked dark hair styled conservatively and wire-rimmed glasses that complemented her scholarly aesthetic. She carried a leather portfolio containing what appeared to be reference materials related to the consultation pretext.

"Detective Chen, Detective Reeves," she greeted them with courteous professionalism. "Fascinating opportunity to observe chronometric artifacts under active temporal field influence. The museum has recorded significant effects on our own collection during recent disturbances—temporal resonance patterns affecting artifact stability across multiple classification categories."

Alice studied the curator carefully as they escorted her through initial security checkpoints. Her enhanced perception detected nothing immediately suspicious in Whittaker's temporal signature—no obvious indications of magical augmentation or technological enhancement that might suggest preparation for sabotage attempt. However, subtle inconsistencies in her demeanor suggested rehearsed responses rather than genuine academic enthusiasm—particularly regarding specific technical terminology that seemed deliberately incorporated into her conversation.

"We've implemented protective measures around particularly sensitive artifacts," Whittaker continued as they approached the mechanism chamber. "Though without understanding the source of these disturbances, our preservation efforts remain somewhat speculative. Your insights regarding the phenomenon's core mechanics would be tremendously valuable from a conservation perspective."

This transparent fishing for implementation details further confirmed Alice's suspicions. The curator was attempting to extract information while maintaining plausible scholarly interest—a sophisticated approach that might have succeeded had they not already identified her potential Society affiliation.

"We're still analyzing the disturbance patterns ourselves," Alice replied noncommittally. "Today's consultation focuses specifically on chronometric artifacts experiencing harmonic resonance disruption—particularly those incorporating temporal alloys similar to what we've observed in the clocktower mechanism."

This deliberate reference to the technical specifications Whittaker had allegedly provided to Harlow produced a subtle but detectable reaction—momentary tension in her expression before professional composure reasserted itself. The curator's gaze flickered briefly toward the western interface where Tobias had been displaced, suggesting specific knowledge of yesterday's events beyond what public information would provide.

"Temporal alloys present unique preservation challenges," Whittaker responded after this telling hesitation. "Their quasi-dimensional properties create conservation requirements that conventional metallurgical approaches can't adequately address. I've developed specialized techniques based on extensive examination of historical examples in our collection."

As they entered the mechanism chamber, Ethan positioned himself strategically near the exit while Alice guided their guest toward the implemented cardinal connection points. Tobias remained at his workstation preparing the intercardinal components, acknowledging Whittaker with professional courtesy that revealed nothing of their suspicions regarding her involvement in his recent displacement.

"The cardinal implementation appears to be stabilizing the surrounding temporal field quite effectively," Whittaker observed, studying the energized connection points with evident interest. "Fascinating integration approach—reminiscent of techniques described in certain historical documents within our restricted archives."

"Which historical documents specifically?" Alice inquired casually. "We've been researching precedents for this implementation methodology and would value scholarly references we might have overlooked."

This deliberate opening provided an opportunity for Whittaker to either maintain her academic cover by providing legitimate references or reveal potential Society knowledge through specific technical details not available in conventional historical documentation. Her response would help confirm the extent of her involvement beyond circumstantial connection.

The curator hesitated momentarily before responding with carefully measured precision. "Several journals from the 1927 period reference similar integration techniques, though without technical specificity that modern implementation would require. The Harlow Collection in particular contains interesting theoretical approaches to chronometric harmonic distribution across mechanical integration points."

The casual reference to "the Harlow Collection" represented significant mistake—confirming a connection to Professor Harlow beyond what her public credentials acknowledged. This collection wasn't cataloged under that name in official museum documentation but represented private archival materials maintained by the Chronos Society outside institutional record-keeping.

"Interesting that you'd reference that collection specifically," Alice noted, maintaining conversational tone while signaling Ethan to move closer. "Particularly given its restricted access protocols and your previously undisclosed familial connection to its namesake."

Whittaker's expression revealed momentary surprise followed by calculation—recognition that her cover had been compromised followed by rapid assessment of available options. Her gaze darted toward the western interface component once more, suggesting continued interest in the technical vulnerability that had enabled yesterday's sabotage attempt.

"Academic interest often follows family tradition," she responded with forced casualness. "Though I've maintained a professional separation between institutional responsibilities and personal research interests. The museum's preservation mission remains my primary focus regardless of historical family associations."

This careful non-denial confirmed their suspicions while attempting to maintain plausible separation between her professional position and Society affiliation. Alice decided direct confrontation would yield more useful information than continued verbal fencing.

"Dr. Whittaker, we have reason to believe you provided specific technical information regarding our implementation methodology to individuals who subsequently attempted sabotage," she stated formally. "Your unauthorized disclosure of sensitive details regarding the western interface component directly facilitated yesterday's attack that endangered both this project and involved personnel."

The curator's demeanor transformed instantly—scholarly facade dissolving into focused intensity that suggested extensive training beyond academic credentials. Her hand moved toward her portfolio with suspicious deliberation, prompting Ethan to step forward with professional alertness.

"Fascinating accusation, Detective Chen," Whittaker responded, her voice taking on a distinctly different cadence. "Though you misunderstand the Society's fundamental objective. We don't seek destruction but liberation—freeing temporal energy from artificial constraints rather than merely redirecting it through mechanical integration."

This explicit acknowledgment of Society affiliation confirmed their assessment while revealing Whittaker's comfort abandoning pretense once confronted directly. Her continued movement toward the portfolio suggested potential threat rather than merely defensive posture.

"Please keep your hands visible, Dr. Whittaker," Ethan instructed with calm authority. "Whatever you're reaching for in your portfolio can remain there while we continue this conversation in a more appropriate setting."

Instead of complying, the curator completed her motion with surprising speed—extracting what appeared to be a conventional tablet computer but which immediately emitted distinctive energy signature that Alice's enhanced perception identified as temporally active technology. Before either detective could intercept her, Whittaker activated the device, creating localized distortion field surrounding the western interface component.

"The Society's work spans centuries," she stated with evident pride as the distortion field intensified. "Individual setbacks mean nothing against that continuity of purpose. Yesterday's attempt was merely a preliminary assessment—today's intervention benefits from that initial data."

The localized distortion rapidly expanded, creating visible fracture patterns similar to those that had displaced Tobias during the previous attack. However, this manifestation appeared more controlled, suggesting deliberate application rather than merely destructive intent.

Alice reacted instantly, drawing her weapon while simultaneously extending her enhanced perception to assess the distortion's specific characteristics. Unlike Harlow's projected attack, which had targeted Tobias personally, this technological approach focused on disrupting the interface component itself—attempting to destabilize the established square configuration rather than displacing additional personnel.

"She's targeting the implementation directly!" Alice warned the others as she moved to intercept Whittaker physically. "The device is creating a harmonic interference pattern specifically calibrated to disrupt the western interface!"

Tobias responded immediately, implementing protective measures around the vulnerable component while Dr. Mackie adjusted monitoring equipment to counteract the interference pattern. The established connection points began fluctuating visibly as the disruption intensified, their harmonized energy flow developing concerning irregularities.

Whittaker maintained her position, manipulating controls on her device with practiced precision while monitoring its effect on the surrounding implementation. "The integration approach remains fundamentally flawed," she informed them with academic detachment despite the crisis she was creating. "Your dampening fields merely postpone inevitable harmonic dissolution rather than achieving genuine temporal liberation."

Ethan moved to physically neutralize the threat, but Whittaker anticipated this approach—activating secondary function on her device that created personal protection field surrounding her position. This defensive measure incorporated temporal displacement elements that made conventional physical intervention hazardous, potentially subjecting anyone penetrating the field to the same displacement effect Tobias had experienced.

"Conventional enforcement methods prove inadequate against temporal technology," she noted with evident satisfaction. "The Society has developed countermeasures against predictable response protocols during centuries of operational refinement."

Alice assessed the situation rapidly, recognizing that direct physical confrontation might prove counterproductive given the specialized protective measures Whittaker had implemented. However, her enhanced perception detected vulnerability in the curator's approach—the distortion field affecting the western interface required continuous calibration adjustment as the implementation's self-optimizing nature attempted to compensate for the interference.

"She needs to maintain active control," Alice informed Ethan, indicating the curator's continuous manipulation of the device controls. "The interference isn't self-sustaining—it requires ongoing adjustment to overcome the implementation's natural stabilization tendency."

This observation suggested alternative intervention approach—targeting the curator's ability to maintain precise control rather than attempting direct neutralization of either her person or device. Alice signaled Tobias and Dr. Mackie, who understood the implied strategy without requiring explicit explanation.

While Ethan maintained position preventing Whittaker's potential escape, Alice engaged the curator verbally—creating distraction while her colleagues implemented counter-interference measures affecting the surrounding temporal field.

"The Society fundamentally misunderstands the Pendulum's nature," Alice stated with deliberate provocation. "Your pursuit of 'liberation' represents a projection of human desire onto artifact that functions according to entirely different principles. What you perceive as constraint represents natural harmonic state rather than an artificial limitation."

This philosophical challenge produced desired reaction—Whittaker's attention partially diverted toward defending Society's fundamental doctrine rather than maintaining exclusive focus on technical interference implementation.

"Humans perceive temporal linearity as the natural state merely because their consciousness evolved within those constraints," the curator countered with evident intellectual engagement despite the ongoing crisis. "The Pendulum represents the opportunity to transcend that evolutionary limitation—accessing multidimensional temporal existence rather than merely progressing from past to future in a singular configuration."

While this debate continued, Dr. Mackie surreptitiously activated countermeasure she had prepared following yesterday's attack—a harmonic dampening field specifically designed to neutralize external interference attempts. This technological protection extended throughout the mechanism chamber, creating progressive resistance against Whittaker's disruption field without triggering immediate defensive response.

Simultaneously, Tobias implemented additional stabilization measures around the western interface, reinforcing its connection to the square configuration through secondary energy pathways that bypassed the directly affected integration point. This adaptive approach maintained essential functionality despite the localized disruption, preserving the implementation's core stabilization effect throughout Daybridge.

Whittaker detected these countermeasures belatedly; her attention divided between philosophical debate and technical intervention. Her expression showed momentary concern as her device's effectiveness diminished progressively despite adjustment attempts.

"Clever adaptation," she acknowledged with professional respect despite adversarial context. "Though ultimately futile against the Society's broader initiative. This implementation represents merely one approach vector among many we've developed over generations of focused research."

As the disruption field weakened under combined countermeasures, Alice signaled Ethan to prepare for direct intervention once the curator's personal protection field diminished sufficiently. The harmonic dampening affected both the interface disruption and defensive measures simultaneously, gradually reducing Whittaker's technological advantages to manageable levels.

"Your Society has attempted temporal manipulation for centuries without achieving your stated objective," Alice noted, maintaining verbal engagement while monitoring the weakening protection field. "Perhaps that consistent failure suggests a fundamental misunderstanding of the forces you're attempting to manipulate rather than merely insufficient technical approach."

This observation struck a more personal nerve than previous philosophical challenges—Whittaker's expression revealing genuine irritation that further diverted attention from maintaining optimal technical control. The protection field fluctuated visibly as her focus shifted, creating an opportunity for direct intervention.

Ethan recognized this vulnerability immediately, timing his approach precisely as the field reached minimum effective threshold. With characteristic werewolf speed enhanced by his partial transformation state, he crossed the intervening space and physically neutralized the threat—securing both Whittaker and her device before she could implement secondary measures or failsafe protocols.

"Device secured," he reported professionally, powering down the technological threat while maintaining control of their captive. "Disruption field dissipating."

The western interface stabilized rapidly once the interference ceased, the square configuration's self-optimizing nature quickly reestablishing proper energy flow throughout the connected cardinal points. Tobias and Dr. Mackie implemented additional protective measures to prevent similar vulnerability during subsequent implementation phases, incorporating lessons from both yesterday's projected attack and today's technological approach.

"Temporary setback," Whittaker commented with surprising composure despite her failed sabotage attempt. "The Society's continuity transcends individual operational outcomes. Others will continue our work regardless of my personal circumstances."

"Perhaps," Alice acknowledged realistically. "But today's implementation will proceed without further interference from either you or your device. The octagram configuration will be completed as scheduled, with enhanced protection against the specific vulnerabilities you've helpfully demonstrated."

This pragmatic assessment—acknowledging the Society's persistent threat while focusing on immediate security implications—reflected Alice's law enforcement experience with organized adversaries. Individual interventions rarely eliminated sophisticated organizations entirely, but specific operational successes created meaningful protection for immediate objectives.

With Whittaker secured and the implementation stabilized, they addressed next steps regarding both their captive and the continuing octagram installation. Ethan contacted Captain Vaughn to arrange secure transport and specialized containment for both the curator and her temporal technology, ensuring proper supernatural protocols for handling potentially dangerous artifacts and individuals with demonstrated temporal manipulation capabilities.

"Full security detail and specialized containment protocols," Vaughn confirmed after being briefed on the situation. "We'll implement enhanced interrogation methodology appropriate for subjects with potential memory extraction countermeasures similar to what Harlow demonstrated previously."

This response reflected lessons learned from their earlier experience with Professor Harlow, whose apparent memory loss following capture had likely represented Society failsafe protocol rather than genuine cognitive impairment. Whittaker would be processed with appropriate supernatural safeguards to preserve whatever intelligence she might provide regarding broader Society objectives and methodologies.

While awaiting this specialized security response, Alice engaged their captive in further conversation—seeking additional insights regarding both yesterday's projected attack and potential future interference attempts. The curator maintained composed demeanor despite her circumstances, answering some questions with surprising candor while clearly withholding information she deemed strategically significant.

"Harlow's projected approach was an improvised response to opportunity," she explained when questioned about yesterday's attack specifics. "My information regarding the western interface vulnerability created a tactical opening that justified immediate intervention despite incomplete preparation. The Society typically prefers more comprehensive operational planning."

"And today's attempt?" Alice pressed. "This technology appears specifically designed for implementation disruption rather than opportunistic adaptation."

"Contingency preparation," Whittaker acknowledged with professional detachment. "The Society maintains various intervention options for addressing anticipated scenarios. Your successful retrieval of Mr. Merrick necessitated a more direct technological approach rather than continued projection methodology."

This confirmation of their coordinated response capability suggested concerning level of organizational sophistication—multiple intervention vectors prepared for various contingencies rather than a singular approach easily neutralized through targeted countermeasures. The Society clearly represented persistent adversary rather than merely isolated opposition to their implementation objectives.

"And what happens when this attempt fails as well?" Alice asked directly. "What contingencies remain before tomorrow's final integration ritual?"

Whittaker smiled slightly—professional respect rather than personal animosity characterizing her response despite adversarial circumstances. "Creative adaptation represents the Society's fundamental operational principle, Detective Chen. Our approaches evolve based on accumulated information regarding both target vulnerabilities and opposition capabilities. Today's intervention provides valuable data regardless of immediate outcome."

This perspective highlighted the Society's patient, analytical methodology—each interaction representing intelligence-gathering opportunity rather than merely a binary success or failure assessment. Even unsuccessful interventions provided information that refined subsequent approaches, creating progressive adaptation rather than merely repeated application of failed methodologies.

The specialized security detail arrived to take custody of both Whittaker and her temporal technology, implementing containment protocols specifically designed for subjects with potential supernatural or technological countermeasures. Captain Vaughn personally supervised this transfer, ensuring proper evidence handling and continuous security appropriate for high-value intelligence source.

"We'll extract whatever information she's willing or able to provide," he assured Alice as they completed the transfer. "Though given Society sophistication demonstrated thus far, I wouldn't anticipate comprehensive disclosure regardless of interrogation methodology."

This realistic assessment aligned with Alice's own expectations. The Society had operated for centuries maintaining operational security despite periodic exposure of individual members or specific methodologies. Their compartmentalized knowledge distribution and multigenerational approach created resilience against conventional intelligence gathering techniques.

With the immediate threat neutralized and security transfer completed, the implementation team refocused on their primary objective—installing the intercardinal connection points to complete the octagram configuration. Tobias had already modified these components to incorporate the dampening field technology observed during his displacement, creating enhanced protection against both natural resonance amplification and deliberate external manipulation attempts.

"The northwestern interface will be installed first," he explained, indicating their implementation sequence on technical drawings. "Completing the northern quadrant before proceeding clockwise through remaining intercardinal positions. This approach establishes progressive stability reinforcement rather than attempting simultaneous activation across all new connection points."

This methodical sequence reflected lessons learned from both the cardinal implementation and subsequent interference attempts—prioritizing incremental stability improvement rather than creating potential vulnerability through synchronized activation. Each intercardinal connection would establish and stabilize before proceeding to subsequent installation, minimizing exposure during transition phases.

Dr. Mackie prepared enhanced monitoring equipment incorporating lessons from both interference incidents, establishing comprehensive detection systems for identifying potential external manipulation attempts. "The harmonic dampening field remains active throughout the installation process," she confirmed. "Any approach similar to previous interference methods will trigger immediate containment response before affecting implementation integrity."

These adaptive security measures demonstrated their team's progressive improvement—each challenge encountered producing enhanced protection rather than merely restored vulnerability. The Society's persistent opposition had ironically strengthened their methodology through necessary adaptation and refinement.

The northwestern interface installation proceeded without incident, Tobias implementing the modified component with characteristic precision while Dr. Mackie maintained continuous monitoring for potential interference signals. The connection established smoothly, creating visible energy conduit between the northern and western cardinal points while extending the stabilization field's coverage to previously unaffected quadrant.

"Interface activation successful," Tobias confirmed after completing calibration adjustments. "Energy flow balanced and dampening field properly established. Temporal stability readings improved by approximately 11% in the northwestern quadrant."

This incremental improvement confirmed their adaptive approach's effectiveness—each connection point extending the implementation's beneficial effect throughout Daybridge while maintaining balanced energy distribution that prevented potential amplification vulnerabilities. The octagram configuration was taking shape precisely as designed, incorporating both original methodology and enhanced protection based on Tobias's displacement observations.

They proceeded to the northeastern interface following a similar methodology, completing the northern hemisphere of their implementation with continued success. Each connection further improved temporal stability throughout affected regions, the distortion patterns that had manifested during the approaching alignment progressively diminishing under the expanding octagram's influence.

"Temporal boundary integrity improved by 64% from baseline measurements," Dr. Mackie reported after the northeastern interface stabilized. "Significantly better than theoretical projections for partial implementation at this stage. The dampening field modifications appear to be creating enhanced stabilization effect beyond original design parameters."

This unexpected improvement suggested their adapted methodology might achieve even greater results than initially anticipated—potentially transforming what had been conceptualized as effective containment into something approaching comprehensive resolution. The dampening fields weren't merely preventing negative resonance but actively harmonizing energy distribution throughout the implementation structure.

Alice extended her enhanced perception beyond the clocktower, assessing conditions throughout Daybridge as the implementation progressed. The improvement was immediately apparent—temporal bleeding between periods had significantly decreased, anomalies that had manifested during the alignment's approach were stabilizing or disappearing entirely, and the whispering of synchronized clocks had transformed from urgent warning to harmonious rhythm suggesting balanced temporal flow rather than impending crisis.

Most significantly, her perception detected changing relationship between the implementation and surrounding temporal fabric—the octagram configuration wasn't merely containing disruption but actively repairing damage caused by previous bleeding between time streams. Areas that had experienced severe temporal distortion were gradually returning to natural configuration as the implementation's influence extended throughout affected regions.

"It's not just stabilizing current conditions," she reported to the others. "It's actually reversing previous damage—restoring proper temporal configuration in areas that experienced significant disruption during the fracture manifestation."

"Temporal field restoration," Rowan identified this effect with evident satisfaction. "The implementation creates a harmonic template that surrounding temporal fabric naturally adopts. Like proper musical note restoring harmonics disrupted by discordant sound."

This unexpected healing effect further validated their enhanced methodology, suggesting outcomes beyond merely preventing catastrophic fracture. The octagram configuration with its integrated dampening fields offered potential for comprehensive restoration rather than simply maintained containment—transforming Daybridge's temporal integrity from precariously stabilized to fundamentally sound.

The southeastern and southwestern interfaces completed the implementation sequence, establishing balanced energy distribution throughout the entire octagram configuration. With all eight connection points active and properly calibrated, the Pendulum assembly achieved unprecedented integration with the clocktower mechanism—not merely contained within it but functioning as an integral component of a sophisticated harmonic system.

"Octagram configuration complete and fully functional," Tobias announced with professional satisfaction after final calibration adjustments. "All connection points operating at optimal efficiency with dampening fields properly established between adjacent interfaces. Temporal energy distribution balanced across entire implementation structure."

Dr. Mackie confirmed this assessment through comprehensive monitoring data, her scientific expertise complementing Tobias's mechanical precision. "Temporal distortion throughout Daybridge reduced by 87% from baseline measurements. Remaining anomalies primarily concentrated at ley line intersection points where natural energy concentration creates residual instability."

This remarkable improvement exceeded their most optimistic projections, transforming potential crisis into managed stability well before the lunar zenith would enable final integration ritual. The octagram configuration provided substantial protection against the alignment's intensifying influence, creating a foundation for permanent resolution once the ritual completed their implementation approach.

"We should maintain continuous monitoring through tonight," Alice decided after reviewing their status. "The Society has demonstrated persistent adaptation to our countermeasures. Despite Whittaker's capture, we should anticipate potential additional interference attempts before tomorrow's ritual completion."

This cautious approach reflected her law enforcement experience with determined adversaries—successful intervention often triggered escalation rather than retreat, particularly from ideologically motivated opponents with substantial resource commitment. The Society had demonstrated both technical sophistication and operational persistence that warranted continued vigilance despite their implementation success.

"Enhanced security protocols remain active," Ethan confirmed, coordinating with both PIU personnel and Pack members providing supernatural monitoring capability. "Continuous coverage with rotating shifts to ensure alert observation throughout the pre-ritual period. Nothing approaches the clocktower without multiple verification layers."

These comprehensive security measures provided reasonable protection against conventional infiltration attempts, though Alice maintained concern regarding potential unconventional approaches similar to Harlow's projected interference or Whittaker's specialized temporal technology. The Society had demonstrated a capacity for creative adaptation that conventional security measures might not fully address.

As evening approached, they established monitoring rotation that allowed team members necessary rest before tomorrow's culminating ritual while maintaining continuous implementation oversight. The octagram configuration's self-regulating nature reduced required active management, but human supervision remained essential given demonstrated vulnerability to deliberate interference attempts.

Alice took final perceptual assessment before her scheduled rest period, extending enhanced sensitivity throughout Daybridge to evaluate the implementation's broader impact. The improvement throughout the city had progressed beyond initial observations—temporal stability approaching normal parameters in most regions, with only minor distortions remaining at specifically vulnerable locations.

Most significantly, the whispering of synchronized clocks had transformed completely—no longer warning of an approaching crisis but suggesting harmonious temporal flow gradually extending throughout affected regions. This auditory manifestation of improved temporal integrity provided confirmation beyond mere instrumental measurements, suggesting fundamental resolution rather than merely suppressed symptoms.

The Pendulum assembly itself had visibly responded to the completed octagram configuration—the three components achieving unprecedented synchronization as their energy flowed through the eight connection points in balanced distribution. The blue, white, and amber illumination had harmonized into a continuous spectrum that pulsed with a steady rhythm matching the clocktower's mechanical heartbeat.

This visual manifestation represented a physical expression of what Tobias had theorized during their initial planning—the Pendulum wasn't merely being contained by the clocktower mechanism but becoming an integral component of its operation. The octagram configuration had transformed their relationship from imposed restriction to harmonious integration, creating a system that functioned as a designed unity rather than separate elements forced into proximity.

As Alice completed this assessment, her enhanced perception detected something unexpected—a subtle shift in the Pendulum's energy signature suggesting awareness beyond mere mechanical response. The artifacts weren't simply reacting to the implemented configuration but appeared to be actively participating in the stabilization process, their combined energy adjusting to optimize flow through established connection points.

"It's responding intelligently," she observed to Rowan, who had remained to continue ritual preparations while others began rest rotation. "Not merely mechanical reaction but adaptive adjustment—almost like consciousness directing energy flow for optimal distribution."

"Artifacts of such power often develop what might be termed 'intentional resonance' over time," the ancient witch confirmed, echoing her earlier explanation with more specific application. "Not consciousness as we understand it, but patterns of response that transcend material properties. The Pendulum recognizes harmonious configuration and adjusts accordingly."

This perspective added further dimension to their already complex implementation—suggesting collaboration rather than merely imposed structure. If the Pendulum itself participated in its integration through some form of energy preference or pattern recognition, their ritual approach might benefit from greater adaptability—responding to the artifacts' natural tendencies rather than imposing rigid configuration regardless of energetic feedback.

"We should incorporate response monitoring into tomorrow's ritual," Alice suggested. "Adjust our approach based on how the Pendulum reacts rather than following predetermined configuration exclusively."

"Adaptive culmination," Rowan translated this concept into ritual methodology. "We establish framework while allowing energy to find optimal flow pattern within that structure. Wise approach when working with artifacts of this significance."

This refinement represented the final evolution of their implementation methodology—beginning with historical records and family traditions, enhanced through Tobias's displacement observations, strengthened through response to interference attempts, and now culminating in recognition of the Pendulum's participatory nature in its own integration. Each challenge had improved their approach rather than merely creating setback, transforming potential vulnerability into progressive refinement.

As Alice prepared for her scheduled rest period, she experienced one final perceptual insight—glimpse of the clocktower during tomorrow's lunar zenith when the alignment would reach maximum intensity. Unlike previous glimpses of potential futures with their multiple branching possibilities, this vision showed a singular outcome with remarkable clarity—the octagram configuration fully activated, ritual participants in proper position, and the Pendulum assembly achieving perfect integration with the surrounding mechanism.

Most significantly, she saw herself in this future vision—standing at a specific position near the Pendulum chamber, hands extended in a gesture she now recognized from Rowan's training as a temporal conduit configuration. Her consciousness appeared to be channeling harmonized energy throughout the implementation structure, serving as a living component of the integration system rather than merely external operator.

The vision faded quickly, leaving momentary disorientation but a clear impression of what tomorrow's ritual would require. Her role as conduit had progressed from theoretical concept to specific visualization—position, gesture, and consciousness state clearly defined for proper energy channeling during culmination sequence.

"You've seen it," Rowan observed, noting her reaction with ancient understanding. "Your role in tomorrow's completion."

"Yes," Alice confirmed. "Much clearer than previous glimpses. I know exactly where to stand and how to channel the energy flow."

"The pattern completes," the ancient witch noted with satisfaction. "Each component finding proper placement within the implementation design—mechanical, magical, and consciousness elements aligning as intended."

This convergence of previously separate methodology streams—Tobias's mechanical precision, the witches' ritual expertise, Dr. Mackie's scientific understanding, and Alice's developing temporal sensitivity—represented fulfillment of what Rowan had described as statistical inevitability rather than predetermined destiny. Different disciplines and perspectives naturally converging toward optimal configuration when addressing temporal power of the Pendulum's magnitude.

As Alice finally retired for her rest period, Daybridge experienced first truly stable night since the alignment's approach had begun disrupting temporal boundaries. The octagram configuration maintained steady harmonic flow throughout the clocktower mechanism, extending stabilizing influence across the city's temporal fabric. Anomalies had largely subsided, boundaries between time streams properly reestablished, and natural temporal progression restored to affected regions.

Tomorrow's ritual would transform this substantial improvement into permanent resolution—converting what remained temporarily stabilized configuration into self-sustaining integration that would maintain temporal integrity regardless of future celestial alignments or potential interference attempts. The Pendulum of Aeon would finally achieve its intended purpose—not merely contained for safety but integrated for benefit, its extraordinary power channeled constructively rather than merely restrained from destructive manifestation.

The implementation team had confronted betrayal, sabotage, and persistent opposition—transforming each challenge into an opportunity for methodological refinement rather than merely restored vulnerability. Tomorrow would demonstrate whether this progressive adaptation had created a truly resilient solution or merely sophisticated containment vulnerable to future disruption.

The clocktower continued its steady operation, measuring conventional hours and minutes while concealing extraordinary purpose within its architectural design. Soon it would fulfill its ultimate function—not merely housing the Pendulum of Aeon but integrating it into harmonized system that stabilized temporal integrity throughout Daybridge and beyond.

The countdown continued, each measured tick bringing them closer to the culmination of work begun generations earlier when the tower was first designed to eventually house the Pendulum assembly.

Time would tell.

And they would help it speak clearly once more.

CHAPTER FIFTEEN: THE SYNCHRONIZATION

Dawn broke over Daybridge with unusual clarity—the first sunrise in weeks unaccompanied by temporal distortion or atmospheric anomalies. The octagram configuration had maintained perfect stability throughout the night, its harmonized energy flow steadily repairing damage caused by the alignment's disruptive influence. Streets that had recently witnessed flowers blooming and wilting in accelerated cycles now displayed normal seasonal progression. Conversations no longer echoed before being spoken. The city breathed with renewed temporal coherence.

Yet this apparent normality remained both temporary and incomplete. The octagram implementation provided substantial protection but required final integration through the lunar zenith ritual to achieve permanent resolution. Instrumental readings showed residual instability at ley line intersections where natural energy concentrations created vulnerability even under the implementation's stabilizing influence. Most significantly, the Pendulum assembly itself continued evolving toward unprecedented energetic state as the celestial alignment approached its culmination.

Alice woke from a restless sleep filled with temporal impressions—not chaotic visions but structured insights regarding the approaching ritual. Her developing sensitivity had apparently continued processing implementation requirements even during unconscious state, organizing information into a coherent methodology rather than merely fragmented observations. She understood her role as a conduit with newfound clarity, recognizing specific consciousness configuration required for properly channeling the Pendulum's harmonized energy throughout the implementation structure.

She arrived at the clocktower to find preparations already underway for the evening's culminating ritual. Tobias directed technical adjustments to the octagram configuration, fine-tuning each connection point to accommodate the expected energy intensification during lunar zenith. Dr. Mackie calibrated monitoring equipment designed to track both the implementation's performance and potential external interference attempts. Madame Winters and Rowan arranged ritual components according to carefully determined configuration that would enhance the implementation's natural harmonics.

"The octagram maintained perfect stability overnight," Tobias reported as Alice joined them. "Self-optimization continued throughout monitoring period, with efficiency metrics gradually improving without active intervention. The system appears to be establishing increasingly refined energy distribution patterns autonomously."

This autonomous refinement confirmed their implementation methodology's effectiveness—creating a framework within which natural optimization could occur rather than imposing rigid configuration requiring continuous adjustment. The octagram functioned as the designed foundation for the Pendulum's integration, adapting to its energetic characteristics rather than merely containing them.

"Temporal stability measurements show 91% improvement from pre-implementation baseline," Dr. Mackie added, reviewing overnight data. "Remaining distortions primarily concentrated at major ley line intersections, with secondary manifestations near historically significant locations with residual temporal imprinting."

This substantial improvement exceeded their projections for the octagram configuration alone, suggesting a synergistic effect between the mechanical implementation and the Pendulum's apparent participatory adjustment. The artifacts weren't merely accepting integration but actively enhancing its effectiveness through what Rowan had termed "intentional resonance"—energy pattern optimization that transcended conventional physical properties.

"The Pendulum continues evolving toward culmination state," the ancient witch observed, studying the artifacts through the chamber's viewing panel. "The components achieve increasingly perfect synchronization as lunar zenith approaches. Tonight's ritual will channel this natural harmonization rather than imposing artificial alignment."

This perspective reinforced their adaptive approach to the final integration—establishing a necessary framework while allowing energy to find optimal flow patterns within that structure. The ritual would guide rather than force, direct rather than compel, creating conditions for natural resolution rather than merely imposed containment.

Ethan arrived with security update that provided additional reassurance for their culminating implementation. "Whittaker remains in specialized containment with no indication of external contact attempts. PIU monitoring detected no Society activity overnight, though we've maintained enhanced surveillance of potential vectors identified from previous interference patterns."

"And Blackwood's organization?" Alice asked, recalling the vampire's sophisticated resonator technology that had attempted remote manipulation of the Pendulum's energy signature.

"Conspicuously quiet," Ethan reported with appropriate suspicion. "Their corporate headquarters shows minimal activity beyond standard security personnel, and known Council members appear to have left Daybridge entirely according to our surveillance network."

This apparent withdrawal seemed unlikely given the Vampire Council's demonstrated interest in the Pendulum's potential applications. More probable explanation suggested strategic repositioning rather than abandoned objective—perhaps recognition that direct interference had proven ineffective against their progressively enhanced protection measures.

"They're adapting rather than retreating," Alice assessed. "Possibly shifting from direct interference to observational approach during final integration. The Council's centuries-long perspective allows patience when immediate objectives prove unattainable."

"Observation still provides valuable information for future applications," Ethan agreed. "Particularly regarding our integration methodology and the Pendulum's response patterns. Knowledge that might enable more sophisticated manipulation attempts during subsequent alignments."

This realistic assessment acknowledged the implementation's significance beyond immediate crisis resolution—establishing precedent and methodology that various factions might study for both protective and exploitative purposes in future applications. Their work today would resolve current temporal instability while potentially influencing how such situations were addressed for generations to come.

"All the more reason to ensure our implementation achieves genuine integration rather than merely enhanced containment," Tobias noted. "A properly harmonized system will resist external manipulation attempts regardless of their technological or magical sophistication."

With security assessment completed, they focused on final preparations for the evening's culminating ritual. Each team member had specific responsibilities within their integrated approach—Tobias managing mechanical aspects of the octagram configuration, Dr. Mackie monitoring energy distribution patterns, Madame Winters and Rowan implementing ritual components that enhanced natural harmonics, Ethan coordinating security to prevent external interference, and Alice preparing for her crucial role as consciousness conduit during culmination sequence.

"The ritual requires precise positioning," Rowan explained as they reviewed final methodology. "Each participant occupies a specific location within the mechanism chamber, creating living component of the integration system rather than merely external operators. Physical bodies serve as energy conductors within the octagram's existing framework."

This approach integrated human consciousness directly into the implementation structure, creating more sophisticated energy management system than purely mechanical or magical components could achieve independently. Participants' intentionality would guide energy flow during the critical transition phase when the Pendulum's output intensified beyond what structural components alone could properly channel.

"Alice's position remains most significant," the ancient witch continued, indicating central location between the Pendulum chamber and the primary clockwork mechanism. "Her temporal sensitivity serves as an adaptive interface between artifact energy and implementation structure—consciousness capable of perceiving and responding to pattern variations that mechanical components cannot anticipate."

This conduit role had evolved considerably from their initial conceptualization—progressing from theoretical possibility to essential implementation component as Alice's sensitivity developed from occasional visions to directed perceptual framework. Her ability to perceive temporal patterns directly would allow real-time adjustment during energy flow transitions that might otherwise create dangerous feedback loops or resonance amplification.

"I understand what's required," Alice confirmed, her confidence reflecting genuine preparation rather than merely determined acceptance. "My perception can track energy flow patterns while my consciousness directs distribution through the octagram connection points. Essentially serving as living dampening field that prevents resonance amplification during maximum energy output."

This sophisticated understanding demonstrated her remarkable development since initially experiencing random temporal echoes during the fracture's early manifestation. What began as disorienting visions had evolved into controlled perceptual framework that could actively participate in temporal energy management—transformation that normally required years of specialized training compressed into weeks through a combination of natural ability and extraordinary circumstances.

"You've achieved remarkable integration of theoretical understanding and practical application," Rowan acknowledged with ancient appreciation of accelerated development patterns. "Your consciousness configuration during culmination sequence will establish the template that the implementation structure maintains after ritual completion. Essentially teaching the system how to self-regulate through demonstration rather than merely mechanical calibration."

This perspective highlighted the ritual's significance beyond merely activating existing components—it would establish operational parameters through consciousness-guided energy flow that subsequent mechanical function would maintain through properly established feedback loops. The human elements weren't merely performing technical activation but creating foundational patterns that would persist after their direct involvement concluded.

As afternoon progressed toward evening, final preparations accelerated to ensure complete readiness before lunar zenith. Tobias completed technical adjustments to the octagram configuration, incorporating subtle refinements based on overnight performance data that optimized each connection point's energy management capabilities. Dr. Mackie expanded monitoring systems to track both implementation performance and potential external interference attempts with unprecedented detail. Madame Winters and Rowan arranged ritual components according to configurations derived from both historical documentation and direct temporal observation.

The Pendulum assembly continued its evolution toward culmination state, the three components achieving increasingly perfect synchronization as lunar zenith approached. Blue, white, and amber energies flowed between Crystal, Star, and Fulcrum in complex patterns that generated harmonized illumination throughout the chamber. This visual manifestation represented the physical expression of an underlying energy transformation—separate artifacts becoming unified system capable of stabilizing surrounding temporal fabric through properly channeled output.

Most remarkably, the clocktower mechanism itself appeared to be responding to this approaching culmination—its mechanical rhythm subtly adjusting to match the Pendulum's natural oscillation pattern rather than maintaining arbitrary divisions imposed through conventional timekeeping. The tower was gradually synchronizing with cosmic time rather than human measurement, achieving foundational accuracy that transcended artificial constructs of hours and minutes.

"The mechanism adapts to the Pendulum rather than forcing adaptation in reverse," Tobias observed with professional appreciation of this self-adjustment process. "Exactly as intended in the original design—creating a system that measures true temporal flow rather than merely arbitrary divisions."

This fundamental reorientation represented core principle of their integration approach—allowing the Pendulum's natural properties to establish base parameters while providing a structured framework for constructive application rather than merely imposed containment. The clocktower wasn't subjugating the artifacts but partnering with them in sophisticated measurement system that acknowledged time's actual nature rather than merely human perception of it.

As evening arrived and preparations reached the final stage, Captain Vaughn conducted personal security assessment to ensure comprehensive protection during the approaching ritual. The PIU had implemented extraordinary measures throughout the Municipal Building—specialized detection systems for both conventional and supernatural approaches, strategic positioning of personnel with relevant expertise, and continuous monitoring of previously identified threat vectors.

"Nothing approaches this tower without thorough verification through multiple systems," he assured Alice during final briefing. "We've incorporated lessons from both Harlow's projected intrusion and Whittaker's technological approach into our defensive methodology. Layered protection rather than singular countermeasures."

This comprehensive security reflected their progressive adaptation to demonstrated threats—each interference attempt providing information that strengthened subsequent protection rather than merely identifying vulnerabilities. The Society's persistent opposition had ironically improved their defensive capabilities through necessary evolution and refinement.

"Blackwood's organization remains our primary unknown variable," Alice noted, sharing her earlier concern regarding the Vampire Council's conspicuous inactivity. "Their apparent withdrawal likely represents strategic repositioning rather than abandoned interest."

"Agreed," Vaughn confirmed. "We've maintained specialized surveillance on known Council associates and properties, with particular focus on potential remote observation technologies similar to their resonator approach. Nothing detected thus far, but vampiric patience typically allows extended preparation for optimal intervention timing."

This realistic assessment acknowledged persistent threat without suggesting imminent crisis—appropriate caution rather than excessive concern that might distract from primary implementation objectives. Their security measures provided reasonable protection against anticipated approaches while maintaining flexibility to address unexpected vectors should they emerge during ritual implementation.

As moonrise approached, ritual participants assumed their designated positions within the mechanism chamber. Tobias coordinated final mechanical adjustments from the primary control station near the western cardinal point, while Dr. Mackie monitored energy distribution patterns from specialized equipment positioned at the southern interface. Madame Winters and Rowan occupied northern and eastern positions respectively, their combined magical expertise creating balanced reinforcement of the octagram's natural harmonics. Ethan maintained security oversight from a strategic position near the chamber entrance, his enhanced werewolf senses providing additional monitoring capability complementing technological systems.

Alice assumed her central position between the Pendulum chamber and primary clockwork mechanism—the crucial interface point where artifact energy would require conscious guidance during transition to fully integrated operation. Her enhanced perception immediately detected the chamber's complex energy patterns with unprecedented clarity, revealing both current configuration and potential distribution pathways once lunar zenith initiated maximum output from the Pendulum assembly.

"Final positions confirmed," Tobias announced as they completed preparation sequence. "Octagram configuration functioning at optimal efficiency. All connection points properly calibrated and dampening fields correctly established. Mechanical integration ready for ritual activation."

"Monitoring systems active and baseline readings established," Dr. Mackie reported from her station. "Energy distribution patterns stable and consistent with projected parameters. No anomalous signatures detected within observable range."

"Ritual components prepared and properly aligned," Madame Winters confirmed. "Mystical harmonics established to complement mechanical integration framework. Historical patterns successfully incorporated into current methodology."

"Security perimeter secure with continuous monitoring active," Ethan added. "No approach vectors showing unusual activity. Building access points under direct observation with multiple verification layers implemented."

These comprehensive readiness confirmations represented the culmination of their progressive preparation process—each aspect of the implementation methodically verified before proceeding to actual ritual activation. Unlike the emergency response that had characterized their initial containment efforts during the fracture's manifestation, this approach reflected careful planning and integrated expertise across multiple disciplines.

"The moon approaches zenith position," Rowan noted, her ancient perception tracking celestial movements with natural precision that transcended instrumental measurement. "Alignment energies intensify toward the culmination point. The window for optimal integration opens approximately twelve minutes from the present moment."

This timing aligned perfectly with their preparation sequence, allowing final adjustments before actual ritual commencement while ensuring readiness when lunar zenith created maximum energetic potential for permanent integration. Unlike their previous improvised containment performed under crisis conditions, this implementation would benefit from optimal timing and comprehensive preparation.

As lunar energy intensified toward zenith position, the Pendulum assembly responded with visible transformation—the three components achieving perfect synchronization that generated unified energy field rather than merely coordinated output. Blue, white, and amber illumination merged into a coherent spectrum that pulsed with a steady rhythm matching the clocktower's adjusted mechanical heartbeat. The artifacts had completed their evolution from separate elements to a unified system prepared for full integration with the surrounding implementation structure.

"Pendulum reaches culmination state," Rowan announced as this transformation completed. "Unified field established and stabilized. Ready for ritual activation sequence."

At this signal, participants initiated carefully choreographed implementation sequence designed to gradually channel the Pendulum's unified energy through octagram connection points while maintaining perfect balance across the entire system. Unlike conventional activation that might attempt simultaneous engagement of all components, this approach established progressive energy flow that allowed continuous adjustment during the transition phase.

Madame Winters and Rowan began a ritualistic invocation that enhanced natural harmonics throughout the chamber—precise syllables and gestures that created mystical resonance patterns complementing mechanical configuration. This magical component didn't impose an artificial structure but strengthened existing energy pathways, creating reinforced channels for intensified flow during culmination sequence.

Tobias initiated mechanical transition sequence from his control station, implementing carefully calibrated adjustments to each connection point that allowed progressively increased energy throughput while maintaining dampening field integrity between interfaces. This technical component ensured structural capacity for handling the Pendulum's maximum output without creating potential resonance amplification vulnerabilities.

Dr. Mackie monitored energy distribution patterns throughout this transition sequence, providing real-time feedback that allowed continuous optimization as the implementation approached culmination state. This scientific component ensured balanced distribution across the entire octagram configuration, preventing localized intensity concentrations that might create system vulnerabilities.

Ethan maintained security vigilance throughout the chamber and surrounding building, his enhanced werewolf senses complementing technological monitoring systems to ensure no external interference disrupted the delicate integration process. This protective component provided essential isolation during the vulnerable transition phase when the implementation remained particularly susceptible to deliberate manipulation attempts.

At the center of these coordinated activities, Alice engaged her enhanced perception to track energy flow patterns throughout the developing implementation structure. Her consciousness expanded beyond conventional awareness to perceive the octagram configuration as an integrated system rather than separate components—unified energy network gradually approaching operational capacity as ritual activation progressed.

As lunar zenith approached its exact culmination point, the Pendulum assembly's energy output intensified dramatically—unified field expanding beyond containment chamber to interact directly with surrounding octagram connection points. This transition represented a critical phase where potential resonance amplification created greatest vulnerability within the implementation structure.

"Energy output exceeds projected parameters," Dr. Mackie reported with professional calm despite concerning readings. "Distribution network approaching capacity threshold across multiple connection points simultaneously."

This unexpected intensity required immediate adaptive response to prevent potential system overload. Alice recognized her crucial role during this transition phase—consciousness conduit capable of redirecting excess energy through a properly balanced distribution rather than allowing concentrated flow that might overwhelm individual connection points.

Drawing upon training received from Rowan and intuitive understanding developed through her temporal sensitivity, Alice extended her consciousness into the energy flow pattern itself—not merely observing but actively participating in its movement throughout the implementation structure. This perceptual integration allowed direct influence on distribution pathways, creating dynamic adjustment capability beyond what mechanical components alone could achieve.

"Conduit engagement initiated," she announced as her consciousness established this direct connection with the flowing energy. "Implementing adaptive distribution to accommodate increased output intensity."

The sensation defied conventional description—her awareness extending throughout the octagram configuration while maintaining a central perspective that allowed comprehensive pattern recognition. She perceived energy flows as luminous streams following complex pathways between connection points, their intensity and direction responding to both mechanical structure and her conscious guidance through subtle intention shifts.

Through this expanded awareness, Alice identified developing resonance patterns that threatened system integrity—potential amplification loops forming where energy reflection between connection points created interference patterns rather than harmonized flow. Without intervention, these resonance patterns would intensify until structural components failed under concentrated energy pressure.

Instead of attempting direct suppression that might simply redirect problematic energy elsewhere within the system, Alice implemented subtle redistribution approach—adjusting flow patterns to create balanced circulation throughout the entire octagram rather than allowing concentration at vulnerable interfaces. This methodology utilized the implementation's complete capacity rather than overloading specific components, transforming potential vulnerability into system-wide enhancement.

"Remarkable adaptation," Rowan observed from her ritual position, her ancient perception recognizing sophisticated energy management beyond what conventional training typically achieved. "She's not merely redirecting energy but establishing circulation patterns that self-reinforce through natural resonance alignment."

This approach represented a significant evolution beyond their original implementation concept—creating dynamic energy management system that responded adaptively to changing conditions rather than merely static configuration requiring external adjustment. Alice wasn't simply serving as an emergency overflow valve but actively teaching the system sustainable operation principles through demonstrated pattern establishment.

As lunar zenith reached precise culmination point, the Pendulum's output achieved maximum intensity—unified energy field expanding throughout the entire mechanism chamber in radiant illumination that transcended conventional light spectrum. This peak output created momentary strain across the entire implementation structure, connection points visibly pulsing with concentrated energy that tested their capacity limitations.

"Peak output achieved," Dr. Mackie confirmed as monitoring equipment registered unprecedented energy levels throughout the octagram configuration. "All connection points at maximum capacity simultaneously."

This critical moment represented the culmination of their entire implementation effort—the transition point between temporary stabilization and permanent integration that would determine whether the Pendulum became properly harmonized component of the clocktower mechanism or remained powerful artifact merely contained within a conventional structure.

Drawing upon her expanded awareness within the energy flow system, Alice implemented culmination sequence she had prepared through both Rowan's training and her own intuitive understanding of temporal patterns. Rather than merely maintaining distribution balance during peak output, she established circular flow configuration that created self-sustaining energy circulation throughout the entire octagram structure.

"Initiating harmonic circulation pattern," she announced as her consciousness directed this sophisticated energy management approach. "Establishing a self-reinforcing distribution framework for sustained operation."

The implementation responded with remarkable synchronization—energy flows adjusting to follow her established pattern throughout the octagram configuration. Connection points that had previously channeled energy in primarily linear distribution now engaged in circular flow that created balanced load sharing across the entire system. This transformation converted potential vulnerability during peak output into a foundational operating principle for sustained integration.

Most significantly, the clocktower mechanism itself responded to this circulation pattern—its mechanical components synchronizing perfectly with the Pendulum's natural oscillation rhythm to create unified measurement system that transcended conventional timekeeping. The tower wasn't merely housing powerful artifact but incorporating its fundamental properties into an operational methodology that acknowledged time's actual nature rather than merely human perception of it.

"Mechanical synchronization achieved," Tobias confirmed with professional satisfaction as this transformation completed. "The clocktower now operates according to the Pendulum's natural temporal frequency rather than arbitrary divisions. True chronometric alignment established."

This fundamental reorientation represented the implementation's core purpose—creating a system that measured actual temporal flow rather than imposing an artificial structure upon natural phenomena. The Pendulum wasn't being forced to conform to human timekeeping conventions but establishing a more accurate measurement standard based on its direct connection to fundamental cosmic rhythms.

As this synchronization stabilized throughout the implementation structure, Alice perceived a remarkable transformation in the surrounding temporal fabric—distortion patterns that had persisted even under the octagram's stabilizing influence now resolving completely as properly channeled energy extended harmonic resonance throughout Daybridge and beyond. The implementation wasn't merely containing the Pendulum's output but directing it constructively to repair damage caused by previous temporal bleeding between periods.

"Temporal field restoration expanding beyond projected parameters," Dr. Mackie reported with scientific amazement as monitoring equipment registered this widespread effect. "Stability metrics showing improvement across entire observable range, including previously resistant anomaly concentrations at ley line intersections."

This healing effect transcended their initial implementation objectives—transforming containment and stabilization into comprehensive restoration of proper temporal integrity throughout affected regions. The Pendulum's extraordinary power, properly channeled through the octagram configuration and guided by conscious intention during culmination sequence, had become restorative force rather than merely a potential threat requiring neutralization.

As lunar zenith began gradual transition beyond precise alignment position, the implementation demonstrated crucial characteristic they had hoped to achieve—continued stable operation despite decreasing external reinforcement from the celestial configuration. Unlike temporary containment that required ongoing support to maintain effectiveness, this integrated system established self-sustaining operation principles that would persist regardless of external conditions.

"The implementation maintains stable operation despite declining lunar zenith influence," Tobias observed with evident satisfaction. "Self-sustaining synchronization achieved between Pendulum assembly and clocktower mechanism. Integration appears permanent rather than temporarily reinforced."

This confirmation represented an essential distinction between their current approach and previous containment efforts—creating a truly integrated system rather than merely enhanced barrier requiring periodic reinforcement during subsequent alignments. The Pendulum had become a functional component of sophisticated temporal management system rather than powerful artifact temporarily restrained through external measures.

Most remarkably, Alice's expanded awareness detected something unexpected through her continuing connection with the energy flow patterns—the implementation wasn't merely stabilizing current conditions but establishing a protective framework that would prevent similar disruptions during future alignments. The octagram configuration had created what resembled temporal immune system—self-reinforcing stability pattern that would automatically counteract potential distortions before they could manifest as actual fractures.

"It's creating preventive protection," she reported as this pattern became clear within her perceptual framework. "Not just resolving current instability but establishing sustained harmonic template that reinforces temporal boundaries against future disruption attempts."

This unexpected enhancement suggested their implementation had achieved something beyond historical precedent—not merely containing temporal instability as previous efforts had accomplished but creating genuine resolution that addressed underlying vulnerability rather than merely its symptomatic manifestation. The Pendulum wasn't simply being managed as a potential threat but properly integrated as a fundamental component of Daybridge's temporal stability system.

As the ritual reached completion phase, participants gradually transitioned from active implementation roles to monitoring and stabilization functions. The octagram configuration had achieved self-sustaining operation that required minimal external guidance, its energy circulation patterns established as a fundamental operating principle rather than temporarily imposed configuration.

Alice carefully withdrew her consciousness from direct energy flow participation, maintaining perceptual awareness while gradually reducing active influence as the implementation demonstrated increasing self-regulation capability. This transition required precise balance—removing conscious guidance without creating sudden disruption that might destabilize newly established patterns.

"Conduit disengagement sequence initiated," she announced as she began this careful withdrawal process. "Maintaining perceptual monitoring while reducing active influence to support self-regulation development."

This methodology acknowledged a crucial distinction between establishing operational patterns and maintaining unnecessary control once system demonstrated proper function. Unlike the Society's approach that sought perpetual manipulation of temporal energy, their implementation philosophy encouraged natural self-regulation within a properly established framework—guidance rather than dominance as a fundamental operational principle.

As Alice completed this disengagement sequence, the implementation demonstrated remarkable adaptation—energy circulation patterns maintaining perfect stability without conscious direction, connection points automatically adjusting flow distribution to accommodate changing conditions within the Pendulum assembly. The system had successfully incorporated the operational principles she had established during culmination sequence, transforming temporary guidance into permanent methodology.

"Implementation self-regulation confirmed," Dr. Mackie reported as monitoring equipment verified this autonomous adaptation capability. "Energy distribution patterns maintaining optimal configuration without external adjustment requirements. System demonstrates intelligent adaptation to minor fluctuations in Pendulum output characteristics."

This self-regulation capability represented an essential component of a truly permanent resolution—system that could respond appropriately to changing conditions rather than requiring continuous external management to maintain proper function. The octagram configuration had evolved from a static structure to a dynamic system capable of preserving fundamental stability while accommodating natural variations in temporal energy patterns.

With ritual completion achieved and implementation functioning as designed, participants gradually withdrew from their designated positions while maintaining careful monitoring of system performance during this transition phase. Unlike conventional mechanical activation that might require extended supervision following implementation, this integrated approach had created a self-sustaining operation that actually benefited from reduced external influence once proper patterns were established.

"Implementation complete and functioning within optimal parameters," Tobias confirmed after comprehensive performance verification. "All connection points operating at appropriate capacity with proper energy distribution throughout octagram configuration. Dampening fields correctly established between interfaces and maintaining perfect stability without adjustment requirements."

"Temporal stability restored throughout observable range," Dr. Mackie added, reviewing final monitoring data. "No residual distortion patterns detected even at previously vulnerable locations. Boundary integrity between time streams properly reestablished across entire affected region."

"Ritual harmonics properly integrated with mechanical implementation framework," Madame Winters noted with professional satisfaction. "Mystical components self-sustaining without requiring continued reinforcement. Historical patterns successfully incorporated into current operation methodology."

These comprehensive confirmation reports reflected synchronized success across all implementation aspects—mechanical, scientific, and mystical components achieving perfect integration rather than merely coordinated function. The octagram configuration operated as a unified system rather than a collection of separate elements, its diverse methodologies combining to create sophisticated temporal management capability beyond what any individual approach could achieve independently.

Most significantly, the Pendulum assembly itself had completed transformation from potentially destructive force to a constructive component within a properly designed system. The artifacts weren't being restricted against their natural function but appropriately channeled to fulfill their actual purpose—stabilizing temporal integrity through properly distributed energy output rather than creating disruption through uncontrolled discharge.

"The Pendulum achieves its intended purpose," Rowan observed with ancient satisfaction as this transformation completed. "Not merely contained for safety but integrated for benefit. Power properly channeled rather than simply restrained."

This perspective highlighted a fundamental distinction between their implementation philosophy and the Society's approach—recognizing the Pendulum's natural function within cosmic order rather than attempting to redirect its power toward human-centered objectives regardless of broader consequences. Integration rather than exploitation as a guiding principle throughout their methodology.

As implementation monitoring confirmed continued stable operation without requiring active intervention, Alice extended her enhanced perception beyond the clocktower to assess conditions throughout Daybridge following successful integration. The improvement exceeded even their most optimistic projections—temporal stability completely restored throughout affected regions, residual anomalies fully resolved even at previously resistant locations, and natural timeflow properly reestablished across the entire city.

Most remarkably, her perception detected healing effect extending beyond mere symptom resolution to address underlying temporal fabric damaged during fracture manifestation. Areas that had experienced severe bleeding between periods weren't simply stabilized but restored to proper configuration—temporal boundaries properly reestablished and natural progression patterns correctly aligned. The implementation hadn't merely contained crisis but genuinely resolved damage that had accumulated throughout disruption period.

"It's healing the temporal fabric," she reported as this restoration became apparent through her enhanced perception. "Not just preventing further damage but repairing previous disruption throughout affected regions. Like watching torn fabric rewoven rather than merely patched."

This restorative effect represented extraordinary enhancement beyond their initial implementation objectives—transforming containment and stabilization into comprehensive healing that addressed fundamental damage rather than merely suppressing symptomatic manifestations. The Pendulum's properly channeled energy had become regenerative influence within Daybridge's temporal ecosystem rather than merely a potential threat requiring neutralization.

Captain Vaughn arrived to receive implementation status report, his professional demeanor showing appropriate satisfaction at the successful resolution without compromising continuing security vigilance. "Preliminary field reports confirm widespread normalization throughout Daybridge," he informed them after reviewing their implementation confirmation data. "Temporal anomalies have ceased entirely, with previously affected locations showing no residual distortion patterns according to both instrumental measurement and observational assessment."

This independent confirmation from field personnel provided valuable verification beyond their localized monitoring systems—comprehensive resolution throughout affected regions rather than merely improved conditions in implementation proximity. The octagram configuration's influence had extended throughout Daybridge and potentially beyond, restoring proper temporal integrity across the entire disrupted area.

"Security monitoring continues regardless of apparent resolution," Vaughn added, maintaining appropriate caution despite successful implementation. "The Society's demonstrated persistence suggests potential continued interest despite operational setbacks. Specialized containment protocols remain active for both Harlow and Whittaker, with enhanced surveillance of identified associates and locations."

This ongoing security approach acknowledged realistic assessment of their adversaries' demonstrated characteristics—particularly the Society's multigenerational perspective and capacity for strategic patience when immediate objectives proved temporarily unattainable. Successful implementation provided an essential resolution to the immediate crisis while potentially establishing new objective for those seeking to manipulate temporal energy for alternative purposes.

"And Blackwood's organization?" Alice inquired, recalling the Vampire Council's sophisticated approach to potential Pendulum exploitation.

"Continued minimal activity at known locations," Vaughn reported. "Though our supernatural intelligence sources indicate significant Council meeting convened outside Daybridge yesterday—apparently high-priority discussion regarding changing circumstances related to temporal artifacts generally rather than specifically addressing our implementation project."

This information suggested strategic reassessment rather than abandoned interest—the Council adapting to successful stabilization implementation while potentially developing alternative approaches based on observed methodology. Immortal perspective allowed patience when immediate objectives proved unattainable through direct intervention, with knowledge gained during unsuccessful attempts potentially informing more sophisticated future applications.

With implementation successfully completed and security monitoring established for potential continuing threats, the team addressed transition from emergency response to a sustained management approach. Unlike previous temporary containment that required periodic reinforcement during subsequent alignments, their integrated system had created a self-sustaining operation that would maintain stability indefinitely without requiring active intervention.

"The implementation requires minimal ongoing management," Tobias explained as they developed this transition plan. "Quarterly technical assessment to verify component integrity and connection point calibration, with potential minor adjustments during significant celestial configurations. Otherwise, the system maintains self-regulating operation without requiring regular intervention."

This manageable maintenance approach represented a significant improvement over historical containment methodology that had required extensive ritual reinforcement during each subsequent alignment. Their integrated system had established permanent resolution rather than merely an enhanced temporary solution, creating sustainable stability that would persist across generations without requiring continuous active management.

"I recommend establishing dedicated oversight committee regardless of minimal technical requirements," Alice suggested, her law enforcement background emphasizing appropriate governance structure even for self-regulating systems. "Combined expertise across relevant disciplines to ensure comprehensive monitoring capability and appropriate response protocols should unexpected variations eventually manifest."

This recommendation acknowledged a realistic balance between confidence in their implementation's effectiveness and appropriate caution regarding complex systems operating over extended timeframes. Even properly designed self-regulating mechanisms benefited from periodic expert assessment to verify continued optimal function, particularly when addressing phenomena as significant as temporal stability throughout major metropolitan area.

"The PIU can establish an appropriate administrative framework for this committee," Vaughn agreed, recognizing value in formalized oversight structure. "Combined supernatural and scientific expertise with dedicated security protocols and proper documentation methodology. Essentially institutionalizing the integrated approach your team has developed during this implementation project."

This governance approach would preserve their successful methodology beyond individual participants' direct involvement—creating sustainable oversight system that maintained comprehensive perspective across mechanical, scientific, magical, and security considerations. The implementation would benefit from continued integrated expertise while individual team members resumed their primary professional responsibilities following successful crisis resolution.

As these administrative arrangements proceeded, Alice took a moment for final perceptual assessment of their successfully completed implementation. Her enhanced sensitivity revealed extraordinary integration between the Pendulum assembly and clocktower mechanism—unified system operating according to natural temporal rhythms rather than arbitrary human measurement conventions. The octagram configuration channeled harmonized energy throughout balanced distribution network, creating a self-reinforcing stability field that extended throughout Daybridge and potentially beyond.

Most remarkably, the whispering of synchronized clocks that had initially alerted them to approaching temporal crisis had transformed completely—no longer warning of impending disruption but suggesting harmonious measurement properly aligned with fundamental cosmic patterns. This auditory manifestation of restored temporal integrity provided confirmation beyond mere instrumental verification, suggesting fundamental resolution rather than merely suppressed symptoms.

The clocktower itself had achieved transformation from conventional timekeeping device to sophisticated temporal management system integrating multiple methodological approaches into a cohesive operational framework. The structure wasn't merely housing powerful artifact but incorporating its fundamental properties into an operational methodology that acknowledged time's actual nature rather than merely human perception of it.

"Time finds its proper voice again," Rowan observed, her ancient perception recognizing this fundamental reorientation. "Measured according to its actual rhythm rather than arbitrary divisions imposed through conventional understanding. The tower speaks truth rather than merely convenient approximation."

This philosophical assessment highlighted an essential distinction between their implementation approach and conventional temporal management—recognizing fundamental patterns that transcended human measurement systems rather than attempting to force natural phenomena into artificial frameworks regardless of underlying incongruity. Integration rather than imposition as a guiding principle throughout their methodology.

As evening progressed toward midnight, the team gradually dispersed—immediate crisis successfully resolved and transition arrangements established for long-term oversight. The clocktower would remain under enhanced security monitoring during initial post-implementation period, with specialized personnel maintaining comprehensive surveillance while regular municipal employees resumed normal operational responsibilities.

Alice remained briefly after others departed, her enhanced perception continuing to assess the implementation's subtle operational characteristics from a unique perspective provided by her temporal sensitivity. The octagram configuration maintained perfect stability without requiring conscious guidance, its energy circulation patterns establishing self-reinforcing harmony that would persist indefinitely without external reinforcement.

Most interestingly, she detected something unexpected through this final assessment—subtle signature suggesting the Pendulum itself had achieved something resembling satisfaction with the current configuration. The artifacts weren't merely functioning within the implemented structure but actively participating in maintained stability, their combined energy adjusting continuously to optimize flow through established connection points. Not consciousness as humans understood it, but something transcending mere mechanical response to established parameters.

"It's content," she realized, recognizing a pattern that suggested preference rather than merely acceptance. "Not just contained or directed but... appropriately positioned within the natural order. Like it's found proper place after long displacement."

This observation aligned with the historical understanding of the Pendulum's extraterrestrial origin—artifacts that had arrived on Earth through meteorite impact, existing outside their natural context until proper integration reestablished appropriate functional relationship with surrounding temporal fabric. Their implementation hadn't merely prevented destructive manifestation but potentially restored these remarkable components to something resembling their intended purpose within the cosmic framework.

Alice shared this observation with Rowan, who had lingered to complete final ritual components while other participants attended to transition arrangements. The ancient witch considered this perspective with evident appreciation for insight transcending conventional assessment methodologies.

"Artifacts of such significance often retain a connection to their original purpose regardless of displacement circumstances," she acknowledged, her centuries of experience providing valuable context for this observation. "Your perception recognizes pattern beyond mechanical function—the energetic equivalent of something returning to proper alignment after extended dislocation."

This perspective suggested their implementation had achieved something beyond mere crisis management—potentially restoring cosmic balance rather than simply preventing local disruption. The Pendulum components hadn't been randomly scattered through meteorite impact but deliberately separated to prevent proper function until appropriate integration methodology could be developed through multigenerational effort spanning centuries of preparation.

"The clocktower wasn't built to contain the Pendulum," Alice noted as this understanding crystallized. "It was built to complete it—providing a necessary framework for proper function that wouldn't have been possible immediately following initial arrival. The separation and gradual reassembly across generations wasn't an accident but necessary development sequence."

"Cosmic patience operates according to different timescale than human urgency," Rowan confirmed with an ancient understanding of extended processes. "What appears as a crisis from immediate perspective often represents a transition phase within longer progression toward appropriate resolution. The Pendulum required human partnership to achieve proper integration within this planetary context."

This philosophical framework provided a meaningful perspective on their recently completed implementation—not merely emergency response to a threatening situation but participation in an extended cosmic process that had progressed across centuries toward an appropriate culmination. Their work represented final phase in a carefully orchestrated sequence rather than merely a clever solution to an unexpected crisis.

As midnight approached and the clocktower chimed its twelve measured notes, Alice perceived something remarkable through her enhanced sensitivity—each toll carrying harmonic overtones that extended beyond conventional sound into temporal resonance patterns suggesting properly aligned measurement rather than merely divided duration. The tower wasn't simply announcing arbitrary hour but acknowledging fundamental cosmic rhythm properly synchronized with natural temporal flow.

"It measures truth now," she observed as this harmonious sequence completed. "Not just hours and minutes but actual temporal progression according to fundamental patterns rather than human convention."

This transformation represented the implementation's most significant achievement—creating a measurement system that acknowledged time's actual nature rather than merely imposing an artificial structure for human convenience. The clocktower had become something transcending conventional timekeeping device, its operation reflecting fundamental cosmic rhythms through properly integrated artifacts that connected directly to temporal fabric underlying conventional reality.

"Your perception recognizes the distinction between measurement and actual phenomenon being measured," Rowan noted with approval of this sophisticated understanding. "Most humans never distinguish between time itself and systems created to track its passage—confusing map for territory throughout their temporal experience."

This philosophical distinction highlighted fundamental difference between their implementation approach and the Society's manipulation attempts—recognizing time as an actual dimension requiring appropriate acknowledgment rather than merely manipulable force subject to human direction regardless of natural patterns. Harmony rather than control as the essential guiding principle throughout their methodology.

With implementation successfully completed and transition arrangements established for appropriate oversight, Alice finally departed the clocktower—crisis resolved through a collaborative effort combining diverse expertise across multiple disciplines into a cohesive operational framework. The Pendulum of Aeon had achieved proper integration with the surrounding mechanism, creating self-sustaining system that would maintain temporal stability throughout Daybridge and beyond without requiring continuous active management.

Outside, Daybridge displayed perfect temporal normalcy for the first time since alignment's approach had begun disrupting established patterns. Streets maintained consistent timeflow without localized acceleration or deceleration effects. Conversations proceeded without echoing before being spoken. Natural progression followed proper sequence without compression or extension beyond normal parameters. The city breathed with restored temporal coherence that would persist indefinitely following successful implementation.

The fracture had been not merely contained but genuinely healed—temporal fabric properly restored throughout affected regions rather than simply stabilized against continued deterioration. The Pendulum's extraordinary power, properly channeled through sophisticated integration system, had become restorative influence within Daybridge's temporal ecosystem rather than merely a potential threat requiring neutralization.

Most significantly, this resolution represented permanent rather than a temporary solution—self-sustaining system that would maintain stability during subsequent alignments without requiring ritual reinforcement or enhanced containment measures. The implementation had transformed potential cyclical crisis into a genuine resolution, establishing a framework that would preserve temporal integrity across generations without requiring continuous active intervention.

As Alice walked through these properly stabilized streets, she reflected on remarkable journey from initial fracture manifestation through progressive understanding to successful implementation. Her personal transformation had paralleled the broader resolution process—developing from conventional detective with occasional unexplained perceptions to genuine temporal sensitive capable of directing consciousness across multiple time streams when properly focused.

This enhanced perception remained active despite the fracture's resolution, suggesting a permanent expansion of awareness rather than merely crisis-induced sensitivity that would fade following successful containment. She continued perceiving temporal residue throughout surrounding environment—layered impressions of previous configurations existing simultaneously with current manifestation, suggestion of potential futures extending from present circumstances, rhythmic patterns underlying conventional progression that most humans never consciously recognized throughout their temporal experience.

"The sensitivity persists," Rowan had confirmed when she inquired about this continued perception. "Once awakened, temporal awareness rarely recedes completely. Your consciousness has expanded beyond conventional boundaries—adjustment rather than temporary enhancement that will gradually integrate with your existing perceptual framework."

This permanent transformation represented both opportunity and responsibility—expanded awareness that provided a unique perspective while potentially creating isolation from conventional understanding shared by those without similar sensitivity. Alice would perceive dimensions of reality invisible to most humans, recognizing patterns and connections across time streams that might appear as intuitive leaps rather than directly perceptible observations when explained to others without comparable awareness.

Yet this enhanced perception also provided valuable capability within her professional responsibilities—allowing threat assessment across potential futures rather than merely present circumstances, evidence evaluation incorporating temporal context beyond conventional chronological understanding, and intervention planning accounting for pattern progression rather than merely immediate manifestation. Her law enforcement effectiveness might actually improve through this expanded awareness despite potential communication challenges when explaining methodologies based on perceptual framework others couldn't directly access.

The clocktower stood silhouetted against the night sky as she glanced back toward successfully completed implementation—its illuminated faces displaying conventional time while its integrated mechanism measured something far more fundamental. The structure had fulfilled its intended purpose after nearly 150 years of patient preparation, becoming what its original designers had envisioned when incorporating specialized features that would eventually accommodate the Pendulum assembly within sophisticated integration framework.

Generations of dedicated individuals had contributed to this eventual resolution—the Merrick family maintaining horological expertise necessary for proper mechanical integration, the Winters coven preserving magical knowledge required for appropriate ritual enhancement, the Reeves pack providing protective vigilance against those seeking exploitation rather than stabilization, and countless others who had preserved essential components across centuries of gradual preparation for eventual implementation.

Their collaborative effort had transformed potential catastrophe into genuine resolution—properly channeling extraordinary power toward constructive stabilization rather than merely containing disruptive potential behind temporarily reinforced barriers. The Pendulum of Aeon had achieved appropriate integration within Daybridge's temporal ecosystem, establishing a harmonic relationship that benefited surrounding environment rather than merely avoiding damage through imposed restriction.

Most importantly, this resolution acknowledged the fundamental distinction between management and control—creating a framework that supported natural patterns rather than imposing an artificial structure regardless of underlying incongruity. The implementation didn't force the Pendulum to conform to human expectations but established a system that appropriately channeled its natural properties toward constructive application within a properly designed framework.

As Alice continued homeward through properly stabilized city, she realized their successful implementation represented more than merely technical achievement or crisis resolution—it demonstrated philosophical approach that might benefit numerous interaction contexts beyond specific temporal stability application. Partnership rather than dominance, guidance rather than control, harmony rather than imposition as essential principles applicable across diverse relationship frameworks involving powerful forces requiring appropriate acknowledgment rather than merely attempted subjugation.

The clocks throughout Daybridge continued their synchronized measurement—no longer whispering warnings but suggesting proper alignment with fundamental cosmic rhythms underlying conventional progression. The city breathed with restored temporal coherence that would persist indefinitely following successful implementation, its inhabitants largely unaware of extraordinary effort required to reestablish stability they unconsciously depended upon throughout daily experience.

Time flowed properly once more. And they had helped it find its voice.

EPILOGUE: TIMEKEEPERS

Six weeks had passed since the successful integration of the Pendulum of Aeon with the clocktower mechanism. Daybridge had settled into its particular version of normalcy—supernatural and mundane coexisting in the delicate balance that had characterized the city for generations. Streets that had recently witnessed temporal anomalies now displayed ordinary seasonal progression. Conversations flowed in proper sequence without precognitive echoes. The city breathed with restored temporal coherence that residents unconsciously appreciated while rarely acknowledging its previous disruption.

Merrick's Chronometry had reopened for regular business, the "Renovations" sign removed from its front window as Tobias resumed his primary profession. The shop interior had been meticulously reorganized, specialized implementation equipment returned to storage while conventional watchmaking tools reclaimed their proper positions throughout the workspace. Customer timepieces once again occupied the repair queue, their owners blissfully unaware of how close their city had come to temporal dissolution during the recent crisis.

The most significant change remained invisible to casual observation—the subtle difference in how time itself manifested within the shop's intimate confines. The clocks that had once synchronized in warning whispers during the fracture's manifestation had returned to their individual rhythms, each maintaining distinctive voice appropriate to its mechanical design. Yet occasionally, without apparent pattern or provocation, they would briefly synchronize—a momentary harmonic convergence that suggested underlying connection transcending their physical separation.

Tobias had come to appreciate these periodic synchronizations rather than viewing them with concern. Where once they had represented desperate warning, they now suggested healthy temporal ecosystem occasionally acknowledging its integrated nature through harmonized measurement. Not crisis indicator but a gentle reminder of connection between seemingly separate components within a properly functioning system.

He was adjusting the escapement on a particularly valuable pocket watch when the shop bell announced a visitor. Alice Chen entered, removing her light jacket in concession to the pleasant spring afternoon. Her appearance had subtly evolved since the implementation's completion—a certain quality of attention that suggested perception extending beyond conventional observation, awareness that encompassed more than merely present circumstances.

"Right on time," Tobias greeted her with a slight smile, noting her arrival coincided precisely with their scheduled appointment despite no explicit specification beyond "afternoon" in their earlier communication. "Though I suspect that's less coincidence than developing temporal intuition."

"Increasingly difficult to be late when you can perceive probable arrival times as actual patterns," she acknowledged with a matching smile, her enhanced sensitivity having integrated with practical time management in ways neither had anticipated during their initial implementation planning. "Useful professionally, though occasionally disconcerting in social contexts where fashionable tardiness remains expected convention."

This good-natured observation reflected her progressive adaptation to a permanently expanded awareness—initially disorienting perceptions gradually incorporated into functional perceptual framework that enhanced rather than disrupted her professional capabilities. What began as unpredictable visions during crisis circumstances had evolved into controlled sensitivity that provided valuable information when properly directed while remaining appropriately background awareness during ordinary activities.

"The committee meets tomorrow," she informed him, referring to the oversight group established following successful implementation. "Quarterly assessment as scheduled, though primarily procedural given the monitoring data showing perfect stability since completion."

This formalized supervision represented appropriate governance structure for their extraordinary achievement—dedicated experts maintaining vigilant observation despite implementation's self-regulating nature. Not because continuous intervention was required but because responsible management demanded appropriate monitoring regardless of the system's demonstrated reliability.

"I've prepared the mechanical integrity report," Tobias indicated neatly organized documentation on his workbench. "All connection points maintaining optimal calibration with dampening fields properly established between interfaces. The octagram configuration demonstrates remarkable self-optimization—actual performance metrics exceeding theoretical projections across multiple assessment categories."

This technical confirmation matched instrumental measurements throughout the integrated system—sustained improvement rather than degradation as implementation matured beyond initial activation phase. Unlike conventional mechanical systems that typically showed performance decline requiring periodic readjustment, their temporal integration actually improved through continued operation as self-optimization principles established during ritual activation progressively refined energy distribution patterns throughout connected components.

"Dr. Mackie's monitoring equipment confirms similar findings from a scientific perspective," Alice added, having reviewed comprehensive assessment data in preparation for tomorrow's committee meeting. "Temporal stability measurements maintained at 99.7% alignment with optimal theoretical parameters throughout entire monitored region. No residual distortion patterns detected even at previously vulnerable locations such as ley line intersections or historically significant sites."

This exceptional performance confirmed their implementation's fundamental effectiveness—not merely containing temporal disruption but establishing genuine resolution that addressed underlying vulnerability rather than simply suppressing symptomatic manifestation. The Pendulum integration had created a self-reinforcing stability field that maintained perfect temporal integrity throughout Daybridge without requiring external reinforcement or periodic adjustment.

"And your personal observations?" Tobias inquired, recognizing her enhanced perception provided assessment capability transcending instrumental measurement. "Your sensitivity offers perspective our monitoring equipment can't duplicate regardless of technical sophistication."

Alice considered this question thoughtfully, her enhanced awareness having continued development following implementation completion. Where once she had experienced unpredictable visions during crisis circumstances, she now maintained continuous subtle perception of temporal layers surrounding ordinary reality—past configurations, present alignments, and potential futures existing simultaneously within her expanded awareness.

"The integration maintains perfect harmony," she confirmed after brief perceptual assessment extending beyond shop confines to encompass broader temporal fabric. "Energy circulation throughout the octagram remains properly balanced with no indication of potential disruption patterns developing even during recent minor celestial configurations. The dampening fields between connection points function exactly as designed, preventing resonance amplification while allowing appropriate energy flow throughout integrated system."

This comprehensive assessment provided valuable confirmation beyond instrumental verification—human sensitivity perceiving qualitative aspects of temporal stability that mechanical monitoring might not fully capture despite technical sophistication. Alice's developed perception recognized patterns that transcended conventional measurement parameters, identifying potential concerns before they manifested as instrumentally detectable variations.

"And your adjustment to this continued sensitivity?" Tobias asked with genuine concern for her personal wellbeing beyond professional capability. "Rowan mentioned permanent perceptual expansion often requires significant adaptation period before achieving comfortable integration with conventional awareness frameworks."

"Increasingly manageable," Alice acknowledged candidly. "The initial disorientation has largely resolved as I've developed appropriate filtering mechanisms for background temporal impressions. I can maintain normal focus during routine activities while accessing enhanced perception when specifically useful—particularly during investigations where historical context provides valuable evidentiary perspective."

This adaptive balance represented a significant achievement beyond mere tolerance of unavoidable perceptual expansion. Alice had transformed potentially disruptive sensitivity into valuable professional asset—controlling enhanced awareness rather than being controlled by it, directing perception purposefully rather than experiencing passive observation without a contextual framework or practical application methodology.

"It's proven remarkably useful for cold cases," she added with professional satisfaction. "I can perceive residual temporal impressions at crime scenes even decades after events occurred—not comprehensive observation but significant fragments providing investigative direction otherwise unavailable through conventional evidence assessment. Captain Vaughn has discreetly assigned several previously unsolvable cases specifically for this analytical approach."

This practical application demonstrated valuable intersection between supernatural sensitivity and conventional law enforcement methodology—enhanced perception complementing rather than replacing traditional investigative techniques, providing additional information layer that strengthened overall evidentiary assessment rather than substituting unverifiable impressions for proper procedural documentation.

"The PIU has created an unofficial designation for this approach," she continued with slight amusement at bureaucratic adaptation to metaphysical capability. "Temporal Forensic Analysis—appropriately ambiguous terminology that satisfies administrative documentation requirements without explicitly acknowledging supernatural perception capabilities extending beyond conventionally recognized investigative methodologies."

Tobias appreciated this characteristic institutional response to extraordinary capabilities—creating an administrative framework that accommodated practical benefits while avoiding theoretical confrontations regarding underlying metaphysical mechanisms. Bureaucracies typically prioritized functional utility over philosophical consistency when addressing capabilities that defied conventional explanatory frameworks but demonstrated practical value within established organizational objectives.

"And Ethan's adaptation following implementation completion?" he inquired, recalling the werewolf detective's significant physiological disruption during the alignment's approach when lunar influence had created unpredictable transformation patterns affecting entire Pack population throughout Daybridge.

"Completely stabilized," Alice confirmed with evident relief regarding her partner's wellbeing. "The lunar cycle has resumed normal influence patterns with transformation responses appropriately aligned to conventional progression. The Pack reports similar normalization throughout their community—predictable rhythms reestablished without residual irregularity even during celestial configurations that typically enhance transformation sensitivity."

This physiological stabilization represented significant quality-of-life improvement beyond merely theoretical temporal integrity—supernatural beings throughout Daybridge experiencing practical benefits from successfully completed implementation through restored natural cycles that supported their distinctive existence requirements. Werewolves, vampires, witches, and numerous other non-human residents had resumed normal biological and metaphysical patterns following disruptive period that had threatened their fundamental functional stability.

As they discussed these positive developments, the shop's clocks experienced another momentary synchronization—diverse mechanical voices briefly achieving perfect harmony before returning to individual rhythms appropriate to their specific designs. This transient alignment no longer created concern but rather appreciation for healthy temporal ecosystem occasionally acknowledging its integrated nature through harmonized measurement.

"They're conversing rather than warning now," Tobias observed with professional satisfaction in this transformed relationship.

"Acknowledging connection without suggesting crisis—healthy communication rather than desperate alert."

"The difference between screaming for help and normal conversation," Alice translated this assessment into human relationship equivalent. "Systems under extreme stress communicate differently than those functioning within appropriate parameters regardless of mechanical or biological nature."

This insightful comparison highlighted a fundamental distinction between their current monitoring and previous crisis response—maintaining appropriate vigilance without experiencing continuous emergency conditions, observing functional system rather than addressing catastrophic failure potential. Their relationship with Daybridge's temporal fabric had transformed from desperate intervention to responsible stewardship—maintaining appropriate oversight while acknowledging system's fundamental stability following successful implementation.

The shop bell chimed again as Ethan entered, his appearance displaying remarkable contrast with crisis-period manifestation. Where once he had shown visible strain from unpredictable transformation impulses, he now presented balanced integration between human and werewolf aspects—amber eye tint suggesting enhanced perception without indicating imminent transformation, slightly elongated canines providing an efficient compromise between human appearance and supernatural capability.

"Committee preparation gathering?" he inquired with characteristic directness, noting their obviously professional discussion despite informal setting. "Or social visit with inevitable professional conversation overlap given our particular shared experiences?"

"Both," Alice acknowledged with a slight smile at this accurate assessment of their evolving relationship dynamic. "Official documentation review for tomorrow's meeting with inevitable conversation extending beyond strictly procedural requirements into broader implications and personal adaptation experiences."

This natural integration between professional responsibilities and personal connection characterized their post-implementation relationship—formal oversight duties providing structure while shared extraordinary experience created a foundation for genuine friendship transcending merely administrative association. They had faced potential temporal dissolution together, implementing a solution that required vulnerable trust beyond conventional professional collaboration, and that shared experience remained meaningful connection point regardless of resumed normal responsibilities.

"The Pack's quarterly assessment confirms complete stabilization throughout the supernatural community," Ethan reported, contributing his formal input for tomorrow's committee meeting. "No residual transformation irregularities even during minor celestial configurations that typically enhance sensitivity patterns. Alpha Lowell extends continued appreciation for implementation success while maintaining appropriate monitoring through designated Pack members with specific temporal sensitivity capabilities."

This supernatural community participation represented an important component within their comprehensive oversight approach—different perception modalities providing complementary assessment capabilities that strengthened overall monitoring effectiveness beyond what any single methodology could achieve independently. Werewolf sensitivity detected different temporal patterns than witch perception or scientific instrumentation, creating a multi-layered verification system that prevented potential blind spots within individual assessment frameworks.

RAE STONEHOUSE

"The museum curator position has been filled," he added with a meaningful glance acknowledging significance beyond merely administrative personnel change. "Candidate with extensive academic credentials and no detectable connection to either the Society or other potentially concerning organizations. Though obviously continued vigilance remains appropriate given demonstrated infiltration capabilities within established institutions."

This update referenced ongoing security concerns following Dr. Whittaker's exposure as Chronos Society operative and subsequent specialized containment under PIU supervision. The Museum of Supernatural Artifacts represented a significant potential vulnerability given its collection of temporally sensitive objects and historical documentation regarding various manipulation methodologies attempted throughout previous centuries. Appropriate personnel oversight remained essential security component regardless of successful implementation completion.

"And Harlow remains in specialized containment?" Tobias inquired, recalling the professor's sophisticated projected intrusion attempt that had temporarily displaced him between time streams during critical implementation phase.

"Secure with enhanced monitoring," Ethan confirmed professionally. "Though his continuing memory issues appear increasingly genuine rather than merely strategic performance intended to prevent useful intelligence extraction. PIU specialists suggest potential permanent cognitive fragmentation resulting from failed projected consciousness return following forcible exclusion during his attack attempt."

This unfortunate development suggested significant risk associated with sophisticated temporal manipulation attempts—even practitioners with extensive experience potentially suffering severe consequences when advanced techniques encountered effective countermeasures during implementation. Unlike Tobias's controlled retrieval following unintentional displacement, Harlow's consciousness had experienced traumatic extraction during active manipulation attempt with potentially permanent cognitive impact.

"The Society itself maintains conspicuous inactivity following implementation completion," Alice noted, sharing current intelligence assessment regarding their primary adversary during the crisis period. "No detected operations within Daybridge municipal boundaries or surrounding regions according to established monitoring networks. Though realistically this likely represents strategic repositioning rather than abandoned objectives given their demonstrated multigenerational operational framework."

This cautious assessment acknowledged realistic perspective regarding sophisticated adversary with a centuries-long operational history—temporary operational suspension following significant setback represented predictable tactical adjustment rather than fundamental strategic abandonment. The Society had demonstrated remarkable persistence throughout historical record, adapting methodologies following unsuccessful attempts rather than abandoning core objectives regardless of temporary implementation failures.

"They're studying what we accomplished," Tobias suggested with a pragmatic assessment of likely adversary response. "Learning from successful implementation methodology to refine their own approaches for future applications. Knowledge gathering rather than immediate intervention following significant paradigm adjustment regarding the Pendulum's proper functional integration."

This perspective recognized their implementation represented an unprecedented achievement beyond merely enhanced containment—fundamental paradigm shift regarding the proper relationship between powerful temporal artifacts and surrounding environment rather than simply improved restriction methodology preventing destructive manifestation. The Society would require significant theoretical recalibration before developing an appropriate response to this transformed understanding regarding temporal energy management principles.

"And Blackwood's organization?" Tobias inquired, recalling the Vampire Council's sophisticated resonator technology that had attempted remote manipulation of the Pendulum's energy signature before implementation completion.

"Officially acknowledging implementation success through diplomatic channels while maintaining appropriate distance from direct involvement," Ethan reported with a slight smile suggesting appreciation for characteristic vampire political positioning. "Council representatives have formally requested eventual information sharing regarding 'stabilization methodology with potential applications for additional temporal anomalies requiring similar treatment' while carefully avoiding any acknowledgment of previous interference attempts."

This diplomatic repositioning represented classic vampire adaptive response following unsuccessful direct intervention—recalibrating approach toward potential collaboration rather than opposition when immediate objectives proved unattainable through unilateral action. The Council's immortal perspective allowed patient strategic adjustment without emotional investment in specific tactical failures, prioritizing long-term knowledge acquisition over immediate operational success when circumstances necessitated fundamental approach revision.

"Translation: they still want the technology but have decided asking nicely might work better than stealing it," Alice interpreted with dry assessment of underlying motivation beyond diplomatic phrasing. "Though obviously appropriate security protocols remain essential regardless of superficially cooperative communication frameworks."

This realistic perspective acknowledged sophisticated adversaries sometimes shifted between oppositional and collaborative approaches depending on specific circumstance evaluation rather than maintaining rigid operational positioning regardless of demonstrated effectiveness assessment. The Vampire Council had existed for millennia precisely because of this adaptive capability—recognizing when strategic objectives required methodological recalibration rather than merely intensified application of previously unsuccessful approaches.

As they continued reviewing current status assessments in preparation for tomorrow's committee meeting, Madame Winters arrived—the elderly witch's appearance showing remarkable vitality despite significant magical exertion during implementation period. Her traditional formal attire remained unchanged, though subtle differences in her demeanor suggested positive effects from restored temporal stability throughout the surrounding environment.

"Unofficial pre-committee gathering," she observed with a slight smile acknowledging their characteristic thorough preparation approach. "Though I suspect formal documentation exchange represents merely a foundational framework for more significant discussions regarding personal observations beyond instrumental measurement capabilities."

This insightful assessment recognized their evolving relationship dynamic—professional responsibilities providing structure while shared extraordinary experience created context for a deeper connection transcending merely administrative association. Their collective implementation experience had transformed initial crisis response team into something resembling extended family with a shared understanding regarding temporal complexity that few others could fully comprehend regardless of theoretical knowledge or professional expertise.

"Rowan sends regards," the elderly witch continued, referring to her ancient counterpart who had returned to semi-seclusion following successful implementation completion. "Her assessment confirms perfect harmonic stability throughout the integrated system with no indication of potential disruption patterns developing within the observable timeframe. Though obviously her perception extends considerably beyond conventional measurement parameters regarding both spatial and temporal dimensions."

This confirmation from their most experienced temporal practitioner provided valuable reassurance beyond instrumental verification—ancient perception recognizing patterns that transcended conventional monitoring capabilities regardless of technical sophistication. Rowan's extraordinary experience with temporal phenomena provided assessment framework that acknowledged implementation quality from perspective spanning centuries rather than merely months or years of comparative observation.

"The coven maintains appropriate monitoring rotation as established following implementation completion," Madame Winters added, referring to formal participation within oversight committee structure. "Regular assessment from magical practitioners with specific temporal sensitivity provides complementary verification beyond scientific instrumentation or mechanical evaluation methodologies. The integrated approach continues demonstrating significant advantages over single-discipline monitoring frameworks."

This multi-methodological verification system represented an essential component within their comprehensive oversight approach—different perception modalities providing complementary assessment capabilities that strengthened overall monitoring effectiveness beyond what any individual approach could achieve independently. Magical sensitivity detected different temporal patterns than scientific instrumentation or mechanical evaluation, creating layered verification system that prevented potential blind spots within individual assessment frameworks.

With all primary implementation team members assembled, their conversation expanded beyond strictly procedural review for tomorrow's committee meeting into broader implications and personal experiences following successful completion. This natural progression reflected their evolved relationship—formal responsibilities providing structure while shared extraordinary experience created a foundation for genuine connection transcending merely administrative association.

"Dr. Mackie regrets missing today's gathering," Alice noted, explaining the physicist's absence from their informal pre-committee meeting. "The university's temporal physics department has experienced significant expansion following recent events, with research funding increased substantially based on demonstrated practical applications during our implementation project. Her administrative responsibilities have expanded accordingly, though she maintains direct involvement with clocktower monitoring systems and data analysis protocols."

This academic development represented positive institutional response to successful implementation—recognition that theoretical temporal physics had demonstrated practical application potential beyond merely speculative research without immediate utility. The university had appropriately expanded support for discipline that had proven essential during potential catastrophic event resolution, acknowledging valuable knowledge development worthy of increased institutional resource allocation.

"Marcus has shown remarkable aptitude for the maintenance protocols," Tobias added, referring to his apprentice who had demonstrated exceptional capability during implementation crisis despite limited previous experience with temporal mechanics. "He's developed an intuitive understanding regarding the octagram configuration's operational characteristics beyond what formal training typically achieves. I've recommended him for official inclusion within the monitoring rotation once his certification process completes next month."

This professional development represented appropriate succession planning within their oversight structure—identifying and preparing next-generation practitioners capable of maintaining the essential knowledge base beyond current implementation team's active participation. Responsible management required sustainable knowledge transfer rather than merely individual expertise that might eventually become unavailable through natural progression circumstances regardless of current commitment levels.

"The Pack has implemented similar capability development," Ethan noted with approval of this forward-thinking approach. "Younger members with demonstrated temporal sensitivity receive specialized training regarding anomaly detection and assessment protocols. Alpha Lowell recognizes sustainable monitoring requires multigenerational knowledge transfer rather than merely current participant expertise regardless of present effectiveness levels."

This parallel development across different community segments represented healthy ecosystem approach to temporal stability maintenance—distributed responsibility rather than centralized dependency, creating resilient oversight structure capable of withstanding individual participant transitions without compromising essential monitoring capability throughout extended timeframes.

As their conversation continued, Alice shared interesting observation regarding her enhanced perception's evolution following implementation completion. "The sensitivity continues developing in unexpected directions—not merely perceiving historical impressions but occasionally glimpsing potential futures with surprising clarity, particularly regarding significant decision points where various probability paths diverge based on specific choices rather than random circumstance."

This capability evolution suggested her temporal sensitivity extended beyond merely passive observation of residual impressions toward more sophisticated interaction with timestream variations—perception recognizing probability patterns that might influence future development rather than simply documenting past configurations without practical application potential. This enhanced capability offered significant practical value beyond merely historical documentation, potentially allowing preventive intervention before problematic circumstances fully manifested rather than merely responsive action following complete development.

"Rowan mentioned this possibility," Madame Winters noted with professional interest in this development. "Natural temporal sensitives sometimes experience capability evolution following significant implementation participation—consciousness that has successfully channeled harmonic energy during integration ritual often develops enhanced pattern recognition regarding potential future configurations rather than merely residual historical impressions. Your particular sensitivity appears especially responsive to this developmental progression."

This assessment provided valuable context for Alice's evolving capabilities—natural progression following significant implementation participation rather than unexpected anomaly requiring concerned evaluation. Her consciousness had successfully channeled harmonic energy during integration ritual, establishing neural pathways that subsequently facilitated enhanced pattern recognition regarding temporal variations across multiple potential configurations rather than merely linear progression perception.

"It's proven occasionally disconcerting but increasingly valuable," Alice acknowledged candidly. "Particularly during investigation planning where potential approach consequences become perceivable before implementation rather than merely theoretical projection based on limited information assessment. Though obviously distinguishing between genuine probability perception and merely subconscious pattern recognition sometimes presents interpretive challenges regardless of apparent clarity."

This balanced perspective demonstrated her characteristic pragmatic approach to extraordinary capabilities—recognizing potential practical applications while maintaining appropriate skepticism regarding interpretive limitations within unfamiliar perceptual framework. Alice neither rejected enhanced perception as mere imagination nor accepted every impression as definitive information, instead developing a nuanced evaluation methodology that incorporated both new sensitivity and established critical assessment skills into an integrated analytical approach.

Their conversation gradually shifted toward forward-looking considerations beyond merely current stability assessment—acknowledging their implementation success while recognizing broader implications regarding Daybridge's supernatural landscape and potential future anomalies requiring similar integrated response methodology. The Pendulum integration had resolved immediate crisis while potentially establishing a precedent for addressing other temporal phenomena that might eventually manifest within a region characterized by unusually high supernatural concentration and complex historical development patterns.

"The clocktower integration represents a significant achievement beyond merely crisis resolution," Tobias observed thoughtfully.

"We've essentially established methodology framework for addressing temporal anomalies through an integrated approach combining mechanical, scientific, magical, and consciousness-based components within a cohesive operational system. Knowledge that might prove valuable beyond this specific implementation context should similar phenomena eventually manifest elsewhere within Daybridge's complicated supernatural ecosystem."

This forward-thinking perspective recognized their work's potential significance beyond immediate application—establishing precedent and methodology that might inform future interventions addressing different temporal anomalies requiring a similar integrated approach rather than merely single-discipline response frameworks regardless of specific manifestation characteristics. They had demonstrated effective integration across traditionally separated knowledge domains, creating implementation model that transcended conventional disciplinary boundaries when addressing complex supernatural phenomena.

"The PIU has already incorporated lessons from our implementation into formal response protocols for potential temporal anomalies," Ethan confirmed, acknowledging institutional adaptation following successful resolution. "Captain Vaughn established specialized cross-disciplinary response team with representation across relevant expertise categories—essentially institutionalizing our integrated approach within a formal administrative framework while maintaining appropriate flexibility for addressing unique manifestation characteristics should different phenomena eventually emerge."

This organizational development represented appropriate systemic learning rather than merely individual knowledge acquisition—transforming successful crisis response into sustainable institutional capability through proper documentation, training protocols, and administrative support structures. The PIU had recognized value in maintaining integrated response capability regardless of specific personnel availability, creating a system that could survive individual participant transitions without compromising essential functional effectiveness.

"The Winters grimoire has been appropriately updated with implementation documentation," Madame Winters added, acknowledging parallel development within magical community resources. "Detailed methodology preservation including specific ritual components, consciousness channeling techniques, and integrated approach frameworks incorporating mechanical and scientific elements beyond traditional magical application boundaries. Knowledge preservation ensuring future practitioners benefit from our experience regardless of potential generational transitions between significant temporal events."

This documentation represented essential knowledge transfer mechanism within tradition characterized by careful information preservation across centuries of accumulated experience. The coven had maintained meticulous records throughout previous temporal interventions, creating an invaluable resource that had informed their recent implementation approach despite generational separation between significant manifestation periods. Their current documentation would similarly serve future practitioners should comparable phenomena eventually require intervention beyond current participants' active involvement capability.

"And my family journals have received comprehensive updates regarding both the mechanical integration methodology and my personal displacement experience," Tobias confirmed, acknowledging his contribution to this multigenerational knowledge preservation approach. "Detailed technical specifications, implementation protocols, and maintenance requirements documented with appropriate clarity for future reference requirements. Though obviously certain aspects require direct experience beyond merely written instruction regardless of documentation quality."

This balanced documentation approach acknowledged realistic limitations regarding knowledge transfer through merely textual preservation—certain capabilities requiring practical application experience beyond theoretical understanding regardless of documentation comprehensiveness. Future practitioners would benefit from their preserved methodology while potentially requiring direct practical development beyond merely intellectual comprehension when implementing comparable interventions during subsequent manifestation periods.

"We've done what we can to prepare those who might eventually continue our work," Alice summarized this forward-looking preparation with characteristic pragmatism. "While maintaining appropriate current vigilance ensuring immediate stability regardless of potential future developments. Balanced responsibility addressing both present requirements and future possibilities without compromising either through inappropriate priority allocation."

This perspective represented mature stewardship approach—acknowledging responsibility spanning both immediate monitoring requirements and potential future intervention preparation without allowing either consideration to undermine effective attention toward remaining obligations. They had successfully resolved current crisis while establishing an appropriate foundation for addressing potential future manifestations through both institutional frameworks and knowledge preservation mechanisms appropriate for sustainable temporal stability maintenance across generational transitions.

As their conversation continued, the shop bell chimed announcing final participant in their informal gathering—Captain Vaughn arriving directly from PIU headquarters with official documentation for tomorrow's committee meeting. His characteristically professional demeanor showed appropriate satisfaction regarding successful implementation outcome while maintaining vigilant attention toward potential continuing security considerations regardless of current stability assessment.

"Unofficial pre-committee gathering," he observed with a slight smile acknowledging their characteristic thorough preparation approach. "Though I suspect formal documentation review represents merely a preliminary framework for more significant discussions regarding matters extending beyond strictly procedural requirements regardless of administrative importance."

This perceptive assessment demonstrated his understanding regarding their evolved relationship dynamic—formal responsibilities providing structure while shared extraordinary experience created a foundation for connection transcending merely administrative association. Vaughn had maintained appropriate professional boundaries throughout implementation crisis while recognizing genuine relationship development beyond merely functional collaboration given extraordinary circumstances requiring vulnerable trust beyond conventional professional interaction frameworks.

"The official monitoring assessment confirms continued perfect stability throughout implementation structure," he reported, providing administrative verification complementing their individual discipline-specific evaluations. "All measurement parameters within optimal ranges with no indication of potential deterioration patterns developing since activation completion. The integrated system maintains self-regulation without requiring adjustment intervention despite minor celestial configurations occurring during monitoring period."

This comprehensive confirmation from official oversight authority provided valuable administrative documentation complementing their individual assessment contributions—formal verification establishing a clear record regarding implementation success beyond merely personal observation regardless of individual expertise credibility. The PIU had maintained rigorous monitoring protocols throughout post-implementation period, ensuring thorough documentation regarding system performance across multiple assessment dimensions regardless of apparent stability during casual observation.

"The Society maintains conspicuous inactivity within observable monitoring range," Vaughn continued, addressing security considerations beyond merely implementation performance assessment. "Though obviously appropriate vigilance continues given demonstrated operational sophistication and historical pattern suggesting strategic repositioning rather than objective abandonment following temporary setbacks regardless of apparent significance."

This security assessment acknowledged realistic perspective regarding sophisticated adversary with a centuries-long operational history—temporary activity suspension representing predictable tactical adjustment rather than fundamental strategic abandonment regardless of implementation success significance. The Society had demonstrated remarkable persistence throughout historical record, adapting methodologies following unsuccessful attempts rather than abandoning core objectives despite temporary operational failures.

"Harlow remains in specialized containment with continued cognitive fragmentation symptoms suggesting genuine impairment rather than merely strategic performance," he added, providing update regarding their primary individual adversary during implementation crisis. "Medical assessment indicates permanent consciousness disruption resulting from traumatic projection termination during attack attempt, with limited potential for eventual recovery regardless of treatment methodology."

This unfortunate development highlighted significant risks associated with sophisticated temporal manipulation attempts—even experienced practitioners potentially suffering severe consequences when advanced techniques encountered effective countermeasures during implementation. Unlike Tobias's controlled retrieval following unintentional displacement, Harlow's consciousness had experienced traumatic extraction during active manipulation attempt with apparently permanent cognitive impact regardless of subsequent medical intervention attempts.

"And Dr. Whittaker?" Tobias inquired, recalling the museum curator's technological sabotage attempt during critical implementation phase.

"Maintained in separate specialized containment with enhanced monitoring protocols," Vaughn confirmed professionally. "Though interestingly her perspective appears to have evolved following observation of successful implementation outcomes. Recent interviews suggest genuine intellectual reconsideration regarding Society methodology rather than merely strategic communication adjustment intended to facilitate potential release consideration."

This unexpected development suggested potential philosophical impact beyond merely operational success—their implementation demonstrating an alternative approach that might influence even committed adversaries through demonstrated effectiveness rather than merely theoretical argumentation. Whittaker's apparent perspective evolution indicated their integrated methodology potentially addressed fundamental questions regarding temporal energy management that transcended merely oppositional positioning between competing operational frameworks.

"Genuine reconsideration or sophisticated manipulation attempt?" Alice questioned with appropriate investigative skepticism regarding this reported perspective shift.

"Uncertain determination despite extensive psychological assessment," Vaughn acknowledged candidly. "Though specialized containment continues regardless of apparent perspective evolution until comprehensive verification beyond reasonable security concerns becomes possible through extended observation period. Appropriate caution without rejecting potential genuine reconsideration given implementation's demonstrated paradigm-shifting characteristics regarding temporal energy management principles."

This balanced approach demonstrated sophisticated security perspective—maintaining appropriate protective measures while acknowledging potential legitimate perspective evolution following significant paradigm demonstration rather than assuming rigid adversarial positioning regardless of possible genuine reconsideration. Effective security required both appropriate vigilance and realistic assessment regarding potential relationship evolution when circumstances presented significant new information potentially affecting fundamental understanding frameworks.

With all participants assembled and formal documentation exchanged in preparation for tomorrow's committee meeting, their gathering gradually transitioned toward more personal interaction—professional responsibilities addressed while allowing relationship aspects beyond merely administrative association to emerge within a comfortable environment characterized by shared extraordinary experience. This natural progression reflected their evolved connection—crisis response team transformed into something resembling extended family through a shared understanding regarding temporal complexity that few others could fully comprehend regardless of theoretical knowledge or professional expertise.

"The clocktower has become something beyond merely architectural landmark or functional timekeeping device," Tobias observed as their conversation expanded beyond strictly procedural considerations. "It's achieved its intended purpose after nearly 150 years of patient preparation—measuring true temporal flow rather than merely arbitrary divisions imposed through conventional understanding. The structure speaks truth rather than merely convenient approximation."

This philosophical assessment highlighted an essential distinction between their implementation approach and conventional temporal management—recognizing fundamental patterns that transcended human measurement systems rather than attempting to force natural phenomena into artificial frameworks regardless of underlying incongruity. Integration rather than imposition as a guiding principle throughout their methodology, creating a harmonious relationship between powerful artifacts and surrounding environment rather than merely imposed restriction preventing destructive manifestation.

"It's become our unofficial meeting place beyond merely committee gatherings," Alice noted with appreciation for this evolved relationship with previously ordinary municipal structure. "The tower represents something significant beyond merely successful professional collaboration—shared understanding regarding temporal complexity that few others can fully comprehend regardless of theoretical knowledge or explained experience descriptions."

This observation acknowledged special connection they had developed with both the implementation structure and each other through shared extraordinary experience—crisis response creating relationship foundation that continued beyond merely resolved emergency circumstances into a genuine connection characterized by mutual understanding regarding experiences others might acknowledge intellectually while never truly comprehending experientially regardless of detailed explanation efforts.

"Time means something different to each of us now," Ethan suggested thoughtfully. "Not merely measured duration but complex dimensional reality with depth and texture beyond conventional perception frameworks. We've glimpsed something fundamental beneath ordinary experience—patterns and connections most humans never consciously recognize throughout their temporal existence regardless of intellectual sophistication or professional expertise."

This insight highlighted the transformative aspect of their shared implementation experience—perception permanently expanded beyond conventional boundaries into awareness that recognized temporal complexity transcending ordinary understanding regardless of subsequent normal activity resumption. They had collectively witnessed reality's underlying structure during implementation process, forever changing their relationship with seemingly ordinary progression patterns that most humans experienced without conscious recognition regarding fundamental dimensional characteristics beneath surface-level perception.

As evening approached and their gathering prepared to conclude in preparation for tomorrow's formal committee meeting, the shop's clocks experienced another momentary synchronization—diverse mechanical voices briefly achieving perfect harmony before returning to individual rhythms appropriate to their specific designs. This transient alignment created appreciative observation rather than concerned evaluation, recognizing healthy temporal ecosystem occasionally acknowledging its integrated nature through harmonized measurement.

"They remind us occasionally," Tobias noted with professional satisfaction in this transformed relationship with his beloved timepieces. "Not warning but acknowledging—gentle reminder regarding underlying connection beneath apparent separation. Healthy communication rather than desperate alert."

"Like friends checking in rather than strangers shouting for help," Alice translated into human relationship equivalent with characteristic insight regarding underlying pattern recognition across different manifestation frameworks. "Confirming connection rather than establishing initial contact under crisis circumstances."

This perspective highlighted their evolved relationship with Daybridge's temporal fabric following successful implementation—maintenance rather than intervention, stewardship rather than emergency response, responsible oversight rather than desperate containment attempt. They had transformed potential catastrophe into sustainable stability through a collaborative effort combining diverse expertise across multiple disciplines into a cohesive operational framework.

As they departed Merrick's Chronometry with plans to reconvene for tomorrow's formal committee meeting at the Municipal Building, each carried awareness regarding their continuing responsibility as unofficial timekeepers beyond merely administrative oversight participants. They had collectively implemented an extraordinary solution addressing temporal instability while establishing ongoing stewardship framework ensuring continued stability regardless of potential future challenges within Daybridge's complicated supernatural ecosystem.

The clocktower stood illuminated against the early evening sky as they glanced toward successfully completed implementation—its conventional faces displaying ordinary time while its integrated mechanism measured something far more fundamental. The structure had fulfilled its intended purpose after generations of patient preparation, becoming what its original designers had envisioned when incorporating specialized features that would eventually accommodate the Pendulum assembly within sophisticated integration framework.

Their collaborative effort had transformed potential catastrophe into genuine resolution—properly channeling extraordinary power toward constructive stabilization rather than merely containing disruptive potential behind temporarily reinforced barriers. The Pendulum of Aeon had achieved appropriate integration within Daybridge's temporal ecosystem, establishing a harmonic relationship that benefited surrounding environment rather than merely avoiding damage through imposed restriction.

Most importantly, this resolution acknowledged the fundamental distinction between management and control—creating a framework that supported natural patterns rather than imposing an artificial structure regardless of underlying incongruity. The implementation didn't force the Pendulum to conform to human expectations but established a system that appropriately channeled its natural properties toward constructive application within a properly designed framework.

As they continued toward their respective destinations through properly stabilized city streets, each carried awareness regarding both their significant achievement and continuing responsibility. They had successfully resolved immediate crisis while establishing an appropriate foundation for addressing potential future manifestations through both institutional frameworks and knowledge preservation mechanisms suitable for sustainable temporal stability maintenance across generational transitions.

The clocks throughout Daybridge continued their synchronized measurement—no longer whispering warnings but suggesting proper alignment with fundamental cosmic rhythms underlying conventional progression. The city breathed with restored temporal coherence that would persist indefinitely following successful implementation, its inhabitants largely unaware of extraordinary effort required to reestablish stability they unconsciously depended upon throughout daily experience.

Time flowed properly once more. And they remained vigilant ensuring it continued its proper course through their remarkable city's peculiar temporal landscape—unofficial timekeepers beyond merely administrative oversight participants, guardians of proper progression beneath ordinary measurement conventions, stewards of balance between powerful forces requiring appropriate acknowledgment rather than merely attempted subjugation.

The Pendulum of Aeon had found its proper home. And they had found unexpected connection through extraordinary, shared experience that would bind them together regardless of resumed normal responsibilities or conventional relationship definitions.

Some partnerships transcended ordinary categorization. Particularly those forged between moments, when time itself hung in the balance.

Copyright:

First Edition

Published by Live For Excellence Productions

ISBNs:

E-book: 978-1-997784-39-5

Paperback: 978-1-997784-40-1

Audiobook: 978-1-997784-41-8

About the Author

Rae Stonehouse turned to fiction writing after establishing himself as a prolific author of self-development and professional growth books.

With over fifty published works helping readers navigate personal and professional challenges, he embarked on a new creative path with the Ethan Reeves Werewolf Detective Series.

When not weaving tales of supernatural sleuthing, Stonehouse continues to share his expertise in personal development through workshops and speaking engagements from his home in British Columbia.

The Ethan Reeves series marks his debut in fiction writing, blending his understanding of human nature with a newfound passion for urban fantasy.

The story doesn't end here. Scan for more books in the Daybridge Chronicles, part of the Ethan Reeves Werewolf Detective Series: https://my.linkpod.site/daybridgechronicles